Blind Date Bride
By Arlene Hittle

Copyright © 2014 Arlene Hittle
Published by Arlene Hittle
Cover Design © Covers by Rogenna 2013
www.rogennabrewer.com
Editing by H. Danielle Crabtree,
http://www.hedanicreations.net

ISBN: 978-0-9911787-1-1

Media > Books > Fiction > Romance Novels
Category/Tags: Romance, contemporary, Reality
TV, comedy

DEDICATION

To everyone who believes in me. May you have as much fun reading Kari and Damien's story as I did writing it.

Chapter One

When the first notes of "The Wedding March" sounded, Kari Parker took a deep breath and forced herself to step down the aisle toward the man who would be her husband for the next three months.

Truth be told, now that she'd seen her husband-to-be close-up, she wasn't so sure she wanted out. He was, well, in a word, perfect. At least he would be if he were just a little less huge. He was too tall and imposing for her taste. At five-eight and three-quarters, she was far from petite, but she preferred someone her own height. She'd rather not have to look up to her man.

Thank goodness her parents were too busy with their restaurant in Springfield to keep a watch on what she was doing in Chicagoland. She definitely didn't want them to know her best friend had entered her in Romance TV's "Get a Love Life" contest — or that she'd won. As far as her folks were concerned, she didn't have a love life, and that was the way she wanted it to stay. They'd definitely object to her sacrificing herself — even temporarily — to bail them out.

Kari grimaced. Not that she had much of a love life to speak of. The few guys she'd dated since college had been chosen mainly because they didn't seem that interested in a physical relationship. That suited her fine.

The seemingly endless walk up the church's aisle complete, she stopped beside the man who'd introduced himself as Damien Walker mere moments ago. She took another deep breath and reminded herself to smile. The cameras were recording their every move, and she didn't want a TV audience of millions to remember her as the terrified bride. Deer-in-headlights wasn't a good look for her, or anyone.

The nervous tension coiled in her gut untwisted a bit when Damien smiled back. Then he reached for her hand and squeezed it.

The jolt that raced through her body took her by surprise again, as it had in the hallway of the church basement. She wasn't used to feeling such instant attraction. In fact, she tried her damnedest to avoid it.

"Dearly beloved, we are gathered here today ..."

****

It was all Damien could do to contain a snort. Beloved? He doubted if he or Kari could count more than a handful of the people in the audience as acquaintances, let alone friends and family.

Even Cody's friendship was in question. If there were a way Damien could disown his best friend, who currently stood beside him with a goofy grin that stretched from ear to ear, he'd be sorely tempted.

How could his buddy do this to him? Even if Cody had put his name in for the "Get a Love Life" contest to win second prize, he'd have to have known how embarrassed Damien would be. Romance TV viewers — all ten of them, by his estimate — would think he was so pathetic that he had to win a wife.

Well, he wasn't. He wasn't pathetic at all. He just chose not to waste time and money on casual dating. He'd done enough of that in college to last a lifetime. He'd always promised himself to start looking for Ms. Right when he was ready for a family. Until then, he had his veterinary practice to keep him busy.

That doesn't keep you warm at night, the voice inside his head nagged. *Or prevent you from being dull as dirt.*

Damien pushed that voice aside and again studied the woman beside him. She was, indeed, gorgeous. Her blond hair was piled atop her head in one of those deceptively disheveled arrangements that had probably taken hours to do, and her dress skimmed her body, hinting at ample hips and small but perfectly formed breasts.

His hands itched to reach under that white silk gown and cup those breasts, to feel her nipples harden under his fingertips.

Damien stopped himself short. It was completely inappropriate to be having such thoughts about a woman with whom he'd only exchanged a few words, even if she was about to become his lawfully wedded wife.

I bet she's great in bed, the voice in his head taunted.

Damien almost turned to scowl at Cody, but stopped himself. He guessed Cody couldn't help what the voice in his head said — even when the commentary came out in Cody's voice.

****

"Will you, Kari Amber Parker, take this man to be your

lawfully wedded husband?"

For a moment, Kari couldn't reply. She couldn't breathe, let alone form the response that would bind her to this giant of a man for life — or at least for now.

Then she remembered everything that would happen if she didn't go through with it: even more public humiliation, a massive bill for the wedding and reception, and her parents losing the restaurant they'd been running since before she was born. She took a deep breath and whispered the words, "I will."

"And will you, Damien Kyle Walker, take this woman to be your lawfully wedded wife?"

"I will."

His voice didn't have even the slightest waver. It rang out as calm and sure as it would be while ordering his favorite meal, whatever that might be. He sounded like he actually meant his vow — for the rest of their lives, not just for the next few months.

It would be nice to have so much confidence, she thought. She was never that sure of herself, unless it was in her work. That was the great thing about accounting; there was only one correct answer. You simply tallied up the numbers, and as long as you didn't enter any of them wrong, you always came up with the right answer.

"It's time to exchange rings," the minister intoned.

A few seconds later, a band of gold joined the network-provided diamond solitaire engagement ring on her left ring finger, proclaiming her status as Mrs. Damien Walker to the world. She had just a second to stare at the gaudy jewelry, wondering how she'd manage to live with this stranger, before the minister announced, "You may now kiss the bride."

Dutifully, Kari turned her face upward and pursed her lips.

****

Damien looked down at his bride, who obviously expected a peck on the lips, and the devil in him prodded him to make their first kiss much more than that.

First, he put his hands on his lovely new bride's waist and pulled her against him. Then he lowered his lips to hers. Instantly, heat flared between them. His fingers tightened their grip on her hips, and his tongue pushed past her lips, demanding entrance into the moist heat of her mouth. When her lips opened on a soft moan, his tongue swept inside.

Then he was lost. Waves of desire washed over him and his

hands dropped to her bottom, settling her even more firmly against him. His tongue thrust deeper into her mouth, imitating the sex act he suddenly wanted to be engaged in.

Damien had no idea how long they stood there, bodies melded together and mouths locked in a kiss, before he felt a tap on his shoulder.

"Slow down, buddy," Cody advised quietly, "before you eat the poor girl alive."

He released his hold on Kari. What the hell had gotten into him? How long had it been since he'd found himself overpowered by desire in the blink of two beautiful brown eyes?

Actually, he couldn't ever remember it happening before. He didn't kiss women he'd barely met as if he'd known them — in the biblical sense — for years.

He was lucky she hadn't slapped him silly. Because that was exactly how he'd kissed Kari, as if they both knew they were destined to do the mattress mambo as soon as possible. And that was patently ridiculous, even if she *was* his wife. He wasn't the kind of guy who jumped into bed with the first warm, willing woman who crossed his path.

Not anymore, anyway.

On the rare occasions he did date, he liked to get to know a girl first, romance her a little. Make that a lot. He was the only guy he knew, except the Romance TV addict at his side, unashamed to admit to being a romantic. He wasn't sure he welcomed the return of his younger, hornier self.

****

For her part, Kari just stared at Damien, dazed. She'd been expecting a sweet, safe little peck. Instead, she'd gotten a wild, passionate ride. That kiss had been an invitation to sin and a promise of hot, sweaty nights to come. It was a kiss for lovers. A kiss like the ones she used to share with Rob, back in college.

She pushed Rob right back out of her mind. She wasn't about to think of that jerk on what was supposed to be the happiest day of her life — even if the wedding was a sham.

She let Damien take her hand, and together they took their first steps as man and wife. When they reached the end of the aisle, they dutifully posed for their wedding pictures. Really, they were publicity shots for Romance TV, but the producer promised Kari and Damien could have as many copies as they wanted.

Like they'd really want any pictures to commemorate this bogus wedding.

She made sure her fake smile remained plastered on, though, as flashes lit the room. She stood and smiled, nodding whenever necessary, while the reporters in attendance asked questions that could only be considered nosy. No doubt this blind date wedding would be news in papers all over the country tomorrow morning.

Thank goodness her parents didn't subscribe to the newspaper anymore. They'd stopped several years ago, claiming too much of the news was depressing. They didn't have cable TV, either.

"So, Mrs. Walker, do you think your luck in love is about to change?"

When Kari didn't respond right away, Damien nudged her. "They're talking to you, sweetheart."

He wanted her to speak in front of all these people? No way! And why was he calling her sweetheart? They barely knew each other.

She leaned over to whisper in Damien's ear. Annoyance flared that she had to stand on tiptoe to do so. "I hate public speaking. I can't address this crowd."

His eyes searched her face. She barely had time to register the half-smile on his lips before he lowered his mouth to hers again. It was another one of those long, soul-searing kisses that made her hunger for more. When the kiss ended, he looked at the throng of reporters. The corners of his mouth quirked up in a satisfied smile.

"Does that answer your question?"

Still breathing hard, Kari stared at her new husband as her mind raced. It certainly answered some questions for her. She refused to give another man the power to humiliate her. Tuning out the reporters' shouts, she turned on her heel and stalked away.

Soon, Damien's footsteps sounded behind her. She didn't slow down.

"Kari, what's wrong?"

She waved him off and kept walking down the church steps and onto the sidewalk. He caught up to her, his long legs making short work of the distance between them. He grabbed her by the elbow and dragged her to a stop. "Would you wait a minute?"

Even as she cringed, Kari hated herself for showing fear. A man like her new husband wouldn't hesitate to twist her weakness to his advantage. When he released her instead, Kari's estimation of Damien crept up a notch.

He took a deep breath, letting it out slowly. "Look, I'm sorry I got carried away back there. I can be a ham."

Half afraid of what she might see, Kari forced herself to search Damien's eyes. He certainly looked contrite. Then again, so had Rob — so many, many times. She took a deep breath and hoped it wasn't a mistake to give this stranger the benefit of the doubt. "Okay."

She willed herself not to pull away when he reached for her hand, and she found she actually wanted him to lace his fingers through hers. When he did, another jolt shot through her fingertips. She caught her bottom lip between her teeth to keep from gasping.

Still, his smile was knowing. "What do you say we find our limo ride to the reception?"

****

"I'm telling you, Beth, that man is trouble with a capital T," she complained later that afternoon, running a thumb over lips that still felt swollen from his kisses. She'd dragged Bethany into the reception hall's bathroom, the one place the TV cameras wouldn't follow, for a few moments of privacy at the Romance TV-sponsored reception.

"Because he reminds you of Rob?"

Kari's thumb froze mid-stroke. Oh yes. Damien's electrifying kisses weren't the only reminder of her ex. For one thing, they both dominated a room, no matter its size. She suspected they both had similar views on women, too: love 'em and leave 'em, but first humiliate them in every way possible.

Wasn't that what he'd done with his public kisses? She certainly hadn't intended to kiss him in full view of millions, and she sure as hell hadn't planned on enjoying his kisses, or craving more.

Even though no one could overhear them, Bethany spoke in a low voice. "Not all big, strong guys are like Rob, Kar. They don't all force—"

"He never really did." Kari's denial was swift and automatic, even if she wasn't entirely convinced it was true. She chose to believe because it kept her from wallowing in self-loathing.

"If not, he came damn close," her friend countered just as rapidly.

She swallowed hard, unable to completely avoid recriminations. Bethany was the only one she'd told about the things that overgrown teenager — she couldn't bring herself to call him a man — had coerced her into doing, all in the name of love. Love? Ha! He'd really only wanted sex, but she'd been a college freshman, thrilled to capture a man's interest and naive enough to believe they shared something special.

She shook her head to dislodge the memories. "I don't want to think about Rob today. Or ever again, for that matter."

"But he's always there, in the back of your mind. That's why you've dated undersexed wimps ever since."

"Spare me your Dr. Phil-induced psychobabble, Beth. I simply like my men more refined."

Bethany snorted. "Right. That's why you and Damien practically went up in flames when you kissed."

Kari opened her mouth to protest, but Bethany cut her off. "Don't try to deny it, Kar. The sparks that flared between you two were visible as far away as Milwaukee."

Kari felt heat course through her veins again as she recalled her phony husband's all-too-real kisses. However, she refused to let the fire of passion rage out of control. No, she didn't intend to let lust lead her to another relationship disaster.

"It doesn't matter, Beth. There's no way I'm going down that road again."

****

Damien's eyes tracked around the cavernous reception hall, looking for his wayward wife. Maybe she'd already tired of the charade and escaped out the side door. Maybe he'd scared the hell out of her with his demanding kisses. The intense desire had surprised him. He had thought his days of just-add-water attraction were long gone.

He was relieved to see Kari emerge from the bathroom, her friend, What's Her Name, in tow. She looked calmer and more relaxed, and he hoped that meant she was as excited as he was starting to be about the next three months.

Because he had to admit, he found the possibilities more than a little intriguing. He watched as Kari wound toward him through the crowded room, her eyes fixed on the floor to avoid conversation. Even with her head down, she moved with grace, her hips swaying gently with each step.

As his eyes followed her progress through the room, he felt blood rushing south and he groaned. His body was behaving as if this was a real wedding, and a real wedding night was just around the corner. His brain knew better, but it was having a hell of a time convincing Mr. Happy that satisfaction would be a long time coming.

Damien shoved his hands in his pockets, embarrassed to be having such an adolescent reaction.

"Wife incoming at two o'clock," Cody whispered. Then he glanced down at Damien's stance and grinned. "But I don't need to tell you that, do I?"

Damien frowned. "You're still on thin ice, buddy."

"It's been several hours. Shouldn't you be ready to forgive and forget?"

He considered that for a moment. Usually, he was quick to anger and even faster to forgive. However, submitting his name for this mockery of a marriage was practically unforgivable. "Why didn't you enter yourself in this contest?"

"Contest rules, buddy. And I quote: 'No self-nomination allowed.' Besides, why would I want to humiliate myself in front of millions of cable TV viewers?" Cody looked horrified by the thought.

"Yet you thought *I* would."

This time, Cody's grin was tinged with guilt. "I didn't expect you to win the grand prize, man. I thought for sure there'd be someone in America with a love life more pathetic than yours. I was hoping you'd win a trip for you and a friend to a singles resort in the Bahamas."

He pursed his lips. "I suppose you thought you'd be the friend I chose?"

"Who else? The rest of our friends are married."

Damn fool was right. Their other friends were off the market. "Maybe my circle of friends needs a wider circumference."

Conscious of the camera approaching behind Kari, he ignored Cody's outraged sputtering and glanced at his watch. They'd been at the reception for two hours already. Surely that was long enough to spend with a bunch of people they didn't know, and probably wouldn't want to meet, either.

When Kari stopped in front of him, he leaned down to peck her cheek, putting on a good show for the camera. Then he whispered in her ear, "I seem to recall promising you a cup of coffee. Ready to try to ditch these cameras and grab one?"

Her lips tipped into a relieved smile and she nodded. "Just let me change."

Cody extended his hand to Kari's friend. "What do you say we head out to the dance floor and put on a show?"

"I'd love to."

****

With Bethany and Damien's shaggy-haired friend distracting the partygoers, Kari and Damien slipped out the side door unnoticed. Fifteen minutes later, she sat across from him in a coffee shop within walking distance of the reception hall.

Having shed her wedding dress for the much more comfortable purple skirt and coordinating baggy T-shirt she'd worn to the church, she now sipped a caramel latte as she tried to concentrate more on what he was saying about life as a veterinarian and less on the mouth forming the words.

She wasn't having much luck. Damien's job was more interesting than hers, for sure. He got to play with animals; she worked with numbers all day. But neither of their jobs was nearly as fascinating at the moment as his perfectly shaped lips.

"I'd better change the subject. Your eyes are starting to glaze over." He waved his hand in front of her face.

The movement captured Kari's attention. "Sorry."

"Don't be. I know I get carried away when I talk about my work." He paused to sip his coffee. "Now that we've explored each other's career choices, let's get down to something really important."

"Such as?"

"Such as why a beautiful woman like you needs to win herself a husband."

Damien was direct; she'd give him credit for that. Kari's cheeks warmed. "That sounds like a compliment."

His eyes raked over her roughly as slow smile spread across his face. "Oh, it is."

Her heart stopped for a moment, then picked up speed. As much as that smile reminded her of Rob's predatory grin, her ex had never looked at her quite like this. The fire in Damien's bright blue eyes made her feel not weak, but empowered.

Her focus zeroed back in on his mouth. Despite the promise she made to herself in the bathroom, she kept remembering the pressure of his lips on hers and wondering what it would feel like to have that beautiful mouth kiss her in other spots.

Kari stopped short. Here she sat, in a brightly lit coffeehouse, and she couldn't stop thinking about her bogus husband's all-too-real kisses. Ridiculous! She hadn't known the man for more than four hours.

Even so, she couldn't help but ponder the likelihood of a repeat performance. She wouldn't mind at all if he took her in his arms and kissed her thoroughly.

"Well?"

With difficulty, she reined in her imagination. "Well, what?"

"You never answered my question."

Ah yes. That question. How could she tell a man who looked at her as if she was a supermodel that she'd never seen herself as pretty? She couldn't, especially when her rational self knew the truth: She was, as Bethany often reminded her, a looker. Her pudgy eighth-grade self just wouldn't accept it. She took another sip of her drink to buy some time.

"I'm shy, remember?"

Damien's eyebrows shot up. "You didn't seem all that shy when you were kissing me."

Oh, God. There was that directness again. Kari bit her lip. How could she handle a man who said exactly what he meant? "Call that an aberration."

Damien shook his head. "I don't think so."

"Trust me. I don't normally act like that."

He leaned across the table, and for a second, she thought he'd kiss her again. Her lips parted in anticipation. However, he merely turned her hand over, palm up, and ran his thumb over the skin at the base of her fingers. She watched it move back and forth, fast then slow, fascinated by the friction-generated heat.

His eyes never left hers, so she saw the instant his desire flickered back to life. Her thighs clenched as her body answered Damien's call.

The dampness she felt provided a rude wake-up call. She clamped her knees together as she jerked her hand out of his grasp, ruthlessly reminding herself how badly her last run-in with lust at first sight had ended.

Seemingly undeterred, he grinned. "You ready to head to

my place?"

"Y-your place?" Surely he wasn't a mind reader.

"Or yours, I suppose."

"My place?" This time, Kari's voice came out in a panicked squeak.

Damien shrugged. "It doesn't much matter to me."

How could he be so ... so ... cavalier about spending the night together? She sought refuge in her latte, savoring its creamy sweetness while she tried to formulate an appropriate response.

Finally, she opted for the obvious. Although Damien's offer, and his kisses, was all too tempting, she wasn't the type of girl who jumped into bed with any guy who paid attention to her. No matter how much her traitorous body wanted her to, she wasn't about to become that girl, either. Not this time. She'd worked too hard to cultivate self-respect in the post-Rob years to throw it away so easily.

"Don't you think it's too soon?"

"Pardon?"

Heat rushed to Kari's cheeks. She certainly couldn't talk with him about sex! She barely tolerated talking to Bethany about the more intimate details of her life. "Um ... uh ... well ... we don't know each other very well."

"We knew each other even less when we tied the knot a couple of hours ago," Damien pointed out, his voice reasonable.

No matter how sensible his point was, or how eager her dirty mind was to stray to an image of the two of them locked in a sweaty embrace, she simply couldn't give in. Well, she probably could, but not if she wanted to hold on to her self-respect.

She took a deep breath and blurted, "Damien, I won't sleep with you."

Chapter Two

Damien's jaw dropped. She thought he was ready to jump into bed with her?

Okay, maybe parts of him were willing, especially after that thing he'd just pulled with her palm. Holy hell, she went up in flames faster than Chicago burned in the Great Fire. But the rest of him — the rational, sensible part he actually tried to listen to most of the time now that he was a mature adult — had miles to go before reaching that point.

Belatedly remembering his mother's saying about catching flies, he closed his mouth. Then he opened it again, and again snapped it shut. How in the hell could he tell a babe like Kari he wasn't interested in a little mattress mambo?

Tougher still, how did he do it without hurting her feelings? Despite the results of this crazy contest they'd won, he doubted she heard rejection often. Women with love-goddess looks like Kari's rarely did.

"You did read the rules of this contest, didn't you?"

"Only about a thousand times."

No doubt to see how she could get out of the wedding, Damien thought. He'd certainly found himself poring over the lines on that stupid pink sheet of paper for just that purpose — when he wasn't pondering the ways a new bride could liven up his boring life, that is.

"Good. Then you know that in order to claim the prize money, we have to live together, starting tonight."

Kari buried her head in her hands. When she finally looked at him again, several minutes later, her face still shone brighter than Rudolph's shiny red nose. "I am such an idiot!"

Damien raised an eyebrow. "Why would you say that?"

"I was thinking—" She stopped and shook her head, then mumbled into the tabletop. "You don't want to know what I was thinking."

Damien studied his obviously embarrassed wife, who was still trying to hide her pretty face behind her hands. Was it possible she didn't know the effect she had on men, on him?

He rolled his eyes. She knew; she had to. Girls like her always grasped the scope of their power over men. He had yet to meet a stunning woman who didn't know exactly how to use that beauty to her advantage.

God knew Teena had certainly exploited *her* looks to get her way while they dated. To the best of his ability, he'd given her everything she'd asked for, everything she'd said she needed: chocolates, weekly bouquets, dinners out, a pricey engagement ring.

But that wasn't enough for Teena. She'd wanted more, demanding his undivided attention. The animals in his care really needed him, but Teena was too selfish to see that, or to understand his vision for his practice.

He wondered if it would be different this time. Would he be able to sustain a meaningful relationship now that his practice was more established? As long as Kari didn't have a heart harder than diamonds …

Damien frowned. He had neither the time nor inclination to think about his ex-fiancée. It was getting late, he was dog-tired, and he and Kari still needed to settle on sleeping arrangements.

Before they made that decision, Damien had to put her at ease. If they were going to survive the next three months together, they at least needed to be on friendly terms.

He reached across the table to reclaim her hand, this time giving her fingers a warm squeeze. "Our thoughts aren't so different."

Kari jerked her hand away again. Her cheeks were still red. "We still can't—"

"I know," Damien rushed to assure her. "That's why I think we should head to my place."

"Why's that?"

"My apartment has two bedrooms."

Her eyes narrowed. "How do you know mine doesn't?"

Did the woman think he had Swiss cheese for brains? He arched an eyebrow. "You told me you share a one-bedroom apartment with your two cats — one black, one white."

"Sorry. I forgot I'd mentioned that." Kari flashed him a mischievous grin that lit her entire face. "Two bedrooms are good."

"Of course, one of them is stuffed with veterinary texts and boxes."

As quickly as it had brightened, her face fell. "Will there be room for me?"

Damien grinned again, amused by how eager his wife was to avoid sleeping with him. "I can make the room. There's already a couch that folds into a bed — once I clear off the boxes that are piled there."

She nodded. "Sounds great."

"Then let's go."

****

When Kari opened her eyes the next morning, she didn't know where she was. Fighting a rising tide of panic, she sat up and glanced around the unfamiliar room.

Yesterday's events came flooding back to her and she remembered: Damien's spare bedroom. Oh, he'd tried to be gentlemanly by offering to let her take his room while he slept on the futon, but she'd insisted on sleeping in the spare room. The thought of spending the night in his bed, even without him in it, overwhelmed her.

He hadn't been kidding about its state, though. It was packed with books and boxes. There was, however, still enough room for her to do her morning yoga stretches — carefully.

Conscious that she'd worn one of Damien's T-shirts to bed because she hadn't thought to pack a bag, Kari eased out of bed and wished for a pair of shorts. She had no one but herself to blame for not having any. She'd been too focused on the unwanted wedding to think ahead to what would come after the ceremony. So, she took a deep breath and sneezed. Loudly. More than once.

She was beginning to get her dust-induced sneezing fit under control when a knock sounded on the door.

The wooden door muffled Damien's voice. "Are you okay in there?"

"Fine," Kari called, raising one leg to do a tree pose. "But you should have warned me about all the dust in here."

"I told you to take my bed."

"I might have, had I known you hadn't cleaned in here for months." No, she wouldn't have, but it sounded reasonable. And, for reasons she didn't care to examine, she wanted Damien to think she was reasonable.

"Well, there's not a lot of reason to dust a room when you're only using it for storage."

Kari giggled and dropped to her hands and knees. "That explains the inch-thick layer of dust."

"Surely it's not that bad."

She craned her neck to glance at the door. He sounded offended. Maybe her new husband was a neat freak. "Actually, it is," she replied, pushing herself up to a downward-facing dog.

"I have to see for myself. I'm coming in."

Her rear end in the air, facing the door, Kari cried, "Wait!"

****

Too late. Damien pushed the door open and his mouth immediately went dry. His wife's long, lean legs went straight up to meet her almost-bare bottom, covered only by a white lace thong.

I doubt the network provided that to go with her wedding dress, he thought, his eyes glued to her nicely rounded glutes.

Squealing, Kari jerked upright and tugged his T-shirt down to cover her butt. Then she glared at him. "You can't go bursting in on people like that!"

"Sorry," he replied, though he wasn't in the slightest. The sight of Kari in her bare-assed glory had been worth the scolding he was sure would come.

"You should be." With that, she plopped on the futon and wrapped the sheet around herself. If she was trying to hide anything from him, it didn't help. The image of her nearly naked rear end now seared his eyelids. "Now, if you don't mind, I'd like some privacy."

Damien regarded her warily. With the way he'd invaded her space, Kari had every right to pitch a fit, so why wasn't she doing it?

"Why?"

"Why do I want to be left alone?"

He shook his head. "No, why should I be sorry? You have nothing to be ashamed of. You're the kind of woman who's meant to run around in nothing but skimpy underwear."

"Not in this lifetime," she muttered under her breath.

He couldn't believe someone who looked like his wife wouldn't want to show off her assets. Lord knows, he sure enjoyed what he'd seen. "Why not?"

"Because you're wrong," she snapped. Still swathed in navy cotton, she left the bed and stalked to the window. "I'm not someone who enjoys being ogled."

Damien couldn't help it; he laughed. He was about as wrong as the Dan Ryan Expressway was "express" during rush hour. She was born to attract men's attention and to revel in it.

"You're still doing it," Kari reminded, turning from the window to cast him a reproachful glance.

"Was I ogling you? Well, then I truly am sorry."

"No, you're not." She turned away from him and toward the window. Her face was half-hidden by masses of blond hair, somehow much curlier than it had been yesterday, but he could still detect disapproval in her posture.

What or who had convinced her she wasn't desirable?

Damien longed to prove to Kari just how alluring he found her. He wanted to plunge his hands into those curls, gaze into her chocolate eyes and tip her face up for a kiss.

No. What he really wanted was to pull the "save the greyhounds" T-shirt he'd loaned Kari over her head to see if her bra matched that thong, or if she even wore a bra. He guessed not.

Damien shook his head to clear the image that was taking shape. His ready-and-willing hormones were just going to have to wait. He wasn't in college anymore, and Kari was nothing like the good-time girls he'd dated then.

Unless, of course, he was wrong and she wanted to fool around. It couldn't hurt to ask, right?

"You're right; I'm not." Damien deepened his voice and let his eyes telegraph an unspoken invitation. "But I can think of a few ways you can punish me."

****

Kari's pulse started racing. For some reason, flirting wasn't scary with Damien. She'd even go so far as to say she felt safe, confident that he wouldn't push her into something she wasn't ready for. Maybe it was because he worked with animals, but she doubted her new husband would intentionally harm any living being — herself included. Wasn't his almost immediate apology for kissing her in front of the cameras and restricting himself to touching her hand after that proof enough?

He couldn't have known her hand was such an erogenous zone. She certainly hadn't.

As long as she felt safe, why not let her inner vixen out to play? Bethany would tell her she'd been repressing that side of her personality for far, far too long.

Maybe Beth was right. For nearly a decade, she'd shied away from men like Damien — guys who made her heart speed up and her flesh ache in places she preferred to ignore. Instead, she'd dated nice, safe, boring men in whose presence her heart rate stayed level and her feet remained firmly on the ground.

What had it gotten her? A string of mind-numbing dates with men she refused to introduce to her parents. She didn't want to bother getting her family's hopes up when she knew they had no future.

She doubted she and Damien had a future together, either — at least not beyond the contest-mandated cohabitation period. Somehow, with him, it didn't matter. She was ready to test her limits.

Kari licked her lips and whirled away from the window. Then she took a deep breath and dropped the sheet. "What did you have in mind, you bad, bad boy?"

For a split second, Damien looked surprised. He hid it well, though, and took a few steps toward her before replying.

"Your choice, sweetheart."

Thinking back to yesterday's encounter on the front steps of the church, Kari knew exactly what she wanted. What she craved. "Kiss me."

"Gladly."

As Damien closed the gap between them and put his hands on her shoulders, Kari shut her eyes. This time, she braced herself for the heat simmering between them, so she was prepared for the jolt of awareness that shot through her when his lips covered hers. She opened her mouth, readily accepting his tongue.

His hands slid off her shoulders, settling on her waist and tugging her against him. She went willingly, allowing her body to melt against his. He felt warm, solid, and his proximity made every fiber of her body sing with awareness.

All Kari's thoughts were focused on the nearly forgotten sensations Damien sent zinging through her system. Her hands tentatively explored the muscles of his neck and back, and then traced a path down his spine to his rear end.

Damien growled low in his throat and responded in kind, dropping his hands to cup her buttocks. Then he slid a finger underneath the edge of her panties and Kari gasped.

He stilled and pulled away, breathing heavily. His gaze held hers. "Too much?"

She shook her head and laced her fingers behind his neck to tug him back to her. She doubted she could ever have too much of this particular man.

This time, she froze. That thought should have scared her, but it didn't. She wanted him — all of him. She dropped her hands to his waist and slid them under his T-shirt, tangling her fingers in his chest hair.

Damien groaned. "Are you trying to make me crazy?"

"Shhh." Stretching up on her tiptoes, Kari kissed his mouth.

His hands dropped to her butt again, and the next thing she knew her stomach was becoming intimately acquainted with a part of his anatomy that appeared happy to see her. As they continued locking lips, he slid his hands up her ribcage and cupped her breasts. When his thumbs brushed her nipples, they tightened even more and she gasped again.

This time, he must have taken it for the encouragement it was, because he didn't stop. Instead, he reached down to grab the hem of her shirt and tugged it over her head before covering her already-tingling breasts with his hands again. She thrust her chest forward, pressing herself more firmly into his hands.

She almost cried out when his hands deserted her breasts for her waist. Then Damien dipped his head and took her left nipple in his mouth. His tongue laved the tight bud before he started to suck. The sensation went way beyond her breast; his suckling seemed to tug at something deep in her womb.

Her breath coming in quick pants now, Kari urged him to give her other breast the same treatment. He appeared about ready to do just that when the phone rang.

Chapter Three

The shrill ringing broke the sensual spell Kari and Damien had cast over themselves, but neither of them had the breath to speak at first. Their rapid breathing and the ringing phone were the only sounds in the room.

"I'd better get that. It could be the clinic." He looked like he'd prefer to ignore the phone. She certainly would.

Kari nodded and struggled to contain her disappointment as she watched him disappear. The minute he was out of sight, sanity returned and she started to wonder what had come over her. She'd been more than ready to drag him on top of her on the fold-out couch.

She rolled her eyes. She knew exactly what had come over her: a bad case of lust, pure and simple. Damien, after all, did have quite the bod.

She ruthlessly shoved that thought aside, determined to force her inner vixen back into the closet. It was where that little tramp belonged for encouraging her to rush into bed.

Of course, Damien wasn't just anyone. He was her lawfully wedded husband.

Shaking her head at the thought obviously planted by the vixen she planned to ignore, Kari retrieved the T-shirt Damien had pulled over her head. After tugging it back on, she bent to pick up the sheet she'd dropped. She was remaking the bed when Damien reappeared in the doorway.

"It's your mother."

"My mom?" Kari repeated. How on earth had her mother gotten Damien's number? And why hadn't she called Kari's cell phone?

She knew why. Her cell phone was back at her apartment. She'd left it there on purpose, not wanting anyone to be able to reach her.

He nodded. "And she doesn't sound happy."

"She must have seen the news," Kari said, sighing. "I'd better talk to her."

"Phone's in the kitchen."

She hurried to the kitchen, acutely aware of Damien trailing her. When he brushed past with a mumbled "excuse me," his fingers grazed her rear end. He flashed her a devilish grin before he began making coffee. "Thought we could both use some."

"Thanks." Kari forced her attention away from her tingling bottom to the phone, wondering why the familiarity didn't offend her. With her mom waiting on the phone, she didn't have time to figure it out. After taking one more deep, calming breath, she picked up the receiver, ready to face a wave of maternal disapproval.

"Hi, Mom. What's up?"

"What's up?" Sara Parker's voice rose an octave. "What's up? You don't think you should have told your parents you were getting married yesterday?"

"Um—"

"I had to hear it from Mrs. Mackenzie. She was too happy to bring us her morning paper today and point to a photo of that spectacle you called a wedding."

Kari winced. Sally Mackenzie was the Parkers' next-door neighbor, and quite possibly the nosiest woman on the planet. She should have known that old bat would take it upon herself to spread the news. "Sorry."

"Well, I can see why you wouldn't want us to know, dear." Her mother's voice was gentler now. "Are you okay?"

"Sure."

"You sound winded." Suspicion tinged her mom's voice. "So did the man who answered the phone."

She latched onto the first excuse that popped into her head. "We just got back from a run."

Damien, still by the coffeemaker, raised his eyebrows and mouthed, "Run?" Kari stuck her tongue out at him. She certainly wasn't going to tell her mom the truth of what they'd been doing. Mothers didn't need to know their children had sex lives.

"I take it that was the new husband? What's his name?"

"Damien," Kari replied. "Damien Walker. He's a veterinarian."

"And he likes to run," her mother added. "Is that all you know about the man? Really, Kari. You're not so desperate that you need to enter a 'Get a Love Life' contest."

Kari sighed. She'd better explain. "I didn't, Mom. Bethany entered for me."

"Bethany thought you needed to get a love life?"

Rolling her eyes, Kari again wished Bethany weren't addicted to Romance TV. Her friend watched that channel, and took note of all its contests and promotions, every chance she got. "She was hoping to win me a subscription to a dating service."

Sara made a satisfied sound. "Bethany's a good girl."

"She is?" That was not what Kari had expected her mother to say.

"Oh yes. When you didn't answer your phone this morning, I called Bethany's cell phone. I know you told me only to use her number for emergencies, but I thought this qualified, dear. For all I knew, you could have been lying dead in the street somewhere. What kind of man would try to win a wife?"

"Mom," Kari interrupted. She wasn't in the mood to hear her mother's imaginings of her untimely demise. Her mother always imagined the worst.

"Sorry, dear. I know you think I worry too much, but apparently, I need to fret a little. Look at the things you get into!" Her mother took a deep breath and continued, "Anyway, Bethany gave me this phone number."

"Figures," Kari muttered, making a mental note to ask her friend how *she* had gotten Damien's number. Surely Damien hadn't given it to Bethany. The two of them hadn't said more than two words to each other all day.

Damien handed her a mug of fresh, hot coffee. Kari squeezed the phone between her shoulder and ear and gratefully accepted the brew. Wrapping both hands around the cup, she inhaled its heavenly aroma.

Eager to get off the phone and enjoy her coffee, she invented an excuse. "Look, Mom, I really need to hang up now. If I don't do some stretching, my muscles will get stiff and I won't be able to move later."

"Okay, dear," her mother replied. Kari thought she heard a smile in her voice. "Just do me one favor, will you?"

"Sure."

"Be careful."

****

Amused, Damien listened as his new wife lied to her mother — again. First running, then stretching. Did she really think her mom was fooled?

Personally, he didn't think Mrs. Parker believed a word of it.

He knew his parents wouldn't. As hard as it was for him to imagine, they'd been hot-blooded honeymooners once themselves. He certainly hadn't been hatched from a pod. Besides, anyone with even a scintilla of imagination could figure out what they had really been doing.

Man, what he and Kari shared had been hot. Once she'd decided she wanted to fool around, she'd gone at it wholeheartedly. He got hard again just remembering the feel of her nipples jutting against his palms.

Damien groaned softly. His hands itched to be filled again; his body clamored to pick up where they'd left off.

He watched as Kari took a tentative sip of coffee, and then smiled. He imagined that liquid sliding down her throat and warming her from the inside. He'd rather he be the one to heat her up, sliding between her legs and —

Kari's voice broke into his reverie. "Would you stop staring at me?"

"Was I ogling again?"

Her lips pursed in disapproval. "You know you were."

"I enjoy looking at my wife. Is that a crime?" He grinned. "Because if it is, you might as well lock me up and throw away the key."

Her cheeks flushed an appealing shade of pink. "Thanks. I think."

"You're quite welcome." Still smiling, he asked, "Ready to get back to that run?"

She shook her head. "I think the moment's past."

Damien could beg to differ, but he wouldn't. This was, after all, only day one of their marriage. He still had eighty-nine more to earn her trust.

Still, he couldn't help doing a little more wheedling. "I'd be happy to help you do some stretching, at least. I'd hate to make you a complete liar."

Kari wrinkled her nose and shook her head. "I had to come up with some reason to hang up. If I hadn't, I'd probably still be talking to Mom when lunchtime rolls around."

"She's long-winded, huh?"

She nodded. "She can ramble for hours about absolutely nothing."

Damien laughed. "My mom's like that, too. Maybe we should get them together to see if they can outtalk one another."

"Maybe." The word was an agreement of sorts, her tone anything but. Without giving him time to pursue the subject, she headed toward the refrigerator. "I'm starved. What's for breakfast?"

Damien took a quick mental inventory of the contents of his bachelor's refrigerator: A half-empty carton of milk that had expired two months ago, two half-finished cups of takeout coffee, a few partial cartons of leftover Chinese food from earlier in the week and a moldy block of cheddar cheese.

He rushed ahead of Kari and stepped in front of the fridge, embarrassed to let her to see how meager its contents really were. When had it gotten so empty, anyway? For a guy who claimed he liked to save money, he ate out way too often.

"Umm, there's not much here. How about I run down to the corner deli and pick up some bagels and cream cheese?"

Her dimples flashed. "That sounds great."

****

A few minutes later, Damien reemerged from his bedroom in blue jeans and a dark green T-shirt emblazoned with a sad-looking basset hound. It probably needed saving, if the shirt he'd loaned her was indicative of a penchant for buying cause T-shirts. As he headed into the late-May morning, Kari strolled back to his bedroom in search of something else to wear.

Really, she couldn't be running around the apartment half-naked. She'd worked hard to be comfortable in her own skin, but that didn't mean she could, or should, flaunt herself in front of Damien.

Even if he did seem to enjoy looking.

She needed pants. She didn't want to put her wedding dress back on. Even in the skirt and T-shirt, she'd feel ridiculously overdressed for a lazy Sunday at home.

Home. Kari tested the word in her mind. It was weird to call this place her home when she hadn't even taken the grand tour yet.

She needed to. Kari wasn't ashamed to admit she was curious to know more about the man she'd been coerced into marrying. She really should explore.

She began by looking around his bedroom. Typically male, with a navy blue comforter and white sheets on the bed, with no dust ruffle or throw pillows. The bed was big and solid, with a heavy oak headboard. It had a built-in bookcase that was filled with carefully arranged books.

The whole room was as neat as the bookshelves. No dirty clothes strewn on the floor or magazines stacked up by the bed, like in her bedroom. She didn't see a speck of dust anywhere, either.

"So his spare room's the only messy one in the place," Kari murmured, remembering the spotless kitchen countertops and the mildew-free shower curtain she'd seen in the bathroom last night. Maybe he *was* a neat freak.

Though she loathed going through Damien's drawers — she wasn't that nosy, for goodness' sake — there was no way around it if she wanted to find something to wear.

"I should have asked Damien for a pair of sweats before he left," she muttered as she crossed the room to the dresser. Too bad she hadn't thought that far in advance. Her only excuse was that her brain was still addled from their romp in her room.

Kari avoided the top drawer, where most people kept their underwear, because she had no desire to see those. Instead, she opted for drawer number two. It was full of T-shirts like the one she was wearing. Drawer number three held jeans. The bottom drawer contained the jackpot. No sweatpants, but jogging shorts were stacked in four neat piles, each one occupying its own quadrant of drawer space.

Hmm. Maybe Damien actually did run. She giggled. If so, she'd have to go with him a couple of times, just to keep things kosher with her mom.

She grabbed a pair of red shorts from the top of the pile and pulled them on, glad the apartment was at a comfortable temperature. At least she wouldn't freeze. As she cinched the drawstring and tied a bow, the intercom buzzed.

"Damien probably forgot his key." She slammed the drawer shut and dashed back to the entryway to answer the call. "Yes?"

"Kari? It's Bethany. Let me in."

Beth? What was she doing here? Knowing she was about to find out, Kari buzzed her friend in and opened the door.

Bethany came through the door a few minutes later, wheeling Kari's suitcase behind her.

"Hey, Kar," she said in greeting. "I figured you probably could use something to wear."

Then Bethany's eyes roamed over Kari's borrowed T-shirt and shorts, and she grinned. "But maybe I was wrong. You look awfully cute in loverboy's clothes."

"Give me that." Kari snatched the suitcase from Bethany and rolled it down the hall to her bedroom. She was glad someone had had enough presence of mind to pack her a bag. "I'll be right back."

Back in the living room in a pair of her own denim shorts and a white, sleeveless shirt, Kari felt much more comfortable. Bethany had even grabbed her cell phone, which indicated a dozen missed calls from her mom, and the pick for Kari's hair.

"Thanks, Beth."

"No problem," her friend replied. "I can bring you some more things the next time I go over to your place to check on Rhett and Ashley, if you want."

"That'd be great."

Bethany grinned again and patted the couch beside her. "Sit down and tell me all about last night."

"Nothing happened," Kari denied, even as she felt her cheeks warm.

"If it was nothing, why's your face getting red?"

Not for the first time, she cursed her fair complexion. Blushes always gave her away. "Because—" She stopped, remembering she hadn't told Bethany where to find her, because she hadn't known herself until after they'd parted for the day. "Stop giving *me* the third degree, Beth. I want to know how you knew where I was."

This time, Bethany's smile radiated satisfaction. "Let's just say loverboy's friend, Cody, was very knowledgeable."

Unimpressed, Kari made a face at her friend. "You mean it was my wedding night and *you* were getting the action?"

Bethany frowned. "Don't tell me you didn't get any."

"With a guy I hardly know? You know me better than that!" Kari shot back, purposely forgetting to mention her early morning interlude with Damien. There were some things that even Bethany didn't need to know, and this was one of them. Beth would never let her hear the end of it.

"But Cody said Damien was really into you, and I know he turns you on."

"That doesn't mean we had to act on it," Kari pointed out, quite reasonably, she thought.

"Doesn't mean you couldn't have, either."

It figured Beth wasn't satisfied with that. She never was,

when it came to needling Kari about her avoidance of the sensual side of life. "Not everyone hops into bed the minute they meet."

Bethany rolled her eyes. "When there's that much attraction between you, you should."

Kari opened her mouth to protest, but Bethany continued. "You two really were hot for each other, Kar, and except for sheer size, he seems nothing like Rob. So what happened?"

"That remains to be seen."

Her protest might as well have gone unspoken, because Beth merely repeated the question. "What went wrong?"

Kari squirmed under her friend's unwavering scrutiny. "Nothing went wrong!"

The instant the words were out, she ducked her head. How was it Bethany could always get her to confess secrets she'd prefer to keep?

Bethany's eyebrows lifted. "Really?"

"Really. We almost did it in his spare bedroom this morning."

"Almost?"

"Mom called and ruined the moment."

"Jeez, Kar. I'm sorry. I shouldn't have asked Cody for Damien's number."

"I would have had to talk to her sometime." Kari shrugged, and then grinned. "Besides, I'm glad something interrupted us. I didn't intend to go that far so quickly. I thought we'd kiss a little bit, but the next thing I knew, he was all over me and I couldn't get enough of him, either."

Bethany brushed away a pretend tear. "Little Kari's all grown up."

"Will you be serious?" Kari poked her friend's arm. "Beth, I wanted to fall into bed with him and stay there all day, and night, long."

Damien's voice rumbled from the entryway. "There's something a guy doesn't hear every day."

Chapter Four

Kari glanced at him and quickly looked away, hiding her flaming-red face behind a cloud of blond curls. Damien shook his head at her bashfulness and walked to the kitchen. She really had nothing to be ashamed of. He'd been just as eager. If that phone hadn't interrupted ...

Unwilling to display a raging hard-on in front of company, he slammed the door on the thought. He deposited bags of bagels, cream cheese and juice on the counter, as Kari's friend, What's Her Name, whispered, "Now that he's heard you say that, there'll be no living with that male ego."

"Come on now," he protested, striding to the living room. "I'm not that bad. To prove it, I'll even invite you to stay for breakfast. There's plenty."

"No thanks. I already had breakfast with Co—" She stopped and rephrased her reply. "I already ate."

Damien shrugged. He didn't care whom she ate with. "Suit yourself."

"I always do," Bethany replied with a wink.

He watched the redhead make an exit, not bothering to try to figure out what she meant by that. Whoever knew what a woman meant by anything?

Especially his beautiful wife, Damien thought, looking back to the couch where she still sat, trying to hide behind her hair. He grinned, supremely pleased to know she really was hot for him. His self-imposed exile from the dating trenches hadn't deadened his instincts.

Those same instincts were telling him not to push her, so he didn't. Instead, he steered the conversation to a less-charged topic. "Since I wasn't sure what you liked, I got plain and blueberry bagels and orange and apple juice. Take your pick."

She raised her head to look at him and tucked her hair behind her left ear. "Blueberry, please," she said with a hesitant smile, probably hoping he was going to ignore what he'd overheard. "They're my favorite."

"I'll keep that in mind." He was willing to let the comment

slide for now. It was enough to be certain he was on the right track where Kari was concerned. If she wanted him as much as he wanted her — and she obviously did, unless she was lying to What's Her Name — they'd get physical soon enough. He could wait.

Damien watched Kari slice a blueberry bagel and pop it into the toaster, and then sighed. He really should find out what her friend's name was. He couldn't go around calling the redhead "What's Her Name" for the next three months.

But he wanted to do it without Kari knowing that he didn't already know the girl's name, because he was sure she'd introduced them at the reception. He didn't want his wife thinking he was absent-minded. He wasn't. He actually had a great memory; he had to in his line of work. The animals' charts only told him so much; it was up to him to remember that Mrs. Trumbull indulged her Persian by feeding it tuna once a week, or that little Timmy Hill tended to make his family's chihuahua even more nervous. Being chased by a kid with scissors tended to do that to a dog.

Back to the issue at hand: How to learn What's Her Name's name.

"Your friend seems nice."

Kari shrugged and retrieved her now-toasted bagel. "She has her moments."

Strike one. Time for a new tactic. "I don't think she likes me very much."

"Like you? She doesn't even know you," Kari replied, looking up from the cream cheese she was smearing on her bagel. "Neither do I, for that matter."

Damn. Strike two, and now Kari was back to denying what little they had going for them in this mock marriage of theirs: the attraction. Damien wasn't about to let that slide. "You know me a heck of a lot better than she does, sweetheart."

He actually heard her gulp before she replied. "I suppose so."

"Oh, I know so," Damien assured her, taking a step toward her. "And she'll never know me the way you do."

Kari countered his step forward with two steps of her own in the other direction. Then she grabbed the cream cheese-covered knife, holding it between them like a sword. "Good to know."

Damien edged backward. It was no fun to try to get cozy with a woman who was threatening to impale him with a butter knife. It was much too early in the morning to risk bodily injury, or possibly even a slow, painful death, if Kari was as jumpy as she seemed.

Besides, he still hadn't discovered What's Her Name's real name. "I don't think she likes men much."

Kari's eyes widened. "Are you kidding me?"

"Well, she obviously doesn't have a high opinion of the male ego."

"What woman does?" Kari responded philosophically before pouring herself some apple juice. "We've all been burned a few too many times." Then, as if she'd said too much, she turned to face the wall over the sink, pretending to be fascinated by the black-and-white tiles of the backsplash.

Interested, Damien studied his wife's back. He could hear her chewing and swallowing pieces of bagel as he contemplated her remark.

So, she'd been burned by some guy with a big ego, huh? He was probably the same jerk who'd given her that raging inferiority complex.

Damien shook his head. There he went, practicing psychology without a license again. He had a tendency to do that. Sometimes he wondered if he should have gone into psychiatry instead of veterinary medicine, but he always came back to the animals. They were so much sweeter and less complicated than humans were, and they gave their love unconditionally.

Sighing, Damien grabbed a plain bagel and put it in the toaster. This wasn't the right time to get to the root of Kari's apparent issues with men. He had a more immediate concern: What's Her Name.

"So your friend likes men, huh?"

Kari giggled. "Very much so."

"Just not me."

"You have to give her some time," Kari said softly, turning to face him again.

Damien gave up. Kari obviously wasn't going to mention What's Her Name by name. Since he wasn't about to admit he didn't know her name, What's Her Name she'd remain — at least for the time being.

Kari spoke again, even more softly this time, and reached for his hand. "We all need a little time, Damien."

Encouraged that his wife had sought out contact with him, Damien smiled warmly at her. Then he whispered in her ear, "There's no hurry, Kari. Time's the one thing we have plenty of."

Yeah. Two months, twenty-nine days and counting, he thought. Plenty of time to get to know the woman Cody and the honchos at Romance TV had thrown into his path.

He already liked her, and Lord knew he lusted after her. Who knew? In another couple of months, their marriage might go from a complete fake to a real union of both body and mind.

He sure hoped so, because she fascinated him. She'd already started to liven up his boring bachelor existence.

****

Kari didn't need the wake-up call when her alarm kicked on the next morning, blaring some obnoxious remake of what used to be a great song.

"Perfect," she groaned. The crappy song playing on the radio was the second sign that today was going to be one hell of a Monday.

The first? The nightmare that had awakened her long before the alarm went off. She'd been lying in bed for a half hour already, staring at the nondescript white ceiling without really seeing it.

Oh, the nightmare hadn't started out as one. In her dream, she and Damien had been finishing what they'd started in what was her bedroom for the time being. And it had been glorious. If she tried hard, she could still summon up the warm glow she'd felt while the dream Damien was kissing her and fondling her and …

Then, in her dream, she'd opened her eyes and it wasn't Damien in the bed with her. It was her ex-boyfriend, Rob, looming over her, taunting her, and pressuring her to …

Kari groaned again as unpleasant memories came flooding back. Rob grabbing her ass in front of her friends, convincing her to let him record them having sex by promising no one else would ever see the tape, then charging his buddies for a "private screening," satisfying himself, then pushing her away with contempt in his eyes.

Her stomach lurched.

"I think I'm going to be sick."

She jumped out of bed and ran for the bathroom. Used to living alone and desperate to reach the commode before she threw up all over the hall, she didn't think about the fact that the bathroom door was partially closed. She simply pushed it open and made it to the toilet just in time.

As she kneeled in front of the toilet bowl, resting her forehead on the cool porcelain, the memories receded and the world started to come back into focus. It was then she realized the water in the shower was running. Scratch that: It was shutting off. The shower curtain rings clinked together as the curtain whooshed back.

"What the—? Kari? Are you okay?"

Her face still buried in the toilet bowl, she mumbled an affirmative. No way was she going to turn her head and get an eyeful of her naked, wet husband. As much as the thought tempted a part her, she didn't need any more fodder for dreams that'd only go bad.

"Are you sure?"

"I'm sure," she told him. "Last night's dinner must not have agreed with me." She mentally crossed her fingers, hoping he didn't remember that they'd shared a frozen pizza. How often did people get sick from eating pizza?

Silence. It stretched out for so long that Kari started scrambling for another, more plausible excuse. No way was she going to attempt to explain the ugly truth. She and Damien were only going to know each other for a couple of months — not nearly long enough for her to trust him with her past.

"Then you think you could move?"

"M-move?"

"Out of the way," Damien explained. "I can't leave the shower with you there."

Figuring there'd be nothing too embarrassing at her eye level, Kari carefully slanted a glance sideways and realized that she was indeed near the edge of the bathtub. She also was treated to a side view of Damien's calf.

A very nice calf it was, too. Muscular but not overly so, and sprinkled with just enough hair.

"Kari?"

She felt her face heat the not-so-cool-anymore porcelain. "Sorry," she mumbled. Still on her knees, she edged toward the door. Behind her, she heard Damien step out of the tub.

A few seconds went by. "Okay."

"Pardon?"

"Off your knees, Kari. It's safe now."

As she slowly stood upright, Kari thought she detected laughter in Damien's voice. She whirled to face him. "Don't you dare laugh at me!"

"Do I look like I'm laughing?"

Kari's eyes roamed over Damien, taking in the droplets of water glistening on his broad chest and the dark green towel slung low on his hips. If it slid an inch or so ...

She gulped and shook her head. "That towel should be banned."

"Oh yeah?"

Kari nodded. "Yeah."

Damien grinned lazily at her, reaching for the terrycloth. "I can take it off, if you'd like."

****

"No!"

Her reply was so quick and so definitely negative that Damien raised an eyebrow. Surely the prospect of seeing him naked wasn't that horrifying. "No?"

Stammering, she rushed on. "I-I d-didn't mean that the way it sounded. I meant that, in that towel, you're bordering on indecent exposure."

"What's so indecent about a little nudity?" Damien teased, ready as always to poke fun at their situation. If he didn't treat it as a joke, he'd go nuts. "We are, after all, husband and wife."

Kari obviously failed to see the humor. "Very funny."

Okay, so maybe their situation wasn't that hilarious. However, he had to laugh to keep from screaming with frustration. What had made Romance TV think a marriage between two complete strangers was a smart idea?

When he voiced that thought, Kari's response was swift and cynical.

"Ratings, Damien. TV's nothing more than a numbers game. I'm sure people tuned in just to see us squirm."

And here he thought it was because the network hoped to make magic for two lonely people. What did he know?

Damien watched, slightly stunned at so much cynicism from a woman so young and beautiful, as she turned toward the sink and grabbed her toothbrush. She carefully squeezed the toothpaste from the bottom of the tube.

As he settled in beside Kari at the sink, Damien smiled to himself. It was good to know that, even if she didn't have a romantic bone in her oh-so-practical body, she did know how to squeeze the tube of toothpaste properly.

It was a start, at least.

****

Kari glanced up from her work when her cell phone rang.

Her morning's premonition was proving right. So far, today had been one hell of a Monday. After her narrow escape from seeing her husband in all his glory, she'd headed to the office, where her coworkers were paying her a ridiculous amount of attention. They'd spent the morning walking past her office to gawk at her, and rooms fell silent when she walked into them. A few brave souls even made rude comments about how she'd spent her weekend.

She sighed. Between the nosy coworkers and her ringing cell phone, she'd be lucky to get any work done at all today. The ringtone, "Wind Beneath My Wings," told her it was her mother calling, so she let it go to voicemail. It was already noon, and she needed to finish this report by the end of the day. She had no time for what was sure to be a lengthy talk with Mom.

She'd just refocused on the paperwork when her phone started playing "Wind Beneath My Wings" again. Kari sighed. If her mother was that desperate to talk to her, she wouldn't get any more work done until she took the call.

Her mother didn't bother to wait for a greeting. "Kari, I need you. Your father's in the hospital."

The word hospital sent panic racing through Kari. Sure, her mom was prone to exaggeration, but a hospital visit was serious business in any case. "What happened? Where are you guys?"

"We're at St. Mary's. Your brothers and sisters are already here."

Dread made Kari sick to her stomach all over again. If her siblings had all left work to gather at the hospital, the situation had to be grave. Her report could wait. "Okay, Mom. I'll be there as soon as I can."

Kari tucked her phone into her purse and grabbed her coat and then stopped by her boss' office to say she was leaving to take care of a family emergency. Twenty minutes later, she was in the ER waiting room at St. Mary's. Her mother sat in the center of the room, surrounded by her siblings. All but one of them was married, and their assorted spouses were in tow.

She swallowed hard. So many Parkers gathered in one place couldn't be a good sign. Her entire family only managed to get together for three occasions: family dinners, weddings and funerals. "What's going on? Is Dad okay?"

Her mother's hands fluttered helplessly, and it pained Kari to see her normally verbose mother at a loss for words. Her sister Shannon's husband, Tim, was the one who explained. "The doctors say Frank had a mild heart attack. He'll be fine, but they want him to cut back on some of the stress in his life."

Soothed by Tim's proper English accent and relieved that it wasn't something more serious, Kari bit back a laugh. "Did you tell the doctors Dad runs a restaurant? Stress is part of the business."

Tim smiled. "I believe your father has spent the last half hour trying to impress that point upon anyone who'll listen."

Kari grinned, even more reassured. If her dad was his opinionated self, the threat to his health wasn't as serious as she'd feared. She sank down next to her oldest sister, Claire, on a black vinyl couch and waited with the rest of the family for the doctors to release him.

Not one of her brothers and sisters needled her about her recent marriage, an indication of just how worried they were about Dad. Any other day, at least one of them would have started teasing her about being desperate enough to win a husband. Kari was used to their mockery, having been the butt of many a joke over the years.

She was glad they were preoccupied but wished it hadn't been at the expense of her father's health. While they waited, she took note of the way Shannon leaned on her husband for support. Her oldest brother, Chris, carried on a quiet conversation with his pregnant wife. Steve disappeared and returned a while later carrying a glass of water and package of crackers for his wife, who'd announced at the last family dinner that she was expecting. Her brother's delivery was so sweet — and demonstrated such devotion.

She heaved a sigh. Seeing all her siblings here, with their loving spouses, made her keenly aware of what she'd been missing. She might insist to Beth she didn't want a man in her life, but the truth was a part of her wanted what her brothers and sisters had. She longed to have someone who would stand by her side at times like this, supporting her in a time of need.

Then why didn't you call Damien?

Kari brushed aside her conscience's question. She'd barely known the man for forty-eight hours. Temporary husband or not, he had no reason to drop what he was doing to sit with her at the hospital. For all she knew, he'd have laughed at her for asking.

Her horrible day didn't improve the next time her cell phone rang just before six o'clock. It was someone from Romance TV, saying her presence was urgently required at the network headquarters for a 6:30 meeting.

Kari made her excuses to the family. She'd already been in to see her dad, and there was nothing she could do for him by waiting around. She could do more good for her family by seeing what the network wanted. With any luck, maybe they'd decided forcing two strangers to live together was a bad idea and were going to hand over the prize money early.

In her rush to get from the hospital to the network's office, she caught her heel in the El platform. Not only did she break the heel on her favorite pair of pumps, but she also twisted her ankle. She barely noticed the red velvet furnishings and dimly lit room when she limped into the lobby of the offices of Romance TV at 6:34.

She almost hobbled right past Damien, who sat on a red velvet, lip-shaped couch in the lobby. Smiling, he rose to meet her, but his smile quickly turned to a look of concern.

"Kari, are you okay?"

"That's the second time you've asked me that today," she reminded him, scowling. "But, no. I'm not. Today's been one of the worst days of my life."

"Mine, too. The only people at work who didn't give me funny looks were the animals I treated. Their owners stared at me like I'd sprouted horns and a pointy tail."

Kari lifted the corners of her mouth in a tired smile. If only her coworkers' stares had been the worst part of her day. "I just spent the last five hours at the hospital. My dad had a heart attack."

When Damien looked stunned, she almost wished she'd called him to give him a heads up. "Is he okay?"

She nodded. "It was only a mild one."

"That's a relief." He reached for her hand and gave it a squeeze. "You could have called me, you know."

Kari looked at him, surprised. She didn't know, but that was okay. They hadn't known each other long enough for her to rely on Damien. She brushed aside her conscience's reminder that she'd have liked to have him with her. "There was nothing you could have done."

His eyes searched her face. "I guess not. Ready to face the network?"

"What do you think they want now?"

Damien shrugged. "No idea. How about we go in and find out?"

Nodding her agreement, Kari slipped her arm through his and together they entered the office of Rick Hayworth, the CEO of Romance TV.

"Welcome, welcome," Hayworth greeted them heartily, rising from his chair and coming in front of his desk to shake both their hands. "How's the happy couple today?"

"Fine," Kari mumbled into the carpet.

"Fantastic," Damien echoed somewhat hollowly.

"Good, good," Hayworth said, flashing a smarmy smile. "I'm glad to hear you're adjusting well to married life. Have a seat."

He gestured to a bank of chairs — black leather, not red velvet this time — in front of his massive oak desk. Once Kari and Damien were seated, he smiled again. "Now I'm going to call in the company attorney, Lucas Nelson, and we can get started."

They exchanged an alarmed glance, but Damien was the one to ask, "What's going on here?"

"There's no need to look so serious, son," Hayworth boomed, pressing a button to summon the attorney. "This is good news."

Kari seriously doubted that. Who needed a lawyer present to share good news? She glanced at Damien, wondering if he was thinking the same thing.

After Lucas Nelson took the last empty seat in front of Hayworth's desk, the CEO waddled to a flip chart set up to the left of the desk. "The numbers are in from Saturday's special, and they were phenomenal, especially for the segment on your wedding." He pointed to a spike in the graph. "This presents an exciting opportunity for all of us."

Kari looked over at Damien, then to lawyer Lucas on her other side. Damien looked tense; the lawyer's face betrayed absolutely nothing.

"What kind of an opportunity?" she asked nervously. The last time someone had mentioned an exciting opportunity to her, it was Bethany and she'd ended up saddled with a too-big, too-sexy husband.

"We want to move our cameras into your home for the duration of your cohabitation period to feature you two in a twice-weekly show called 'Just Married.'"

Chapter Five

"You what?" Damien roared. Then he winced. The dull ache behind his temples that had started at work suddenly morphed into a full-blown, throbbing headache.

"We want you to—"

He cut Hayworth off. "I heard you the first time. I just couldn't believe what I was hearing."

"Now, son—"

"Don't 'son' me!" Damien interrupted again, reminding himself not to shout. Yelling wouldn't accomplish anything, except to make his head pound even more than it already did. "It wasn't enough to coerce us into this farce of a wedding? Now you want to invade my home, too?"

"Our."

The soft, feminine voice clearly belonged to Kari. Damien turned to look at his wife, whose skin was almost as pale as the lawyer's blindingly white shirt. "Pardon?"

"You said 'my home,'" she explained, her voice barely above a whisper. As she continued, she looked up from the floor to meet his eyes. "It's not just yours anymore. It's our home."

For an instant, Damien thought he saw a spark of challenge in her rich, brown eyes. But it was gone so quickly that he had to have imagined it. Even so, when she was right …

"You're right," he told her, reaching over to squeeze her hand. "I'm sorry."

She rewarded him with a small smile. Then her eyes took on a mischievous glint. "I like a man who can admit he's wrong."

"Happy to oblige, sweetheart," Damien replied with a grin. He liked Kari's playful side. Too bad it didn't come out more often. In the three days they'd known each other, he'd only seen it a couple of times. He was amazed it had come out tonight, though, when she was worried about her father's health.

"That's great," Hayworth broke in. The man's tone was fake hearty, the voice of a man trying too hard to convince them to go along. "It's just the kind of thing Romance TV viewers will love. You two are naturals!"

Damien glowered at the pesky TV exec. How could he have forgotten, even for an instant, that the creep was in the room with them?

But he had. When Kari smiled at him, everything else in the room ceased to exist. Damien groaned. This wasn't supposed to happen. If he didn't get a handle on his lust, he was never going to make it through the next two months and twenty-eight days without embarrassing himself or his wife.

"My — our home is closed to camera crews," Damien said firmly. Being firm was the only way to deal with pushy people.

"You would, of course, be compensated accordingly."

Beside him, Damien felt Kari freeze. No wonder. Getting paid to humiliate themselves twice a week on TV? She was likely as appalled by the suggestion as he was. "Money isn't every — "

Kari pressed a finger to his lips. "Let the man talk."

"Surely you're not actually entertaining the idea," Damien said, turning to gape at his bride. "I thought you hated being the center of attention."

"I do, but we should at least hear Mr. Hayworth out," she said. Her face was still pale and her breaths were shallow and rapid, but her lips were set in a determined line. "We need to hear his offer."

"Sensible girl," Hayworth approved, beaming at her. "Lucas, why don't you run down the terms?"

Damien heaved a sigh. If Kari was that interested in the cash, she was more like his ex-fiancée than he wanted to admit. The thought disturbed him more than it ought.

Still, he settled back in his chair to listen. Hearing the man out was the least he could do. "This should be good."

The lawyer opened his mouth for the first time to utter three little words: "One million dollars."

****

"O-o-one million d-dollars?" Kari stammered, unable to believe what she'd just heard.

"Each," Lucas Nelson confirmed with a crisp nod. "And that's on top of the original $500,000 prize the two of you will split if you successfully complete the cohabitation period."

She whistled. That was a lot more dough than she had ever expected to see in her lifetime.

The lawyer continued. "At two episodes per week for twelve weeks, that's twenty-four shows, or — "

"Almost $42,000 an episode," Kari concluded gleefully, thinking of how much even one episode's pay would help on her upcoming trip to Alaska. Three weeks' worth would pay off the balance of her student loans and put her firmly on the path of the financially secure, and after a month, her parents would never have to worry again.

Kari suspected financial stress had contributed to her father's heart attack. With her pulling in that kind of cash, her parents easily could hire someone to manage the restaurant so her father could follow doctor's orders to slow down. Knowing him, he probably wouldn't, but at least she could give him the choice.

Besides, it'd help take the edge off her guilt. She suspected another reason for Dad's attack was the marriage she hadn't wanted them to know about. In hindsight, maybe warning her folks would have been better, but it was too late for that now. All she could do was agree to this deal so she could provide her folks with some much-needed cash.

She finally noticed the lawyer gaping at her and tapped her temple. "I'm an accountant. I can do math in my head."

"Oh. Very good," lawyer Lucas replied, erasing all traces of confusion from his face. Kari suddenly had the feeling that he was an excellent gambler. Then again, lawyers probably took a class on how to bluff. "Now, if you agree to accept this payment, a camera crew will move into your home and film you round-the-clock."

****

"No way!" Damien burst out. When Kari turned questioning eyes on him, he defended himself. "I'm not going to let millions of TV viewers watch me go to the bathroom."

"The bathroom will, of course, be off-limits to our crew, just like it was at the wedding reception," the lawyer said smoothly. "Millions of people have no desire to see you use the bathroom."

"Of course they don't, son." Hayworth's voice was still hearty. "They want to see you two interacting, getting to know each other and maybe even falling in love. We are, after all, Romance TV."

"Misguided though you may be," Damien mumbled, rubbing his temples. His headache had gone from bad to worse. The pain stabbing at his temples could probably qualify as a migraine, though he'd never had one before.

The exec cocked his head. "Pardon?"

"This is my life you're monkeying around with," Damien shouted, finally giving up the struggle to keep from yelling. He jumped out of his chair and continued his tirade, throbbing head be damned. "Okay, mine and Kari's. You threw us together hoping we'd make good TV, and now that we have, you want to invade our privacy again so we can continue to entertain your audience."

Hayworth's cheeks shook with indignation. "Plenty of people would love to be in your place, young man."

"Yeah? Well plenty of people smoke crack, too," Damien muttered. "That doesn't make it right."

****

Kari glanced from the sputtering, red-faced TV executive to the equally stormy features of her husband, and she knew that if she didn't do something, her financial future would be a lot less secure.

Years of watching her parents count their pennies each month to keep their restaurant open had taught her the value of having a nice, fat nest egg. It was the reason she'd chosen a stable profession like accounting. Well, that and the fact that she could hide behind her desk, crunching numbers, and not have to do much interacting with strangers.

Now, dangling just out of reach was the tantalizing promise of never having to worry about money again, and of being able to help her parents do the same. She wasn't about to let anything get in her way — not even an angry, oversized husband.

Suppressing a shudder at the thought of Damien's size, Kari reached out to lay her hand on his arm. "Damien?" she said hesitantly. When he looked down at her, she asked, "Can we talk?"

He nodded and she turned her attention to Hayworth and his lawyer. "Mind if we have a few minutes alone?"

"Of course not," the executive said, beaming at her. He obviously sensed she was willing to go along with the network's plan. No surprise there: Kari had never taken a class in bluffing. "We'll just step outside for a moment."

Once they'd vacated the room, Kari pointed at the chair Damien had recently leapt out of. "Sit."

Damien raised an eyebrow. "That sounds like an order."

"Please," Kari amended. "I'd like to have a civil

conversation, if you don't mind."

Damien had the grace to blush. "I kind of lost my temper with Hayworth, huh?"

"With good reason. You're right. They are just using us to garner ratings for the network."

"You agree? But I thought—"

Kari held up her hand. "Still, let's be practical. Think of all the money we'll be throwing away if we turn down this offer."

"Money isn't everything, Kari," Damien said softly. "It causes more problems than it's worth."

"Spoken like someone who's never had to worry about not having enough of it," she snapped.

****

Damien paused to consider that. True, his family had been what his mother called "comfortably well-off." When his parents weren't busy with school, they'd taken family vacations to Greece and Ireland, then explored the United States one state at a time. And, when he graduated from veterinary school, his dad had floated him a loan to buy the practice he loved.

"I have bills to pay. Rent, utilities, my veterinary practice ..." Kari didn't have to know that his dad had told him not to worry about repaying the loan for ten years. He felt a little guilty about that, actually. His parents could be using that money for any number of things, from traveling more to helping his mom's pet cause, Hope House.

Of course, if he and Kari did agree to this TV show, he'd be able to pay his father back right away and have money left over to buy that new state-of-the-art X-ray machine he'd been eyeing for the practice. He'd also be able to join some of his colleagues in setting up a no-kill shelter just outside of the city. They'd asked him to help, and he wanted to get in on the worthy cause, but he didn't feel his practice was established and secure enough for him do so. With this kind of cash, he had no excuse.

"Maybe," he began slowly.

Kari smiled at him. "Yes?"

"Maybe I could find a use for some extra money."

"Does that mean ...?"

Damien rolled his eyes and nodded. "God help us, we're going to be stars of our own reality show."

****

That night, as she stood across what seemed to be the

world's smallest king-sized bed from Damien, Kari wished she hadn't been so eager to accept Romance TV's offer. She wasn't normally impulsive, so why hadn't she thought this through?

She couldn't even excuse this decision with a lust-addled brain, she thought with disgust. Greed-addled, maybe. But what was so wrong about craving financial security not just for herself but also her parents?

"I can't do this!"

Despite her best effort to sound calm, Kari's voice still came out in a panicked hiss. Really, how else was she supposed to sound now that her new roommate had also become a bedmate? With the camera crew around twenty-four-seven, taking over the spare bedroom, she and Damien actually had to sleep in the same room, and Kari knew what that meant.

She could no longer bank on coasting through the network's cohabitation period by avoiding her unwanted husband. The urge she felt to jump Damien's bones would only strengthen. With every minute they spent together, her reasons for wanting to avoid him would dim, replaced by the sheer lust she felt every time she remembered how incredible it felt to be in his arms.

"Of course you can," Damien assured her. She noted crossly that he sounded a lot more relaxed than she felt — just like at the wedding. How could he so readily accept this new life they'd been handed?

He reached down and pulled back the bedding. "All you have to do is take off your slippers and climb into bed."

"With you," she added, her voice flat.

"Yes, with me. You don't think I'm going to spend the next three months sleeping on the floor, do you?"

"I'd rather you did," she muttered under her breath, half-hoping Damien wouldn't hear.

He did. "Tough. That's not gonna happen."

"Why don't I sleep on the floor, then?"

Damien shrugged and perched on the edge of the bed. "Suit yourself."

"Fine," Kari retorted. She sank to the floor and slid her feet out of her fuzzy blue slippers. She was about to stack them up to use as a pillow when a navy-cased pillow landed in her lap with a thud. "Thanks."

"No problem."

Kari plumped her newly acquired down pillow, stretched

out on her back and stared up at the ceiling. The ceiling fan whirred lazily, making only a few slow circles before Kari was convinced that no one would be spending the night on Damien's floor. The hardwood floor wasn't just rock-hard; it was also freezing cold. Kari didn't know how that was possible when it was in the low eighties outside, but if she didn't climb into Damien's bed soon, her boxer-clad butt was going to end up with a severe case of frostbite.

Her eyes darted from the ceiling to the bed, where Damien still sat, watching her intently.

"Stop looking at me like that!" she snapped at him.

"Like what?"

"Like you're on a diet and I'm a hot fudge sundae!"

Damien rolled his eyes. "You think you're that irresistible, huh?"

"Well," Kari began. More concerned with her own response to the look he was giving her, she hadn't considered how conceited the complaint would make her sound.

"Because I have news for you, sweetheart, I can resist. No problem."

She stood and sat on the edge of Damien's bed opposite him, but not before scowling at him. "You don't have to be such a jerk about it."

He glowered right back. "Why shouldn't I be? You're basically saying you don't trust me to keep my hands to myself, right?"

"Uh—"

"Because I've never had to force my attentions on an unwilling woman before, and I don't intend to start anytime soon. So until you decide you want my hands on you, you have nothing to worry about."

With that, Damien turned his back to Kari and punched his pillow into shape. The bedsprings squeaked under his weight as he tried to make himself comfortable on a sliver of what used to be his king-sized bed.

Kari swung her legs onto the bed and laid her head on a pillow. Then she pulled the sheet up to her chin.

Her unwanted husband's declaration should have been making her feel a lot better about having to sleep with him. After all, if he were going to wait for her invitation, he'd have a long, long wait. She had absolutely no intention of asking Damien to lay his hands on any part of her. Ever. She'd been down that road once before, and her ex used her desire to humiliate her.

Yes, Damien's promise should have made her happy. She could sleep worry-free; he wouldn't be planning any stealth attacks on what was left of her virtue.

So why did she feel so awful?

Chapter Six

Damien was still awake long after his bogus bride's breathing became deep and regular. Staring into the darkness, he wondered again what had happened to Kari to make her so distrustful.

Someone, somewhere, had done something to shatter her sense of self and her ability to let go. Despite the fact that she practiced yoga — adorably, he thought — the woman was wound so tightly that she was likely to self-destruct if she didn't loosen up a little. He knew she was capable of loosening up. That Sunday morning encounter in the spare bedroom had more than proven her ability. What he didn't know was how to get Kari back to that place where she was willing to have some fun.

He rolled onto his other side so he could watch his sleeping beauty and maybe pick up a clue as to what made her tick. No such luck. In sleep, she looked relaxed. Her hair fanned out over the pillow, begging him to run his fingers through it. Her lips were soft and oh-so-kissable, and underneath the ratty blue T-shirt she had on, her pert breasts rose and fell gently with each breath.

Damien briefly wondered what, if anything, she was wearing underneath the T-shirt. His mind obligingly conjured up a picture of how she'd looked the morning after the wedding, breasts bared to his hungry gaze. They were small but full, tipped with rosy nipples.

His cock began to stir and he groaned. With such sweet temptation lying inches away from him, how would he ever manage to keep his promise to keep his hands to himself?

Yet he had no choice. He certainly didn't want to add to her obvious issues with men. Besides, he'd always prided himself on being uncomplicated and easy-to-read, the kind of guy who said what he meant and meant what he said.

And he'd said she could trust him.

Okay, he'd said it under duress. He'd been ticked off that she believed the worst of him. After all, he'd done nothing to deserve her mistrust.

Nothing except think of sex nonstop since you first saw her, Damien's conscience gibed. As if wanting to add to the chorus, Mr. Happy jutted against the fabric of his sweatpants.

"Oh, shut up," he grumbled, rolling over again. But he soon realized that removing Kari from his line of sight wasn't going to be enough.

Damien glanced at his alarm clock. It was 11:58 p.m., a ridiculous time to be saddled with a hard-on the size of Florida. Scowling, he got up to take a cold shower. At least the camera crew wasn't set to arrive until morning.

"This is going to be a long three months."

****

Thud! Thud! Thud!

Still half asleep, Kari cracked one eye open and tried to make sense of the noise that had awakened her.

Thud! Thud! Thud!

When she opened the other eye and stretched, two bits of bad news became clear: Someone, most likely the network's camera crew, was at the door and, even worse, she was snuggled comfortably in Damien's arms. Her head was tucked under his chin and his hips cradled her bottom. Their legs were tangled, too.

They fit together perfectly, like two pieces of a jigsaw puzzle.

Thud! Thud! Thud!

This time, she welcomed the banging on the door. It allowed her to push that disturbing thought out of her mind. They couldn't be a perfect fit. He was nothing like her type.

Unfortunately, the knocking also roused Damien this time around. He responded by mumbling something unintelligible and tightening his hold on Kari's waist.

The extra pressure was all it took for Kari to shift from feeling safe, though disturbed, to trapped and panicky. She struggled against Damien's arms and only succeeded in enticing him to hold on even more tightly.

"Let me go!"

His only response was a snore.

Knowing Damien wasn't even awake did nothing to alleviate Kari's panic. Her breath came in quick pants, and her stomach got queasier by the second. If she didn't escape soon, she was likely to throw up all over Damien's bedding. How would she explain that?

Thud! Thud! Thud!

"We're coming!" Kari shouted between pants. Then she resumed her struggle. When her wriggling succeeded in doing nothing but arousing her unwanted husband, as evidenced by what was now jabbing at her backside, Kari wanted to scream.

Instead, she bit her lip and did something she swore she'd never do again.

"Let me go," she begged. "Please." Then she started sobbing.

****

"What the—?"

Kari's cries were a jarring wake-up call. He released her the second he realized he'd been holding her hostage. She scrambled across the bed so quickly that she'd have left skid marks, had she been a car.

"I'm sorry. I didn't mean—"

She kept her eyes firmly fixed on the floor. "We need to let them in."

Her refusal to look at him was unsettling. It wasn't as if he'd wrapped his arms around her on purpose, after all. "I wasn't even awake, K—"

"I know that!"

"Then what's the problem?"

Thud. Thud. Thud.

Still staring at the floor, Kari brushed aside the question with an impatient wave, and then jumped to her feet. "We really should open the door before they wake up everyone on this floor."

Damien sighed and followed his wife to the door. She was right, and he knew it. He could already imagine the angry phone call he'd get from Ned Applebee, his neighbor across the hall, should the knocking continue much longer. Ned worked nights, so he'd be sound asleep now.

What Damien didn't know — and, at the rate he was going, would probably never understand, he thought with a grimace — was why Kari was so bent out of shape. It wasn't as if she could hold him responsible for what happened while they were sleeping, after all.

Hell, for all he knew, Kari could have been the one to snuggle up to him. Both being asleep at the time, they'd never be sure who started what.

At the sound, she stopped and turned to look at him. He was surprised to see her brown eyes filled with sadness and what looked to him like a touch of fear.

Stepping forward, Damien reached out to grab her arm. "Kari, I—"

"Don't," she hissed, taking three steps backward for each step he advanced. "Just don't."

Damien gasped as she edged closer and closer to the couch. "Kari, wait!"

****

The warning came too late. Kari bumped into the arm of the couch and tumbled backward, landing on the offending piece of furniture with her legs waving in the air.

"Beautiful!" a strange voice boomed from the doorway. "This will make great TV."

Not bothering to hide her mortification, as if that were even possible, Kari struggled to a seated position and watched as Damien scowled at the beaming man.

"How'd you get in here?" he demanded.

Though Damien's fierce frown was enough to make her want to run to a corner and hide, the man in the doorway kept right on smiling.

"When it took you so long to answer the door, I rummaged around and found a key on the top of the doorsill," he explained, advancing into the room and motioning the camerawoman following him to do the same. "The name's Sam — Sam Stewart. And this is my wife, Stacy."

Kari felt her cheeks get hotter. No doubt he'd been hoping to catch her and Damien in a compromising position. Surely *that* would have made even better TV.

Thank goodness there was no chance of that! She wasn't even in danger of indecent exposure this morning — unlike Sunday. She congratulated herself on having worn pajama shorts and a T-shirt to bed the night before. That was something else to be thankful for. At least America wouldn't be seeing her panties.

Kari rose from the couch and went to stand by a still-scowling Damien's side. No doubt her unwanted husband wished he could yell at their camera crew without making himself look like a complete jerk.

But he couldn't, and if he was trying to protect her, he needn't bother. After all, it wasn't his fault she'd made a fool of herself by tripping over the couch. Not really, anyway. Her own somewhat irrational fears had prompted her escape attempt.

Tentatively, Kari reached for Damien's hand and gave it a squeeze. Then she offered Sam and Stacy a smile. "Welcome to our home."

****

An hour later, Sam and Stacy had moved a bank of monitors into Damien's spare room and were all set up to spy on him and Kari. They distributed sound equipment throughout the apartment and set up remote cameras in strategic spots to capture any action that went down while they weren't present.

Damien sighed and spread shaving cream on his face. He and Kari crowded into the small bathroom as they both got ready for work. With the bathroom and bedroom being the only camera-free rooms in his space, he'd better get used to the cramped quarters. He'd probably be spending more time there than usual.

He slanted a glance sideways to watch his wife swipe on a little mascara and lip gloss. She was smiling and appeared to have forgotten their altercation — until he looked more closely. Then he could still see traces of fear in her beautiful brown eyes.

He cursed softly as he picked up his razor. Day three of their mockery of marriage, and Kari was still running scared. How would they ever start to build a real relationship if she saw him as the Antichrist? He should apologize.

Wait a minute. How could he apologize? He had no idea what had set her off.

Still, it might improve things if he tried, since he was beginning to want their farce of a marriage to become something more.

"Kari, I'm sorry."

She turned to look at him, startled. "Why?"

Damien set the razor on the counter and faced his wife. "For doing whatever I did that scared the hell out of you earlier."

Her cheeks turned pink. "It's not you. It's me."

He puzzled over the cliché for a few moments, but it didn't do any good. He still couldn't figure out what had her so disturbed. "What's that supposed to mean?"

"You didn't really do anything." She sighed. "I just overreacted."

It was Damien's turn to ask why.

Kari stared at him for a long time before finally opening her mouth again. "Let's just say my taste in men hasn't always been the best." With that, she turned back to the mirror and started fiddling with her hair.

Damien watched her twist the blond mass and start arranging curls atop her head. So, they were back to the jerk from her past.

Whatever that guy had done to her, it had made her scared to death of anything that remotely resembled intimacy. Damien wished he knew who it was. The creep should pay for the damage he'd done.

Resisting the urge to gather Kari into his arms and kiss away her fears, Damien instead picked up his razor and went back to shaving. However, before they left the bathroom, he gave her a peck on the cheek.

"Don't work too hard," he said with a grin.

He was glad when she smiled back, then winked at him. "Don't worry. I never do."

****

"I am such a liar!" Kari groaned to herself, surveying the stacks of papers on her desk later that morning.

What had possessed her to tell Damien she didn't work hard when nothing could be further from the truth?

She shoved the question aside. With so much work to do, she didn't have time to contemplate her motives for making her fake husband think she was more fun than she really was.

She glanced at her watch. It was already 12:30, and she'd been working nonstop since her 8 a.m. arrival at the office. Her morning coffee, now stone cold, sat untouched on the far side of the desk.

She briefly considered heading down the hall to the office microwave to warm it up, then reconsidered. Why bother when she'd be taking a lunch break in another half hour?

The thought of lunch made her stomach rumble. The blueberry bagel she'd split with Damien at 7:30 this morning had long since been digested, and she was actually looking forward to lunch.

That was a good thing, too, since she had a lunch date with Bethany. Kari knew Beth wouldn't let her beg off because of the workload. She'd just storm into the office and drag Kari away from her desk, kicking and screaming, if necessary.

She checked her watch one more time before flipping open yet another file, her tenth of the morning, and starting to scan the papers inside. She was still poring over them when Bethany knocked on the door.

"Let's go, Kar." Bethany's voice was already impatient.

Kari barely looked up. "I only have one more page." She broke off when her friend snatched the folder from her hands and snapped it shut.

"No way! Lunch at Italia doesn't wait for boring paperwork, or anything else," Bethany reminded her. "Besides, you've been awfully quiet these last few days. I need the scoop on what you and loverboy have been up to."

Kari, who'd been reaching into her desk drawer for her purse, froze. She'd been so busy dealing with her move into Damien's bedroom that she had yet to fill Beth in on the latest developments. She finished retrieving her purse and followed her friend through the hall and down the block to their favorite Italian bistro.

As they walked, she said, "You're not going to believe this."

"What won't I believe? That you and Damien are going to star in your own reality show?"

"How'd you …?" Kari trailed off, remembering Bethany watched Romance TV constantly. The network had probably started airing promos for the show the second she and Damien had agreed to do it.

"You could have told me," Bethany said while they were following the maître d' to a table. "I didn't much like seeing your big news in a thirty-second sound bite."

Kari slid into the seat across from her friend and bowed her head. "Sorry, Beth."

Bethany giggled. "Jeez, Kar, it's not that big a deal!"

"It's not?"

"Nah. I just thought it'd be fun to watch you squirm a little. Can you imagine how surprised I was when I saw that ad for your show?"

"Probably not nearly as shocked as I was when they asked us to do it."

"So you two will be on camera all over the apartment?"

Kari nodded. "The bathroom will be the only truly private space we have." She lowered her voice to a whisper. "I get the feeling Damien plans to spend a lot of time in the bathroom."

This time, Bethany chortled. "As much time as possible, I should think. I know I would."

The comment killed Kari's laughter. "This won't be much fun, will it? I mean, having the cameras around all the time. They're even going to monitor the sound in the bedroom, but they can't come in unless we say so."

"I imagine you'll get used to it," her friend assured her. They broke off their conversation long enough to give the waiter their order — fettuccine Alfredo for Bethany and pasta primavera for Kari. Then Bethany picked it up again. "But why on earth did you agree to do it? As shy as you are, I never thought you'd agree to do reality TV."

Kari gave her friend a meaningful glance. "I owe it all to you."

"Me?"

"Yes, you. You're the one who entered me in that stupid 'Get a Love Life' contest."

"But a twice-weekly TV show wasn't part of the deal."

"They made us one heck of an offer," Kari confided. "A million dollars."

Bethany spit the water she'd been sipping back into the glass. "A million?"

Kari nodded. "Each."

"Holy crap, Kar!"

"I know. My cash flow problems will be over — forever! And so will my parents'. Dad will be able to slow down and get the rest the doctors say he needs."

Now Bethany nodded. "I couldn't figure out why you agreed to it, but now I understand."

"Money's a great motivator," Kari agreed cheerfully. Thank God the waiter was finally arriving with their salads and breadsticks. It was the perfect excuse to change the subject before she gave in to the temptation to dissect the nuances of every conversation she and Damien had carried on since signing the deal. "I'm starved. Let's eat!"

Chapter Seven

"I hate to tell you this, sweetheart," Damien said. A pair of adoring brown eyes looked up at him as he continued, "It's time to start you on a diet."

This female's response wasn't what most would consider typical. Instead of getting huffy, she thumped her tail and licked Damien's face.

Too bad her owner wasn't as receptive.

"Come on, man!" Cody protested, reaching over to scratch behind his dog's ears. "Chelsea does not need to lose weight."

Damien looked pointedly at the rotund mutt's middle. "Refresh my memory, Cody. Which of us went to veterinary school?"

"You did, but—"

"But nothing. Face it, man. Chelsea's been hitting the kibble too hard. She needs to lose at least five pounds to be at a healthy weight."

Cody sighed and started stroking the dog's soft, brown fur. "I can't make her stick to a diet, dude. You know me. I'll cave the first time she stands by her empty food bowl and looks at me like she hasn't eaten in a month."

Damien clapped his friend on the back. "You'll have to be strong. You know, being overweight is as risky for our pets as it is for us." He glanced at Cody's slight beer belly. "Maybe you two should start taking more walks."

Cody rewarded him with a glower. "Just because you like to jog doesn't mean I have to."

"Did I say anything about jogging? I said to take a walk."

"I know what you were really thinking," Cody said with a shake of his head. Then he changed the subject. "Ready to grab some lunch?"

Glancing at his watch, Damien was surprised to see it was already after one. Cody's appointment was his last before the lunch break; he'd set it up that way on purpose, since he and Cody had kept getting wires crossed lately.

In fact, they hadn't exchanged more than three or four

sentences since the wedding reception. If Damien were a betting man, he'd lay odds that Cody avoided him on purpose.

Well, he was about to find out. He clipped a leash to Chelsea's collar and led her to the door. "I'll take Chels back to boarding. Then we can go."

Ten minutes later, they sat in their customary booth at their favorite pizza joint, waiting for the usual — a Deluxe Meat Lover's Special. Damien poured himself a glass from the pitcher of Coke that sat on the table between them.

He took a long drink, wishing it were a nice, cold beer instead. But because he had to be back at work in an hour, he'd just have to be content with the pop.

Finally, he spoke. "The camera crew set up this morning."

"Camera crew?" Cody looked supremely confused. "What camera crew?"

Damien groaned. He'd forgotten that Cody was clueless about his reality-TV-star status. Already he disliked the effect this whole blind date wedding thing was having on him. His memory was beginning to rival that of a politician who forgot he wasn't supposed to take lobbyists' bribes.

Still, he couldn't resist taking a little jab at his friend. "What's wrong? Haven't been getting your Romance TV fix lately?"

Cody made a face. "You know I don't watch that channel now that the cast has come off my leg."

"I know you say you only watched because you were stuck in bed with a broken leg." Damien grinned. "But I also know, from reading those rules twelve thousand times, that the contest you entered me in didn't even start until three weeks after the cast came off."

"Give a guy a break," Cody protested, laughing. "I had to wean myself slowly."

"Then you don't know."

Cody sipped his drink. "Know what?"

"Kari and I are going to be featured on Romance TV twice a week for the duration of our marriage. The camera crew, a man named Sam and his wife, arrived this morning."

"You're going to be on TV? Again?"

Damien nodded. "Unfortunately so. The network thinks we'll be a big hit. The audience will want to see it all: How we get along, how well we get to know each other—"

"Your first big fight," Cody chimed in. Then he grinned. "Man, I'm so glad it's you and not me."

"You?" Damien scoffed. "Aren't you forgetting something? You're lacking something for that kind of show."

"What's that?"

"The woman, you idiot."

Maybe he was faking it, but Cody actually looked hurt. "Why don't you ask me why I've been out of touch lately?"

This time, Damien was the one who felt confused. What did Cody's avoidance tactics have to do with anything? The waitress slid their pizza onto the table and dished up the first two slices while he tried to puzzle that one out.

Not wanting to lose sleep over his buddy's riddles, he had to ask. "Okay, Cody. Tell me what you've been doing."

"Rephrase that question," Cody instructed through a mouthful of pizza.

"Huh?"

Cody swallowed his food, and then tried again. "It's not what. It's who."

"Who what?"

"What I'm doing."

Damien's head was starting to throb again. He needed to do a better job of watching his stress levels, he thought absently, rubbing at his temples. His first de-stressing step? Getting a straight answer from his best bud. "Will you please tell me what — or who — you're talking about?"

"Beth."

"Beth? Who's Beth?"

Cody's grin was wider than Damien had seen it since their sophomore year of college, when his pal had single-handedly beaten the school's best beer pong team.

"She must be something special, if you're this happy."

"She is, Damien. She is," he replied before helping himself to another slice of pie.

Damien made a mental note to find out more about this Beth. But right now, he needed to make headway on his pizza before it got cold. His male pride was at stake. There was no way he could let Cody, who was already a slice ahead, out-eat him.

Hours later, Damien paused outside his apartment building, loosening his tie. His shoulders sagged. After spending the afternoon with animals that needed his undivided attention, including an elderly, ailing Doberman that he'd had to put down, he was mentally and physically exhausted.

Top that off with the fact that Cody had managed to polish off five pieces of pizza to his three, after he'd decided he didn't want his gut to start getting as big as his buddy's, and passing several long hours entertaining his new camera crew was the last thing he wanted to do.

"Why did I say yes to this TV show again?" Remembering the look of joy on Kari's face when he'd agreed, and the payoff that would allow him to not only reimburse his dad but also upgrade his practice and establish the shelter to save hundreds of unwanted Chicagoland pets, Damien squared his shoulders and entered the revolving door.

Still, the thought of that damn camera crew made him drag his feet. He dawdled through the lobby, taking time to look at the newest paintings on the walls. Who knew? Maybe he'd like one of them enough to get a copy for his office.

He stopped suddenly, his gaze drawn to a blonde sitting on the bench by the mailboxes, her head bent over a magazine. There was something familiar about that cloud of blond hair.

With each step closer to the bench, Damien became surer it was his bride. He cleared his throat. "Kari?"

Using her finger to mark her place, she closed the magazine and looked up. She offered him a shy smile. "Hi."

He grinned back, happy that she at least seemed glad to see him. "What are you doing down here?"

"You're probably not going to believe this," she began. Her small smile quickly reversed itself as she dropped her gaze to the floor.

"Try me." Damien suspected he had a good idea why Kari was hiding out in the lobby. Sitting next to her on the bench, he extended his legs in front of him and put his hands behind his head. Then he waited.

Kari bit her lower lip and fiddled with her reading material, which Damien now saw was a travel magazine. The biggest headline on the cover screamed "Alaskan Adventure Done Right." "I'm a little ashamed, really. After the way I pushed you into doing this TV show—"

"You don't want to go upstairs, either, do you?" Damien interrupted. He wanted to put her out of her self-imposed misery as quickly as possible. Why make her suffer when he felt the same way?

Finally meeting his gaze, she shook her head. "Not really. At least not yet."

"Then let's not," Damien said, jumping up from the bench. "There's no rule that says we have to come straight home from work, right?"

"I don't think so."

"Good. Then let's think up a reason not to." He glanced at his watch. "It's nearly six o' clock. You hungry yet?"

A half smile played on Kari's lips. It wasn't her full-fledged playful grin, but it was a start. "I could eat."

"Okay, then." Damien grabbed Kari's hand to pull her to her feet. She resisted for a moment while she tucked her magazine into her giant leather tote, and then gracefully rose from the bench.

They'd only taken a few steps toward the door when she stopped again. "Where are we going?"

Damien shrugged. "Does it matter?"

"Anywhere is fine, as long as it's not here." A beat later, she lowered her voice to a whisper and confided, "I'm terrified of making a fool of myself in front of the cameras."

He folded his wife's smaller hand into his. "You're not the only one, sweetheart."

****

Kari let Damien lead her down the block. At first, she was too glad to be escaping the camera crew to question their destination further. Then her stomach rumbled, reminding her lunch had been hours ago.

She slanted a glance at Damien, hoping he'd missed her stomach's protest. They didn't know each other well enough for him to be privy to her bodily functions. The grin on his face told her he'd heard the gurgle.

"I worked though my afternoon snack," she explained defensively.

His grin widened. "That was you? I thought it was me." He leaned closer to whisper in her ear. "I didn't get my snack either."

Before she could stop herself, she blurted, "You don't snack!" There was no way he could, looking the way he did.

Damien stopped walking, so Kari did the same, all the while giving herself a mental kick. She didn't want him to know how attractive she found him. If he knew that, he'd surely find a way to use it against her.

"I do. Scout's honor," he insisted, holding up three fingers in the universal scout salute. "But only on Tuesdays."

Kari's curiosity was piqued. "Why Tuesdays?"

"It's the day Sarah, my receptionist, brings in something homemade. Today it was chocolate-chunk macadamia nut cookies for us and cheese biscuits for our furry patients."

"She bakes for the dogs?" As much as she loved her cats, Kari had a hard time imagining baking for the beasts. They turned their noses up at everything but the most expensive brand of cat food.

"Cats, too," Damien confirmed. "Of course, they're pickier. The only things they'll eat are tuna-flavored crackers shaped like fish."

No doubt Rhett and Ashley would find them delicious, Kari thought, suppressing a grimace. They did nothing for her appetite, though. "Let's talk about something else."

Damien's nod was knowing. "They don't smell any better than they sound, but my feline patients love 'em." After a brief pause, he added, "What would you rather talk about?"

Before Kari could reply, her stomach registered another loud protest. She blushed and ducked her head so her hair fell forward, covering her face. "Um, any ideas where we should go for dinner?"

Damien took her hand and they began walking again. He explained as they strolled, "Three blocks from here, there's a whole street full of restaurants. We can have whatever you want."

They continued down the street in companionable silence for about two and a half blocks. That was when Kari saw — correction, smelled — it: a small storefront with the name "Stavros'" painted on the window.

She stopped mid-stride, pulling Damien to a stop as well. "Do you smell that?"

Damien sniffed the air. "Smells Greek."

"It smells heavenly," Kari corrected, savoring the aroma. She looked from the menu posted in the restaurant's window to her husband. "How do you feel about Greek food?"

****

Damien looked at Kari, watching him with such a hopeful

expression. She clearly wanted to eat at Stavros'.

He sighed. He had no heart to tell her he'd prefer to eat somewhere else.

It wasn't that he disliked Mediterranean cuisine. But with a somewhat traditional Greek father, he'd eaten so much Greek food growing up that he could go years without seeing — let alone tasting — more hummus and dolmas.

"Greek's good," he assured her, comforting himself with the thought of enjoying a big chunk of sweet, sticky baklava for dessert. It was the one Greek dish he'd never lost a taste for, likely because he only got it as a special treat. And since he'd missed his sweet snack this afternoon ...

Damien reached around Kari to push open the door. "Let's eat."

Chapter Eight

Kari followed Damien into the dimly lit restaurant. As her eyes adjusted and she got a good look at the place, she started to wonder if eating here was such a good idea after all.

The food smelled wonderful, but the restaurant was a real dive. The tables appeared to be a good fifty years old, with scarred Formica tops, and the vinyl chair cushions were split in several places. Even her cash-strapped parents had found the money to redecorate a couple of times in the last several decades.

A short man with a bushy black mustache bustled out of the kitchen to greet them at the same time she turned to look at Damien. "Maybe we should—"

****

"This'll be fine," he said firmly, nodding to the chef and guiding Kari to a window table.

Damien could tell with one look that the man, most likely the restaurant's owner, was proud. He would take it as an insult if his customers — the only ones in the place — left.

Besides, he'd caught a glimpse of the baklava in the dessert case near the front door. Just the sight of the flaky pastry drizzled with golden honey made his mouth water. Definitely worth sitting in a dingy booth for.

The rest of dinner didn't smell so bad, either. It had been, oh, about a year since he'd eaten anything Greek, and the aromas wafting from the kitchen reminded him what he'd been missing.

He looked across the table at Kari, who studied the menu intently. Her blond curls hid most of her face, but Damien could see her mouth. Her slightly parted lips were pale pink and shiny, just begging to be kissed.

Whoa! Damien shifted in the booth. Where'd that thought come from? They were supposed to be having a relaxing get-to-know-each-other dinner away from their camera crew. Thoughts of his new wife's lips, and other parts, were strictly off-limits.

Firmly shoving aside the last of his lustful thoughts, he hoped, Damien cleared his throat. "What're you having?"

****

Kari looked up, startled. She'd been so busy concentrating on the menu that she'd forgotten Damien was with her.

That wasn't entirely true. She'd been focusing on the menu so she could try to forget the way he'd so easily manhandled her into staying.

Her objections to the restaurant had disappeared now that she'd had a little more time to look around. Despite the old-fashioned decor, the place was neat and clean — a lot like Damien's apartment. Still, she resented being overpowered. If Damien could force her to do what he wanted to here, what was to stop him from doing the same thing somewhere else?

A chill rushed down Kari's spine and she shuddered. Never again.

So here she sat in a booth, across from her too-big, too-strong husband, trying to forget his existence. She might have been successful, too, had his leg not kept brushing hers under the table. Every time it did, despite her vow to ignore the brute, butterflies began tap dancing in her stomach.

It was one of those shivers of awareness that Damien had interrupted with his question — a question for which, she realized, he was still awaiting an answer. The man from the kitchen had joined them, and he, too, waited for her reply.

"The moussaka sounds good," she said, offering them both a shy smile. "I'll also take some tabbouleh and an order of spanakopita."

When she saw Damien trying to hide a smile, she defended her choices. "I told you I was hungry. And I love Greek food."

"I'll take the moussaka, too, with a side of hummus and pita bread," he told the waiter. Then he grinned at Kari. "I hope you're saving room for dessert."

Despite her misgivings about Damien, Kari felt her smile widen. He had at least one thing going for him: Apparently, he wasn't going to tell her she needed to diet.

"Of course! You can't leave a Greek restaurant without having baklava."

****

An hour later, Kari polished off her last bite of baklava, and then groaned.

"That was incredible."

Damien nodded in agreement. Dinner and dessert had been delicious. But what he found truly remarkable was the way Kari savored every bite.

She was unlike any other woman he'd known. His ex-fiancée, even his mother, always ordered salad for dinner, and then picked at it. He hated that. What was the point of eating out if they always ordered the same thing, then barely ate two bites? It was nice to see a woman actually revel in a meal for a change.

He found himself thoroughly enjoying watching her. Something about the way Kari ate made him wonder if she savored other, more carnal pursuits with the same abandon. If her response to him the other morning in the spare room was any indicator, the answer to that question was "yes." All he had to do was figure out a way to tap into his lovely wife's wild side.

Realizing his mind had been wandering, Damien refocused his attention on the conversation he was supposed to be having.

"I'm glad you liked it. This restaurant was a great idea."

Another one of those genuine smiles bloomed across Kari's face. Damien loved those smiles. He promised himself he'd see more of them in the next two months and twenty-seven days.

"It was, wasn't it? I admit that I had a few doubts at first. But anyone who can make baklava that melts in your mouth like that doesn't need up-to-date furnishings."

"If you think Stavros' baklava is good, you should taste my mother's. It's out of this world."

Kari straightened in her seat. "Your mom can make this stuff?"

"Sure. It was my dad's favorite dessert, so my grandma taught her how to make it right after they got married," Damien explained.

"I wish I knew how to make baklava."

Damien immediately picked up on the wistful note in Kari's voice and saw a way to get his favorite dessert more often.

Mentally crossing his fingers, he offered, "I bet Mom would be happy to show you how."

"Really?"

Damien sighed. He couldn't lie, not even to get more of the best dessert on the planet. "She wouldn't exactly be happy," he admitted. "She always complains that baklava is more work than it's worth."

"Then I couldn't ask—"

"Sure you could," Damien interrupted. He couldn't quite give up on the idea, not with squares of homemade baklava dancing through his head. "For my wife, she'll take the time."

He watched as Kari's expression immediately dimmed. When she spoke, her voice was bleak. "I'm not your wife."

"Actually, you are."

"Only temporarily."

"My mother doesn't know that."

He saw the appalled look on Kari's face and rushed on. He didn't want his bride to think he was some kind of monster, not when his intention was merely to spare his mother three months of anxiety. If Mom knew the truth, she'd just worry. "I don't intend to tell my parents our marriage isn't real. Are you telling yours?"

"No, but they saw the news coverage."

"Maybe so. But they don't have to know we're planning to go our separate ways after three months, do they?"

"I guess not."

"Good. Then I'll call Mom and see if she has time to give you a lesson in baklava-making this weekend."

"Y-you want me to meet your parents?"

Damien tried not to shoot his new bride an impatient glance. It was tough, but he just about managed. "Yes."

"This weekend?"

Not sure why Kari considered it such a big deal, he shrugged. "Why not this weekend? We can't avoid our families for three months."

"I suppose not." A frown marred her face. "But I'd sure like to try."

****

Kari looked from her now-empty latte cup to her rather drowsy-looking husband. They'd been sitting in a bookstore cafe near their apartment building for the last hour, talking.

Kari couldn't help thinking it was the way they should have talked before making a lifetime commitment to one another. Unfortunately, they hadn't had the luxury. "I hate to break up our party, but I think we've played hide-and-seek with the camera crew long enough."

Damien checked his watch, and then nodded. "We probably should go. It's getting late."

"Late?" Surely the sun hadn't been down that long. Kari glanced down at her watch to confirm her suspicion. "In what universe is eight o'clock considered late?"

"The one where I get up at five in the morning for a run before heading to the office at seven," Damien replied without missing a beat. He stood.

Confused, Kari also rose to her feet. "I thought you went in at eight."

"Not on Wednesdays. That's my surgery day."

Kari tossed her cup into the trash before returning to Damien's side. "Then let's get you to bed." When she saw Damien's brows lift in surprise, she blushed and started stammering. "I d-didn't me—"

He put a finger to her lips. "Shhh. I know what you mean."

He reached out for Kari's hand, and she let him take it. The warmth of his hand covering hers was reassuring somehow.

As they left the coffee shop, she wondered why it was she couldn't keep her foot out of her mouth around Damien. She was really going to have to try harder, because every time she opened her mouth, something incredibly stupid, such as "Let's get you to bed," slipped out.

Kari blamed lust for her lapses into dimwittedness. Constant awareness of her too-sexy husband was scrambling her brain, and if she weren't careful, Damien would find out just how much she wanted him. She couldn't let that happen, because then he'd be in control.

No man would ever have that kind of power over her again. She glanced at Damien, standing beside her in the elevator. Sure, he seemed harmless enough now, but she knew from experience how that could change in a heartbeat.

And Kari wasn't going to let a man, especially someone like Damien, take charge of her life. Not this time. That meant keeping a lid not only on her attraction to Damien, but also on suggestive comments.

The elevator dinged and the doors slid open. Kari followed him off the elevator and down the hall, muttering, "Maybe I need a muzzle."

"Pardon?"

Kari started. She hadn't meant to speak aloud. She scrambled for an explanation. What rhymed with muzzle? Puzzle!

"I said maybe we should do a puzzle." Damien looked at her doubtfully. "It'd be something for the camera crew to film."

This time, he chuckled and leaned close to whisper in Kari's ear. "I hate to break it to you, but they're hoping to shoot something more exciting than us assembling a jigsaw puzzle."

****

Damien heard Kari's breath quicken and saw her eyes darken with unspoken passion. Armed with the unmistakable evidence of her desire, he decided to do what he'd been longing to all night. He captured her lips for a kiss.

She resisted for a moment, likely taken by surprise, before looping her arms around his neck and allowing his tongue to slip inside her warm, wet mouth.

That was all the encouragement he needed. In seconds, he'd backed his hot, sexy wife against the nearest wall. Damien deepened the kiss and pressed himself against the full length of her body. Her nipples tightened and brushed his chest, making him want more, so he dropped his hands to her rear end to pull her even closer. She came willingly, seeming to melt into his embrace. She twined her fingers in his hair and kept on kissing him.

He groaned. Kari was so responsive when she loosened that tight lid she had on herself. Now that she had, he planned to take full advantage of it.

What he really wanted was to bare her breasts, but he couldn't do that here, in the hallway. That'd come later. Instead, he settled for the next best thing.

He kissed her again and again until he lost himself in the depths of her eyes. Practically mindless with need, he pushed one of his thighs between her legs and slipped his hands under her skirt. He cupped her bottom and was rewarded with a soft sigh.

Wanting more, more, more, he started to pull down her panties. Her murmur of protest reminded him they were still in the hall. It was then that he tore his mouth from hers long enough to make a breathless suggestion.

"Let's get to bed."

When Kari dazedly nodded her agreement, he took her by the hand and turned toward the door to their apartment. But it wasn't a closed door he saw. Sam and Stacy stood in the doorway with a camera trained on them.

Sam motioned for them to carry on. "Pretend we're not here."

Damien glanced at his wife, who'd gone from looking

thoroughly kissed to slightly nauseated in less time than it took a hungry dog to snap up a treat.

Right. Neither he nor Kari was in the mood anymore. "I think the moment's past."

"That was great. You two are hot together!" the director enthused. His smile was as wide as the state of Texas.

Since Sam was either oblivious to their change in mood or pretending ignorance, Damien glowered at him. How dare the camera crew interrupt his and Kari's private moment? "How'd you know we were out here, anyway?"

"We heard voices in the hall, then silence. Silence usually means something is up," Sam explained. He looked pointedly at Damien. "And it was."

Damien rolled his eyes. "Well, it's not anymore, so you can leave us alone."

With that, he stalked past Sam and Stacy and into the apartment, dragging Kari behind him. Once they were in the bedroom, he locked the door. It wouldn't prevent the crew from monitoring the sound in the room, but it would at least keep the camera at bay.

He looked at Kari, who now perched on the edge of the bed. Her face was still a little green, and he cursed.

"Sorry about the interruption, sweetheart."

Something that looked suspiciously like relief flickered in Kari's eyes before she replied. "That's okay. Tonight just wasn't meant to be."

Damien searched her face for a clue as to her feelings, but drew a blank. She was maddeningly tough to read. He grumbled another curse and then shrugged. There was no use raging against something he couldn't change.

Besides, he still had almost three months to get to know Kari. The upbeat thought was immediately replaced by a sinking feeling he'd need every minute. His wife was a complex woman, and he hadn't even scratched her surface yet.

"I'm going to take a cold shower," he told her. He pressed his lips to her forehead. "Wait up for me if you change your mind."

****

Kari watched Damien disappear through the bedroom door. The instant it thumped shut, she flung off her clothes and jumped into a pair of pajamas. Then she got into bed and tightly closed her eyes.

No way did she want him to think she'd changed her mind. She still wasn't sure what had made her agree to go to bed with him in the first place.

Her eyes flew open. Wait. That wasn't entirely true. Bethany's voice responded in her head, telling her it wasn't true at all.

She knew exactly why she'd said "yes" to Damien. It was lust, pure and simple. His kisses melted her resistance. They practically liquefied her bones — until she forgot her reasons for fighting her attraction. She almost forgot her own name.

Kari felt ill when she thought about how quickly she'd given herself over to Damien's kisses. Not five minutes after her pep talk, and she was kissing him like ... like she was drowning and he was her sole source of oxygen. No one else had ever kissed her the way Damien did — not even Rob.

Thank goodness the camera crew had been there. The interruption had given her a much-needed chance to come to her senses.

The Bethany in her head snorted and Kari sighed.

All right, she wasn't a hundred percent glad for Sam and Stacy's interference. A part of her — the part that wanted her to strip off her pajamas and lounge naked on the bed, eagerly waiting for Damien to return — was disappointed. That part of her longed to let him have his wicked way with her. He could start by kissing her mouth, then her breasts, then ...

Kari groaned. It was a good thing she'd locked that vixen back in the closet of her mind. That was definitely where that fool belonged. To make sure she didn't make a break for it, Kari pulled the sheet up to her chin and squeezed her eyes shut again.

When Damien came back into the room, she heard him pause at the foot of the bed. After a long moment, he whispered, "Sweet dreams, Kari," and walked around to his side of the bed. The mattress dipped and the sheets rustled as he settled in for the night.

Kari released the breath she'd been holding and tried to relax enough to get some sleep.

Chapter Nine

Kari paused outside the door to the apartment she now called home and took a deep breath. As Wednesdays go, it hadn't been too terrible. She'd even ceased to be the hottest topic for office gossip now that two interns had been caught kissing in a supply closet.

"Thank goodness for small miracles." The reprieve wouldn't last long. As soon as the first episode of "Just Married" aired Thursday night, she'd jump back to the top of the gossips' list.

Kari took another deep breath to fortify herself to face the camera crew, and then let herself into the apartment. When a series of ferocious barks greeted her, she froze.

The source of the racket came barreling down the hallway and straight toward her. Kari screamed. Repeatedly.

Her yells brought Damien running from the bedroom.

"What's wrong?"

She pointed at the dog. "That thing attacked me."

"Sunny attacked?" Damien frowned and motioned at the animal. It plopped its butt on the floor. "I don't think so. She doesn't have an aggressive bone in her cuddly little body. Besides that, she's injured."

Kari looked at the dog, which she now noticed had a cast on her leg and what appeared to be a lampshade on her head. The animal didn't look nearly as scary as she had a few minutes ago, running toward her at full speed. A big pink tongue lolled out of her mouth and she extended a paw in what looked like greeting.

Kari scowled at Sunny. The dog was making her look ridiculous. She tried not to sound sullen as she amended her complaint. "The dog scared me."

****

Ignoring the TV camera as best he could, Damien looked from the friendly yellow Lab to his definitely frightened wife. He'd heard Sunny bark a greeting when the door opened, but it wasn't an aggressive bark. He figured he'd let the two of them get acquainted without his presence.

Apparently, that had been a mistake. Kari was breathing

heavily and eyeing Sunny warily. He commanded the dog to lie down, and she responded immediately. Then he beckoned Kari to follow him. With Sam and Stacy trailing behind, they headed to the kitchen.

"You have a problem with dogs?"

When Kari nodded slowly, Damien took a deep breath. He needed to get to the bottom of her issue before telling her Sunny would be staying for a while.

"What happened?"

"I once saw a neighbor kid get bitten. It was awful. The dog was snarling and the kid was crying and bleeding," she broke off. "I think I was about three. I've been terrified of dogs ever since."

Damien frowned. Her fear didn't bode well for his announcement. He took a deep breath, and then expelled it. "I wish I'd known that." There was no way he could have, of course. They hadn't even known each other for a week yet.

"Why?" Her gaze was curious.

"Sunny's a stray." He raked a hand through his hair. "Someone brought her into my office after watching her get hit by a car that kept on driving."

"Who would do such a thing?"

Damien glanced at his wife. Now she looked dismayed. Good. At least she didn't wish dogs harm.

"I wish I knew. Whoever it is deserves to be punished." When Kari nodded in agreement, he continued with his explanation. "I set Sunny's leg and gave her an e-collar to keep her from chewing on the cast, but she won't be adoptable until she's fully recovered."

"Poor thing."

Sympathy was good. He hoped it'd make what he had to add more palatable. "I agreed to foster her."

Kari's eyes widened. "So Sunny will be staying here? With us?"

"For at least six weeks," he confirmed with a nod. "But you don't have to be scared of her. From all I've seen, she's well-trained and not at all aggressive."

Kari looked at the dog, who hadn't budged since they entered the kitchen. Then she looked back at Damien. "That's easy for you to say. You like dogs."

He chuckled. His wife was no pushover. He liked that about

her. No matter how scared she was, she stood her ground. "I like you, too."

"Not as much as you do dogs."

He shook his head. "More."

"Yeah, right."

"Right," he agreed softly. Quickly, he leaned forward to brush his lips against hers. Then he grinned. "I guarantee you I don't do that to my patients."

He was glad to hear Kari giggle. It meant, hopefully, that her fear had dissipated.

"I should hope not!" she said, laughing again. "There's some kind of rule against that, I'm sure."

Damien grinned. "Dozens."

When Kari's smile widened, he was struck again by his wife's beauty. He wanted to take her into his arms and kiss away the worry that still shadowed her eyes.

A bark reminded him why they were having this talk. He cleared his throat. "Listen, if you're that terrified of Sunny, I'll find her another foster home. One of the vet techs will—"

"Shhh." Kari stopped him in midsentence, reaching out to touch his arm. "I'm sure Sunny and I will get along fine."

****

The next morning, Kari smelled coffee in the air before she opened her eyes. The heavenly aroma enticed her to stretch and sit up in her — their — bed.

She shook her head, glad that she hadn't vocalized that slip. After all, she'd been the one to point out to Damien that it was now "their" place and not just his. However, it was hard for her to get used to having a so-called "better half."

Not so sure the description fit, Kari shook her head a second time. Then she stood and headed for the kitchen. If she was separated from her morning coffee for much longer, she was going to get cranky, and after a nightmare-free sleep, she was in too good a mood to be cranky.

"Damien?" she called as she approached the kitchen, hoping he'd be able to have a full mug waiting for her when she got there. It'd save a few precious seconds and allow her to have that first sip just a little sooner.

No answer.

"Where could he be?" she wondered aloud. She knew he wasn't in the bedroom, and the bathroom door had been wide open as she walked past. She turned to scan the living room. Nope. He wasn't there, either.

Kari shrugged and hurried to the coffeemaker. She wasn't about to launch a full-scale search for her wayward spouse before she had her coffee. After pouring herself a steaming wake-up call, she took two steps to the left, to the fridge, to see what kind of breakfast she could scrounge up. When it came to his kitchen, Damien still lived like a bachelor. If she expected more choices, she was really going to have to start stocking the refrigerator for him.

That was when she noticed the note stuck to the door.

"Office called," she read aloud. "Emergency. Couldn't walk Sunny. Please help."

Kari glanced up from the note — there was more — to look around the apartment. Where was the dog, and why hadn't she barked? After spotting Sunny sitting by the window, she turned her attention back to Damien's scrawl.

"Cody coming for show tonight. Invite anyone."

Kari groaned. So much for her good mood. For a brief, shining moment, she'd forgotten tonight was the premiere of "Just Married." Well, she'd just have to call Bethany. No way did she want to sit there watching it with just Damien and his buddy. She'd need someone to share her pain.

Speaking of pain, Kari turned to look at Sunny again. The dog stood and ambled toward the door. Then she sat and thumped her tail on the floor.

"I bet you have to go outside, don't you?"

Sunny responded with what might have been a happy bark.

"Okay, then."

After taking two steps toward the door, Kari stopped. Sunny would need a leash, just like her cats, Rhett and Ashley, used when they went outside. Rhett actually enjoyed his walks, parading down the street with his tail held high; Ashley was more reluctant, hissing and spitting as she led him around. She glanced around the living room before spotting the required restraint on the table by the door.

She picked it up and looked at the dog. When Sunny looked right back, her big pink tongue lolling and her brown eyes shining, Kari could almost believe Damien's assertion that the dog was well-trained. She didn't appear the least bit menacing.

"You can do this," Kari assured herself, ignoring the quaver in her voice. "This dog is friendly."

She took a deep breath, and then reached for the mutt's collar. When Sunny didn't so much as twitch a whisker, Kari clipped the leash to the collar and pushed open the door.

Faster than a smoking skillet melted butter, the dog was out the door and barreling down the hallway. Kari let herself be dragged halfway down the hall before she realized they were going in the wrong direction.

"Come on, girl," she said, tugging on the dog's leash. "The elevator's this way."

She stopped to close the apartment door, and then led the slightly more sedate dog outside. After Sunny took care of business, they returned to the apartment and a ringing phone. She picked up the receiver. It was Damien.

"Sorry I had to leave you with Sunny," he apologized. "I had to head out in a hurry."

Even as she marveled at the concern in his voice, she reassured him. "Don't worry about it. Once I stopped letting her drag me down the hall, we got along fine."

Damien's chuckle rumbled in her ear. "I'm glad to hear it. Don't worry about dinner tonight. I thought I'd pick up some pizzas. We can eat while we watch the show."

"That sounds like a plan," Kari agreed. Then she caught a glimpse of the clock. She still had plenty of time before she had to be at work, but it was later than she'd like. "Listen, I have to get ready for work. I'll see you tonight."

"You bet."

Kari hung up the phone. Even though she dreaded watching herself and Damien on TV later, she was still looking forward to their date.

"You can't really call it a date when Bethany, Cody and the camera crew will be there," she reminded herself.

The reminder didn't keep her from smiling as she got ready to go to the office.

****

"Shhh. The show's about to start," Cody hissed as the first notes of a theme song began to play.

Damien heard the music and frowned. Couldn't Romance TV have picked something with a little more, well, something a lot less cheesy? The song made their life sound like a 1970s sitcom.

He looked over at Cody to see his friend's head bobbing along to the song. Great. If Cody liked it, at least the channel had its audience pegged.

Turning to Kari, he asked, "Where's your friend?" He still didn't want to admit he didn't know the girl's name.

"Hmm?"

"You know, the one you invited over here to watch the show with you. The one we're holding the pizza in the oven for."

Kari shrugged. "She's on her way. She called from the El."

Foiled again! Why wouldn't Kari mention What's Her Name by name? "Well, she'd better get here soon, or Cody's going start the party without her."

Kari looked over at Cody, who laughed aloud as her onscreen self tumbled over the back of the couch. "I think he already has," she muttered to Damien.

Cody hushed them again. "I'm trying to watch the show here, guys."

"We've kind of already seen it," Damien pointed out — reasonably, he thought.

Obviously annoyed, Cody replied, "Then why don't you go somewhere else so I can enjoy it? Why not go to the kitchen and bring me back some pizza?"

Yes, why not? He hadn't been kidding Cody: He really didn't need to see the last couple of days unfold again onscreen. He'd managed just fine without watching the rerun of the original wedding special, after all, so why had he thought a viewing party was a good idea?

Damien turned back to Kari. "Shall we?"

Kari was quick to jump up from her chair, obviously just as eager as he was *not* to watch the show. "Let's go."

As they left the room, Damien heard Cody laugh again. Apparently their life was a lot funnier onscreen than it was while it was happening. Either that or Cody had taken a hit of laughing gas before he arrived.

Damien was willing to bet it was the former. Sighing, he admitted to himself that the sitcom theme song might not have been such a bad choice.

****

Standing in the kitchen a few seconds later, Kari reached into the cabinet for a stack of plates. They were definitely a man's dishes, oversized and hunter green, but she liked them. When she ate something from one of them, she felt like she'd had something substantial — even if she'd only picked at a handful of grapes.

Once she placed the plates on the counter, beside the pizza box Damien had just deposited there, she fixed her husband with a stare. "Can we *not* have people over to watch anymore?"

"I was thinking the same thing." He grinned. "Better yet, let's not watch it at all."

"I'd be fine with that." They were on the same page again. How could two people with nothing but a pair of meddling friends in common think so much alike?

Kari ignored the camera in the doorway as she pulled out a giant bowl and poured a bag of salad into it. She added a handful of cherry tomatoes and a splash of Italian dressing while Damien carried pizza number one and the stack of plates to the living room.

The salad had been her idea. She knew Bethany would thank her for it — if Bethany ever arrived, that was. And from the short time she'd known Damien, she knew that if she didn't serve up a salad, he wouldn't think to eat any vegetables.

She couldn't understand how a guy who looked like her husband did could live on carbohydrates and fat — and not the good ones. His diet seemed to consist mainly of pasta, potatoes and cheese, all the things that, if Kari let them, would make her pile on pounds faster than a microwave melted chocolate chips.

In fact, Kari thought her pants had started getting tighter since she'd moved in with Damien. She was going to have to start keeping a closer eye on what she ate. Even at her height — or maybe because of it — she had to be extremely careful to avoid weight gain.

"No more than two slices of pizza tonight," she muttered to herself, not for the first time, as she brushed past the camera with the salad bowl in her hands.

When Kari deposited the salad on the coffee table, both men were already chowing down on the pizza. Sighing, she went back to the kitchen to grab four forks. She doubted they'd all be used, but she grabbed enough for everyone anyway.

As she nibbled on her salad, she saw Cody slip part of a pizza crust to Sunny, who sat expectantly near the humans' feet. Her husband's glare also didn't go unnoticed — at least by her. Cody seemed oblivious to it, though, until Damien shook his head.

"And you wonder why your dog needs a diet."

Cody dismissed the comment with a wave and took another slice of pizza. "Chelsea's weight is fine," he said between bites. "Now be quiet. I don't want to miss a minute of this."

When the bell rang ten minutes later, Kari jumped up to answer it. Onscreen, she was about to be attacked by the least threatening dog on the planet, and she really didn't want to relive that humiliating moment. Why did the funniest onscreen moments always seem to make her look like an idiot?

"I'm glad you finally made it."

Bethany hurried toward the living room, with Kari close behind. "Sorry I'm late, but the El was delayed. There was some sort of accident somewhere."

"That's okay. It hasn't been too awful so far," Kari assured her, only lying a little bit. "Help yourself to the pizza and salad."

Bethany stopped in mid-step and reversed course, dragging Kari into the kitchen.

"You didn't tell me *he*'d be here," she whispered.

"Of course he's here. It's his apartment," Kari replied.

"Not Damien, you goof. His friend, Cody."

Kari had to vocalize her confusion. "I thought you and Cody were getting along great."

"*Were* is the operative word in that sentence," her friend informed her, her lip curling in what could only be called a sneer.

"I thought you said he was 'very knowledgeable.'" After all the teasing she'd endured from Bethany over the years, Kari couldn't resist throwing her friend's description back at her.

"He was — at first," Bethany admitted. Then she glanced toward the living room. "Can we talk somewhere else?"

Doubtful that Cody would notice anything but the TV screen he'd been glued to since the start of "Just Married," Kari snorted. "He's not paying a bit of attention to us, you know. But if it'll make you feel better ..."

Kari walked back toward the living room and looked at Sunny. "Do you have to go outside?" When the dog headed for the door, Kari said to Damien, "We're going to take Sunny for a walk."

Damien nodded. "Okay. Just remember she's recovering. Don't keep her out too long."

Chapter Ten

Once they were in the elevator, with no chance of being overheard, Bethany looked at Kari with raised brows. "I thought you hated dogs."

"Been petrified of dogs, yes, but I've never hated them. This one, however, is about as scary as the Snuggle bear," she explained. Realizing Bethany was trying to change the subject, she narrowed her eyes. "You're not getting off that easily, missy. Last I knew, you and Cody were setting off fireworks between the sheets."

Bethany simply nodded. "Then Mr. Jump-the-Gun Jackson asked me to go with him to see the new 'Star Trek' movie."

"That's a problem why?" Kari still didn't understand her friend's objection. Bethany was a diehard Trekkie — a fact she must have mentioned to Cody, and the movie was going to be one of the summer's biggest blockbusters. Theaters had been showing the trailer for months, hyping it as "the best 'Star Trek' movie yet." Never mind that *every* "Star Trek" movie released was "the best yet."

The elevator dinged and the doors slid open. With Sunny barely tugging the leash, the two friends walked through the lobby and into the late-May evening. Only then did Bethany reply.

"That movie doesn't open for two more weeks!"

It was Kari's turn to freeze. She ignored Sunny's whine at being stopped so suddenly. Damien had just said they shouldn't go far anyway.

"You mean to tell me you're avoiding Cody because he dared to ask you to commit to something that doesn't happen for two weeks?" When Bethany nodded again, she said, "That's messed up, Beth."

Her friend fixed her with a stare. "About as messed up as you throwing away a great relationship with Damien because he reminds you of your ex."

"That's not the same thing at all."

"Sure it is. I have an aversion to commitment; your aversion is to alpha males. We're both nurturing natural distaste."

"But your distaste is for a normal relationship," Kari pointed out, sure that she was in the right. Bethany couldn't possibly be making sense. Kari had been hounding Beth about her commitment phobia almost since they'd met, and she hadn't changed. If anything, she'd gotten wilder since college graduation, rarely going out with anyone more than twice. That was why Kari had been glad to see her friend spend so much time with Cody.

"You think yours isn't?"

Her mind flashed back to her time with Rob, and Kari couldn't help but shudder. "That relationship was anything but normal."

"Rob lied to you and manipulated you into doing things you'd rather not admit to, yada, yada, yada." Bethany waved her hand dismissively.

Kari wasn't offended. She knew Beth had heard the argument before many times. Bethany was the only one who knew even half of how badly that jerk had treated her. "Right."

"Ever since, you've used that as an excuse to avoid getting anywhere near anyone with more than a teaspoon of testosterone."

"So you keep saying."

"Kari, you know I'm right."

Scowling, she shook her head. She wasn't about to admit it and give Bethany any more ammunition in her quest to permanently loose Kari's inner tramp. Kari liked keeping that sleaze locked in the closet of her mind, where she belonged.

"Face it, Kar. Damien is nothing like Rob. He takes care of sick animals, for God's sake." Then Bethany's voice dropped to a whisper. "And as much as I hate to admit it, a creep like your ex would never have a friend like Cody."

Recognizing her chance to help Bethany break through her fear of commitment, Kari jumped on it. "Then why don't you give the guy a break? You know you want to see that movie anyway. You've been hounding me about going for months."

"But what if I don't want to see it with him? The wrong companion could ruin the whole moviegoing experience."

Kari grinned. Her friend was nothing if not stubborn. Too bad for Beth, she could be equally obstinate. "I think I'm busy that night."

A glint lit Bethany's eyes, and Kari knew she'd somehow misspoken. She tensed, waiting for Beth to drop a bombshell.

"You make a date with Damien for that night and I'll go out with Cody."

She relaxed again. A date she could handle. She and her much-too-large husband could order in Chinese food and play Monopoly. The camera crew might complain about the lack of action, but it'd be her kind of date. Safe and non-threatening. "Done."

"Forget family game night, Kar," her friend said firmly, apparently reading her mind. "I mean a real date. The kind that has a real possibility of ending with the two of you getting naked and sweaty together, in bed or any other room of your choosing."

Bethany's words immediately conjured a picture in Kari's head: She and Damien were tangled together in his — their — king-sized bed, naked and panting.

Kari swallowed. What had she just gotten herself into?

****

Damien glanced from the clock to the silent telephone sitting on his desk. He had ten minutes to spare before his next patient was due to arrive, and he really needed to return his mother's phone call.

He'd put it off long enough. She'd called him Wednesday, and it was now Friday. He couldn't reasonably delay any longer, especially if he wanted to introduce Kari to his parents this weekend.

"I still can't believe Cody got me into this," Damien grumbled under his breath as he picked up the receiver and started to dial. He wasn't ready to admit — even to himself — that his buddy had probably done him an immeasurable favor.

The part of him hoping his mom wouldn't be home cringed when the phone was picked up on the third ring.

"You finally decided to call me back, huh?"

"Sorry, Mom," he said. "I've been swamped with patients this week."

He swore he heard his mother sniff on the other end of the line. "If you say so."

"You think I'm sitting here twiddling my thumbs all day?" Damien asked, hurt that she didn't believe his excuse. Sure it was flimsy, but he didn't fib to his mother often enough for her to doubt his word.

"I didn't say that, dear," his mother replied. "But I'm pretty sure your furry patients haven't been keeping you nearly as busy as your new wife has."

Damien expelled a breath. If his mom was bringing it up, at least he didn't have to break the news of his blind date wedding. "You heard about that, did you?"

"Did you expect to keep your marriage a secret, Damien? Your father and I can read the newspapers just like everyone else, you know."

"I know." Damien sighed. "I was trying to figure out how to tell you guys, but how do you explain to your parents that you won a wife?"

There was silence on his mother's end of the line. Finally, after what seemed like hours, she said, "I can see where that would pose a dilemma. So you were just going to ignore us until you were back to your bachelor self?"

"Actually, I was hoping to bring Kari out to meet you this weekend."

"Really?"

His mother sounded surprised. "Yes, really, Mom. Kari and I might have met somewhat unconventionally, but we're making the best of this and that means trying to make it work." This time, her "really" was even more shocked. "I like this woman — a lot."

"Well, she's certainly pretty," his mother conceded. "Just don't let lust blind you to defects in her personality."

"Kari doesn't have a defective personality," Damien retorted. Then he took a deep breath to calm himself. His mom was just trying to protect him. "Look, I have to go. My next patient is due shortly. We'll be there around noon tomorrow. And be sure to look good, because we'll have the camera crew in tow."

With that said, Damien quickly hung up the phone. He didn't want to have to explain that one.

Too late, he remembered he was supposed to ask his mom to show Kari how to make baklava. Maybe his memory *was* going. Maybe Kari had introduced What's Her Name at the reception and he just forgot.

Nah, that couldn't be. His mind was still sharp as ever. He could recall details about his patients, no problem. Besides, there'd be plenty of time for his mom to teach Kari how to make his favorite dessert.

If he got his way, they'd have the rest of their lives.

****

"Happy one-week anniversary, wife," a voice rumbled in Kari's ear.

She opened her eyes to see Damien standing beside the bed, holding out a coffee mug. She took it and sniffed the heavenly scent. After taking a sip of brew that tasted even better than it smelled, she said, "Thanks."

As the coffee percolated through her system, she became more alert. That was when she noticed Sam standing in the doorway, camera rolling. Her hand flew to her hair, which she was sure was a mess.

"You look beautiful," Damien told her.

Kari rolled her eyes. She knew her hair well enough to know that until she ran a pick through it, she was going to look like she styled her hair with an eggbeater.

"Nice try, buster," she said, punctuating her statement by poking Damien's arm. "So what's on our agenda today?"

"I thought we'd drive out to the 'burbs and visit my parents."

"Y-your parents?" When Damien nodded, Kari squeaked, "So soon?" She'd only known Damien for a week. No way was she ready to meet his folks, even if he had suggested it earlier in the week. She figured he'd been joking.

"There's no time like the present. I can't avoid them for the next three months, and believe it or not, my mom is eager to meet you."

"Two fibs in one morning?" Kari teased. She had to do something to keep panic from setting in, and cracking jokes was the best she could come up with. It sure beat heading to the kitchen for a pint of Ben & Jerry's that'd go straight to her hips. "You'd better not go outside during the next lightning storm."

Damien frowned at her. "I'm not kidding, Kari. Mom read all about the wedding."

"And I'm sure she can't wait to see what kind of girl would try to win herself a husband."

Damien quirked an eyebrow. "Okay. I won't tell you the subject didn't come up. But I explained to her that we're going to make the best of this mess our friends got us into, and that means trying to lead as normal a life as possible under the circumstances."

"And that means I get to meet your parents today." Sighing, she resigned herself to what was sure to be an ordeal. Whether she was ready or not, this was going to happen — kind of like her wedding. Life had a tendency to steamroll her these days, and she wanted it to stop — soon.

However, today was not the day. She was about to try to make a good impression on Damien's parents.

"I can be ready to leave in about an hour."

****

A little more than an hour later, their stomachs full of blueberry bagels and orange juice, the couple sat in Damien's blue Honda Element, speeding toward the suburbs.

With every mile the car got closer to his parents' house, Damien could tell Kari's nervousness was increasing. He tried to quash some of her nerves by telling her about his parents.

The stories he shared were carefully chosen to emphasize his parents' humorous sides, including one about the time his mom, a history professor, staged a coup in the department. She'd managed almost single-handedly to convince everyone the current department head was losing touch with his students, with the material and probably even with reality itself. And she'd done it not just because Professor Dunham was all those things, but also because, as she liked to say, he was an obnoxious little man who'd had the temerity to insult her brownies at a departmental tea.

When Kari didn't laugh, Damien stifled a curse. He really hadn't expected the story to make her more nervous. Obviously it had, though, because Kari's voice sounded unsteady when she said, "Your mom sounds like a *formidable* woman."

So *that* was it; his mom scared Kari. Well, to be honest, his mom still frightened him from time to time — not as much now as she had when he was younger and always seeking her approval, but still.

"Don't worry. Mom's mellowed out some since she retired from the university to head up Hope House."

"Hope House?"

"It's her pet charity, a shelter for women trying to escape abusive relationships."

This disclosure seemed to put Kari at ease. "So your mom's

against spousal abuse, huh?"

"Isn't everyone?"

"Not everyone."

The tone of her reply disturbed Damien. He took his eyes off the road long enough to cast a glance at her face and saw that she was positively green.

Fearing for the car's upholstery, which he'd had to clean just last week after one of his patients got sick on the seat, Damien guided the Element to the shoulder of the road and turned on the hazard lights. Then he hit the button to roll down the passenger side window.

"Take a couple of deep breaths," he instructed.

Kari complied, and Damien watched as her complexion returned to normal. He couldn't help thinking the wife he hadn't known he wanted had just given him a clue to her mysterious past.

His eyes locked with her brown ones. He held her gaze until her cheeks reddened, and she bowed her head so masses of blond curls obscured her face.

He wanted to say something to put her at ease. But what? Some guy had obviously mistreated Kari at some point.

"Sweetheart, I don't know what you've been through, but I can promise you I wasn't raised to resolve problems with violence." Then he grinned. "Besides, you can bet my mom would tan my hide if she ever heard that I raised a hand to a woman."

Chapter Eleven

As Damien pulled the Element back onto the road, Kari forced herself to smile. She couldn't explain to him why she reacted violently to what his mother did for a living — not when she couldn't even explain it to herself.

Really, she needed to get a grip. Damien was not Rob, and she knew that. Truly she did.

At least part of her did. Another part of her was still frightened every time her too-large husband loomed into the room. It wasn't that he'd purposely done anything to spook her, either. On the contrary, he continued to act like the perfect gentleman.

Truth be told, it was beginning to annoy her. She knew Damien appreciated her, thanks to the morning after their wedding and that night after dinner at Stavros'. Yet he seemed perfectly happy to make good on the promise he made the night she moved into his bedroom that he'd keep his hands to himself.

Just as well, Kari told herself firmly. Despite what her inner tramp wanted, she really didn't need to get too cozy with her temporary mate.

But right now, her husband was the least of her problems. Here she was, about to meet his parents, and the camera crew would be filming the moment for posterity. With her track record, that meant *something* was bound to go wrong.

Kari leaned back in the seat and closed her eyes, willing herself to remain calm. The visit would go much more smoothly if she didn't give in to panic before they even arrived.

Only when she felt the car slow did Kari open her eyes again. But it wasn't a house they were coming to; it was a grocery store parking lot. She looked questioningly at Damien.

He shrugged. "I thought it'd be nice if we showed up with dessert. I know better than to ask for homemade baklava on a normal Saturday."

"Baklava's a lot of work," Kari said, nodding. She'd been reading up on the subject so when Damien's mom did give her that lesson he'd volunteered her for, she wouldn't be a complete klutz in the kitchen. It seemed like a lot of trouble, even for the small slice of heaven that was baklava.

"Right. She usually makes it for major holidays like Christmas or Easter." He shut off the car's engine.

"Yet you think she wants to teach me to make it." Kari shook her head.

"Sure she does. What's that saying? The more the merrier?"

"More like misery loves company," Kari muttered under her breath as she got out of the car and shut the door firmly — perhaps a little too firmly. She still was out of sorts about this whole meet-the-parents scenario. Sure, she knew they had to meet eventually, but not this soon. She'd dated guys for months without ever meeting their families, or introducing them to hers.

Then again, Damien was more than just some guy she was dating. He was her husband, and, for better or worse, that meant that once she got through the ordeal of meeting his parents, she'd have to introduce him to hers. No way would her boisterous, loving family let her get away with making three months' worth of excuses for skipping family dinners.

Speaking of her husband, the man in question was making a beeline for the back of the store. He obviously needed to use the bathroom.

"Wait," she called after him. He turned around. "What should I get?"

"Whatever looks good. I'll meet you back at the car." With that, he turned again and sped off, leaving Kari to head to the bakery.

Kari stood in front of the cake display, silently cursing Damien. She didn't even know Damien's favorite dessert, let alone what his parents liked.

"What looks good to me is immaterial," she muttered. Even so, she grabbed a Black Forest Cake. The ruby-colored topping glistened atop fluffy white frosting, beckoning her. *You can't go wrong with cherries, chocolate and whipped cream.*

By the time the Element rolled to a stop in Damien's parents' driveway fifteen minutes later, Kari had herself convinced that she could do this. Parents were people, too — just like anyone else.

Never mind that Kari had problems meeting new people, period. She was choosing to overlook that fact.

You're going to do this, and you're going to make a good

impression.

After giving herself that pep talk — about her thirtieth since they'd left the apartment — Kari got out of the car and smoothed her sweater. The short-sleeved, lightweight lavender sweater was one of her favorites. She'd bought it at Target last summer, marked down 75 percent.

With that done, she took one last deep, calming breath and started to follow Damien, who was already several steps ahead. He must have heard her footsteps crunching on the gravel drive, because he turned around. The cake in one hand, he held out the other to Kari.

When she slipped her hand into his, Damien squeezed her fingers. Then he winked. "Don't worry. My mom won't bite."

Kari laughed nervously, and together they walked toward the door. Painted a hunter green, it was adorned with a wreath of vines and pink and white flowers. She registered that the house at least looked welcoming before she noticed Sam standing on the porch, to the left of the door, his camera at the ready.

No doubt he was hoping to catch some spectacularly embarrassing moment. Even though she wasn't particularly religious, Kari said a silent prayer that there would be none of those.

The door swung open before Damien got close enough to knock. Kari's first impression was of a stout woman with salt-and-pepper hair. Then she noticed the short-sleeved lavender sweater his mom wore was the same one she had on.

She halted abruptly, dragging Damien to a stop as well. "Look!"

Damien looked at his mother, then back at Kari and at his mother again. When he looked back at Kari a second time, she could tell he was trying not to smile.

"This isn't funny."

Before Damien had a chance to reply, his mother stepped forward. She smiled warmly and reached out to take Kari's hand.

"You must be Kari. I'm Ella." She paused, then added, "My son didn't tell me you had such good taste."

Kari was so grateful to Ella for trying to put her at ease that she almost missed what Ella said next. "Of course, he didn't tell me much about you at all."

Eager as she was to make a good impression, Kari had to say

something in Damien's defense. She didn't want to cause a rift between a man and his mother. "It's not his fault we don't know each other that well yet. Blame Romance TV." Then, to steer the conversation back to safer territory, she smiled. "I got my sweater on sale last summer."

"Me, too — 50 percent off."

Kari hesitated, but decided to confess. If Ella was still smiling at her now, after she'd just mouthed off, finding a better bargain wasn't likely to dim her smile. "I must have waited a little longer than you to buy. Mine was discounted 75 percent."

Damien chuckled. "See Mom? You've been right all these years: Patience *is* a virtue."

****

Damien steered both women into the living room, trying hard to ignore the fact that Sam was trailing right behind them. So far, this meeting was going about as well as could be expected. At least fur wasn't flying between the two most important women in his life. Not that he'd expected it to. He might not know Kari well, but he was sure she was much too polite to disagree with the woman of the house.

Once his mom was ensconced in her favorite armchair, Damien sat next to Kari on the couch. He tried to sit close enough to be reassuring, but not so close that it made Kari more nervous than she already was. It was a fine, fine line.

"Where's Dad?"

"Where he always is: in his study, doing research."

Familiar as he was with his father's tendency to get lost in research, to the exclusion of everything else, Damien was still annoyed. It wasn't every day he brought someone home to meet his parents, especially when that someone was his wife.

"Isn't he going to take a break to meet Kari?"

Ella waved. "He'll come to lunch. Until then, the three of us can have a nice chat."

At least he was planning to make an appearance. Damien supposed that would have to suffice, since it was all he was going to get.

In a few minutes, his mom knew how things were going at the vet's office, what Kari did for a living and how many siblings she had — five, it turned out. Three brothers and two sisters, all but one of them happily married and producing grandchildren. Why hadn't he thought to ask her that himself?

You've had other things on your mind, he reassured himself. Things like trying to figure out What's Her Name's name and coaxing more smiles out of his wife. And let's not forget that whole learning-to-deal-with-the-cameras-filming-every-aspect-of-his-life thing.

He darted a glance in Sam's direction. Sure enough, the camera's little red light was blinking. Damien doubted any of this footage was going to make it into the next episode of "Just Married," though. Heck — even he was finding most of it dull. He could imagine what the viewers would think.

Not that he cared about the viewers, he told himself quickly, again wishing Cody hadn't gotten hooked on Romance TV. Damien guessed TV had been one of Cody's few options while he lounged on the couch nursing his broken leg. But why couldn't Cody be a normal dude and tune in to "Sportscenter"?

As he turned his attention back to the conversation, he realized Kari had asked his mom about her work with Hope House.

"I can't give you any specifics, dear," his mother was saying. "But the house has a six-resident capacity, and just two of the beds are filled."

"Does that mean fewer women are being abused?" Kari asked. Damien thought he detected a note of hope in her voice.

His mom shook her head. "More likely, it means fewer women are ready to get out. Or it could be that I need better publicity."

Kari's answering "oh" was small. Even having known her for a mere week, Damien could tell she was starting to get upset. It was time for him to change the subject.

"Breakfast was hours ago, Mom. I'm starved."

His mom checked her watch and stood from her chair. "Give me ten minutes to put the finishing touches on lunch."

Once his mom had disappeared into the kitchen, Damien squeezed Kari's hand. "You're holding your own."

"I like your mom," she replied, gifting him with one of her wide smiles.

"Good, because I think she likes you, too."

When Kari's smile brightened, it was all Damien could do to keep from wrapping his arms around her. He settled for dropping a quick kiss on the tip of her nose.

"You're beautiful when you smile like that," he told her,

watching as her cheeks colored and she ducked her chin to her chest. He wondered again why she didn't know the effect she had on men — on him.

Damien used his thumb to raise Kari's chin, insisting, "You are."

When a throat was cleared behind them, Damien jumped up guiltily. Even though nothing untoward had happened, he felt like a teenager again, getting caught in a compromising position on his parents' couch.

"Don't let me interrupt," his father said dryly.

"Hi, Dad." He helped a now red-faced Kari to her feet and made the introductions. "Dad, this is Kari. Kari, my father, Vic."

Chapter Twelve

Mortified, Kari stumbled her way through a greeting. Then she followed the men into the kitchen.

It figured. Since Damien's mom actually liked her, something had to go wrong when it came to his dad. Now she knew what: He thought they couldn't keep their hands off one another — or at least that Damien couldn't keep his hands off her.

There are worse things than a husband who can't keep his hands off his new wife.

Kari shoved away the thought — obviously coming from her inner tramp — and took a seat beside Damien at the table. It was beautifully set, complete with lavender cloth napkins, fancy water goblets and pink tulips in a vase that matched the glasses. The dishes, a sage green, reminded her in size and heft of the plates at Damien's.

The food looked lovely, too. There was a bowl heaped with salad, another one full of herbed new potatoes and a platter of — oh no — it looked like salmon in some kind of sauce.

The fish was Kari's least favorite, but she vowed she'd eat it anyway. She didn't want to get on Damien's mom's bad side now by turning her nose up at the older woman's cooking — especially after what Damien had said that morning about his mom and the prof who didn't like her brownies.

"Everything looks delicious." It wasn't much of a little white lie, because it did *look* good. She just doubted it would taste that way.

"Thank you, dear," Ella said.

After Damien's father led the family in grace, Kari helped herself to generous servings of salad and potatoes. She hoped no one would notice that she took a tiny piece of fish.

Damien noticed. "That's not much food."

"I'm not really that hungry," she lied, trying not to hold her breath. She hoped he'd forget that she'd been so nervous about meeting his parents that she'd only eaten half a bagel for breakfast.

Apparently satisfied, Damien turned his attention back to his plate. Kari relaxed and attacked her salad. Then it was time to try the salmon. She took a small bite and — surprise — it tasted as good as it looked. The tangy, lemony sauce had just a hint of dill.

Kari quickly polished off her first piece of salmon, thinking that if her salmon tasted like this, she'd be a lot less reluctant to eat it.

Maybe I should ask Ella for the recipe, she thought as she took a second, slightly bigger, piece.

His parents were wrapped up in a conversation about university politics, but Damien took note of Kari's second helping. He raised an eyebrow. "I thought you weren't very hungry."

She shrugged. "Guess I'm hungrier than I thought."

"Are you sure you're not just trying to impress Mom with your love of her cooking?" he teased.

"That too," Kari agreed easily. There was no point in denying the truth.

As the meal continued, Kari started to relax. Apparently, Damien's father wasn't going to make a big deal about what he'd seen. Not surprising. Now that she'd had time to process what had happened in the living room, she realized he hadn't seen much.

When Ella rose to get dessert, Kari jumped up, too. "I'll help."

Kari cut the cake while Ella readied four plates. Both women were mindful of Sam hovering in the doorway.

"I don't know how you do this, dear," the older woman said, shooting a worried glance in the camera's direction.

Kari busied herself with putting a cake slice on each plate. "Once your wedding's been on TV, it gets easier, but it's still not much fun."

"I can imagine," Ella replied as she picked up a plate in each hand. "You two have no privacy."

"Not much," Kari agreed, grabbing the other two dessert plates. "The cameras are barred from the bathroom."

"That's not enough room for you and Damien to—"

Seeing where this conversation was about to go, Kari slammed on the brakes. The last thing she needed was for the world to see her discussing her love life with her new mother-in-law. "We don't."

"Pardon?"

Ella looked confused — though Kari couldn't fathom why she'd automatically assumed her son was getting busy with a woman he barely knew. Didn't most mothers like to pretend their children weren't having sex? Hers certainly did. Of course, in Kari's case, it was the truth.

Without going into detail, she tried to explain. "Damien and I don't know each other well enough for that yet."

"But Damien said you two were trying to make this marriage work," Ella protested.

We are? Kari recalled their conversation about not telling their families it was temporary and masked her surprise. "I guess we are."

She slid her slices of cake back on the counter, motioning for Kari to do the same. Realizing that she was going to have to discuss the subject with her mother-in-law — in full view of Sam's camera, Kari reluctantly complied.

Ella put an arm around her shoulders. "You're young and inexperienced, so I'm going to give you some advice: What goes on in the bedroom can make or break a marriage."

Now it was Kari's turn to be confused and a little angry. Damien's mother was supposed to champion women, so why was she advocating such nonsense? She pulled away. "Are you saying I need to put out?"

"W-what? Of course not!" Ella sputtered. "I'm merely saying that sex is part of marriage — an important part. You can't truly be trying to make your marriage work if you're ignoring what should be happening in the bedroom."

Slightly mollified, Kari tried to smooth things over with Damien's mother. "I'm not saying Damien and I will never — uh — make it into the bedroom. But I think we need to know each other for more than a week before we do."

Ella patted Kari's hand and smiled. "Good things come to those who wait, dear."

Suddenly, Kari had the feeling that she'd just passed some kind of test. Now, if only she could win Damien's father's approval, too.

Perhaps dessert would help.

****

What was taking Kari and his mom so long in the kitchen?

Damien was on the verge of getting up to check on them when Sam moved away from the door. His mother entered the dining room first, followed closely by Kari.

The two of them looked awfully cozy, Damien thought. It worried him for all of two seconds. Their closeness wasn't necessarily a bad thing. He wanted Kari and his parents to get along. That was just one more hurdle to clear in making their marriage real — the outcome he wanted more with each passing day.

Kari placed a slice of cake in front of him. Chocolate, cherries and whipped cream? *Great choice,* Damien thought as he eagerly dug in.

He took one bite, then another. It was while he was chewing his third bite that he realized the cake was more than chocolate, cherries and whipped cream. It had nuts, too.

"Dad, stop!" he said. For once he was glad his father was the slowest eater on the planet. That quirk — the one that had annoyed Damien to no end as a kid, because he couldn't leave the table to go play until everyone was finished eating — just may have saved Vic's life.

Vic stopped, his fork halfway to his mouth. "What?"

"What kind of nuts are these?" Damien demanded.

"Nuts?" Ella said at the same time.

A confused-looking Kari offered, "Black Forest Cake sometimes has walnuts."

Vic put his fork down and pushed the plate away. "Thanks, son."

"No problem, Dad," Damien replied. To Kari he explained, "Dad's allergic to walnuts."

Kari scowled at him. "You could have told me that before you let me pick out dessert."

Damien was taken aback. He supposed he could have mentioned that fact — had he not been in such a hurry to get to the bathroom.

"Sorry, sweetheart," he apologized. That'd be the last time he downed a Big Gulp on the way to his parents' house. Apparently, his bladder wasn't as young as it used to be.

Kari accepted his apology with a nod. To Vic, she said, "I'm sorry."

Vic waved his hand. "Don't worry about it. You didn't know."

BLIND DATE BRIDE

"But I could have killed you."

"Despite what my son the drama king would have you believe, eating walnuts won't kill me."

Damien had to break in. "Come on, Dad. You have to admit I saved you a lot of discomfort." He turned to Kari and winked. "Dad puffs up like a blowfish and his skin gets blotchy."

"Still, I wouldn't have kicked the bucket," Vic insisted stubbornly. He smiled at Kari. "I'm not going to let you make the poor girl feel bad because *you* forgot to tell her about my allergy."

Damien fought to keep from rolling his eyes. It was a good sign that his dad was defending his wife. He wondered if she realized she'd just gotten the parental stamp of approval.

Chapter Thirteen

"It was awful," Kari complained to Bethany over the phone later that night.

"Come on, now," her friend cajoled. "Surely meeting Damien's parents couldn't have been that bad."

Kari snorted. "Take the worst thing you can think of and multiply it tenfold."

"Something had to go right."

"You mean the part where I tried to kill Damien's father, or the part where his mom and I had a sex talk in the kitchen?"

"You did what?"

Bethany's screech made Kari pull the phone away from her ear. She settled it again and explained. "Damien neglected to tell me his dad's allergic to walnuts, so I tried to feed him Black Forest Cake. With walnuts."

She hoped her voice sounded more patient than she felt, because what she really wanted was to climb into bed and pull a blanket over her head until the disastrous day was a distant memory.

"That's bad all right," Bethany commiserated. "But I was more surprised by your other revelation."

"Believe me — no one was more surprised than I was. I'm not even sure how the topic came up, but the next thing I knew, she was telling me that what goes on in the bedroom can make or break a marriage."

"She's right, you know," Bethany choked out after she stopped laughing.

Kari groaned. "I should have known you'd be on her side."

"It's true."

"Like you know anything about marriage," Kari grumbled under her breath, half hoping Beth wouldn't hear.

"I heard that."

Of course she did. Why wouldn't the luck of the day continue its hold? At least Beth didn't sound offended. Thank goodness they'd been friends long enough to speak their minds.

On the other end of the line, Bethany was saying, "Keep a

man happy in the bedroom, and he'll keep you happy out of it."

Kari rolled her eyes. She knew Bethany couldn't see it, but she couldn't help herself. "You sound like a throwback to the '50s."

"If it ain't broke—"

Kari cut her off. "I refuse to believe sex is that important."

"Just because you're a prude doesn't mean there's no truth to what she said," her friend objected. "And you pretending sex doesn't matter at all is just as off base as me using it as the sole basis for a relationship."

Beth admitted she could be wrong? That brought Kari up short. "You might be onto something there."

"Of course I am," Bethany replied, sounding more like herself again. "And speaking of me being right, have you made a date with Damien yet?"

"What?" she asked absently, still mulling her friend's previous statement.

"Oh no you don't," Bethany said. "I kept my end of the bargain and agreed to see 'Star Trek' with Cody. Now it's your turn."

"Oh. That."

"Yes, that. And don't forget, it has to be something good," she prodded. "No family game night allowed."

"Okay, okay," Kari agreed, knowing her friend wasn't going to give up. Still, she wanted to stall. Anything to keep that disturbing image of herself and Damien from popping back into her head. "That's still nearly two weeks away."

"If you don't plan now, Damien might make other plans."

"He's my husband for the next almost three months, Beth. I don't think he *can* make other plans."

"You have a point there," she conceded. "Still, it'd be considerate of you to actually make a date."

"I will," Kari promised. As Bethany disconnected the call, she was already thinking about what she and Damien could do. It had to be something more interesting than Scrabble, but just as safe.

After depositing her phone on the nightstand, she unrolled her yoga mat at the foot of the bed. It was past time to unwind from her stressful day.

That was when it hit her: Her gym offered a couples yoga class on Friday nights. She and Damien could take the class together, and then sit across a table from one another for dinner.

Smiling, she began her evening yoga routine. That would work out just fine. No full-body contact necessary.

****

"She wants you to do what?" Cody asked, stopping in mid-stride.

"Don't sound so surprised," Damien said crossly as he kept on walking. "You heard me the first time."

"Oh, I heard you," Cody said. The two of them were walking Chelsea and Sunny in the park across from Damien's office. "I just can't believe you agreed to take a yoga for couples class, especially on the night 'Star Trek' premieres."

"Yeah. Why on earth would I want to spend time with my adorable wife when I could be watching 'Star Trek' with you and a theater full of other sci-fi geeks?"

"Uh, are you forgetting your adorable wife just told all of America you're not getting any?"

Damien groaned. "Don't remind me." Despite what he'd told Kari the night of the premiere party — and against his better judgment — he'd decided to tune into their show Sunday night. Even three days later, part of him was glad he had, because it meant he got to find out what had kept Kari and his mom in the kitchen for so long.

He had to admit, Kari had handled the conversation, well, better than he would have for sure. The thought of discussing his love life with his mother — he'd rather go through another semester of organic chemistry or struggle through the euthanasia talk with one of his pet parents. Still, he wished the Romance TV audience didn't know about his lack of a love life.

"You've always been a bigger fan of those shows than I have," Damien told Cody, not for the first time. He was more upset that his friend's dog had gained a pound in the week since he'd told Cody to put her on a diet than he was about the show or the yoga class he'd be taking. "Besides, yoga could be fun."

"If you call tying yourself in knots fun."

Wondering when Cody had developed such an aversion to fitness, Damien ignored the comment. "You're forgetting I've seen Kari practice yoga."

"Dude, you don't get to sit back and watch. They'll expect you to do those poses too."

Now it was Damien's turn to pause in mid-step. Perhaps he

ought to rethink this thing. "Guess I'd better get some practice before class, then. I'd hate to look like a complete idiot in front of Kari."

Cody chortled. "Or the TV cameras. Don't forget them."

"I haven't forgotten," Damien said, groaning. There was no way he could forget that damn camera when Sam was always around, that red light blinking steadily, catching his every moment on film.

He was just grateful that his life was generally boring, so a lot of what the camera captured never made it into the show.

Tired of thinking about the show, Damien changed the subject. It was time for an intervention, before poor Chelsea got to be thirty pounds overweight and desperately unhealthy. "Cody, you have to stop overfeeding Chelsea. No more table scraps."

"But—"

"No buts, man. Your dog's diet is a disaster," he said firmly. "A few more walks like this one wouldn't hurt, either."

"You know I don't always have time to meet you before work," Cody protested.

Damien snorted. "No one said I have to join you and Chelsea on your walks. Work them into your schedule at your convenience."

"But—"

Damien cut him off again. He hated it when people tried to argue they didn't have time for their pets. "Cody, you shouldn't have adopted a dog if you didn't have time to take care of her properly." He paused, and then added, "You're doing Chelsea a real disservice, because she's not healthy."

"She's happy," Cody insisted stubbornly.

"She'd be a lot happier if she weren't carrying around six extra pounds," Damien countered.

Obviously sensing he wasn't going to back down, Cody sighed. "I know you're right. I just hate to see her looking hungry. Can I send her to your house for a few weeks so I don't have to watch her starve?"

"You don't need to starve her, man. Just check the dog food bag and feed her ten percent less than it suggests for the weight she should be," Damien informed him. "And stop feeding her table scraps. She's not a receptacle for the food you don't want."

****

Kari sat at her desk later that afternoon, poring over a catering firm's annual report. Even though tax season was already over, she was busier than ever. An accountant's work never ended.

She started adding up a column of monthly income, so she could compare it to a list of monthly expenses. Her ringing cell phone interrupted her progress. Recognizing the ring as Bethany's, she was tempted not to answer. It was fifteen minutes to five, and she wanted to leave work on time for once. This was the last task she had to finish before she could go.

But Kari if she didn't answer, the phone would just keep ringing. Less hassle to take the call.

"Hey, Beth. What's up?"

"Kari, I'm so glad you answered."

Her friend sounded breathless — not a usual thing for Bethany. "What's wrong?"

"I don't know how to tell you this, but when I stopped by to feed your cats today, I couldn't find Rhett anywhere."

"What?" Panic made her imagine her poor black cat wandering the streets, cold, wet and starving.

"Don't jump to conclusions," Bethany said. "I'm almost certain he didn't escape. I didn't see a little black furball race past when I opened the door."

Even Bethany's uncanny ability to read her mind didn't impress Kari. "He's pretty fast, you know."

"Well, I promise I wasn't being careless."

Knowing yelling wouldn't help bring Rhett back, Kari took a deep, calming breath in and out. She tried to keep the panic out of her voice when she replied, "Beth, my cat has been in your care for a little more than a week and you've lost him. If that's not careless, what is?"

She should have known better than to entrust Rhett and Ashley to Bethany's care. Her friend couldn't keep a houseplant alive for a month, let alone watch two cats for three of them.

"Just stay there. I'm leaving the office now." Courtney's Catering was just going to have to wait until morning.

An hour later, Kari had been searching for Rhett for thirty minutes. She'd checked behind the living room curtains, on top of the kitchen cabinet — all of Rhett's favorite hidey-holes. But he was nowhere to be found.

What next? She asked Bethany, and her friend gave her a

pointed look.

"Your husband's a vet. Maybe you should ask him."

Kari scowled at Bethany. Why hadn't she thought of that herself? Her only excuse was that Rhett's disappearance was making her scatterbrained.

She dug her phone out of her purse and dialed Damien's cell phone number. This call was too important to be filtered through the office receptionist. She listened as it rang several times and went to voicemail.

"Damien, I can't find my cat. I've looked everywhere. Help!"

Chapter Fourteen

Damien saw his last patient back to the waiting area and strode to his office. He made a few notes on the cat's chart and filed it away. Then he noticed a missed call on his cell phone.

He dialed his voicemail and listened to the message. Kari sounded frantic, and no wonder. He couldn't imagine misplacing a pet.

Hmm. He hadn't even known Kari had a pet, he thought as he eased the Element into rush-hour traffic.

Wait. Vaguely, he remembered Kari mentioning her cats on their wedding night. One was black and the other white, he recalled triumphantly. His memory was just fine.

Just then, Damien recalled Sunny was still at the office. He made his way to the right lane so he could drive around the block and pick up the dog, who'd had fun visiting with the other canines being boarded at his office that day. It was convenient having his own doggy "day care" so Sunny didn't have to hang out at the apartment alone while he and Kari were at work.

The mutt licked his face while she stood waiting for him to help her into the SUV. With the cast on her leg, she didn't want to jump up there herself — a good thing, because she wasn't supposed to.

"I'll be glad when this cast comes off, girl," Damien told her as he hoisted her hind end into the vehicle. He was doubly glad that Sunny wasn't carrying extra weight like Cody's Chelsea. He'd probably strain his back if he had to move that oversized mutt into his car.

With Sunny safely in the vehicle, he headed toward home. Halfway there, it occurred to him that there were no cats in the apartment. He'd definitely remember that, even with his apparently failing memory.

He dialed Kari's number, and she answered on the first ring.

"I got your message," he said quickly, wanting to get right to the point. "But I don't know where your apartment is."

Kari gave him the address. It was in the same general direction from his office as his own. He was glad, because it meant he could rush to the rescue that much faster.

He had no doubt he could save the day. He was an expert on cats and their hiding places. Felines got into more strange hiding places than any other animal he treated. Just today, his last patient, a tiger-striped male named Tigger, had managed to get into a closed cabinet in the exam room.

Damien swung his SUV into a parking place near Kari's apartment and took the stairs two at a time. When he knocked on the door, Kari called, "Come in. It's open."

"He's here somewhere," What's Her Name was saying as he walked into the living room. "He has to be."

He took one look at his wife's tear-stained face and immediately wanted to gather her into his arms and kiss away her pain. However, finding the cat would go a lot further toward making her feel better than his caresses would.

"I'm sure he is," Damien agreed. "Why don't you show me where you've already looked for — what's the cat's name?"

"Rhett."

As Kari led him on a walking tour of her apartment, he took note of the furnishings and décor, as well as of potential hiding places she might not have checked yet. It was a nice place, neat and clean. Definitely feminine, with frilly curtains and an abundance of throw pillows in every room.

Maybe Rhett got smothered under a pile of them. He knew better than to voice the thought. Women didn't like criticism of their interior decorating skills, especially when they were already overwrought.

Really, it wasn't a bad place. Toss out about three dozen unnecessary pillows, and Kari's apartment would be very habitable. The walls were a soft, buttercup yellow and the plush carpet was a lush green. He felt a little like he was in a sunny, warm forest.

With the tour complete, Damien had a few ideas of where to look for the wayward feline. He also knew all their lives would be a lot easier if Rhett were to come out of hiding voluntarily. The atmosphere in the apartment was too chaotic for that, though.

While Kari wasn't paying attention, he motioned for What's Her Name to join him in the kitchen. Once she arrived, he quietly suggested, "Why don't you take Kari to that coffee shop I saw around the corner?" He held out a twenty-dollar bill. "My treat."

The woman shook her head. "She's not going anywhere while her beloved Rhett is AWOL."

He pressed the money into What's Her Name's hand. "She will if I have anything to say about it."

Damien strode to where Kari stood by the living room window, staring unseeingly into the mid-June dusk. He put a hand on her shoulder.

"Sweetheart?" When she turned to him, he continued, "You guys have been here a long time. Why don't you take a break?"

"How can I relax when my cat can't be found?"

"You called me because you trust my judgment, right?" he asked her. She nodded. "I think Rhett will be more likely to let himself be found if things quiet down around here. So you two go linger over some coffee, and by the time you come back, your feline family will be back intact. Promise."

****

Knowing Damien was probably right, Rhett would keep hiding until things calmed down, Kari reluctantly followed Bethany down the stairs. They headed around the corner, to the coffee shop where Kari had been a regular until recently.

By the time they got to the counter, the barista had already made Kari's favorite, an iced latte with sugar-free caramel syrup.

"You remembered," she commented, accepting the drink with a grateful smile.

"Sure did," the girl said, smiling back. "It's not every day we get to serve a celebrity."

"I'm not—" Kari curtailed her objection as soon as it occurred to her that the people in her neighborhood probably did consider her famous.

That would take some getting used to. In her mind, she was the same woman she'd always been — albeit with a husband she wasn't sure she wanted and now a missing cat she did.

"I hope it never gets to the point where people recognize me on the street," she murmured to Bethany. That would be sheer torture.

"Don't worry. You have a few more weeks until that happens," Bethany told her, grinning.

Kari groaned. "That's what I'm afraid of."

She headed to her favorite table, in the quietest corner of the coffee shop, and took a seat. She sipped her drink and tried to believe in Damien's skill with animals. If he couldn't find Rhett, the cat was truly gone.

They nursed their drinks in silence. Bethany, she knew, was subdued because she felt terrible about losing Rhett.

Kari knew it wasn't Beth's fault. Sure, she couldn't keep a houseplant alive, but Kari wasn't so great at that herself. And, for a creative type, Bethany was reliable. She even paid Kari back every time she borrowed a few bucks.

Kari took a deep breath. Time to apologize. "Beth, despite the way I've been acting, I know it's not your fault."

Bethany waved away the apology. "I'd be ticked off too, if you lost my pet."

"It's hard to misplace a fish," Kari pointed out, giggling. "But seriously, Beth, Rhett loves to play hide and seek. He's just not usually so hard to find."

"He's probably mad that you haven't been around."

Kari pondered that as the two of them made their way back to her apartment. Rhett could be hiding because he missed her. She hadn't seen him for more than a week, after all.

She pushed open her apartment door and stepped inside, holding her breath. She hoped against hope that Damien had been able to coax Rhett out of whatever hidey-hole he'd burrowed into.

Sure enough, Damien was sitting on the couch with Rhett curled up on his lap. The cat's purr was so loud she heard it from the doorway.

****

"You found him!"

Damien could feel her relief as Kari ran toward him and plopped down on the couch. He nodded. "He was holed up in the storage space under your waterbed."

The waterbed had surprised him — not at all what he'd expected Kari to spend her nights in. She seemed more like a canopy-bed type to him. But as soon as he'd seen the setup, he suspected the cat was hiding there.

Sure enough, when he'd opened the cabinet door, two glowing green eyes stared back at him.

"Why didn't I think to check there?" Kari wondered aloud as she scooped Rhett off his lap and cuddled him against her chest.

"If it's not one of his normal hiding places, I'm not surprised you didn't check it," he assured his now much more relaxed wife, trying not to wish he were in the cat's place.

She finally looked up, right into his eyes. Her smile was radiant. "Thank you."

"I'm glad I could help." He was, too. Seeing Kari's beautiful smile was all the reward he needed.

A hug like the one she just gave the cat would be nice, too, the voice in his head, the one that sounded like Cody, prompted. Damien silenced that voice, because he was curious about something.

"Why have your cats been here without you?"

"I made sure someone stopped by to check on them every couple of days, to make sure their food and water bowls are filled."

He couldn't help himself; the veterinarian in him took over and he frowned. "That's no substitute for your daily care. You should have brought them with you when you moved in."

Kari frowned right back at him and he knew he was in for a challenge. Funny how he could read her so well already. "You're forgetting that I didn't know a thing about you when we got married. For all I knew, you could have been a kitty serial killer."

He had to admit she had a point. They'd known absolutely nothing about one another, except a panel of experts that included Danielle Steel and Dr. Drew said they had the worst love lives in America. "Okay, what about once you knew I was a vet? Most veterinarians don't go around killing cats — at least not on purpose."

"That's true enough," she agreed. "But we've been a little preoccupied, don't you think?"

Damien reviewed the last few weeks in his mind. First there was the wedding and reception, then the call to do the TV show, bringing home Sunny, taking Kari to meet his parents, and he couldn't forget the time they'd spent trying to get to know one another. "It *has* been a busy couple of weeks," he conceded.

"Exactly!"

She appeared pleased that he seemed to understand, but he wasn't all that understanding. "Your cats are important to you, so they should be with you."

For just a moment, Kari looked stunned. Then she leaned in and gave him a peck on the cheek before dropping Rhett back on his lap.

"Thank you, Damien," she said. "You hold Rhett while I go

pack up their gear."

Damien watched her leave the living room, slightly stunned himself. Apparently, Kari's two cats were going to join Sunny at their apartment.

It was a good thing the dog got along with felines. He'd witnessed that firsthand at the office. Now, if only Rhett and Ashley turned out to be dog lovers, the transition would be seamless.

Chapter Fifteen

The cacophony of barks and hisses coming from the apartment as Kari approached the closed door after work that Friday evening were proof that the relationship between Rhett, Ashley and Sunny was still rocky.

Kind of like my relationship with Damien.

Like her husband, Sunny was overly friendly, always wanting to play. Rhett and Ashley, not used to dogs, wanted nothing to do with her. Kind of like Kari, unused to big, strong alpha-male types, wasn't quite sure what to do with Damien.

"I'm self-aware enough to admit that," she muttered as she unlocked the door and pushed it open. The question was: What should she do about it?

The scene that greeted her had Rhett perched on the arm of the couch, hissing. Sunny was sitting on the floor at the cat's feet, her tail thumping happily, and Ashley was crouched inches from the dog, his little white paw swiping at Sunny's nose.

Kari rushed to grab the cat before he shredded poor Sunny's schnoz. "Bad kitty," she scolded. "You're going to have to start getting along with this dog, because she's in your life for now."

She deposited the cat next to his brother, who'd jumped to the back of the couch. She had a sinking suspicion she'd just answered her own question. She needed to get along with her too-large husband because he was in her life to stay, at least for the time being.

Wait a minute. Wasn't that what she'd been trying to do for the last week and a half? It's not as if she'd been acting as if Damien had cooties or something. No, nothing like that.

After pausing to scratch Rhett behind the ears, Kari turned around. Before she could take two steps, she bumped into the man she couldn't stop thinking about.

"You startled me!"

Damien apologized and took a step backward. The room immediately felt two sizes larger, and Kari relaxed. "I just got off the phone with Hayworth."

Uh-oh. He did not sound happy. Bracing herself against the

displeasure, she asked, "What does he want now?"

"Our presence is requested down at Romance TV headquarters."

"Do I have time to change out of my work clothes?" Kari asked. She really didn't want to head back downtown in a suit and heels.

He checked his watch. "Make it quick."

Kari dashed down the hall, kicking off her pumps and shedding her jacket as she went. What to wear? A laundry basket — full of folded, apparently clean clothes — sat in the middle of the bed. Glad that Damien had found the time to do a load of laundry, she grabbed a pair of jeans.

Not even two full minutes later, she was back at Damien's side in the entryway. "Let's go."

Damien grabbed his jacket as they headed out the door. "Where'd you learn to change so quickly?"

"You really want to know?"

Damien raised an eyebrow. "I wouldn't have asked if I didn't."

"Two words: marching band." When Damien merely looked confused, she elaborated. "You learn to change pretty fast, and without exposing anything, when you have to get dressed on the band bus."

Damien stopped in mid-stride, forcing Kari to do the same. After what seemed like minutes — but was probably really only a few seconds — of enduring his gaze, she narrowed her eyes. "You're ogling again."

"Was I?" he asked, beginning to walk toward the El stop again. "Sorry. Just trying to figure out what you played." A few steps later, he stopped and grinned. "Color guard!"

Kari shook her head. "Guess again."

"You definitely weren't a tuba player," he said, waggling his eyebrows. When she just rolled her eyes, he suggested, "Flute?"

She giggled. Kidding around like this was fun. "That's your third strike."

"I've never been good at playing baseball," Damien replied, shrugging. "Trumpet, yes. Baseball, not so much."

"No way you were a band geek," Kari told him. "You have jock written all over you."

He shrugged again. "Sorry to disappoint you, dear, but I didn't discover my athletic side until I got to college. That's when

I took up running and tennis."

"You really played trumpet?"

"All through middle school and high school. I even had a solo in the Christmas concert one year." He turned away to swipe his pass and walk through the turnstile. Task complete, he added, "It's harder than you might think to get a trumpet to sound like a whinnying horse."

Kari had to get herself through the turnstile, and then rush to catch up to Damien. Turned out he was a fast walker. When she reached his side again, he was more than halfway to the loading platform.

She picked up the conversation where they'd left off. "Are you by chance talking about 'Sleigh Ride'?"

Damien nodded and Kari groaned. "Our first chair trumpet player only managed to get it right about half the time. When he didn't, it sounded like the horse was dying."

"I had a few of those dying horse moments myself," Damien said, chuckling. "Thank goodness I came through in the actual performance."

"So did Dave, but I'm pretty sure we were all holding our breath." ·

Just then, the train arrived. After they boarded, Damien said, "I don't know why band directors torture kids with the same holiday songs year after year."

"There *are* a limited number of Christmas carols to choose from," Kari pointed out. "But if you want to talk torture, try that bell song. You play the same four notes, over and over again until you're ready to scream — and then you get to do it again."

"I remember that one," he said, nodding. "Sounds like you were doing the flute part."

Kari shook her head. "You already guessed that."

"Okay, I give. What did you play?"

"The bells."

"Bells, huh?"

Kari waited while Damien pondered her revelation for a moment. Even though they were sitting side by side, she could feel his gaze roaming over her body. It was a strange feeling, but not entirely unwelcome.

Finally, he spoke. "I can see you — a younger version of you, anyway — in the pit."

"Well, that makes one of us who looks the part," Kari told

him with a grin. "Because I still don't think you look like a band geek."

"You should have seen me before I got contacts and started working out — total nerd," Damien confided, winking at her. "Don't forget both my parents were college professors."

Kari giggled again. "Remind me to ask you to show me a picture. I want to see that."

"My high school yearbooks are packed away in the spare room. Maybe later tonight, we can boot Sam and Stacy out for a while and hunt them down."

Kari doubted Sam and Stacy would agree to leave. "They'll probably want to film the moment for posterity."

"You're probably right. I guess there are worse things they could air."

"Like me talking sex with your mom in the kitchen?" Kari suggested mischievously. Despite telling Damien she didn't care to watch "Just Married" when it aired, she'd tuned in. And she had to admit, when she saw the visit with his parents on TV, it didn't seem nearly as bad as it felt while it was happening. If she squinted and held her breath, she could almost believe both his parents liked her. Almost.

Damien nodded. "Exactly like that. I can't believe Mom went there."

"You saw it?" The thought made Kari blush.

He nodded again. "I couldn't help myself. I had to catch it."

"Me, too. It's like one of those accidents you pass on the highway. You tell yourself not to look, but can't help yourself."

Damien squeezed her hand. "Next time, let's watch together, but without Cody."

"Sounds like a plan," Kari agreed. Even if he was good for Beth, that man seemed to enjoy their antics a little too much.

****

The train rolled to a stop and Damien stood. "We're here."

He led Kari out the door and into the late-afternoon sunshine. Not for the first time, he wondered why they were being summoned to the Romance TV headquarters. Maybe the show's ratings were so bad Hayworth wanted to pull the plug. They could only be so lucky.

Pushing open the glass door, Damien was assaulted by the same terrible décor that had greeted him on his first visit to the office. Who in their right mind would put a red, lip-shaped couch in the lobby?

"The same people who would call a blind date wedding quality TV," he muttered in answer to his own question.

"Pardon?"

He looked down at the top of Kari's head. How could he have forgotten, even for a second, that she was beside him? Temporary blindness caused by the too-bright couch, perhaps? "Sorry. I was just wondering why the lobby looks like it belongs in a tacky hotel."

Kari scanned the room. "Was it this bad last time?"

"It was," he confirmed. "How'd you miss it?"

"I was a little out of it. Remember?"

He remembered, all right. She'd almost limped right past him on her way through what had to be the world's ugliest lobby. "I think that day was rough for both of us."

At that, Kari sighed. "This one's probably not going to be much better. We'd better get in there and see what's up this time."

Together, they walked through the heavy wooden door that led to CEO Rick Hayworth's office. Damien was relieved to see that Hayworth was alone — no lawyer this time. That had to be good news.

There were three chairs in front of the CEO's desk, and Damien chose the leftmost one. He was surprised, but glad, when Kari sat next to him instead of leaving a chair between them. That, too, was a good sign.

At least he planned to take it that way. They *had* just bonded over band memories, after all. Smiling to himself, Damien shook his head. Why was it so hard for her to believe he'd been in the band?

Probably the same reason it's tough for you to believe she doesn't know how beautiful she really is, his Cody-conscience gibed. If she'd been a band geek too, he wasn't the only one who'd had to grow into his looks. Maybe she was still growing.

He needed to get his mind off Kari's sex appeal before something else started growing. Keeping that in mind, Damien focused all his attention on Hayworth, who was saying, "I'm glad you two were able to come in so quickly."

"What's going on?"

The question came not from him but from Kari. Damien admired her for wanting to get to the point. Left on his own, the executive would probably waste time making small talk.

"It has come to our attention that you, Mrs. Walker, are planning a three-week trip to Alaska." When Kari nodded her confirmation, Hayworth continued. "We regret to inform you that the trip will result in nullification of our agreement."

****

Kari stared at the CEO of Romance TV, unable to comprehend what he was telling her. "Excuse me?"

"If you leave Chicago for three weeks and your husband doesn't go with you, you'll forfeit the prize," Hayworth explained.

"I can't cancel the trip now. It was in the works long before I won this contest. The reservations are all made."

"The rules clearly state that you two must live together for the three months following the wedding," he reminded her.

"And if I'm in Alaska and Damien's here, we're not living together."

"Now you're catching on," he said, offering her a smile.

Kari had to struggle to keep from narrowing her eyes. Hayworth was smarmier than she remembered. She turned to her silent husband, wondering what he was thinking.

Damien's countenance gave her no clue as to what was going on inside his head. Great. He'd be no help at all.

Then again, it wasn't his vacation that was threatening to ruin everything. It was hers — so by rights, she should be the one to handle it.

Kari looked back at the CEO. "Thanks for the heads up, Mr. Hayworth. We'll work something out."

Hayworth beamed at her. "I knew you would. You're a sensible girl."

This time, Kari did narrow her eyes at Hayworth. She couldn't help it; she hated to be called a girl. She was a full-grown woman.

Maybe it was time to start acting like one.

That thought brought Kari up short. Where had it come from? It certainly sounded like the inner voice she'd been trying to silence — with increasing difficulty — since meeting Damien. Only this time, it wasn't urging her to explore her sensual side.

And this time, it might actually be right. An adult would not have panicked quite so much when her cat disappeared, or whined about changing her vacation plans. So what if she had to forfeit a few fees? The money she was going to win more than made up for those surcharges.

A full-grown woman also wouldn't run in the other direction every time her husband put the moves on her.

Okay. *That* sounded more like the vixen, and that she could handle. She ruthlessly pushed the thought, along with its cousins, to the far corner of her mind.

"Is that all?"

Kari looked over at Damien, who'd asked the question. She teased, "He speaks!"

When Hayworth merely nodded, Damien frowned. "You called us all the way down here just for that? You could have shared that information over the phone."

"We thought it was important to tell you in person."

"Damien's right," Kari chimed in, as eager as he apparently was to avoid being summoned to HQ at Hayworth's whim. They both had better things to do with their time. She'd missed her after-work yoga session and she desperately needed to unwind. "It took us longer to get downtown than it did to have the whole meeting."

Damien rose to his feet, holding his hand out for Kari to join him. She did, without hesitation. "Next time, think again."

Hand in hand, they left the CEO's office together, letting the door shut behind them with a satisfying thump.

Once they were back on the sidewalk, Kari grinned at her husband. "You really told him!"

"You have to be firm with people like that. Otherwise, he'll be calling us downtown for meetings every time we turn around. I don't know about you, but I'd rather not spend all my free time riding the train downtown."

Kari rose up on tiptoes and planted a kiss on Damien's forehead. Realizing that even that small action generated heat between them, she quickly pulled away. "Well, thank you for telling Hayworth exactly how I felt."

"I'm just glad we're on the same page," Damien told her, squeezing her hand.

Kari didn't try to fight the tingle sparked by his touch. "As long as we're downtown, why don't we grab some dinner? We have a vacation to re-plan."

Chapter Sixteen

"I know I can't ask you to cancel your entire trip," Damien told Kari forty-five minutes later over a deep-dish sausage and pepperoni pizza from Uno's. "But I also can't take three weeks off from work."

"Of course not," she agreed, sounding incredibly sensible.

He liked that about Kari. Despite her new-agey interest in yoga, she was infinitely practical. Even her push to get him to agree to do the show had been motivated by realism. She wanted the money not to go on a shopping spree or to buy a flashy new car, but to help her folks and build up her savings — always sensible ideas.

"So how long do you think you can break away?" After asking the question, Kari took a big bite of her second slice of pizza, washing it down with a swig of light beer. She'd agreed to split a half pitcher because, she said, beer and pizza went together like peanut butter and jelly. He suspected their little chat with Hayworth had rattled her more than she wanted to let on.

As Damien watched her eat, he hid a smile. His wife certainly had an appetite. He just wished he knew where she kept putting it, because it definitely wasn't going to her hips — or anywhere else, as far as he could tell. Her body was perfect. The curve of her breast, the flare of her hips below her nipped-in waist, her rounded bottom. His body leapt to attention as he contemplated her charms.

Guiltily, he realized his mind had been wandering. Kari was watching him expectantly, waiting for a response. He shifted in his seat and did some quick calculations. He knew a couple of colleagues who'd be willing to help in his absence, so ... "A week?"

When Kari's face fell, he knew she'd been hoping for more. Well, it'd be worth a little extra sacrifice on his part to see her smile. He took a deep breath and committed — at least as much as he was able without contacting his colleagues first. "Two weeks will be a stretch, but I think I can swing it."

There it was: Kari's widest, brightest smile. He was quickly coming to love that look of pure joy.

"Thank-you-thank-you-thank-you!" she said in a rush. "I've been wanting to see Alaska since I was eight and my parents starting watching 'Northern Exposure.'"

"I'll start making the arrangements with my replacements first thing in the morning," Damien said, smiling back at her.

"And I'll rearrange the itinerary. Want want me to go ahead and get your plane ticket?"

Damien, who'd been about to take a bite of pizza, froze in mid-bite. He gulped. "Plane? As in airplane?"

"How else are we going to get to Alaska and back in a week and a half? By time machine?"

His eyebrows shot up at the note of sarcasm in his beautiful wife's voice. But as quickly as they went up, he forced them back down. She was entitled to bristle when he asked such a stupid question.

She was right. Of course driving would take too long.

"Go ahead and get the ticket," he told her, forcing a smile. "I'll write you a check when the credit card bill comes through."

That was that. For the first time in a long time, he was taking vacation — to Alaska, a state he'd never had much desire to see. And he'd be traveling by, God help him, airplane.

Damien finished his slice of pizza and drained his glass of beer before pouring himself another one. He just hoped he'd survive the experience.

****

Later that night, Kari unrolled her yoga mat at the foot of the bed. She sat, lotus-style, and took a few deep breaths as she meditated on the events of the day.

It had been surprisingly easy to work out a vacation compromise. She was glad Damien had been so accommodating. Being in Alaska for only two weeks wasn't much of a sacrifice — not when the whole reason for her trip had changed.

Yes, she had wanted to see the state, as she'd told Damien over dinner. However, when she'd planned her Alaskan sojourn, she'd been single. After reading enough romance novels set in the state where men outnumbered women — and with more than a little encouragement from Bethany — she'd hoped she might stumble across the man of her dreams.

Obviously, now that she had a husband — albeit a

temporary one — she wouldn't get the chance to meet any nice, single men. Having Damien around would really cramp her style.

Kari's snort interrupted a controlled exhalation. It wasn't as if she had a style to cramp. What had she been thinking? Mr. Right was just going to drop from the sky onto the road in front of her rental car?

That's the last time I let Beth help me plan a vacation.

She unfolded her legs and did a few more gentle stretches before rerolling the mat. She really needed to start jogging with Damien, especially if she intended to continue eating like he did. No way had a few easy yoga moves burned enough calories to make up for two slices of deep-dish pizza and two glasses of light beer.

After checking that the bedroom door was locked so Damien couldn't walk in unexpectedly, Kari changed into the ratty shorts and T-shirt that now served as her pajamas. Then she unlocked the door so Damien *could* get in and climbed into bed, wishing she could still sleep in the nude, the way she preferred. She missed the freedom and the sensual feeling of bare skin against soft cotton.

When Damien still hadn't joined her a little while later, she checked her watch. It was after ten — much later than his usual bedtime. So where on earth was he?

Just then, the bedroom door swung open and Damien entered the room. He was carrying a bright red, oversized book.

"It took awhile, but I finally found my freshman yearbook," he said, thrusting the book in question at her. "Check out page thirty-two."

Eagerly, Kari flipped to the correct page. There, in full color, was the proof of Damien's band geek-dom. He must have been at band camp, or at least at a summer rehearsal, because he was wearing shorts and a tank top. He was all scrawny arms and legs, his trumpet dangling from bony fingers at his side. His glasses, complete with thick, black frames, dominated his thin face.

She bit back an inappropriate giggle. "Are those braces I see?"

The bed dipped under Damien's weight as he sat down and stretched out beside her. "Unfortunately, yes."

Kari whistled. "Now I believe you. You really *were* a band

geek."

"I hate to say, 'I told you so.'"

She put a finger to his lips to stop him, trying not to shudder at the jolt of awareness that shot through her at the contact. "You earned it, so go ahead and say it."

"Okay, then. I told you so," he said, grinning. After a pause, he added, "Now that I've shown you mine, it's your turn."

Kari caught her lower lip between her teeth. Even if she wanted to let him see the frizzy hair and chipmunk cheeks she'd had at fourteen, before she'd discovered quality hair products, a healthy diet and an exercise she enjoyed, she couldn't.

"I'd love to," she fibbed, "but my yearbooks are at my place."

Damien sighed. "I was afraid of that."

"Next time I swing by the apartment, I'll grab them," she promised, mentally crossing her fingers. Hopefully, he'd forget by then, because she had no plans to head over there anytime soon. With Rhett and Ashley here with her and Bethany picking up her mail, she had no reason to make a time-wasting trek to her place.

He smiled. "I bet you were adorable at that age."

"Nope. I was a complete geek too."

"Complete geek?" Damien clutched at his heart with his hand. "That hurts!"

"If the shoe fits."

"Can't you give a guy a break?"

Kari laughed. When she was kidding around with Damien like this, she almost forgot his extreme maleness. "Well, I've always been partial to geeks."

But only almost. In an instant, the energy in the room changed from playful to sexually charged. Her breath quickened as Damien gazed into her eyes. The next thing she knew, he was no longer beside her. He was straddling her waist and swooping in to kiss her.

When he pulled away moments later, she breathlessly demanded, "What was that for?"

Still hovering over her, he apologized. "I couldn't resist, especially not when you just admitted geeks are your type."

As Kari looked up at her hunk of a husband, a part of her was wishing he hadn't stopped. Still, she didn't need him thinking he could just kiss her whenever he wanted to. Her defenses weren't strong enough to withstand sneak attacks like that.

She pushed at his chest and he moved away, much more easily than she expected him to. That he settled on his side of the bed without a lot of urging made her feel a little better. Maybe he really wouldn't use his size and strength against her.

But Kari simply couldn't take that chance. Not yet, anyway.

"I hate to break it to you, but you're not a geek anymore."

When Damien scowled at her, and not in a playful way, Kari flinched, wondering if she'd just pushed him too far. However, he merely got up and strode from the room. On his way out the door, he grumbled, "You can't blame a guy for trying."

****

Damien was greeted by silence when he let himself into the apartment Thursday afternoon. He was glad, because it meant that, after a week of living under one roof, Sunny and the cats were finally making peace with one another. Even better, now he could get to his reason for ducking out of work early without having to organize a feline-canine peace treaty.

"If I were a yoga DVD, where would I be?" he muttered as he headed to his first-choice location: the entertainment center.

Bingo! Several DVDs were lined up in the space next to the TV, and they were all exercise-related. Good. Kari was as unimaginative as he was when it came to multimedia storage.

He perused the line of titles. There were a couple of Pilates DVDs, a boot camp workout and — what the hell? — strip aerobics?

"That's a surprise."

On second thought, it wasn't such a shock. He already knew his temporary wife was hot enough to be an exotic dancer. He just didn't think *she* was aware of it. She couldn't know and keep such a tight lid on her sexuality. Strip aerobics just didn't jibe with her buttoned-up persona.

Now the sex kitten he'd coaxed out to play a couple of times was a different story. He bet *she* had a lot of fun with that workout.

Damien shook his head at the direction of his thoughts and went back to scanning the titles. He couldn't afford to waste his precious practice time fantasizing about his wife doing a striptease. At the end of the row, he found the title he was looking for.

"'Yoga for Beginners. That's me."

He pulled the DVD off the shelf. The back cover promised simple moves to improve flexibility, balance and focus.

Damien grinned. It sounded like the perfect way to keep him from looking like a complete fool when he and Kari took that yoga for couples class Friday.

He popped the disc into the DVD player and headed to the bedroom to change into shorts and a T-shirt. When he returned to the living room, the guy on the DVD was twisting himself into some sort of pretzel, with his left calf up around his ear.

Damien shook his head and headed to the kitchen. If this workout would be that strenuous, he needed to stay hydrated.

Finally back in front of the TV with a bottle of water in hand, he was stunned to see the instructor springing up into a handstand.

"This can't be a beginning yoga DVD," he said to no one in particular. Sunny, who was lying in a sun patch near the window, yipped her agreement.

He stopped the DVD player and checked the disc. Sure enough, it was titled "Yoga: Beyond Intermediate."

Definitely not up for that challenge, Damien checked the case with that title and found the "Yoga for Beginners" disc. He slipped the new disc into the DVD player and pressed play. Almost instantly, a female instructor was asking him to sit cross-legged on the floor and breathe deeply.

He smiled to himself. "This is more my speed."

He followed the woman through several minutes of breathing exercises and breezed through the spinal twist and cat/cow poses. He couldn't help but smile while rolling from side to side, legs in the air, for something called "happy baby."

Damien had trouble with downward-facing dog. His legs refused to straighten the way the instructor's did. His canine patients made *that* look a lot easier than it was.

Next came a series of standing poses. He wobbled a couple of times, but managed to stay upright. He dropped from a folding forward bend to another down dog, again wondering why the pose wasn't as comfortable as dogs made it look. They seemed to enjoy the deep stretch.

So did Kari, for that matter. It was the pose he'd walked in on her doing that first morning of their marriage. Unwilling to let his mind stray to *that* subject, no matter how pleasant the interlude had been, Damien forced himself to concentrate on the DVD's instructions.

He dropped to the floor for a cobra pose — also not as comfortable as it looked, and then sprang back up to another down dog. It seemed to be the instructor's go-to position.

Why couldn't the instructor like "happy baby" half as much as downward-facing dog?

Once he was fully upright, it was time to make like a tree. After having struggled with the other balance poses, Damien wasn't looking forward to the challenge.

Slowly, he raised his left foot and rested it on his right ankle. No wobbles there, so he raised his leg to mid-calf. Now he was shaking, but only minimally. *That* he could handle.

"If you're unsteady, tighten the muscles in your core," the woman onscreen intoned.

Damien was surprised that, when he did as instructed, he stopped wavering right away. He smiled and raised his left leg to his right knee. Once he was certain that he wouldn't topple over, he closed his eyes to concentrate on his breathing.

Slowly, he breathed in and out, trying to visualize himself as a giant oak tree standing proud, stretching tall while putting roots into the floor.

"Feel yourself growing taller as you stretch your spine."

That last part seemed more than a little silly, but he was determined to get the full yoga experience. If that meant pretending to be a mighty oak, so be it. At least no one was around to see him looking foolish.

As if fate wanted to have a laugh at his expense, that was the exact moment he heard a key in the lock. Sunny heard it too, because she barked and raced toward the door to greet whomever was coming in.

With his eyes still closed as he focused on putting down his roots, Damien didn't see that the dog was heading straight for him. Too late, he felt Sunny run into him.

He toppled over, groaning as his rear end hit the floor — hard. He kept his eyes closed, not wanting to know whether it was Kari or Sam and the camera who'd just witnessed his tumble. He'd almost rather have Romance TV's viewers — all several thousand of them — see him fall on his butt than embarrass himself in front of the wife he was trying to impress. That was why he'd wrangled a private practice session in the first place. Figuring out when Sam was going to be absent from the apartment for a production meeting hadn't exactly been a piece of cake.

He heard footsteps approach and cracked one eye open. The sight of a woman's pump greeted him. Unless Sam was suddenly sporting women's footwear, it was his wife, then. Great.

When he opened both eyes and looked up, Kari was staring down at him trying, unsuccessfully, to hide a smile.

She'd definitely seen him fall. At this point, there was nothing he could do to save face, so he decided to crack a joke.

"So much for the mighty oak tree," he said with a grin.

Kari giggled as she offered her hand to help him up. "You fell so fast I didn't even have time to say 'timber.'"

Chapter Seventeen

"Do we really have to go in there?"

Kari rolled her eyes, exasperated by the question she'd heard at least a dozen times — in as many different ways — since walking in on Damien's spectacular fall the afternoon before. She gave him points for creativity, at least.

"There" was Eve-olution Yoga, Kari's regular studio. She was comfortable inside its walls, because it specialized in female-only classes. She liked the way it was marketed: as a safe place for women to get in touch with their inner goddesses — though Kari was starting to wonder if her inner goddess and inner vixen were working hand in hand.

Every so often, the studio branched out with classes like tonight's "Yoga Date Night," which encouraged couples to practice yoga together. Kari had been itching to try Yoga Date Night since she'd first seen the poster months ago, but until tonight, she'd been lacking one crucial requirement: a date.

"Yes, we have to go in there," she said, her voice as firm as she could make it. "They don't hold the class in the parking lot."

"Sure you wouldn't rather skip class and have an early dinner instead?"

The look on Damien's face was so hopeful that for a moment, she was tempted to agree. But her curiosity won over the fleeting desire to please him. Now that she had the date she needed, she wasn't about to miss her chance to finally see what Yoga Date Night was all about. She no longer had to feel like the sorority she wanted to join wouldn't have her.

Besides, she had to uphold her end of the bargain with Bethany. Her friend was on her way to the theater with Cody to watch the new "Star Trek" flick, and she'd promised Beth date night with her husband.

"We're going in, and that's final."

"But—"

Kari narrowed her eyes at him. "You promised."

"I know I did," Damien replied, sighing, "but right now I can't imagine why. Yoga is much harder than you make it look."

Ah, so that explained his sudden reluctance to follow through. "You're worried you'll look stupid."

Damien arched his eyebrows. "It is a valid concern, considering that just yesterday I toppled over while attempting a simple tree pose."

Kari dismissed his complaint with a wave of her hand. "You didn't do that on your own; Sunny contributed to your downfall."

"Saying I got sacked by my dog doesn't make me look any better."

Kari had to concede he had a point. But darn it, so did she. "Damien, *everybody* looks like an idiot the first time they try yoga."

"I bet you didn't."

"Oh, but I did," she insisted. Maybe sharing her first-day-of-yoga story would make him feel more comfortable about what they were about to do. "The first time I tried to do Warrior II, I could barely stay upright. The instructor asked me if I'd been drinking."

"Really?"

"Yes, really." When Damien still looked doubtful, she asked, "You think I'd make up something that embarrassing?"

"Probably not. But how do you make it look so effortless now?"

"I've been doing yoga since college, so I've had years to perfect my form."

She'd taken her first yoga class while still dating Rob, and it was the strength — both mental and physical — she'd gained in that class that had given her the courage to finally cut that jerk out of her life. Not that she was planning to share that tidbit with Damien. Rob was in her past, and there was no reason for her temporary husband to know what had happened back then.

No reason at all — except that then he could better understand what makes you tick, the voice in her head piped up.

Kari shook her head at the errant thought. She didn't want or need Damien to understand her that well.

Suddenly aware that the husband in question was watching her intently, Kari grinned. She was well aware what he'd been doing — checking out her "perfect" form. Well, she'd set herself up for that one.

"You're ogling again." He didn't need to know she wasn't as

perturbed by his stares as she used to be. "At least we won't have to worry about Sam and his camera."

"We won't?"

She smacked her forehead. "I forgot to tell you: The studio refused to consent to taping the session."

****

At Kari's revelation, some of Damien's tension drained away. Sure, he still dreaded what was to come, but Sam's absence was at least something to savor.

"Thank God for small favors. At least if I do end up looking stupid, there won't be a camera around to preserve the moment."

With that said, Damien again looked at the squat brick building. Funny. It didn't look like a torture chamber. If he didn't know better, he'd think it was a preschool, or something equally benign.

Since Kari was adamant about this class, there was no point in further delaying the inevitable. He squared his shoulders and turned back to his increasingly impatient wife. "Let's go."

They covered the distance from the parking lot in less than a minute, and then Damien was somewhere he'd never expected to be — on the inside of his first yoga studio.

He took a quick look around, noting that it was exactly what he expected. Soft lights cast a dim glow over the hardwood floor; lavender-scented candles flickered in a mirrored wall that dominated the front of the room, and new age music tinkled softly in the background.

Unsure what to do next, he looked for Kari. She was in the far corner of the cavernous room, stuffing her shoes and socks into a cubbyhole. He crossed over to where she was and did the same thing.

The door opened and in walked a short, curvy woman in a black unitard. She, too, was barefoot, and her dark hair was pulled back in a braid that hung down her back, past her shoulder blades.

"Class will begin in five minutes," she said in a melodic voice. "Please find spots for yourselves and sit quietly to meditate on what you hope to get out of this session."

Damien let Kari lead him to the center of the room. He watched her unroll her yoga mat before kneeling to unroll the one he'd borrowed from her. Then he sat on the mat, cross-legged, and closed his eyes. After taking a few deep breaths, he opened them again. He'd much rather study his wife than contemplate his inner eyelids.

He was still doing what Kari, if she'd seen him, would define as ogling when the instructor began to speak several minutes later. Feeling guilty that he'd wasted so much time meditating on his wife's charms, he focused on the older woman's instructions.

"Couples yoga is a very special kind of yoga," she began after introducing herself as Lillith. "For the next ninety minutes, I want you and your partner to communicate candidly, through not only words but also touch and breath. By the end of your time together tonight, you will have a better understanding of yourselves and each other, an understanding that will deepen your intimate bond."

Beside him, Damien thought he heard Kari take a deeper-than-necessary breath, but when he glanced in her direction, her eyes were still closed and her features serene.

"And don't forget, the less flexible partner is always in charge."

Damien nudged Kari and whispered, "That'd be me."

Her eyes flew open and the look in them could only be described as panicked. What the hell? She'd been practicing yoga for years; of course he was going to be the less flexible one.

He was about to ask her what was wrong when Lillith said, "Now let's begin."

Their first pose, a seated facing twist, was pleasant enough. They faced one another, knees touching, and twisted to the right, grabbing each other's hands to deepen the stretch. After holding the position for five deep, slow breaths, they released and twisted to the left.

The instructor led them through several more seated poses, none too terribly uncomfortable, before telling them to rise to their feet.

"Now we're going to do a double standing straddle. This pose opens your hamstrings, stretches your lower back and neck, and lengthens the spine. And because your head is below your heart, you can use it whenever you need relief from headaches or sinus pressure."

Damien followed instructions, standing with his back to Kari, his feet a little more than hip-width apart. On Lillith's three-count, they both folded forward. Damien had to stifle a groan when he felt the deep stretch in his hamstrings.

"I really thought I was in better shape than this," he whispered to Kari as they reached through their legs to grasp one another's hands.

She responded with a smile, but no words. In fact, she'd been strangely silent throughout the experience, despite Lillith's instructions at the start of class.

Damien shrugged and concentrated on what the instructor was telling them to do. So far, things were going better than he'd expected. The poses were actually easier than the ones he'd attempted with the DVD, maybe because Lillith kept circulating through the room, stopping from time to time to make adjustments in the placement of various limbs.

They went through another several positions, each one more challenging than the last, before Lillith rang a bell at the front of the room.

"For the last ten minutes of class, I want you and your partner to sit facing one another in straddle position, sole to sole and palm to palm."

They'd been here for almost ninety minutes already? Huh. He hadn't expected the time to fly.

He parked himself on the floor across from Kari and did what Lillith said. Once everyone was in position, the instructor spoke again. Her voice was soft yet firm.

"Now I want you to look into one another's eyes as you breathe deeply. Match the rhythm of your breath to your partner's. Imagine that breath as a thin cord binding the two of you together. With each successive breath, it thickens and strengthens until it is a lifeline connecting you, a lifeline through which you draw strength and deliver comfort."

Damien did as he was told, to the best of his ability. This couple's yoga thing was like anything else in life: There was no point in doing it halfway. If the instructor wanted him to visualize, then visualize he would, no matter how ridiculous he felt doing it.

As the exercise continued, he watched Kari's beautiful brown eyes widen and then flutter closed. When she opened them again, just an instant later, her breaths were coming more quickly. He wondered what she was thinking, wishing the so-called lifeline stretching between them would allow him to read her mind.

Arlene Hittle

With the way she kept holding back, mind reading was the only way he'd ever know what his lovely wife was thinking. Too bad it wasn't on his list of accomplishments, because he suddenly wanted to get to know her much, much better.

That wasn't entirely true. His desire to get to know Kari wasn't sudden at all. He'd wanted to get into Kari's head — and pants, as long as he was being completely honest with himself — ever since they'd been thrust together by that farce Romance TV called a wedding.

Lucky for him, Kari was exhibiting signs that she, too, was interested in getting cozier. At least he *thought* she was half the time. The other half, she treated him as if he had a scary and highly contagious disease.

He just hoped their dinner tonight would be one of the former half, not the latter. After sharing this class with Kari, he felt closer to her and he wanted that feeling to continue.

****

When the bell chimed softly to signal the end of the class, Kari remained seated. Trying to block out the sounds of people packing away their gear, she closed her eyes and took several more deep, cleansing breaths. She needed them to calm the pulse that had started racing during all that prolonged eye contact with her too-sexy husband.

Yoga Date Night was a lot more intense than she'd expected it to be. It definitely wasn't the place for the casual, safe date she thought she'd planned.

"Good to know," she muttered under her breath before she opened her eyes.

As she expected, Damien was still sitting across from her, his eyes devouring her with that hungry gaze of his. Yep. Definitely not the effect she'd hoped class would have.

She offered him a shaky smile. "That was intense."

"It sure was," Damien agreed easily.

Looking for a way to hide her annoyance at Damien's seemingly unflappable mood, Kari turned away to roll up her yoga mat. After a class like that, he should be feeling as unsettled as she was.

Instead, he looked like he'd just spent a day getting pampered at the spa, and she was as jittery as a first-year teacher on the first day of school. That just wasn't fair.

Kari peeked over her shoulder and saw that Damien, too,

was packing up his mat. He moved slowly, almost languidly, rolling the mat into a tight cylinder. She turned back to her work, even more annoyed that he was better at rolling a mat than she was. Her years of yoga experience should have given her an edge, but not against her athletically gifted husband.

"He looks like the pro, and I look like a first-timer," she muttered, aiming a glare at her suddenly uncooperative mat. After two more false starts, she finally had the darn thing compact enough to slide into its carrying case.

With that done, Kari rose to her feet. Conscious of Damien looming behind her, she turned around. Despite having just spent ten minutes sharing prolonged, unnatural eye contact with him, she forced herself to look into his eyes again. "Are you ready for dinner?"

His nod was enthusiastic. "I'm starved."

"What are you in the mood for?"

The instant the words left her mouth, Kari wanted to take them back. The smoldering look that darkened her husband's eyes did nothing to change her mind.

She took a step backward. "I meant—"

"Relax." The grin on Damien's face diffused the moment. "I know what you meant." Another pause. "I'd be willing to do another downward-facing dog for some chips and salsa."

Kari knew how much he disliked that pose — one of her favorites — because he'd mentioned it more than once since yesterday. She also knew Mexican food was his favorite.

"I know a great Mexican place just a few blocks from here," she replied, glad he wasn't going to push the innuendoes. "And lucky for you, they don't ask their customers to do yoga before seating them."

"That's good."

"They're also known for their margaritas," Kari told him as they headed to the parking lot and his Element. "The 'Three Amigos' comes in a glass bigger than your head."

Damien didn't miss a beat — or a step. "Even better. I could use a stiff drink."

Kari took a moment to process the comment. Maybe their yoga experience *had* affected him more than he let on. She wasn't sure if that was a good thing.

When they got to Damien's car, he handed her the keys. "You drive."

Kari looked at the shiny, new Element and refused to take them. "I couldn't."

"Of course you can." He pressed the keychain into her hand and curled her fingers around it. "I trust you. You know the neighborhood and it'll be easier than you telling me where to go."

Kari shot her pushy husband an annoyed look and pocketed his keys. She'd like to tell him where to go, all right. "I have a better idea. Since the restaurant's just a couple of blocks away, let's walk. After dinner, we'll come back to the car and I'll drive your margarita-filled self home."

"Aren't you going to have one?"

"Are you kidding me? I can't finish one of those suckers!" she said. The one time she'd come close, out with Bethany one Friday night after yoga, she'd had the worst hangover of her life the next day. She didn't care to repeat that experience. "I'll just have a few sips of yours, if you don't mind."

Damien gestured at the Element, then at himself, and grinned. "What's mine is yours, wife of mine."

Kari rolled her eyes and started walking. When she didn't hear him following, she turned around. "I thought you were hungry."

"Oh, I am," he replied, fixing her with that sexy stare of his — the one she was finding it harder and harder to resist with each passing day.

Then why do it? the vixen in her head piped up. Kari mentally swatted the voice away. She didn't need to give in to her growing lust for her too-large, pushy husband. That was sure to lead to disaster.

Kari broke eye contact by turning back around. "Let's go. If we hurry, we might still beat the dinner rush."

Chapter Eighteen

Ten minutes later, Damien and Kari walked through the door at Casita del Sol, a trendy Mexican restaurant Damien had heard of but never had a chance to try. He was surprised that Kari not only knew of it but also seemed to be a regular customer.

The hostess greeted his wife like a long-lost friend, leaving her podium to give Kari a hug. Kari surprised him even more by chatting in Spanish with the woman, whose name tag said she was Anna.

As he wondered why Kari seemed to be fluent in Spanish, Anna led them to a cozy corner booth. Then she handed them each a menu and brought a basket of chips and three kinds of salsa.

"You ordering a Tres Amigos tonight?" she asked in English.

Shaking her head, Kari said, "Not for me, thanks. But Damien is going to try one."

The waitress looked in his direction for the first time. "What flavor?"

"What do you have?"

She rattled off the list quickly: "Regular, raspberry, mango or prickly pear."

Damien looked at Kari. "What do you recommend?"

"The prickly pear," she quickly replied.

"Then that's what I'll get."

"A very good choice," she replied. Turning back to Kari, she whispered something in Spanish. With the restaurant's noise level, Damien didn't hear everything, but he was able to make out the words "lucky," "husband" and "enjoy."

He watched Kari blush and duck her head so she could hide behind her voluminous curls. While she was in hiding, he busied himself by devouring several chips with salsa and soaking up the restaurant's atmosphere. He liked its trendy brick-red walls and peppy ethnic music. He liked the cozy booth that cocooned them into their own private space even more.

When Kari finally emerged from her cloud of curls, her cheeks still adorably pink, she said, "You understood that, didn't you?"

"Enough of it," he confirmed. He'd taken several years of Spanish in order to communicate better with the immigrant pet owners who sought his help.

His wife blushed again. "Don't listen to Anna. She doesn't know what she's talking about."

"I happen to agree with her, Kari. You are one lucky woman, and I'm a lucky guy."

When Kari merely stared at him, her jaw halfway to the floor, he tried to explain. "That yoga class we just took made me think. And if I'm honest with myself, I'm beginning to believe our friends did us a favor when they entered us in that stupid contest."

A waiter brought their drink. Kari was right. The glass the margarita came in was definitely bigger than his head. He had no time to marvel at that fact before Kari snatched the straw and took a big gulp of the bright red concoction.

Apparently, she's not ready to be that honest with herself.

That had to be why she was downing a fair amount of the margarita she'd said she didn't want. If she kept consuming the drink at her current speed, he was going to have to order another one just to get a taste.

Hiding a smile, he turned his attention to the menu. It offered typical Mexican fare, from tacos and burritos to taquitos and, his favorite, fajitas.

When Kari finally relinquished the straw, Damien took a sip. "This is really good."

"Thanks." She offered him a nervous smile. "So what are you having for dinner?"

"You're the regular here. What do you recommend?"

She thought for a moment before offering, "The fish tacos are a house specialty."

He shook his head. "Sorry, I don't do fish tacos. Ever tried the fajitas?" The look on her face was one of pure panic. "What's wrong with fajitas?"

Her voice was a mere whisper. "Everyone stares at you when they come to the table."

Damien regarded Kari silently. He wondered again how someone as beautiful as his wife could fear being the center of attention. Plenty of women plainer than Kari still commanded every room they walked into.

Not Kari, though. She clearly would rather remain invisible. Sighing, Damien resigned himself to foregoing his favorite Mexican dinner. Settling for a loaded steak burrito was a small price to pay to see his wife's smile.

****

When the waiter arrived to take their order, Kari was relieved to hear Damien ask for a burrito. A guy who changed his order just to allay her fear of being stared at couldn't be all bad. Of course, she wasn't ready to kiss Bethany's feet for giving her the opportunity to get to know him — despite what Damien had just said. No, she was still far from admitting their wedding had been a good thing.

But that didn't mean she couldn't acknowledge Damien's positive traits. She knew he had a few. After the waiter left the table, she said, "Thank you."

"No problem. I'm not in the mood for fajitas tonight anyway."

Sure that was a fib, Kari smiled anyway. It really was sweet of Damien to try to spare her embarrassment. Maybe he was more than an overbearing, too-powerful man.

The thought unsettled her, and she took another sip from the giant margarita, which was already about half-gone. She'd better slow down, or she'd be nursing one hell of a headache come morning.

She pushed the glass toward Damien, hoping he'd take the hint and start drinking more. He did, and she nibbled on a few chips with salsa.

While they waited for their meal, they chatted about everything and nothing. They made good progress in emptying the basket of chips and the giant margarita glass. With each passing moment, Kari felt herself relaxing more.

Spending time with her husband was actually painless. Even yoga class had been okay, until they started visualizing a deep connection that — against her better judgment — she was starting to feel.

Kari shoved another chip, this one covered in spicy bean dip, in her mouth. Had she actually just admitted to herself that she was connecting with the husband she hadn't wanted? No, that had to be the alcohol talking. It was making her imagine

Arlene Hittle

warm, fuzzy feelings where there were none.

You know that's not true, her inner voice prodded. Inner vixen or inner goddess? Kari was beginning to think they were one and the same, both pushing her to kick her relationship with Damien into high gear.

When their meal arrived, Kari watched Damien attack his burrito. He masterfully separated a piece from the whole and put it in his mouth. He chewed slowly, then swallowed and took another bite.

She found herself wondering what it would be like to give in to her growing lust. Would Damien go about pleasuring her as methodically as he dismantled that burrito? She suddenly longed to give him a chance. He was, after all, her husband — at least for now. And he was, as Anna had pointed out when she'd greeted Kari in the lobby, cute.

Perhaps too cute. This time, the voice in her head brought her up short. Damien was the kind of guy she would have loved to be seen with in high school, when she'd had no chance, but that was before Rob taught her good-looking and powerful was also cruel.

She frowned at the unwelcome thought. She didn't want Rob to intrude on what was shaping up to be a nice evening with the husband she was starting to want.

"What? Do I have cilantro stuck in my teeth?"

Damien's question caught her off guard. "Pardon?"

"You just scowled at me."

Kari shook her head. "I wasn't scowling at you. I was a million miles away."

"I must not be much of a dinner companion, if you're not focusing on the here and now."

He actually looked hurt. "I'm sorry," she apologized, reaching across the table to touch his hand. Instantly, heat flared.

For once, Kari didn't want to fight it. She couldn't tell whether her subconscious feelings — the ones she'd been trying to tamp down for weeks — were finally bubbling to the surface or the alcohol was obscuring her better judgment.

Suddenly, she didn't much care. She was tired of constantly holding Damien at arm's length, just because he might hurt her. He hadn't done anything hurtful yet. In fact, he'd been nothing but kind and considerate — like tonight, when he'd ordered a burrito instead of fajitas.

BLIND DATE BRIDE

Kari vowed to relax. It was time to put herself in her husband's more than capable hands and see what developed.

She took a deep breath and smiled, warmly, she hoped. Squeezing his hand, she promised, "I'm here now."

****

Damien gaped at his ever-surprising wife, who'd just shocked the hell out of him again. If he wasn't mistaken — and he didn't think he was — she'd just given him the go-ahead to put the moves on her.

He decided to test his theory. After taking another sip of margarita to fortify himself against potential rejection, as unlikely as it seemed, he turned her hand over and brushed his thumb across her palm.

Encouraged when Kari didn't immediately pull away, he continued stroking her palm. When he felt a shiver run through her, he suggested, "What do you say we skip dessert?"

Kari's eyes widened. A shadow flitted across her features before she dipped her head slightly. "I'd like that."

That was all Damien needed. He signaled the waiter for their check. While they waited, he sent a quick thank-you heavenward. Whatever had flipped that switch in Kari's head, the one that gave sexy Kari the go-ahead to come out and play, deserved his gratitude. He planned to take full advantage of his playmate while she was here.

As they walked the three blocks back to the Element — an inspired idea on Kari's part, he had to admit — they held hands. He nuzzled her ear and gladly obliged when she turned toward him for a kiss.

The touch of her lips on his was electric. It jolted through Damien, rooting him to the sidewalk. When he broke free, as soon as he was able to move again, he settled his hands on Kari's hips and dragged her against him. He settled her firmly against his arousal, glad that the thin material of the pants they were both wearing didn't provide much of a barrier.

He watched as her big brown eyes first widened in surprise, then darkened with the same passion he felt for her.

"Mmm, that's nice," she murmured, pressing her lips to his throat. Then she slid her hands under his shirt and caressed his back. In response, his hands snaked from Kari's hips to her rear end — that round, yoga-firmed booty that he enjoyed ogling so much. It felt just as good as it looked. Maybe better.

"Beautiful," he whispered.

She opened her mouth, probably to protest, but Damien refused to give her the chance. Instead, he swooped in for another kiss. It was a long, drawn-out one, and by the time they separated, they were both out of breath.

"Let's get ourselves back to the car," Damien panted.

Kari nodded and slipped her hand back into his. Then she eagerly took off down the street, practically dragging him along.

Not that he needed much encouragement, he thought ruefully. He was more than ready to get his wife into the relative privacy of his Element. It might not be an ideal place to get it on, but considering this moment had been weeks in the making, it would do fine.

It had the added bonus of being away from the prying lens of Sam's camera. That was a huge mark in the blue SUV's favor.

When they got back to the car, Damien could wait no longer. He reached into Kari's pocket and retrieved his keys. Then he clicked the remote to unlock the doors, and threw open the back door.

"Get in," he ordered.

Kari's brief hesitation before climbing into the backseat of the vehicle made him wonder. He was making a mental note to ask her about the pause some other time — a time when they weren't about to do what he'd been wanted to do since they met — when she leaned back against the far side of the passenger compartment. She grinned at him, her dark eyes flashing a challenge. "What are you waiting for?"

"Absolutely nothing," Damien replied, scrambling into the Element and shutting the door.

He quickly divested himself of his T-shirt and stripped off Kari's tank top, exposing a somewhat unsexy sports bra. Refusing to let neon green cotton spoil the mood, he stripped that off, too, tossing it aside. Finally, her breasts were again bared to his hungry gaze.

Damien took a moment to relish the scene. With her eyes shining, chest heaving and rosy nipples at full attention, his wife was a vision of passion.

He kissed Kari on the lips several times before turning his attention to her pretty pink nipples. He took the left one into his mouth while he lightly pinched the right.

Kari gasped and arched upward. Then, tentatively, she

BLIND DATE BRIDE

traced the muscles of his shoulders and back. Slowly, her hand trailed to his rear end and then around front to flutter over his now-raging hard-on.

It was Damien's turn to groan. Even that featherlight touch through the fabric of his yoga pants was driving him wild. Roughly, he yanked her pants down over her hips and cupped the mound of her sex.

When she made a soft sound of protest and pushed his hand away, he groaned again. So, she wasn't quite ready yet. He captured her lips again, stroking her face, shoulders and thighs as his tongue plunged in and out of her mouth in an imitation of the sex act he wanted to be engaged in.

Slowly, he felt Kari's resistance melting. Sending another thank-you into the universe, he pushed down his pants and positioned himself between her thighs.

Bright light flooded the Element.

"What the—?" Damien spat a curse.

A split second later, he had his answer. Sam's voice announced cheerfully, "Found 'em."

Chapter Nineteen

Kari's newfound, margarita-fueled daring evaporated the moment she realized she was about to get caught on camera with her pants down — literally — and she whimpered.

The pathetic sound made Damien look down, and suddenly she was all too aware that he was looming over her. Right away, her pulse sped up and she silently cursed her absurd reaction to a perfectly normal situation.

Not that there was anything normal about having a guy with a video camera rudely interrupt an intimate interlude.

"Don't worry. I won't let anyone see you like this," Damien promised as he yanked his pants back up and used his body to keep her hidden from the camera's view.

For once, Kari was glad for Damien's size. He was large enough that he made an excellent shield while she scrambled back into her clothes.

The pants were easy. She just slid them back up over her hips. However, she had no idea where Damien had thrown her bra. How the bright green garment could be invisible, she didn't know. But when a quick look around the well-lit SUV yielded no results, she slipped into her shirt without it.

"Thank you," she whispered once she was decent. She brushed her lips against his cheek. "I owe you one."

Damien waggled his brows. "I can think of a couple of ways you can repay me."

Still reeling from the effects of what they'd just been up to, Kari wanted nothing more than to oblige, but they had to be sensible. Sam and his camera weren't going to go away, and she wasn't crazy enough to consummate her marriage in full view of the Romance TV audience.

"Let's get ourselves out of this situation first. Then we'll see."

"Somehow I think the moment will be gone."

"I'm sure you're right," she agreed, disappointed by the thought. "The moment," as Damien had put it, was already slipping away and her doubts were creeping back in. Chief among them: his size. Damien really was huge — big enough to do her real harm if he so chose.

Yet he didn't. He used his size to protect you instead.

Kari digested the thought, accepting it with little resistance. Her conscience was right for once. She smiled brightly at Damien. "Shall we open the door for Sam?"

Damien's eyes raked over her before he answered. "It depends."

"On what?"

"If you want America to see you looking like you've been thoroughly kissed."

Kari sighed heavily. "People are going to imagine we've been up to much more than that, you know."

"I know." He grinned. "We were."

It was her turn to say it: "I know. I'd just rather not let all of America in on that secret."

Damien reached over and started rearranging her curls. What seemed like several minutes later, he kissed the tip of her nose. "Now you're presentable again."

"Then let's present ourselves." She handed Damien his T-shirt. There was no point in delaying the confrontation any longer.

Once Damien was fully dressed, he pushed open the door. Sam stood there grinning, his camera's red light blinking away.

"Welcome back to the real world, you two," he said, sounding way too chipper.

Kari watched Damien's expression darken, and was glad his scowl was directed at Sam and not her.

"How'd you track us down?" he demanded crossly as he got out of the Element. Kari followed suit and stood beside him, close but not too close. Not close enough for Damien, who snaked an arm around her waist and tugged her to him until they stood hip to hip.

His nearness was distracting. Kari had to struggle to focus on what Sam was saying, because she, too, wondered how the cameraman had found them.

"It wasn't easy," Sam said. "You were supposed to call in to let Stacy and I know where you were going for dinner so we could meet you there."

Kari groaned. With yoga class scrambling her brain, the scheduled check-in with Sam and Stacy had been the last thing on her mind. "Sorry. I forgot."

Sam acknowledged her apology with a nod. "Because I tried to get the okay to film at the yoga studio, I knew where it was, so I came by earlier. When I saw your vehicle in the parking lot, I knew you'd be back eventually and I was right." He paused and grinned. "I just didn't count on catching you in flagrante delicto."

Kari could feel the tension flowing through Damien as his features darkened even more. "You didn't."

"Close enough," Sam said with a shrug. "This is going to make great TV."

"Fantastic."

Kari could practically see the sarcasm dripping from her increasingly grumpy husband's one-word response.

She couldn't blame Damien for his reaction. She felt the same way. Talking about sex in the kitchen with his mother — as bad as it had seemed at the time — was merely awkward; getting caught in a compromising position in the SUV was positively humiliating. When Bethany saw this episode, Kari was never going to hear the end of it.

Hmm, maybe Bethany didn't have to see it. If she were lucky, no one would have to see it. It wouldn't hurt to ask.

"Sam, is there any way to keep this, umm, interlude off the show?"

When Sam merely looked at her, bushy black brows raised, Kari knew the answer to that question was a big, fat no.

"It was worth a shot," she insisted, offering the cameraman a tentative smile.

Damien squeezed her waist. His comment was a mere whisper in her ear. "Good try, sweetheart."

"Obviously not good enough," she muttered back, trying hard to do it without moving her lips. Maybe it was a skill she needed to perfect. As long as their audience couldn't read lips, she and Damien could communicate undetected.

Fat chance. The network would probably just close caption the show — if it didn't already.

Kari sighed. Time to resign herself to another round of nationally televised embarrassment. Unfortunately, it was something she was getting used to.

****

Aware that Kari had downed more margarita than he had,

Damien drove home. As the Element steadily ate up the miles, he found his anger at Sam's interruption receding. The cameraman was only doing his job, after all.

Besides, it was barely nine o'clock on a Friday night. Not even he went to bed that early, so they had plenty of time to recapture the moment.

If the way Kari kept stroking his thigh was any indication, she was as eager as he was to do just that. He captured her hand in his, redirecting it to another part of his anatomy that would appreciate the caresses a lot more.

Again, she resisted for a split second before she let her fingers flutter over the growing bulge in his pants. He heard a hitch in her breath as she wrapped her fingers around Mr. Happy and squeezed.

Holy hell! His hands jerked on the steering wheel and the Element swerved. Damien regained control and cleared his throat. "Umm, maybe we should wait until we get home."

Immediately, Kari released her hold on him, and just as immediately, he wished she hadn't. He wanted to pull the car over and finish what they'd started, not just now but before Sam had rudely interrupted them.

But with Sam and Stacy following them, he knew they'd have more privacy in the apartment — at least once they finished entertaining the camera crew and escaped to the bedroom. Although Sam and Stacy did constantly monitor the sound in the room, the camera was only allowed in by invitation — thank God. And he and Kari had yet to issue that invite.

A too-long fifteen minutes later, he and Kari were finally home. Stacy had volunteered to walk Sunny for them, no doubt so Sam could capture more "great" footage.

Well, with Kari standing there undressing him with her eyes, he wasn't about to disappoint. He wrapped his arms around her and pulled her close, whispering in her ear, "Now who's ogling?"

She giggled even as she urged him closer, spreading her thighs so his all-too-willing Mr. Happy could nestle near the promised land. "Your bad habits must be rubbing off on me, because I can't seem to stop staring."

"Look as long as you want, wife." The words came out more growl than intelligible, but Kari didn't seem to notice. No, she was too busy tugging him toward the couch.

Arlene Hittle

Damien didn't mind at all. He gladly let her push him down and straddle him, as eager as she was to recapture the moment. But when Kari started to pull off her shirt — in full view of the camera, even though he knew she wasn't wearing the bra that he'd found balled up beneath the Element's brake pedal — Damien had to stop her. He stilled her hands and jerked his head in Sam's direction.

"You don't really want to do that, do you?" he asked softly.

Kari reared back, looking like he'd physically struck her. "I thought you ..." She trailed off, unwilling — or unable — to finish her thought. That was when Damien regarded her more closely and realized how much she'd had to drink. Her breath reeked of margarita, and her eyes were bleary and unfocused.

Even so, she seemed determined to have her way with him. She shifted positions and plunged her hand into his pants.

Damien bit his lip, needing the pain to distract him from the pleasure his beautiful wife was so stubbornly trying to provide. There was no way he could take advantage of Kari now, no matter how much his body clamored to consummate their marriage. His conscience would never shut up if he did.

Besides, if he didn't put a stop to Kari's ministrations soon, Romance TV would end up showing the footage on their sister porn station — if they had one. Damien wasn't sure. He didn't want to find out, either.

With that thought in mind, Damien extricated her hand from his pants. He kissed each knuckle in turn before guiding her hand to his shoulder — a much less sexually charged resting place.

"Sweetheart, I'd love nothing more than to finish this."

She pouted and tried to reach between his legs again. "Then why fight it?"

Damien blocked the attempt and captured her face between his hands. His eyes held hers. "When we finally make love, I don't want either of us to have any regrets."

****

His office hours at the veterinary practice complete the next morning, Damien sat at his desk and pulled up the screen for his favorite Internet search engine. He waited for it to load on his somewhat slow Internet connection, thinking high-speed was a misnomer. When the website finally loaded, he tapped in a search term: "fear of flying treatment."

Almost immediately, a list popped up. Damien clicked on a link and started reading.

Sweaty palms? Heart palpitations? Labored breathing? Yep. He had all those symptoms — and more — when he got near a plane.

Annoyed that the site was telling him something he already knew, he backed out of the page and clicked on a different link.

"I don't need to know my symptoms, I need to know how to overcome them, and fast." He and Kari were set to leave for Alaska in a week and a half.

A few clicks and several minutes of reading later, Damien was frustrated again. The preferred treatment, cognitive behavioral therapy, took years he didn't have.

A place in L.A. offered virtual reality therapy, guiding patients through every aspect of a flight — from getting a seat on the plane and taking off to flying in bad weather and landing — using a virtual reality simulator.

Again, that took time, and he'd probably have to fly there to start treatment.

"Not gonna happen," he muttered, trying another link. No luck there, either.

Still irritated, as much by last night's aborted attempt at finding heaven as by his futile search for treatment, Damien picked up his office phone. He dialed Cody's number, tapping his fingers on the desk impatiently until his buddy answered the call.

When he did, his "Hey, Damien. What's up?" sounded out of breath.

"I hope your panting means you've been out walking with Chelsea," Damien told him.

"Sure," Cody replied. His answer was so quick that Damien was immediately suspicious, but now, he was more concerned with his dilemma than whatever Cody was doing. "What do you need?"

"Information," Damien replied. He took a deep breath and pushed out the question in a rush, not giving himself a chance to chicken out. "Did you ever finish those flying lessons you started?"

"A couple of months ago." Cody's voice turned suspicious. "Since when are you interested? You were the one who told me—"

Arlene Hittle

Damien finished his friend's sentence. "If humans had been meant to fly, we'd have been born with wings." Even if his memory wasn't what it used to be, he didn't need help remembering that statement. "I still believe it."

"Then why do you care if I have my license?"

"I'm flying to Alaska next week with Kari."

"Alaska?"

"Her choice, not mine," Damien snapped, annoyed that Cody made the state sound like outer Mongolia. Once he got there and had his feet on solid ground, it wouldn't be that bad. "She's had this trip planned for months, and our friends at Romance TV say I have to go, too, or we forfeit the prize money — and you know I have plans for that cash."

Cody snorted. "Boring ones. You should plan a tropical vacation or buy a bitchin' convertible."

Damien rolled his eyes. He'd heard Cody's suggested spending plan before, and it didn't hold any more appeal the second time around. "That money will allow me to pay my dad back, buy a new X-ray machine and buy into the shelter."

"Dude, the contest was called 'Get a Love Life,'" Cody reminded him. "With that attitude, you're never going to get a life — love or otherwise."

Damien leaned back in his chair and put his feet up on his desk. This conversation was going to take awhile. "Are you forgetting who entered that contest? I wasn't looking for a wife."

"And I wasn't trying to win you one," Cody countered. "I just wanted you to take a vacation."

"Well, you got your wish. I'm headed to Alaska."

"That's not the vacation spot I had in mind."

Damien sighed. "Me, either. But it's where I'm going." Now the conversation had come full circle, and he was back to the reason for the call. Damn. He'd hoped for a longer diversion. "That's where you come in."

"Huh?"

"I need you to take me up in your plane." When Cody laughed, Damien scowled. "I'm not kidding."

"I know you're not, but you do know the plane I fly is only a two-seater, right?"

Damien gulped. The smaller the plane, the bigger his phobia. Large jets he could tolerate — barely — without totally cracking up. However, the smaller the plane, the harder it was for him to handle.

He forced himself to say, "A two-seater is good."

"Really?" Doubt dripped from Cody's reply.

Damien swallowed hard again. "Sure. It'll make any commuter flights once we get there seem like a jumbo jet."

Now if only he could make himself believe that, he'd be all set.

"Okay, then. I was planning to go up tomorrow anyway. I'll pick you up at your place at 8:30."

"So soon?"

"If you leave next week, there's no time to waste," Cody pointed out.

Damien sighed. When Cody was right, which wasn't often, he was right. "Sorry. I was just hoping to have a little more time to get used to the idea."

"The airport diner has great food," Cody said. "If you get through the flight without barfing, lunch is on me."

Great, Damien thought. *Something to look forward to.*

Chapter Twenty

Kari was still mostly asleep when her cell phone started to ring Saturday morning. She'd just started to stir, and had time to register that she was alone in bed.

"Damien must be at work already," she muttered, glancing at her watch. No wonder. It was 11:30. He'd been up for hours, hard at work, while she slept the day away.

Recognizing the ringtone she'd assigned to her sisters, Kari groaned. Then she rolled over, trying to burrow under the covers so she could ignore the chiming phone. The last thing she wanted to do was talk to one of her sisters, especially on the morning after she'd consumed enough prickly pear margarita to make her forget every reason she was avoiding getting intimate with her too-large mate.

Oddly enough, the thought of Damien brought a smile to her face. He'd demonstrated remarkable self-control last night — twice. First, he hadn't killed Sam for interrupting their romantic interlude in the Element. That was what she'd wanted to do — well, what part of her had wanted to do, at least. Her sane, sensible side wanted to thank the cameraman profusely for breaking things up.

Then, on the living room couch later, when the alcohol-inspired tramp inside her had tried to get the momentum going again, Damien put the brakes on it. Thank goodness one of them had shown some sense last night!

Putting a halt to such a sure thing was an incredibly gentlemanly thing for him to do. She doubted most guys would have stopped. Rob certainly wouldn't have.

The phone stopped ringing. Kari congratulated herself for dawdling long enough to avoid the call.

It wasn't that her older sisters, Shannon and Claire, weren't good people. They were both caring mothers and loving daughters. However, Kari couldn't set aside how awful they'd been to her growing up. Just two and three years older than she was, they'd tormented her mercilessly as kids, calling her "chunky" and teasing her about never getting any dates.

BLIND DATE BRIDE

With a flash of self-awareness, Kari realized they'd probably contributed to the raging inferiority complex that made her easy pickings for a creep like Rob. Good. That gave her another reason to avoid Shannon and Claire. It made her life easier not to have to hear how happy they were with their husbands and adorable children.

You have a husband, too.

The phone began ringing again, chiming tones of "The Funeral March." That meant whichever sister was calling wasn't giving up. Kari reached for the phone: Caller ID said Tim St. Lawrence.

Great. So it was Shannon calling. Of the two, Shannon was her favorite. Being the two younger sisters, they'd both been on the receiving end of Claire's teasing from time to time. She might as well answer it and see what Shannon wanted badly enough to call twice.

Besides, as the tramp had pointed out, she did have a husband of her own now. If Shannon got too obnoxious, she could always start talking about how wonderful Damien was.

She wouldn't even be stretching the truth that much, she reluctantly admitted. So far, if she discounted his sheer size, he was Mr. Perfect. He'd even been a band geek, so they had that in common.

She pressed the button to answer the call. "Hello?"

"Chunk-Chunk!" Shannon exclaimed. "I was beginning to wonder if I was interrupting something."

Kari sighed. "I've asked you before to stop calling me that. It might have been cute when I was five, but now it's not even accurate." She wanted to add that Shannon was carrying more extra weight than she was these days, but refrained for the sake of family harmony.

"Uh-oh. You're grumpy enough for me to believe I did interrupt."

"The only thing you broke up was my sleep," Kari admitted grudgingly. She really didn't want either of her sisters to know the intimate details of her life.

"Still asleep when it's nearly noon?" Shannon laughed. "You must have had a good night, then."

Kari made a noncommittal sound. Anyone who watched the show would know soon enough what she'd been up to Friday night, and she had no doubt her sister was glued to Romance TV during the airing of "Just Married." She and Claire probably watched it together so they could dis her wardrobe. "To what do I owe the pleasure of your call?"

"Do I need a reason to call my baby sister?"

"Usually? Yes."

Now, Shannon was the one who sighed. "Guilty as charged. Mom has been driving both Claire and I crazy with questions about when you'll be bringing Mr. Wonderful home for family dinner."

"What?" Kari hated the panicked squeak her voice had suddenly become. "It's too soon for that."

This time, Shannon's laugh was harsh. "Sis, I hate to break it to you, but you're already married. That's a much bigger commitment than introducing him to the family."

"I know that," Kari snapped, annoyed that Shannon thought she was unaware of such a simple fact. "I just don't want to subject the poor man to the Parker family madhouse yet."

"Again, you're already married, so he can't run in the other direction screaming and never call again."

The reminder made Kari giggle. That was exactly what had happened when Shannon introduced her first serious boyfriend to the family. As a freshman in college at Eastern Illinois University, Shannon had brought a guy named Dexter home for Thanksgiving. After all three of their brothers ganged up to tackle Dexter during a post-dinner game of touch football — ostensibly because they didn't like something he'd said at the table, though Kari couldn't remember anything offensive — the poor guy rode away in a cab. It was three weeks before he'd return any of Shannon's calls, and even then, he refused to be in the same room with her.

"Dexter was an idiot," Kari said to commiserate.

"Not so much. He's actually a rocket scientist," her sister replied. "But that's okay. If Dexter had stuck around, I'd never have been lucky enough to end up with Tim, who's—"

Kari finished the sentence for Shannon. "A real prince."

Literally. Shannon met him while she was studying overseas, and they fell in love before she knew he was royalty in some small European country. As a younger brother, though, he was just a minor prince and had no real duties, so no one minded when he moved to Chicago to take a job with the American Medical Association.

"You got it, Chunk-Ch—" Shannon stopped herself. "Sorry. So can I tell Mom to expect you and your new husband — what's his name? — for dinner?"

"It's Damien," Kari said, pleased that Shannon had caught her use of the hated nickname. Maybe there was hope for their relationship yet. "What night?"

"Everyone except Chris can make it tomorrow."

Tomorrow? That was awfully soon, and to make things worse, the next episode of "Just Married" aired that night.

On second thought, her parents had no cable and that meant no one in the family would be watching the show. Therefore, they wouldn't have a chance to see her in a compromising position.

Upon realizing that tidbit, Kari didn't have to fake her enthusiasm. "Sounds great. Just let me check with Damien, and I'll get back to you later today."

****

Damien pushed open the door to the apartment and paused to pat Sunny on the head. After scratching behind the dog's ears, he turned into the kitchen. Now that he was married, the fridge was always full — a good thing when he came home from work hungry. He no longer had to wait for delivery every time he wanted to eat something more substantial than coffee and crackers.

A few minutes later, ham and Swiss sandwich in hand, he headed to the living room couch. Once he sat down, Kari's black cat, Rhett, jumped up beside him and started using his two front paws to knead Damien's thigh.

At least the cat wants to get close to me, he thought, grinning, as he turned on the TV. He wondered where Kari was and what she was doing.

The sandwich was half-gone and Damien was engrossed in a Cubs game when she emerged from the bathroom wrapped from head to toe in a blue flannel robe, her hair up in a towel.

Even as covered up as she was, she was a vision. As she approached, he shifted over so she could sit beside him on the couch. She did, and he dropped his arm around her shoulders.

Well aware just how much she'd had to drink at Casita del Sol, he asked, "How are you feeling?"

"Better now that I've had a shower."

"I'm glad to hear that," he told her honestly, giving her

shoulders a quick squeeze.

He was encouraged when Kari tolerated the embrace. "I could have used some more sleep, though."

"You were sleeping pretty soundly when I left," he said, adding with a grin, "Some people would say you were sawing logs."

"I don't snore!" She nudged him in the ribs. "The phone woke me up."

"What did your friend want this time?" He was resigned to never finding out What's Her Name's name. In fact, he half suspected Kari was aware he didn't know and was purposely avoiding calling the other woman by name. Maybe she got some kind of thrill from keeping him out of the loop. She did, after all, seem to prefer being in control.

"It wasn't her; it was my sister, Shannon," Kari corrected. "But she did want something."

"What?"

"Us to go to dinner at my parents' house tomorrow night."

Damien froze. "Tomorrow?" When Kari nodded, Damien took a deep breath. With a flight in the morning and dinner with Kari's family later on, it appeared Sunday would be a trying day.

"So I can accept the invitation?"

Damien slanted a sideways glance at his wife. She actually thought he'd say no? "Of course. You don't have to ask me for permission to see your family."

"I was more worried about whether *you* wanted to see them," she countered.

"Since you've already met my parents, I can't very well say no."

"You have no idea what you've agreed to," Kari warned. "En masse, my family can be a bit much to take."

Damien eyed Kari warily. They'd produced her, and she was a great person — smart, funny and sweet, even if she was a little shy. "How bad could they be?"

Kari raised her eyebrows at her poor, unsuspecting husband. "You have no idea."

"Enlighten me."

****

How much could she say without scaring Damien? She decided to start with the basics. "There are six of us altogether, so any meal is chaos. Add in my siblings' spouses and eight kids —

and Mom and Dad's three cats — and no matter what happens, it's going to be a madhouse."

She saw Damien swallow, hard, and quickly added, "My brother Chris isn't going to be there, though. That means two and a half fewer to contribute to the confusion."

"Two and a half?"

"Chris' wife Lana is pregnant, so I was counting the little one," she explained.

"How much trouble can someone cause if they're not even born yet?"

Kari grinned. "Lana could go into labor any day now."

"Maybe that's why your brother will be staying home," Damien suggested.

"Could be," Kari agreed. "My brothers can be rather *protective*." That was putting it mildly. Overbearing, obnoxious and downright scary were other words she'd use to describe their attitudes toward defending the women in their family.

Of course, they did what they did out of love. Kari had no doubt they thought they had Shannon's best interest in mind when they scared Dexter off. And maybe they had. After all, Shannon found a better man.

She also knew unequivocally that, had she ever told just one of her brothers about some of the things Rob had put her through, they'd have teamed up to scare him off, too. The videotape fiasco alone would have earned Rob a trip to the hospital. Had her brothers known even half of what he'd done, they'd have killed him. Kari shuddered at the thought. No way was that creep worth any of her family spending time in the slammer.

Damien's voice broke into her straying thoughts. "So you're saying I should be prepared for anything, huh?"

"Nosy questions from the adults and weird observations from the nieces and nephews, yes," she admitted, eager to push Rob back out of her mind. "And if my brothers suggest a game of touch football after dinner, watch out."

Kari launched into Dexter's story, finishing with, "But they're all older and wiser now."

"I sure hope so," Damien said, "because I doubt I could fend off three angry Parkers."

"You won't have to," Kari assured him with more confidence than she felt. She rose from the couch and headed to the bedroom to change and make a call. "Chris won't be there, so it'll only be two. But I'll have Shannon put out the word that you're not to be harmed."

Once she was alone, she dialed her sister's number. Shannon picked up on the first ring.

"Hi, sis," Kari said. "Damien said he'd be happy to have dinner with the family tomorrow night."

"He did?" Shannon sounded surprised. "Did you not warn him?"

"I did. I also told him you'd ask the boys to behave."

"Okay, then," Shannon said. "We'll see you at my place at six o'clock, then."

Kari frowned. That wasn't the plan. "Your place? I thought we were meeting at Mom and Dad's."

Shannon laughed. "Are you kidding? Mom and Dad don't have cable, and none of us want to miss your Sunday night show."

"Fantastic," Kari groused. So much for her brilliant plan. "I can't wait."

"Us, either," Shannon said brightly. "See you tomorrow."

****

"I think we need to rethink this plan," Damien said as Cody made the turn to enter the airport parking area.

"Sorry, dude," Cody replied. "I'm not letting you back out of this one."

"Seems to be a theme with you lately," Damien grumbled. "You didn't let me back out of the wedding, either."

Cody pulled his Camaro into a vacant parking place and cut the engine before countering, "You should thank me for that, with the way it's turning out."

"Was I complaining?"

His friend opened the driver's side door and stepped out of the vehicle. Once Damien reluctantly followed suit, Cody continued the conversation. "Good, because from what I've seen, you're starting to fall for your wife."

Damien pondered his buddy's observation as he trudged toward the hangar. His feelings for Kari were that obvious, were they? For the usually oblivious Cody to pick up on them, they had to be.

Great. Just what he needed: for all of America to be privy to his crush on his wife, especially when he wasn't sure she felt the same way.

That wasn't entirely true. At times he was certain she wanted him as much as he wanted her — if not more. Then again, there were other times when she held him at arm's length. Arm's length? Hardly. She kept him farther away than that.

No point in thinking about the puzzle that was Kari Parker-Walker right now, though. He had more pressing things to worry about, such as his impending death by small aircraft.

He followed Cody through the hangar, wishing his buddy would slow down. "We're not in a hurry, are we?"

Cody stopped and turned. His gaze was steady and coolly appraising. "I have to get you in the air before you change your mind."

When he turned back around and started walking again, his pace was even faster than before. Damien sped up to keep up, wishing he'd thought to pack some liquid courage to help him get on the plane. The one saving grace of this misadventure was that Sam wasn't tagging along. Cody, perhaps realizing how rough it would be on him, had somehow convinced the cameraman the plane wasn't big enough for three, and to let them film themselves with a small, handheld device. If Damien had his way, they'd lose the footage.

A minute later, he stood in front of the plane Cody had rented, eyeing it doubtfully. "You weren't exaggerating. This thing is no bigger than a Tonka toy."

"Actually, this plane is just the right size."

"For a coffin, maybe."

Cody opened the door. "Cut that out. Everything will be fine."

"Easy for you to say," Damien grumbled as he stood at the bottom of the steps that would allow him to board the plane.

There were five of them. Just five not-so-steep steps separated him from a seat on the too-small aircraft. How hard was it to advance five small steps? His racing heart and the gnawing in the pit of his stomach gave Damien the answer he didn't want to hear. It was going to be well nigh impossible.

He stood frozen at the foot of the stairs, unable to twitch so much as an eyelid.

"What are you waiting for?" Cody asked from behind him. "We're not getting any younger here."

"I can't."

Cody's cheerful response was, "Of course you can."

Damien was still paralyzed by the thought of boarding an airplane, especially this airplane barely big enough for two. "Seriously, man, I can't. I literally cannot move here."

There was a pause. As it stretched between them, Damien figured Cody must have been considering his options. Damien used the time to try — unsuccessfully — to convince his brain to stop running through all the ways he could meet an untimely end.

Suddenly, a hand on his rear end had him racing up the stairs and into the aircraft he hadn't wanted to board. He turned to glare at Cody, who was still on the ground. "What was that?"

Unperturbed, Cody grinned and climbed into the plane behind him. "I figured that'd get you moving."

"Well, it worked."

Still chuckling, Cody closed the cockpit door. Damien barely had time to reflect on the ominous-sounding thud the door made as it slammed shut before Cody secured Sam's camera to the dash and gestured at one of the two seats. "Sit there and buckle up. We'll be in the air in no time."

Damien looked at the seat. Funny. It didn't *look* like a torture device. Still, he had a feeling facing the Inquisition would be easier than planting his butt in that chair.

"Sometime today would be great. I have dinner plans."

He scowled at his buddy, who suddenly thought he was the "Last Comic Standing" or something. "I'm working on it."

Cody turned away, and after rummaging around behind the pilot's seat, held out a bottle of tequila and a shot glass. "I thought you might need some liquid courage."

Without hesitation, Damien accepted the offering. He twisted off the cap and poured a more-than-generous splash into the glass, downing it in one gulp. Two more gulps later, he'd mustered the courage to take his seat. He fumbled with the safety belt before it finally clicked into place.

That wasn't so bad, he thought. Maybe he would survive this ordeal.

Fat chance. As Cody started to taxi the plane down the runway, Damien's stomach plummeted to his feet.

"We don't actually have to go up in the air," he said in a last-ditch attempt to avoid takeoff. "I've made remarkable progress just by boarding the plane."

Cody didn't take his eyes off what he was doing. "Sorry, dude. You're leaving for Alaska in less than a week. If you want to get there without looking like an idiot in front of your wife, you need to get over your fear of flying now."

"Um, maybe she likes guys who hate to fly."

Cody snorted. "She strikes me as more the world-traveler type."

"You spend a lot of time thinking about my wife, do you?" Damien slanted a glance at his buddy, who wasn't too focused on takeoff to roll his eyes.

"Jealousy's an ugly emotion, dude. You don't want to be putting off bad vibes when you're surfing the sky."

"Surfing the sky, huh?" That was an apt description. Flying had to be at least as dangerous as surfing. Probably more so.

"Don't change the subject," Cody snapped, sounding a lot less laid-back than usual. He actually sounded offended. "I'm not after your wife."

Just then, the plane's wheels left the ground. Damien gulped and poured himself another shot. Was it his fourth or fifth? He'd lost count.

That wasn't all he'd lost when he boarded this aircraft. He'd apparently also lost all capability for rational thought. Of course Cody wasn't interested in Kari. Last he checked, complex blondes weren't his buddy's type. Cody was more a bubbly brunette kind of guy.

"Sorry, man. I guess I'm touchier than I should be."

Back to his easygoing self, Cody shrugged. "You can't help how you feel, dude. If you're falling for your wife, you need to do something about it."

"Like what?"

"Try telling her how you feel."

Now, Damien was the one rolling his eyes. "What good will that do? Ours isn't exactly a traditional marriage."

Cody chuckled. "But it *is* a traditional marriage of convenience, and we both know how those often end."

"We do?" When Cody nodded, Damien arched an eyebrow. "You forgetting I'm not the one who watches Romance TV?"

"You don't have to watch cheesy television shows to figure that out, Damien."

"Really?"

This time, Cody didn't stop at a chuckle. He full out

chortled. "You two are going to end up together, happily ever after."

Was that how marriages of convenience ended? With two people who hadn't even known they were looking for love suddenly finding it? "I'm beginning to hope so."

Cody suddenly stopped laughing. "I never thought I'd hear you say that."

Damien sighed. Sure, he hadn't always believed in love, or in happily ever after, especially after he'd had to choose his career over his ex, Teena.

After that, he spent a couple of months reliving his early college years. His freshman and sophomore years were when he took up tennis and running and finally grew into his lean, lanky body, and soon found it was a bod every girl on campus was hot for.

It went straight to his head. He went a little crazy and started dating. A lot. Sometimes three or four different girls a week.

His adult self hated to admit it, but he told them all that he loved them. Maybe he did, in a way. But not in a way that mattered. His late-blooming, hormone-packed self had just wanted to score.

And score he did. Often. Until one morning near the start of his junior year, he woke up next to a redhead whose name he couldn't remember and realized how empty his life was. He wanted more than a series of one-night stands. Even though he always had company, he was lonelier than he had been growing up as an only child.

Even then, the armchair psychiatrist in him had recognized his promiscuity as an attempt to fill a hole in his life. It also told him encounters with nameless, faceless women would never make him feel any less lonely. He needed to seek out a real companion, someone in whose presence he didn't feel alone.

So he started dating more selectively, met Teena in his first year of vet school and settled in for what he thought was the long haul. It wasn't. She couldn't handle the fact that he spent so much time working and gave him an ultimatum: her or the animals. He picked his patients and never looked back.

A brief return to his lothario ways reminded him why he'd sworn off such behavior, and he threw himself into his work. If he was always busy working, he didn't have time to dwell on what he was missing.

"Dude? Did you fall asleep over there?"

Cody's voice intruded on his thoughts, and he apologized again. "I'd like to think I've grown up over the years."

"Of course you have," Cody told him. "You're the most mature guy I know."

Damien snorted. Cody worked with at-risk teens. "That's not saying much."

"But it's something." Cody grinned and tugged off the headset he'd been wearing. "You know what?"

Damien didn't like the look of that. Surely his buddy should still be in contact with traffic control or something. "Uh, shouldn't you keep that on until we land?"

Cody shot him a look that could only mean one thing: Duh. "Look around, D."

Reluctantly, Damien glanced out the window and saw that the plane had landed and was slowing to a stop. When, and how, had that happened?

When he asked Cody as much, his friend smiled. "You were lost in thought there for quite a while."

He considered that for a moment. First, he'd stewed over his jealousy. Then he'd taken a long and not necessarily pleasant trip down memory lane.

"You did that on purpose!"

"Guilty as charged," Cody admitted with a grin. "I figured you'd handle your airtime a lot better if I gave you something else to think about."

"Right again," Damien mumbled. Damn. Cody was starting to make that a habit. He wasn't sure he liked that.

Cody grinned again. "Now that you managed to make it through the flight without losing your breakfast, let's go grab some lunch."

Chapter Twenty-One

Damien followed Cody off the plane, which he *still* thought was too small, and into the airport's café, where they chased an order of buffalo wings with a pitcher of beer. Damien was starved. He'd been too nervous about the flight to eat breakfast.

When the pizza arrived, hungry as he still was, Damien almost decided not to eat any of it. He was, after all, meeting Kari's parents in a few hours, and he knew dinner was on the agenda. With her parents being in the restaurant biz, they'd probably be offended if he wasn't hungry for whatever they served.

Pizza was the perfect companion to another glass of beer, though, and he didn't want to drink any more on an empty stomach. He wouldn't be able to make a good impression on them plastered, either.

Still, no one would deny him a little something to take the edge off his nerves, right? He deserved it after staring down his fear of flying.

So, he sat in the airport café with Cody, continuing his excursion down memory lane, chowing down on pizza and drinking beer until his buddy checked his watch and cursed.

"I promised Kari I'd have you home by three. If we rush, we should just be able to make it."

"By all means." Damien popped one last bite of now-cold pizza into his mouth and drained the dregs from another glass of beer. Then he lurched to his feet.

The room started to spin. Shit. Maybe he'd had too much to calm his nerves. He shook his head in an attempt to stop the spinning, and it seemed to do the trick. "We shouldn't keep my lovely wife waiting."

****

Kari paced the apartment as she waited for Damien to put in an appearance. It was now 3:30, and she'd expected him by three. To be on time for dinner, they needed to leave for Shannon's by four — 4:15 at the absolute latest.

"Where is he?" she mused aloud for about the hundredth

time in the last ten minutes. She pulled aside the curtain to peer out the window again, aware of Sam following her progress with the camera. She thought, not for the first time, how bored viewers were going to be watching her wear a path in the carpet.

Perhaps that wasn't the real question. She really wanted to know what Damien and Cody had *had* to do this morning that was so all-fired important.

Why do you care? her conscience taunted.

Good question. Damien was a free man. She had no right tell him what he could or couldn't do.

Not true, the voice inside her head piped up again. *The ring on your finger gives you that right.*

She glanced down at the ring in question. The princess-cut solitaire winked up at her as it caught the sunlight streaming in the window. Provided by Romance TV, it was bigger than any wedding ring she'd ever seen — surely larger than Damien would be able to afford on his own.

Not that the size of the ring mattered. The sentiment behind it was what really counted.

Kari scowled. The ring was probably a fake, just like her sham of a marriage. She'd do well to remember that. Falling for Damien could only end in disaster.

The ringing doorbell startled her.

How odd, she thought. Damien had never forgotten his key before.

She hurried to the door and yanked it open. Cody stood there, holding up her husband.

"Are you drunk?" She glared first at Damien, who was barely able to stay upright, let alone notice her displeasure, then at Cody. "How could you let this happen?"

Cody shot her a sheepish grin. "We split a couple pitchers of beer with lunch."

"Forgot the tequila," Damien piped up.

Tequila and beer? It made Kari even more curious just what her husband and his buddy had been up to. However, she didn't have time to figure it out right now.

"We're supposed to leave to meet my parents in—" She paused to check her watch. "—less than forty-five minutes."

"Don't just stand in the doorway, Kari. Help me get him inside and into the shower."

As Kari stepped forward, she was struck again by Damien's

size. At nearly 5 feet, 9 inches tall, she was far from petite, but he made her feel positively dainty.

Together, she and Cody wrangled Damien down the hallway and into the bathroom. The instant he was propped up against the sink, Cody backed out of the room.

"You can take it from here. I'll go make some coffee."

Kari watched Cody beat a hasty retreat to the kitchen. He obviously wasn't eager to see Damien naked. Guys were funny about that kind of thing. Why, she didn't know. They both had the same equipment, so it wasn't anything Cody hadn't seen before.

What made Cody think she was any more capable of undressing Damien than he was?

You're Damien's wife, dummy. You're supposed to see him naked.

Kari gave the vixen a mental swat and then cast a doubtful glance at Damien. She wasn't even sure how to get him out of his shoes, let alone the rest of his clothing.

Best to start from the bottom up. "Damien, can you sit?"

"Okay," he mumbled. He shifted over and plopped down on the toilet seat. Thank goodness the lid was down.

She knelt at his feet and tugged off first his left Nike tennis shoe, then the right. Easy enough. His socks were next. White crew-cut deals, they, too, came off without much trouble.

Kari rocked back on her heels, contemplating her next move. The pants would have to go, but she wasn't ready for that yet. The shirt would be much easier to remove. She did, and her heart stuttered at the sight of Damien's bare chest.

Cut that out. She didn't have time to get turned on. She had to try to get her husband to sober up enough to meet her parents in less than two hours.

She saw Damien fumbling with his fly and took it as a good sign. If he was alert enough to help at least a little bit, maybe he wasn't too far gone to sober up.

Then he looked at her with a drunken grin. "Are you gonna help me out here or what?"

When she reached down to unbutton his jeans, Damien caught her by the wrist and guided her hand lower. She yanked away from him and stepped back.

"What do you think you're doing?" She didn't need to ask. How dare he try to put the moves on her now, when he was drunk and they had somewhere to be?

Damien looked more confused than anything else. "You started undressing me."

"To get you into the shower to sober up."

"Oh." After a pause, he asked, "So you don't want to pick up where we left off Friday?"

For a split second, Kari was tempted. Oh so tempted. She'd give anything to recapture the feelings she'd had in the Element. The thrill of discovery. The heat of passion. The glow of desire, and being desired.

But the timing was all wrong. They needed to leave for her sister's house in less than thirty minutes. Besides, Cody was in the kitchen, making coffee, and Sam was probably hovering right outside the bathroom door.

"We can't, Damien. At least not now."

"Later?" He shot her a hopeful grin.

"Maybe."

Damien seemed satisfied by that, until he glanced from Kari to the shower and back again and waggled his eyebrows suggestively. "You sure you don't want to join me?"

Kari nodded. "Positive. You take a nice, cold shower. I'll be back in a few minutes to make sure you haven't drowned."

Without bothering to make sure he was doing what she asked, Kari beat her own hasty retreat. She had to get out of there before her defenses collapsed and she found herself sharing the shower — and herself — with him.

When she reached the safety of the kitchen, Cody handed her a mug of coffee. "You look like you could use some."

"Thanks." Kari took the mug and took a sip. When the temperature was right, she took a deeper swallow. "This is as good as mine!"

"Now I'm the one who should say thanks, because Damien says your coffee's the best." Cody stared at the floor tiles for a moment and then raised his eyes to meet her gaze. "You deserve an explanation."

"I do. But shouldn't it be coming from Damien?"

Cody shrugged. "Probably, and I doubt he'll thank me for telling you what we were doing."

Kari's heart plummeted to her toes. That didn't sound at all promising. She hoped they hadn't been hanging out at some strip club, because she couldn't stand the thought of scantily clad women shaking things in her husband's face. It'd be too easy for

Damien to get what she was still reluctant to give.

But to go searching for cheap thrills the same day he was supposed to meet her family? Surely he wouldn't be that callous. Damien was a nicer guy than that.

Even with that reassurance, Kari couldn't keep her voice from shaking when she spoke. "Dare I ask?"

"We were flying."

Flying? Was that some kind of man code for watching strippers? "Pardon?"

"I rented a plane and took Damien up in the air for thirty minutes."

That was a relief, strange, but a relief all the same. She had to ask. "That's an odd thing to do on a Sunday morning, and it still doesn't explain how Damien ended up drunk."

Cody's grin was somewhat sheepish. "That's what he doesn't want you to know. He's afraid of flying. I had to ply him with tequila shots before he'd let me get the plane off the ground. And once we landed, he drank more than his share of a pitcher of beer 'to calm his nerves,' he said."

"Oh." Kari's mind was racing. So *that* was why he'd acted so strangely about flying to Alaska. She patted Cody's shoulder. "Thanks for letting me know."

Cody's cheeks flushed as he handed Kari another, much larger, mug. The thing was so huge she could barely lift it. "You'd better get that to our hate-to-fly boy."

Kari nodded and picked her way toward the bathroom, careful to keep the brew from sloshing over the side of the mug. As she walked, it struck her that Sam had been filming the conversation. How the heck could she have forgotten the camera's presence?

Strange. Was the camera now such a part of her life that she didn't notice it? She never dreamed that day would come.

Regardless, she wasn't the only one who now knew about Damien's fear of flying. Millions of Romance TV viewers would soon know, too. She hoped Damien wouldn't be too pissed at Cody when he discovered his buddy spilled the beans on national TV.

As she neared the closed bathroom door, she heard the water shut off. Wanting to give Damien plenty of time to wrap up in a towel, she counted to fifty before putting her hand on the knob and pushing the door open.

He wasn't wearing a towel. He wasn't wearing anything at all. Since their exploit in the Element had been in semi-darkness, this was the first time she'd gotten a good look at Damien in all his glory. And he was magnificent.

Kari gulped, wishing she'd counted to a hundred and fifty instead. She swallowed again, seeking to soothe her suddenly parched throat. Her hand shook, reminding her that she was holding Damien's industrial-sized vat of coffee. She stole a sip, certain that he wouldn't miss it from a mug that size.

Speaking of large …

No! Kari refused to let herself go there. Locking her eyes on his face, she stepped into the room, shut the door and held out the mug. "Cody thought you could use this."

He took it from her, and Kari felt a jolt as his fingers brushed hers. "Thanks. I'm already feeling more like myself."

"That's good, because we leave for my sister's in about fifteen minutes." She tried to ignore the electricity humming in the air between them, and the part of Damien that seemed happy to see her.

Kari reached behind her husband for a towel and held it out, too.

He didn't accept it nearly as readily as he had the coffee. Instead, he arched an eyebrow. "Have something you want to tell me?"

The rat! He seemed to be enjoying her embarrassment. Kari was glad to see that he was starting to act more like himself, but annoyed at the same time. She had no time to be teased.

She shook the towel at him. "Could you please put this on?"

"For you, sweetheart, I'll do anything." He took the towel and wrapped it around his waist.

Kari smiled her thanks and hid a sigh. If only he meant that, they might have a chance after the contest's three-month cohabitation period. Despite this current fiasco, it was something she was starting to think she wanted.

****

A short time later, Damien and Kari were on their way to her sister's house. Still not quite sober, he'd insisted she be the one to get behind the wheel of the Element.

Not for the first time, he wondered how he'd managed to get so drunk. He certainly hadn't intended to.

Losing track of the number of tequila shots he'd consumed

on the plane was partly to blame. The beer afterward also hadn't helped.

Thank God for cold showers and hot, strong coffee. With their help, he might still manage to get through this meeting with Kari's family without making a complete ass of himself.

Too bad he couldn't go back in time and avoid doing the same thing with Kari. What in hell had possessed him to make a pass at her in the bathroom?

He blamed Cody. It was that trip down memory lane his buddy had sent him on. Remembering what he liked to call the Don Juan years had made him think every woman wanted him.

But Kari wasn't every woman. She was his wife — his very complicated wife, whom he was going to need years, not a mere three months, to figure out. His first task? Learning why she kept running scared every time they approached anything resembling intimacy.

Unfortunately, now wasn't the time. First, he had to apologize for being such an idiot.

"Kari, I'm sorry."

She glanced over at him. "Why?"

"For being a jerk back there."

She shrugged. "Don't worry about it."

"I'm serious. You didn't deserve me hitting on you."

"Damien, let it go. It's fine." She turned away so her hair obscured her face.

It wasn't fine. Hiding behind her hair was her biggest defense. Even knowing her for as short a time as he had, he already knew that. Still, he wasn't ready to let it go. "I want to make it up to you somehow."

She didn't look at him, instead keeping her eyes glued on the road. "You can repay me by making a good impression on my folks."

Damien nodded. He wasn't surprised that the impending visit weighed heavily on her mind. She'd been a basket case before meeting his parents. To hear her tell it, her family was much, much worse than his. The worst his parents were guilty of was indifference.

Now that he was sobering up, he was confident in his ability to impress the family. It couldn't be that hard.

An hour later, sitting beside Kari on her sister's living room couch, he was no longer so sure of himself.

Sure, the visit had started out okay. He'd exchanged smiles and pleasantries with Kari's parents, Frank and Sara, and sisters. Her brothers-in-law had nodded and her brothers had waved without looking away from the White Sox game they were watching.

Damien took a seat with them while Kari disappeared into the kitchen with her mother and sisters. They'd be talking about him, no doubt. Soon he was as engrossed in the game as everyone else.

The trouble started when he made a smart-aleck comment about the Sox. He should have known better, but as a die-hard Cubs fan, he couldn't help himself.

The comment earned him a glare from Sean. "You don't like the White Sox?"

Damien shrugged. "Sorry. I grew up watching the Cubs."

Kari's other brother, Steve, chuckled. "We'll forgive you — this time."

"Thanks, I think."

After the game wrapped up with a White Sox win, which Damien tried his damnedest to look happy about, Steve and Sean both turned to look at him. Sean was the one who issued the invite. "Let's walk."

Damien stood and followed Kari's brothers outside. The minute the door closed behind them, Sean's formerly friendly countenance darkened. "Shannon said Kari wanted us to be nice to you."

"What kind of man asks his wife to fight his battles for him?" Steve chimed in.

Damien stopped walking. "Wait just a minute. I did not ask Kari to tell you anything."

"So you're not scared?"

He leveled a gaze at Sean, who'd asked the question. "Nervous, sure. Who wouldn't be, facing down an entire roomful of in-laws? But not scared."

Steve chuckled again. "Told you he didn't know Kar asked us to take it easy on him."

"That's something," Sean grumbled as they started walking again. "At least our sister didn't marry a Cubs fan *and* a complete chicken."

Steve's grin vanished. "Exactly who did she marry?"

Sean answered his brother's question before Damien had a

chance to speak up. "A veterinarian who felt the need to win a wife."

"What kind of guy does that?"

They were talking about him as if he wasn't standing right beside them, Damien thought, annoyed. "A busy one."

He thought it best not to mention the fact that he hadn't actually entered the contest. Better her brothers thought he'd taken the initiative. He didn't want them to think he had no control over his life — even if it was true.

Sean, obviously the "bad cop" of the two, leaned in, invading his space. "You obviously weren't too busy to waste time watching TV."

Damien held his ground, glad he'd brushed his teeth before he and Kari left the apartment. At least now Sean wouldn't get a whiff of beer breath. He couldn't back down now that he'd said he wasn't scared, so he looked Sean in the eye. "When you get home from work that late, there's not much else to do."

"What self-respecting man watches Romance TV?"

It was all he could do to keep from laughing at Steve's question, considering how many times he'd asked Cody the exact same thing. "Would you believe it's my only vice?"

"I doubt that," Sean grumbled as they turned back toward the house.

Damien chose not to respond. As they walked, he reflected on the conversation. Given a chance, he could like Kari's brothers. They both seemed like solid guys — for White Sox fans, anyway. And he sensed Steve could become a real ally.

He just might need one of those in a family like this. He couldn't believe how protective they were of Kari.

"Guys, I promise I won't hurt your sister."

While Steve responded with a pleasant nod, Sean scowled. "Don't make promises you can't keep."

It occurred to Damien then that they might know why Kari kept backing off whenever he got close. He stopped walking and waited for them to do the same. When they both looked at him, their raised eyebrows making them look identical, he asked, "Did something happen to Kari that I should know about?"

Sean shrugged. "Nothing I know of."

But Steve looked more thoughtful. "What about that jerk she dated in college? What was his name? Slob?"

"I think it was Bob," Sean supplied. "He was a jerk. I was

glad when she stopped bringing him around."

"Did he do something to her?"

"Not that I know of," Steve said. "But he didn't treat her like he should have."

Sean added, "She was always waiting on him, fetching him drinks and stuff."

Steve grinned. "And ol' Bob the slob didn't like baseball at all — so you have one up on him."

Damien supposed he should be grateful for that. However, he was too busy puzzling over what he'd just learned. It wasn't much, but at least he now knew her ex, Bob, was a chauvinist. It didn't explain her skittishness, though. Unless …

"Did Bob ever smack her around?"

Sean snorted and walked off, but Steve fixed him with a stare that spoke volumes.

Damien held up his hands. Of course her brothers wouldn't have stood for that. Look at how they were grilling him! "Sorry, man."

****

Kari watched Damien follow Steve and Sean out the door before heading to the kitchen, where the rest of the Parker women were already gathered. Stacy trailed her like a prospective student stuck to the campus tour guide.

Good thing she was getting used to ignoring the camera. When she took a seat at the island and picked up a paring knife to chop salad veggies, Shannon winked at her. "I can see why you've been eager to keep Damien to yourself."

Their older sister, Claire, rolled her eyes. "Please. Kari doesn't know what to do with that man."

"I do too!" Kari's protest was swift. How dare Claire insinuate she was clueless about sex! It was like high school all over again.

"Do not," Claire countered calmly. "If you did, you two would be burning up the sheets."

"Who says we're not?"

"You."

"I did not!"

Shannon broke in. "I hate to break it to you, Kar-Bear, but you did … unless you were lying to the new mother-in-law."

"And lying to your mother-in-law is never a good idea," Claire added.

Kari felt her cheeks flush. How had she forgotten her sisters knew as much about her love life as she did? She cursed Romance TV and the prize money she wished she didn't need. If only her parents hadn't taken out that second mortgage on the restaurant to help Steve buy a house. But that was who they were — willing to do anything to help their children make their way in the world.

"I wasn't lying to Mrs. Walker," Kari admitted reluctantly.

Claire lifted her nose in the air. "I didn't think so."

Shannon waved her hand at them both. "Girls, we're forgetting the point here."

"What would that be?" Claire prompted.

Shannon giggled. "That I bet Kari's husband will give the boys — even my Tim — a run for their money in the annual shirtless Parker contest."

At the mention of her brothers' summer tradition, Kari's heart started racing. Every year at the family's Fourth of July barbecue, her brothers — and now brothers-in-law — took off their shirts and paraded around, trying to outdo one another to get the most applause. Her family loved competition, and the boys had dreamed this one up years ago.

It couldn't be July Fourth weekend already. No way would she have agreed to bring Damien to dinner for that spectacle. She tried to sound casual. "Is that this weekend?"

Claire looked at her as if she'd just asked if a gigolo was a musical instrument. "Those unfulfilled hormones running through your veins are making you stupid, Kar-Bear. You need to get yourself laid — and soon."

Kari made a face at her sister. Thank God she and Damien would be in Alaska by then. There'd be no embarrassing Shirtless Parker contest for him. Good. She didn't want to have to explain that family quirk. "You're not funny."

Claire grinned. "You'd find me a whole lot funnier if you and that hot husband of yours were getting it on."

Kari's cheeks grew hot again. She hated the way, even after so many years, Claire could make her feel so stupid, helpless and unable to defend herself.

Besides that, she knew that in no time at all, her entire family — including her parents, unless she could figure out a way to get them out of the room — was going to see exactly what she and Damien had been up to Friday night.

Just then, her mother returned to the room. She'd obviously been listening at the door, because she waved at Claire. "Stop pestering Kari, dear. I think it's good that she's not jumping into bed. You young people have sex at the drop of a hat and then wonder why you can't get a man to commit. Men are never going to buy the cow when they get the milk for free."

Kari's eyes widened as she stared at her mother. Well, it *looked* like her mother, but she'd never heard anything like that come out of her mom's mouth before. Maybe some alien had invaded her body.

Before she could formulate any kind of coherent response, Shannon giggled again. "Mom, Damien already bought the cow. If he doesn't start getting milk soon, he'll trade her in."

Kari dropped the knife and buried her flaming face in her hands. She started to retreat deep inside herself, the way she always did when her family got to be too much to handle. They were so big, so loud, so outspoken that it was no wonder she responded by going the opposite way. She couldn't compete with them.

Of course, her sisters wouldn't let her be. She felt a nudge and raised her head to find Shannon looking at her. Her eyes were filled with what looked like concern.

"Kar? You always wondered what we old married women were doing in the kitchen — well, now you know."

Kari frowned. How could she have forgotten that it was her first time in the kitchen with the big girls? One of the rules in the Parker house was that only married women were allowed in the kitchen. For years, she'd wondered what they were doing when they disappeared in there. "You mean, all this time, you've been in here chatting about sex?"

Shannon nodded and leaned in to whisper, "You'll get used to Mom's shocking statements. She's surprisingly hip, even if her attitudes are a little dated."

Somehow, Kari suspected her mom and Damien's mother would have a lot in common.

Damien suddenly burst in through the back door. The room fell silent as four pairs of eyes turned to look at him.

"I get the feeling I'm interrupting something."

Kari rose and walked to where he stood, planting a kiss on his cheek as she pushed him back onto the step. She didn't miss the fact that her brothers were standing by the big oak tree in the yard, trying hard to look innocent. "No men in the kitchen. It's a rule."

"Then why …?" Damien trailed off and frowned. "Steve and Sean have been hazing the new guy. They insisted I come in through the back door."

Kari squeezed his hand. "That means they like you."

"If that's true, I'd hate to see what they do to a guy they don't like," Damien grumbled under her breath.

She giggled. "Remember Dexter?"

"How could I forget about Dexter?" Damien smacked his forehead with the heel of his hand.

She gestured toward Steve and Sean. "Take those two jokers back around front and keep Dad company for a little while. Dinner will be ready in about fifteen minutes. Then, after dinner, Shannon wants us all to watch the show."

The I-just-smelled-something-bad look on Damien's face told Kari he was no more thrilled by that prospect than she was. No wonder. The idea of sitting there with her family while they watched what could only be described as soft-core porn was not her idea of fun. It wasn't even on the same continent as her idea of fun.

"If you can think of a way to escape, I'm all ears." Kari offered him a smile.

Damien grinned back. "I'm on it."

When she got back to the kitchen, Shannon nudged her again. "You have him eating from the palm of your hand, Kar-Bear. Take advantage of that."

Kari nodded and started slicing tomatoes for the salad. For fear of looking stupid in front of their other sister, she didn't ask Shannon the obvious question: How did she do that?

Chapter Twenty-Two

Damien sat next to Kari at the dinner table, trying to make himself feel at home. It wasn't easy with her sisters ogling him and her brothers giving him the stare of death, all under the steady gaze of Sam's camera. Kari hadn't been kidding when she said her family was a bit much to take. At least Frank and Sara seemed to like him.

Now he knew why being ogled bothered Kari so much. During the Don Juan years he'd spent the early afternoon reminiscing about, he'd enjoyed it, but tonight it made him uncomfortable.

They sipped after-dessert coffee and chatted about Frank and Sara's restaurant, which apparently wasn't doing so well.

They probably didn't want to broadcast their business in front of a stranger — his parents certainly wouldn't have. Damien tried to change the subject. "That meal was fantastic."

Sara beamed at him. "Thank you, dear."

He wasn't lying. A delicious beef stew, salad and home-baked bread had been followed by the best coconut cream pie he'd ever tasted. He'd enjoyed every bite, even if he now felt uncomfortably stuffed. He should have known not to order pizza and wings at the airport café.

Come to think of it, he had known. Yet he chose to ignore the little voice inside his head, saying, "Don't do it."

Suddenly, one of Kari's sisters — was Shannon the one who lived here? — checked her watch and jumped up. "Five minutes until 'Just Married'! Into the living room, everyone. We can finish our coffee there."

Yep. Definitely Shannon. Kari had said she was eager to tune into the show.

Damien stood with everyone else, snaking an arm around Kari's waist to ensure she couldn't lead the way. Not that she seemed all that eager to change rooms. He took a deep breath. This was his only chance to avoid certain embarrassment.

"Guys, I hate to be a wet blanket, but you all seem to be big on tradition — and Kari and I have one of our own."

Shannon narrowed her eyes, glancing from him to Kari. "What's that?"

"Kari and I don't like to watch 'Just Married.'" When Shannon looked ready to protest, he quickly added, "Think about it. Why should we watch something when we just lived it not even a week ago?"

Shannon snapped her mouth shut. "You do have a point."

"And that's why Kari and I thought Frank and Sara might like to join us on a walk around the neighborhood."

"It's a beautiful evening," Kari added, apparently eager to help him out.

"But, Kari dear," her mother protested, "I was kind of looking forward to seeing the show. You know I can't watch it at home because we don't have cable."

Damien felt her stiffen slightly. "You and Dad really should come with us. You haven't gotten much chance to get to know Damien yet."

Shannon must have sensed the "help us" vibes his wife was sending because she chimed in. "Mom, I'll record it and you can watch when you get back."

"Okay, then." Sara's agreement was cheerful. "Let's take a walk."

When her parents left the room, Kari turned the full force of her smile on him. She pushed herself up on tiptoe and whispered, "Thank you."

He dropped a quick kiss on her lips. "Don't thank me yet. We haven't saved ourselves from complete embarrassment if Shannon's going to record it."

Kari merely smiled again. As she walked past Shannon, she muttered something that sounded like, "Lose the recording."

Shannon laughed and winked at them both. "Sure, sis. Whatever you say."

Damien, Kari and her parents shared a pleasant walk through Shannon's neighborhood. With its large shade trees and white picket fences, this was like the suburban neighborhood he'd grown up in, and the one he wanted to settle down in eventually.

He was so enchanted with the location that he took note of a "for sale" sign in the yard of one of the houses they passed. Sure, it'd make for a long commute to his practice, but not that much longer than his current drive when the city was gridlocked.

When they got back to the house thirty-five minutes later, Kari and Damien exchanged a glance. She took a deep breath and whispered, "Here goes nothing."

Damien pushed open the door and was immediately greeted by Sean's hostile stare. Steve, however, flashed him a thumbs-up, mouthing the words, "Good job."

Kari's other sister greeted them with a harsh laugh. "I stand corrected."

Beside him, Kari's face flamed fire engine red. Damien narrowed his eyes at the other woman. For some reason, he didn't like this sister much.

It was then that Shannon came rushing to the rescue. "Mom, I have some bad news: The DVR malfunctioned."

Sara Parker stamped her foot in frustration and looked at Kari. "I so wanted to see you in action, dear."

Kari sucked in a breath at her mother's word choice. Even Damien found it unfortunate. He was about to say something to come to her rescue when her brothers threw in their two cents' worth. Sean tried unsuccessfully to stifle a snort and Steve quipped, "Trust me, Ma. You didn't miss a thing."

Damien felt himself relax, reassured that even if Kari's brothers and sisters annoyed her to no end, they loved her enough to do whatever it took to protect her.

At that thought, he glanced again at the other sister, the one he didn't like and whose name escaped him. She was watching him with something akin to a predatory gleam in her eye. At least most of the family would protect Kari, he amended, giving the older woman a sarcastic salute as he pulled his wife closer to him.

"We'd better hit the road. It's a long drive back into the city," he said. "Shannon and Tim, thanks for your hospitality. It was good to meet you all. Kari has told me so much about you that it was nice to finally put some names and faces together tonight."

When they were back in the Element heading toward the apartment, this time with Damien behind the wheel, Kari sighed and leaned back in her seat. "You didn't have to lay it on so thick back there."

"What are you saying?"

"'Kari has told me so much about you ...'" she mimicked. "They're going to know you're lying."

Damien glanced over at her for the briefest of moments. He didn't miss the way her eyes shone in the streetlights they drove under. "You've told me more than you think, sweetheart."

"You barely knew I had a family!"

"That in itself tells me volumes."

Kari considered that for a moment. "Like what?"

"Like you get overwhelmed by your family and wish like hell you were an only child. But I'm here to tell you, being an only child isn't all that great."

As a kid, he'd wished for a brother or sister to keep him company while his parents were busy with their research. However, he'd remained an only child through middle and high school, meeting Cody his freshman year of college, when they were assigned to the same dorm room. They bonded like brothers, and he hadn't felt alone since.

She was silent for so long that he worried he'd offended her. That wouldn't do. "Kari, it's okay if you don't like your brothers and sisters. I'm not sure if I like them, either."

Kari giggled. "It's not that, Damien. My relationship with them is *complicated*."

"All family relationships are complicated, Kari. It's the nature of family. They're the people who know you best, and who you sometimes wish didn't know you quite so well."

****

Kari stared at Damien, who kept his eyes on the road, wondering when he'd gotten to be so insightful. When she asked him as much, he glanced over at her again.

"I considered becoming a psychiatrist."

"Why didn't you?"

Damien smiled. "I prefer patients who don't talk. It makes my days a lot easier."

"You're joking, right?" Kari didn't believe for a minute that his motivations were that transparent.

"Sorry. If you have to ask, it wasn't that funny."

She persisted, even though she wasn't sure why it suddenly mattered so much to her. "So why did you opt to be a vet?"

"I've always loved animals. It's that simple. I get a lot of satisfaction from helping people make sure their pets are healthy and happy."

Kari looked at Damien — really looked at him — in the half-light that filtered through the car's windshield. The smile on his lips softened his somewhat formidable profile, and she found herself thinking about what was and what could be.

He'd just said her attitude toward her family told him a lot about her, but his outlook on his work told her something, too. It told her that, unlike Rob, Damien truly was a gentle man.

Her flight instinct, the one that kept screaming Damien was going to hurt her, was quieting down. She was starting to believe he would never harm her — on purpose, anyway. This afternoon's drunken episode notwithstanding, he'd never crossed any lines, never done anything she hadn't been completely on board with. And the minute she started resisting, he backed off. Even today, when he was drunk, he didn't push.

That was the complete opposite of Rob, who had refused to take no for an answer, pestering her to do whatever it was he wanted until she finally gave in. It was easier for her to give in than to stick to her guns and get what she wanted for a change.

Kari frowned, shoving that unwelcome memory aside. She refused to let it intrude on the warm fuzzy feelings she was having for Damien. He was her husband, after all. Why was she fighting her attraction to him so hard?

Because he's only your husband for a short time.

Now her inner tramp was the voice of reason? She shook her head. She wasn't going to listen — not this time.

"Damien, stop the car."

"Excuse me?" He looked confused. "You forget something we need to go back and get?"

She rolled her eyes. "Just pull over." When her husband did as she asked, she leaned over and kissed him on the lips. Her hand slid down to the button on his jeans. "Now say 'thank you' for the gift you're about to receive."

****

Damien shifted uncomfortably in his seat. What had gotten into Kari all of a sudden? That sexy, raspy voice ... her sudden interest in making out.

A part of him didn't care. If visiting her family made Kari horny, they needed to see her family more often. Mr. Happy was more than willing to oblige.

His mind, however, was more reluctant. He put his hand over Kari's, trapping her fingers against his fly.

"Let's not do this here, sweetheart."

"But—"

He silenced her protest with a kiss that left him wishing he didn't have to put the brakes on this. But for both their sakes, he did. He still didn't want either of them to wake up with regrets.

"There's a time and place for everything, and I don't think the Element on the side of the road with traffic whizzing by every few seconds is the right place for this." After a pause, he added, "Besides, you know Sam and Stacy will be along soon. If they see us parked on the side of the road, they're just going to pull in behind us to get more footage."

"You're right about that," Kari conceded.

Damien smiled encouragingly. "And I don't know about you, but I don't want America to think I have a fetish for getting it on in the car."

This time, she giggled. "I can see where that might be a problem."

He lifted the palm of Kari's hand to his lips, brushing it with a kiss, and then gently placed her hand back in her lap. "Then we're agreed."

Kari giggled again. He was coming to love that carefree sound. He'd have to figure out how to make her giggle a lot more often. "Let's head home and see what comes up."

Chapter Twenty-Three

When they got to the apartment, they started with chores. Damien walked Sunny and Kari cleaned Rhett and Ashley's litter box. By the time she'd done her evening yoga routine and unlocked the bedroom door so Damien could come to bed, the moment had passed.

Kari admitted, at least to herself, she was glad. Whatever had gotten into her in Damien's SUV, sanity was back now that she stood staring at the bed. It was a huge bed, plenty large enough to stand up to some spectacular bedroom acrobatics.

It was good to hear her inner tramp up to her old tricks, Kari thought as she shoved the unwelcome thought aside. Instead, she clung to the thought of sweet, sweet sanity.

When a vision of what Damien had looked like that afternoon, naked, flitted into her mind, she reminded herself that theirs was not a real marriage.

When Damien came up behind her, wrapping his arms around her waist and planting a kiss on her neck, she reminded herself of that fact again. She broke away from him and turned to look him in the eyes.

She bit her lip, knowing she was about to do something some men — men like Rob — considered unforgivable.

Damien backed up a few steps. "This isn't going to happen tonight, is it?"

Kari shook her head, by now biting her lip so hard she was surprised she didn't draw blood "I'm sorry, Damien."

"You don't have to apologize to me for changing your mind, Kari." He rubbed his thumb over her and a little thrill rippled through her. "Your mind is your own, and you can change it as many times as you want to."

She looked at him in disbelief. Saying things like that, he really was too good to be true. "You don't need to pretend. I know you're angry."

Damien snorted. "Angry? No. Disappointed? Yes."

"But—"

When he put a finger to her lips to silence her protest, she couldn't help thinking it wasn't nearly as fun as when he'd kissed her for that same purpose.

When he spoke, his voice was measured. "I was looking forward to, as you said, seeing what comes up. But I can't and won't force you to follow through if you're no longer willing." Then he grinned. "Now if you'll excuse me, I'm going to go take a cold shower."

With that, Damien spun on his heel and left the bedroom, leaving Kari behind to think about what had happened.

I really need to get past my past. Her inability to put her experiences with Rob behind her disgusted her. That man had no place in her life anymore, yet he haunted her.

Grow up.

Damien and Rob couldn't be more different. Sure, they were similar in physical size, but that was where the similarities ended.

Rob had used his size to intimidate her; Damien used his to protect her. Rob had imposed his will on her more times than she could count; Damien let her call the shots at every turn. Rob had never understood what she wanted and needed; Damien seemed to be almost as adept as Bethany at reading her mind. And Damien, too, had been a band geek in high school — just as she had.

Kari smiled to herself. If she hadn't seen the photographic proof, she still wouldn't believe it, but pictures like that didn't lie. Her still-too-large husband had once been a trumpet-toting, card-carrying geek. She wondered if she should take that as more proof that he wasn't going to hurt her.

Damien had shown remarkable restraint by walking out instead of cajoling her to change her mind. That was what Rob would have done, and if persuasion hadn't worked badgered her into submitting. He never took "no" for an answer.

The memory made Kari shudder. She took a deep breath. Maybe Beth was right and she did need a therapist to exorcise Rob from her life. She obviously wasn't succeeding on her own.

Tomorrow, she promised as she dropped into a tension-taming downward-facing dog pose. *I'll look for a therapist first thing.*

****

When Damien walked back into the bedroom, he was greeted by Kari's rear end. Her butt was up in the air in what he now knew was the dreaded down-dog. She sure made it look more comfortable than it was.

The sight banished any effects from the cold shower, and he groaned, wishing he'd dawdled in the bathroom just a little longer.

He quietly shut the door behind him and made his way to his side of the bed. Kari was still oblivious to his presence, her eyes closed as she breathed deeply.

God, she was beautiful. He leaned back to watch his wife decompress. Her long legs rose up to meet her perky little bottom and her hair hung down, brushing the floor by her head.

He longed to run his fingers through those long blond curls. He wanted to kiss her and caress her and — Damn! Why had she changed her mind?

Damien shook his head. The why didn't matter. All that mattered was that she *had* changed her mind. He'd meant what he said. She had the right to vacillate as many times as she wanted to.

That didn't mean he couldn't try to get her to change it back.

The errant thought brought a scowl to Damien's face. If he didn't change the direction of his thoughts, he was going to need another cold shower, and if he kept that up, his next water bill was going to be triple digits. Maybe even quadruple ones.

Kari finally straightened up and opened her eyes. She focused on Damien. "You were ogling again, weren't you?"

Damien felt himself grin, the scowl quickly forgotten. "Guilty as charged."

"It's okay. I'm getting used to it."

What? His lovely wife had just managed to surprise him again. Good thing he was a quick thinker. He came back with, "That's good, because you have a body that's meant to be ogled."

Kari glanced down at her flat stomach and frowned. "I

won't if I keep eating the way I have been the last few weeks."

Damien found himself frowning, too. He liked the fact that she normally didn't seem to be hung up on her weight. "You don't have anything to worry about, sweetheart."

When she gave him a look that said, "Yeah, right," he patted the bed beside him. "Come here, Kari." He saw the hesitation in her eyes and held up his hands. "Just to cuddle. I don't have anything else in mind."

Her gaze strayed down to his lap and she grinned. "I think we both know that's not entirely true."

Damien glanced down, too, even though he knew what he was going to see: Mr. Happy, clamoring for a little attention. He locked his eyes on Kari's, steadily holding her gaze. "I don't have to act on that, you know."

He could feel the doubt rolling off her in waves, and he couldn't help thinking that maybe her brothers didn't know everything that went on between Kari and that Bob guy. *Something* had certainly happened to make her mistrust men, and he was willing to bet his share of the "Get a Love Life" prize money Bob was somehow involved.

He took a deep breath, then let it out slowly, the way he'd learned to do in yoga class. There was something to that deep breathing thing; it really did help him release tension. "Kari, nothing is going to happen unless you want it to."

Still she hesitated, glancing from his face to other parts of his anatomy.

Damien took another deep breath. He wasn't into making promises he couldn't keep, so he'd try like hell to keep the one he was about to make. A case of blue balls was a small price to pay if he could help rebuild his wife's trust in men.

Finally, she crawled into bed beside him, putting her head on his shoulder.

Success! Damien slid his arm around her waist, letting his hand rest on the flat abdomen she seemed to be so worried about. "Nothing, Kari. Not unless you make the first move. I promise."

****

When Kari woke up the next morning, she was struck

by two thoughts. The first: She was alone again. Damien must have gotten up early to go on a run. If she wanted to keep eating the way she'd been eating, she was really going to have to ask him to take her with him on his runs. The yoga routine wasn't cutting it in the calorie-burning department.

She found the fact that she was alone especially disappointing in light of her second thought: Damien had kept his word.

Sure, there had been a few iffy moments when she'd first gotten into bed. Though Damien had shown no real signs of starting something, she'd worried that he wouldn't be able to control himself. Slowly, as seconds ticked into minutes and he did exactly what he'd said, cuddled and nothing else, she'd relaxed into his embrace and fallen asleep.

Now she'd awakened — alone. Well, she really couldn't blame him for vacating the bed as soon as he could. He was probably frustrated as a one-legged man in an ass-kicking contest by now.

Truth be told, she was getting annoyed, too — mostly at herself and her inability to get past her ex. Rob had been out of her life for more than nine years, so it was long past time for him to stop haunting her.

That thought spurred her out of bed. Time to start looking for that therapist.

First, Sunny needed attention. The dog was whining at the door, obviously wanting to go out. She clipped the leash to Sunny's collar and off they went, thumps of the dog's cast alternating with the rhythmic click of nails on the tile floor.

They met Damien in the apartment building's lobby. As she suspected, he'd been running. His face glistened with a fine sheen of perspiration.

Kari rolled her eyes. It was unfair that her husband looked so good after a run. She'd have been red-faced and gasping for air with sweat pouring off her face. He looked like he'd just been out for a pleasant jaunt.

He held out his hand. "I'll take Sunny."

She shook her head. "That's okay. I need the exercise."

Damien shrugged. "Have it your way."

"We'll be back in fifteen minutes."

Arlene Hittle

Kari took Sunny down the block to the park. As they strolled among the tree- and tulip-lined paths, she marveled again at how sedate and well-behaved this dog was. And, despite the cast on her leg, she wanted to keep going and going. She'd been missing out on a great walking partner by being so afraid of dogs all these years.

Just like you're going to miss out on a life partner if you don't get over your fear of men.

Kari turned back toward the apartment building and scowled at her inner tramp. She didn't need the heavy-handed comparison to know it was time to get help.

Where, exactly, did one go to find a therapist? The phone book?

She vowed to call Bethany before the morning was out to seek some advice. Having been in and out of therapy for years, Beth would surely know where to find a doctor.

When Kari got back to the apartment, bacon scented the air. Her favorite. She took a deep, appreciative sniff.

Damien stepped out of the kitchen, a spatula in hand. "Welcome back. Since it's still early, I thought I'd whip up my special breakfast."

Kari was curious. "What's that?" Whatever it was, it smelled delicious.

"Denver omelet with bacon instead of ham."

She smiled. "You really know how to get to me. Bacon is my kryptonite. I can resist sausage and ham, but never bacon."

Damien grinned back at her with a mischievous glint in his eye. "So you're saying I should rub myself all over with bacon?"

Kari's eyes widened and her heartbeat picked up speed. It was amazing how quickly her imagination took off. "Isn't it a little early in the morning for comments like that?"

He shook his head. "It's never too early to have fun with bacon."

This time, she laughed. Somehow, he seemed to know exactly what to say to create tension *and* dispel it. "You are incorrigible."

"That's exactly what my mother used to say."

Kari chuckled again. "I knew I liked her."

Breakfast was as delicious as it sounded. They enjoyed

their omelets under the watchful gaze of Sam's camera, and then readied themselves for work. Once they'd gone their separate ways, Kari settled into a seat on the El and took out her cell phone. It was time to call Bethany.

She answered on the third ring. "Kari, you naughty, naughty girl!"

Kari cringed. She should have known Bethany wouldn't let Sunday's show go unremarked upon. "Hi, Beth."

"I hope you two managed to finish what you started," she said, her voice sly.

"Not yet." Kari sighed. "Actually, that's why I'm calling."

Bethany snorted. "If you can't seal the deal after that, you two might be doomed."

"That's not what I needed to hear this morning, Beth." Maybe her friend would pick up on her serious tone.

She did, and her next comment was much more supportive. "What can I help you with, Kar?"

"Therapy."

"Pardon?"

Kari took a deep breath. She might as well get this over with. Bethany had been pestering her about going into therapy for years, and she knew an "I told you so" was in the works. "I'm ready to find a therapist to help me finally get over Rob and thought you might know someone."

"I sure do!" She readily supplied the names of her last five therapists.

Kari giggled. "You change doctors almost as often as you change men."

Bethany ignored her. "Dr. Spaulding's my favorite. She helped me realize that I've been seeking affection from men that I didn't get from my absent father."

"Wait a minute. Where's your 'I told you so'?"

"Why would I say anything to deter you from getting the help you so obviously need?" Kari heard the grin in her friend's voice. "If your Rob hang-up is keeping you from getting it on with that hunky husband of yours, you need to get over it — fast."

With that, Bethany rattled off the doctor's number and hung up with a request. "Do me a favor and wait a few minutes to call Dr. Spaulding."

Kari counted to a hundred and then dialed, managing to set up an appointment for lunch hour the next day. Someone, probably Bethany, had just canceled, so the immediate opening was available.

Suspicious, Kari called Beth again to ask if she'd just canceled her appointment with the therapist.

Bethany laughed. "You needed it more than I do, Kar. My love life is right on track."

The comment jogged Kari's memory. Bethany had gone out with Cody on Friday night. Her promise to Beth that she'd make a date with Damien if her friend went out with Cody was why she and Damien had been found in a compromising position in the Element. "How was 'Star Trek'?"

Bethany's answer was swift. "Awesome."

"And the company?"

"Couldn't have been much better," she admitted.

"Beth, I'm so happy for you!" She was, too. "Cody really is a good guy." He had to be to be willing to help Damien get over his fear of flying like that.

Bethany sighed. "That's what I'm afraid of."

"Excuse me?"

"With my track record, I'm starting to worry that I'm going to hurt him."

Kari considered that for a moment. Considering what Bethany put men through, it was a real possibility. But if Cody was anything like Damien — trustworthy, caring and strong — he'd more than likely be able to stand up to Beth. "I think maybe Cody's stronger than you're giving him credit for. Hasn't he already persisted through your initial kiss-off attempt?"

"Only because my deal with you made me change my mind."

"But when you agreed to go to the movie with him after telling him you wouldn't, he still went," Kari pointed out.

"That's right! So you think Mr. Jump the Gun Jackson is going to stick around?"

"I think he just might be in it for the long haul if you are." As Kari hung up the phone, she wondered if she could say the same thing about Damien.

Maybe her new therapist would be able to shed some

light on that.

****

When lunchtime rolled around the next day, Kari stood outside Dr. Spaulding's office, staring at the closed door. She had ten minutes until her appointment time, and she had a feeling she'd need every second of that time to muster up enough courage to cross the threshold.

She'd waffled most of the night, wavering between excitement to meet the doctor and finally put her past behind her and fear of what might lie ahead.

She wasn't stupid. She knew that it could take years to reach a breakthrough, but she didn't have years. She was working with a limited schedule. In about two months, she and Damien could go their separate ways, and would, especially if she couldn't stop comparing him to Rob. Kari wouldn't blame Damien for getting fed up with her.

She really didn't want to keep disappointing him. That made it imperative she succeed at this therapy thing.

Kari took a deep breath and reached for the doorknob. Time to get this over with. She pushed open the door and got her first look at Dr. Vivian Spaulding, the woman she hoped could help her kick Rob out of her head once and for all.

When Dr. Spaulding rose to greet her, Kari's first impression was that she was tall — taller than most women and even some men. She might even be taller than Damien. Figured Bethany would send her to the biggest doctor she knew. Beth probably thought it'd help her get over her size complex that much faster.

The doctor's faded red hair was scraped back in a severe bun, but her blue eyes were kind. She smiled a greeting.

"Welcome, Mrs. Walker." She gestured to the beige couch. "Please, make yourself comfortable."

"You can call me Kari." As she took a seat on the surprisingly soft couch, she saw Dr. Spaulding scribble something on her notepad. "Did I say something wrong?"

The doctor smiled. "No, Kari. Nothing you say here can be wrong. This is a safe place for you to say whatever you want."

"Then why —?"

"When I saw your name in my appointment book, it seemed familiar. Then, when the network called for permission to film here, I familiarized myself with the show. I'm sorry I had to tell them 'no.'"

"I'm not. I can't imagine talking freely with Sam behind me."

"I'm not either, actually. I protect my patients' privacy." The doctor's eyes crinkled when she smiled. "I do, however, find it interesting that you're so eager to disavow your married name."

Kari sank back into the couch cushions and sighed. She should have known "Just Married" would come up. Of course Dr. Spaulding watched the show. It seemed as if everyone in Chicago watched that blasted show. Strangers were starting to recognize her more and more often.

She sighed again. "I'm being ridiculous, I know."

Dr. Spaulding shook her head. "Your feelings are what they are. Acknowledge what you're feeling — no matter what that might be — and then move on." She paused to take a seat behind her desk. "Now why don't you tell me what brought you here?"

"Actually, I need help moving on."

"From what?" the doctor asked.

Kari hesitated. She'd kept the details of her relationship with Rob from everyone but Bethany for so long, it was hard to bring herself to share them with anyone else.

That's why you're here, her inner voice piped up, sounding impatient.

The tramp was right. She hadn't made an appointment with Dr. Spaulding to talk about the weather.

Still, Rob wouldn't be easy to talk about. Even Beth didn't know everything. She'd never told Bethany about the shame and helplessness she felt every time she gave in to Rob's will, or her rage at herself for not being strong enough to stand up to him. However, that was why she was sitting in Dr. Spaulding's office, on a too-comfy couch, getting ready to spill her guts. Kari took a deep breath and began to speak.

She told the therapist how she and Rob met, and how he acted like a model boyfriend — for at least five minutes. He was the first guy to pay attention to her, and she, being inexperienced, was blind to his flaws. She thought he was Mr. Right, that he would always love her and never do anything to hurt her.

She told Dr. Spaulding how he wasted no time controlling her. At first, it was all mental. He had her convinced that she'd never find another guy like him. Looking back, she sure as hell hoped not! Soon he was using his sheer size to intimidate her into doing his bidding.

Finally, she described how yoga helped her find the strength to banish Rob from her life.

"But he's still here in my head." She tapped her temple. "He's making it impossible for me to let Damien in. I keep flashing back to what things were like with Rob whenever Damien gets too close."

Kari looked expectantly at the therapist, waiting for her to hand over the key to freedom. But Dr. Spaulding merely asked, "Do you really want to let Damien in?"

She considered the question. From everything she'd seen so far, she believed wholeheartedly that Damien was the great guy he seemed to be. With Rob for comparison, she knew what a real creep looked like.

"I think so, yes."

The doctor smiled. "Then we'll work on that."

They spent the rest of the hour going over ways to keep Rob from intruding on her new life. She decided to try a little aversion therapy. She'd wear a rubber band around her wrist and snap it every time thoughts of Rob surfaced.

Kari made another appointment for three weeks later, once she returned from her Alaskan vacation. She actually found herself looking forward to another session with Dr. Spaulding. Beth had been right. Talking to her was a little like dishing with a good friend, and she felt better after getting all that off her chest — lighter, somehow. Maybe there was something to therapy. Why had she resisted for so long?

Chapter Twenty-Four

After work that night, Kari headed home to finish packing for the trip to Alaska. They were set to leave late the day after next.

Damien was already in the bedroom, filling a suitcase. She watched him tuck his winter hat, gloves and a pair of long johns into the suitcase.

"What are you doing?"

He raised an eyebrow at her. "What do you think I'm doing? Packing for Alaska."

She giggled. "It's not going to be that cold."

"But it's Alaska!"

Kari shook her head. "They have four seasons up there, too. This is late June. Daytime temperatures should hit the mid 60s."

"Are you sure?"

This time, she nodded. "I spent a lot of time researching this trip. You'll need jeans and long-sleeved shirts in the evenings, but shorts and T-shirts should do fine for daytime. And we'll be doing a lot of hiking, so don't forget your hiking boots."

Grumbling, Damien took the gloves and long underwear back out of the suitcase. "Okay. But if I freeze to death, I'm holding you responsible."

Kari smiled, secure in the knowledge that what she was about to propose could never happen. "If you start to freeze to death, you have my permission to cuddle with the bears."

"I'd rather get close to you."

With that, Damien stepped up behind her to nuzzle her neck, resting his hands on her hips. Her skin burned at the touch of his lips, sending a sizzle down her spine.

She spun in his embrace, snaking her arms around his neck and turning up her lips for the kiss she suddenly wanted more than anything. When he obliged, an inferno blazed to life deep inside her.

Such intense feelings. Kari hadn't ever felt passion like this, not even—

Before she thought the name, she reached for the rubber

band on her wrist. She was glad her hands were behind Damien's head, so he couldn't see what she was doing.

He did, however, hear the snap. He paused and cocked his head. "What was that?"

Kari froze. How was she going to explain that noise? She certainly wasn't ready to tell him the ugly truth. Sharing that with one person a year was enough. She opted to keep things light. "Are skyrockets going off in your head, too?"

A dark brow arched. "That was definitely not fireworks."

Frantically, she racked her brain for another explanation. "Rice Krispies?" Pathetic, she knew, but it was all she had.

Damien shook his head. "Snap, Crackle and Pop are like Sam and his camera — not allowed in the bedroom."

Kari laughed, just the way he probably wanted her to. But as she did, she still scrambled for a believable way to explain the snapping sound away.

Maybe she could get away with simply changing the subject. She eased out of his embrace and started toward his suitcase.

"Want me to help you pack?"

"I can think of things I'd rather do." Damien caught her by the wrist and pulled her back toward him. He rubbed his thumb over the thick rubber band on her wrist. "I'm pretty sure I just found the source of that mysterious snapping sound."

Caught. Kari winced. She refolded a pair of jeans lying on the bed and tucked them into the luggage. Better he thought she was neurotic about food than about intimacy. "I've been snacking way too much lately, so whenever I have the urge to eat between meals, I'm going to snap the rubber band."

He raised both eyebrows, adopting an almost comical look of disbelief. "You mean you were thinking about food while I was kissing you?"

****

His lovely wife nodded in response to the question, but he didn't believe that for a second — not with the way she'd been kissing him back. She had to be using aversion therapy to keep him at arm's length.

Damien sighed. Here he thought he'd been making some headway with Kari, and now she was snapping herself when he turned her on.

That was just great for his ego. He sighed. Unfortunately, there was nothing he could do about it. As he'd already told her,

her feelings were her own. She had a right to feel what she wanted to feel and do what she thought she had to do.

His ego wasn't quite ready to let her feeble excuse stand, though. "You're kidding, right?"

The rubber band slapped Kari's wrist with a resounding thwack as she shook her head at him. "Nope. I just thought about walking down to the corner for an ice cream cone."

So that was the story she was sticking to. If that was what Kari wanted, there was no point in his getting upset. He still had seven weeks, two days to get her to come around.

With that thought in mind, he grinned lazily at her. "You know that if you walk a block to get the ice cream, it has fewer calories, right?"

"Nice try, Damien, but I'd have to jog for an hour to burn off the calories in one of those cones."

"What's stopping you?"

She stared at him as if he'd just sprouted horns and prodded her with a pitchfork. "Pardon?"

"There's still plenty of time before it gets dark. Let's go for a run."

She regarded him with what looked like suspicion in her beautiful brown eyes. No wonder — he'd gone from packing to making out to suggesting they work out. He was kind of wondering what he was up to himself.

But if it helped Kari feel better about herself — and got him some of his favorite frozen custard from Milo's on the corner of Broadway and Twenty-Fourth — he was willing to go for his second jog of the day.

He added one more enticement. "Wouldn't it be fun to see Sam trying to keep up with us?"

Damien chuckled along with her as he imagined the portly director trotting along behind them with a camera on his shoulder.

When she stopped laughing, she said, "Okay, Damien. You win. Let's go running."

"I'll go warn Sam to put on his tennis shoes."

An hour and fifteen minutes later, the sun was starting to sink below the horizon as he and Kari strolled back to their apartment building, cones full of custard in hand. Stacy, who'd accompanied them on the run because she was in better shape than her husband, walked several steps in front of them, holding the camera over her shoulder backward to catch them on tape.

Damien was peeved that he didn't get to see Sam try to jog. However, it was hard to stay annoyed for long with a big serving of his favorite pineapple custard in his hand. The only way this evening could get much better would be to end it in bed.

He glanced over at Kari, trying to gauge her mood. Would she be more receptive to starting something once she was full of ice cream?

She gave him one of her brightest smiles, the ones he wanted to see more of, and he couldn't help but smile back. Maybe she would.

"I'm glad you talked me into that run," she said, "because now I get to enjoy this chocolate-peanut butter cone guilt-free."

He watched as Kari licked her ice cream, her tongue circling the cone with long, firm strokes.

Idly, he wondered if she understood what the display was doing to him. When her eyes darted in his direction and a sly smile played on her lips, he realized she did, indeed.

Hmm. Maybe he was wrong about the aversion therapy thing. If she were trying to avoid getting closer to him, she wouldn't be eating ice cream so suggestively.

He cleared his throat. "Have I told you lately how beautiful you are?"

Kari shook her head and then smiled. "But you can keep compliments like that coming. True or not, that's something a girl likes to hear."

"You are, you know."

She blushed and took another bite of ice cream before quickening her pace. "Right."

Again wondering what had happened to make her doubt that, Damien, too, sped up. He caught her by the elbow. "I'm serious, Kari."

She shook him off and dropped the remainder of her ice cream cone into a trash can as they passed it. Then she took off at a jog.

"Let's go. I'll race you the rest of the way home."

Damien scowled at her sudden change of heart. His wife blew hot and cold faster than a malfunctioning air conditioner. Still, he picked up his pace. No sense in letting her run away. She did enough of that already.

But he held onto his custard. No way was he going to let the rest of a perfectly good cone go to waste. It wasn't until later, when he saw himself on "Just Married," that he thought about how ridiculous he looked, jogging down the street carrying an ice cream cone. It reminded him of the day he'd seen an overweight man in running clothes "walking" his dog by driving slowly down the street while holding the leash out the window.

The health care professional side of him had wanted to give that guy a piece of his mind, but he'd decided against it. There was no telling how he would have reacted, and Damien didn't want to risk life or limb for some guy who obviously wasn't firing on all cylinders. At least the dog was getting exercise!

Damien beat Kari back to the building, but only by a hair. His wife really could run. He'd have to remember that and invite her to go with him more often. It wasn't often he ran with someone who kept up with his pace. Those long legs of hers were good for something besides ogling, he thought idly as he went back to his packing.

He had to admit, the thought of seeing the great state of Alaska was somewhat exciting. He liked visiting new places, and this trip was going to be full of discoveries. From Fairbanks and Denali National Park in Alaska's Interior, they planned to head down to Juneau and Sitka, finishing up with several days in the big city of Anchorage. Sightseeing was high on the agenda, with plenty of hiking and lots of good food.

He just preferred to take his trips by car, not plane. Unfortunately, Alaska was so big that they'd still be traveling by plane once they arrived, and Kari had said something about taking a floatplane tour.

Yeah, right. Damien knew he'd be coming up with an excuse to get out of *that* adventure. He didn't care if he had to get himself mauled by a bear. No way was he going to get on a plane as small as the one Cody had taken him up in.

Remembering the flight with his buddy made him shudder. Sure, it went off without a hitch, but that didn't mean the next one would. Of course, he would be flying with a seasoned airline pilot — not his best friend who'd only recently been licensed.

Wait a minute! Why was he so worried about a commercial flight? Surely the jaunt he'd taken with Cody was more dangerous than a flight planned and executed by professionals who made hundreds of flights a year.

He looked over at Kari, who was also putting things in a

paisley-print suitcase, and grinned. "I can't wait to go on this trip."

****

Brave words coming from a chicken, Damien's conscience mocked him two days later as he paused outside exam room two. Perhaps he'd been a little hasty in dismissing his fear. A hard lump of dread sat in his stomach, growing every time he thought about how he'd be on a plane to Alaska in less than four hours.

He took a deep breath. His last patient of the day, a cat named Spirit, waited inside with her owner, but he needed a moment.

It had been a trying day, with an emergency surgery to remove a roll of quarters from a Weimaraner mix's intestine. The procedure was a success, thank God, but he still needed to catch his breath. Spirit was a smart, lively girl, and he'd need every ounce of energy he could muster to keep up with her.

He allowed his mind a moment to skip ahead to quitting time. He planned to meet Kari at the apartment. From there they'd drop Sunny off with Cody, who'd agreed to dog-sit while they were gone. Damien knew she'd be in good hands with his buddy, and he wouldn't have to worry about Sunny getting overstimulated, like he would if she spent a week and a half boarded at the office.

Then it was off to O'Hare. They'd be at the airport by five, with time to get through security and enjoy a leisurely dinner before their flight left at 8:30. Of course, that assumed his stomach would be settled enough to eat.

He forced his thoughts back to the office. He'd kept Spirit and her owner waiting long enough.

"Hi, Stephanie. What seems to be the problem?" Damien asked the question as he stepped into the exam room and scratched the cat behind her ears.

Spirit's owner, Stephanie Simpson, wrung her hands. "I'm moving to California. We leave tomorrow and I can't figure out how to keep Spirit calm for the drive."

He glanced at Spirit, who was leaping from the exam room table to the counter and back repeatedly. She meowed loudly as she darted in and out of her carrier. "I can see where she might need a little help in that department."

This problem was a no-brainer — a nice, easy way to end the

day. "I'll give you a sedative called Diazepam. Give it to Spirit as prescribed and she'll stay calm and quiet while you're on the road."

Stephanie frowned. "Isn't that Valium?"

Damien nodded, surprised. "Most people I talk to don't know that."

"My mother used to take it. The bottle was always on her nightstand."

That explained it. "It also comes in a generic, so you can save a little money."

"Thanks, doc," Stephanie said as she ushered a now-reluctant Spirit back into her carrier. It figured. The moment you wanted a cat to do something, it wanted to do the complete opposite. "This cross-country move is already costing me an arm and a leg. The U-Haul truck alone is almost a thousand bucks."

Damien whistled. "I've enjoyed caring for Spirit. Be sure to contact us when you get settled and we'll forward her records to your new vet."

Stephanie hoisted the soft-sided carrier bag onto her shoulder and pushed open the exam room door. "Thanks again."

As Damien wrote the prescription for his vet tech to fill for Spirit, he paused. Diazepam worked for animals that were nervous to travel, so why not take some for himself? Maybe it'd help him stay calm on his flight.

Why not? His conscience supplied a good answer. *It's a controlled substance. You can't just help yourself.*

Ah, but he did have the power to write himself a prescription. More accurately, he'd be writing it for Sunny. No one would know he planned to take the pills himself.

You can't do that!

His conscience was right. Too bad he wasn't the type to abuse his power. Valium and vodka would have been a perfect prescription to get him through hours on a plane without making a fool of himself.

Chapter Twenty-Five

"Not again." Kari groaned as she paced from the apartment door to the window, waiting for Damien to arrive home. They'd planned to leave for the airport ten minutes ago, but he was still MIA.

Just then, her cell phone chimed the generic ring she had set for most incoming calls. She checked the display, and when it said Damien was calling, she jumped to answer it.

As she asked him where he was, she idly considered giving him his own ringtone so she could identify his calls without looking.

How about "Hunka Hunka Burnin' Love?"

The rogue thought startled Kari so much that she almost missed his explanation about getting stuck in traffic.

"Now I'm only five minutes away. We can make up for lost time if you meet me in the parking garage."

"With both our suitcases and Sunny?"

"I guess not." He sighed again. "Sorry. I'll be up as soon as I can."

Kari disconnected the call and stared at the phone. Her big, strong, always-so-sure-of-himself husband sounded completely frazzled. The thought of fourteen hours of plane travel must really be wearing on him. Poor guy.

She wheeled the suitcases to the door and clipped the dog's leash to her collar. It was the least she could do when he was being so accommodating.

Really. He was about to do something that scared the hell out of him, just because she wanted to do it. She wasn't sure she'd be willing to go to such extraordinary lengths for him, and she knew Rob would never have done anything like that for her.

There was that name again. She snapped the rubber band on her wrist for about the thirtieth time since she'd started wearing it a day and a half ago. That averaged out to about once an hour.

Kari groaned. "If I don't stop comparing Damien to the Evil One soon, my wrist will be rubbed raw."

When Damien walked through the door a few minutes later,

she was running through a mental checklist to make sure she'd packed everything. Yep. All was accounted for — even her cell phone charger. After leaving it behind for a weekend getaway with Bethany last year, she wouldn't forget that again.

"Are you ready to go?" When she nodded, Damien picked up the suitcases. "I'll get the luggage if you grab Sunny."

Kari nodded again and bent down to get the dog's leash. She glanced into the kitchen to make sure everything was turned off — ceiling fan, coffeemaker, oven. They were going to be gone for a week and a half; she wanted to make sure they had a home to come back to.

She waited in the Element when Damien dropped Sunny off with Cody, watching him stride to the door with easy confidence. Either he hid his fear well, or Cody had exaggerated Damien's fear of flying.

She wouldn't put something like that past Cody. Damien's friend wasn't stupid. He'd probably realized she was upset that Damien came home drunk and made up the "he's afraid of flying" story to soften her anger. Guys tended to stick together like that — at least her brothers did. Rob sure hadn't cared enough about her to spare her feelings.

Damn! She snapped the rubber band on her wrist yet again, wincing as it landed on the delicate skin at the base of her palm. She was going to have to exorcise her ex from her thoughts — and soon.

"Cody promised to take good care of Sunny," Damien announced when he got back in the car. "Now, on to O'Hare."

Kari looked over at her husband, who sounded way too chipper for someone about to stare major fear in the face. That's it. Cody had to have lied.

Well, she didn't intend to tell Bethany that. She didn't want to give Beth a reason to write Cody off, because she still thought he was a good guy. Jerks didn't go to such lengths to protect friends.

Kari snickered. Jerks didn't even have friends. Not real ones, anyway. That she knew from experience. Cody, on the other hand, was a good friend to Damien. He was sure to be a nice, stable influence on her wild-child friend.

Soon they were parking at the airport. As organized as ever, Damien jotted down a note about their parking spot and took off for the ticket counter, both suitcases in tow. She trailed behind, still marveling at how well he was taking his impending date with the big, scary airplane.

She almost opened her mouth to ask him about it, but changed her mind. If he'd somehow dealt with his fear, she didn't want to dredge it up again.

It was better that she just watch and wonder. Kari quickened her pace to catch up with Damien. When she fell into step beside him, she smiled. "I can't wait to start this trip."

"Technically, it's already started."

She pushed her hair behind her ear so she could get a better view of Damien. "I know that. But I want to be in Alaska, taking in the sights. There's so much to see that I don't want to waste a minute."

Damien stopped, his eyes searching her face. For what, she didn't know. She'd never admit to the real reason she'd planned an Alaskan vacation. No point, because now that she had a husband, that purpose was moot. Finally, he smiled. "Then it's a good thing we'll be taking off in a little more than two hours."

They checked in and got through airport security in about thirty minutes — not bad at one of the country's busiest airports. Ten minutes after that, they were sitting at a table in Chili's, waiting for a waitress to take their order.

A ponytailed brunette bustled up to the table, engulfing them both with a friendly smile. "Hi, I'm Annie. Can I start you with something to drink?"

Damien pounced on the offer. "Vodka on the rocks."

Kari raised her eyebrows in surprise. Straight vodka? On top of his coming home drunk Sunday afternoon, she wondered if Damien had a drinking problem she was only now discovering. Considering how little she knew about her husband, it was entirely possible.

Realizing the server was waiting for her to order, Kari started. "Just water with lemon, please."

As the woman walked away, Damien grinned. "Learned your lesson, did you?"

Kari nodded. After drinking more than her share of Damien's giant margarita Friday night and suffering from the mother of all hangovers Saturday, she didn't even want to look at alcohol. "I've had my quota of booze for the month."

After the server returned with their drinks, Damien stared into his glass for a moment before he lifted it to his lips to take a sip.

He made a face. "To tell you the truth, so have I. But I'm not much of a flier."

"I know."

"You do?" He looked surprised.

"Cody told me Sunday afternoon while you were in the shower."

He took another sip of vodka. "I should have known you'd want an explanation for my boorish behavior." He paused, looking thoughtful. "Have I apologized for that yet? I should have known better than to try to conquer my fear of flying and meet your parents all in the same day."

Kari shrugged. "Everything worked out okay, so there's no need to apologize."

"Yes, there is," he insisted. His bright blue gaze was steady. "I can't imagine how panicked you felt when I stumbled in drunk, and I'm sorry for making you feel that way."

Uncomfortable with the conversation and the way he was able to discern feelings she wasn't even ready to admit to having, she focused her attention on the menu. "What are you ordering?"

He gave the menu a cursory once-over. "The Southwest chicken, but don't try to change the subject. I'm trying to apologize here."

"And I'm trying to tell you that you don't have anything to apologize for," Kari shot back, agitated. Why did he keep insisting on an unnecessary apology? "Shannon said our mom couldn't stop talking about you after we left. That means she liked you. And if you're in with Mom, you're okay by Dad, too. So even though you may have still been a tiny bit tipsy when we arrived, you passed the parent test with flying colors."

"I'm glad your parents liked me, Kari." He paused to sigh — patiently, it seemed to her. "But I'm trying to tell you I'm sorry for making you even more nervous about the visit than you already were. I'm sure I made an already trying experience even harder on you, and I shouldn't have."

Kari looked at Damien, surprised once again by how perceptive he was. Had he always been such a sensitive new age guy? And did she really want a man who sometimes knew her better than she knew herself?

Aware that he was still watching her, his steady blue-eyed gaze fixed on her face, she smiled. "Apology accepted."

"Thank you." Damien's broad smile transformed his until-then serious countenance as he added, "I don't think Sean liked me all that much."

Kari rolled her eyes. The family had long ago dubbed her middle brother "the difficult one." "Sean doesn't like anyone. There's a reason he's thirty-three and single."

Damien affected a hurt look. "Hey, now. Until recently, I was thirty-three and single, too."

Sensing his serious mood was behind him, she laughed. It felt good to lighten the atmosphere at the table. "Trust me, Damien. You're nothing like Sean. He once dumped a girl because her *sister* didn't change the oil in her car often enough."

For a moment, he looked surprised. Then he grinned. "Don't you know a girl whose sister doesn't maintain her car correctly can't be trusted?"

"I did not know that," Kari said, giggling. "Does the same go for guys?"

Damien nodded solemnly. "You bet."

"Then I hope Cody knows when to change his oil."

This time, Damien was the one who laughed. "My man Cody might not give his dog enough exercise, but he is a car maintenance freak."

Suddenly feeling shy, Kari offered Damien a small smile. "I'm glad."

"Me, too."

****

A couple of hours later, Damien sat beside Kari on the plane, waiting for it to take off and wondering if convincing her to split an order of queso and chips before dinner had been such a good idea. The cheese, or maybe it was the chicken, lumped in his stomach, making him queasy.

Well, at least the vodka and Vicodin Cody had pressed into his hand when he dropped off Sunny — pain meds left over from Cody's broken leg — were working their magic. Aside from being slightly sick to his stomach, he was feeling fine. He might as well be sitting on his couch as in an airplane. In fact, if he closed his eyes, he could pretend he was relaxing in the living room.

He let his eyelids flutter shut, visualizing his couch. He pictured the soft brown cushions, now covered with animal hair, courtesy of Sunny and Kari's two cats. He saw the cats curled together on one arm of the couch, blithely ignoring the dog. It seemed the two of them had reached some kind of détente. At least they were no longer sniping at each other every few minutes.

In his mind's eye, he brushed aside copies of *Newsweek* and *Entertainment Weekly* and put his feet up on the coffee table.

Damien was amazed that he felt so completely relaxed. This visualization thing really worked!

It's more likely the vodka and Vicodin.

The voice was probably right. Whatever was doing the trick, he planned a repeat performance every time he got on a plane.

He returned to the couch in his head. He was still lounging there with his feet up when the plane began rolling down the runway. It picked up speed.

Okay. Nope. Not okay.

Panic started to set in. He took a few deep, yoga-type breaths, but suddenly all he could visualize was their plane exploding in a ball of flame.

He needed to distract himself. Turning to Kari, he could only choke a single word past the lump of fear that had shot from his stomach to his throat. "Help."

Kari looked up from the travel magazine she'd been perusing. Her annoyance immediately turned into concern. "Are you okay?"

He managed a complete sentence this time, even though the plane was now barreling down the runway at breakneck speed. "Distract me."

"How?"

Damien gut rolled as the plane's wheels left the ground. He clutched at his armrest so hard that his knuckles instantly turned white. "Just do it. Please."

His "please" was an afterthought, but at least it was some kind of coherent thought. He took that as a good sign. He hadn't completely lost it if he was still able to consider Kari's feelings in the grip of intense fear.

For just a moment, she looked as panicked as he felt. Then she started talking, telling him stories about growing up with her two sisters and three brothers. For a moment, he envied her big, happy family, practically a "Brady Bunch" existence, but with a whole family instead of two halves. He'd have loved to have brothers and sisters.

Then she told him a little about some of the mean things Claire and Shannon, especially Claire, had done and said to her, and he was a little less jealous. Dare he believe she was giving him a clue about the root of her poor self-esteem?

As his mind raced off on that tangent, he congratulated himself on a successful distraction. He figured diversion would do the trick, since Cody had used it so effectively Saturday. There were advantages to being an amateur psychologist.

A torturous seven hours later, the plane touched down. He glanced over at his lovely wife. Even though she'd talked herself hoarse three or four hours ago, she was like the Energizer Bunny — still going and going. He now knew more about Kari's wonder years than he did about his own.

That wasn't the torturous part of the flight. No, he'd actually enjoyed hearing more about what Kari had been like growing up. It helped him better understand what made his complex and confusing wife tick.

No, it was the air travel itself he found excruciating. Even the sedative effect of the pills and vodka couldn't make the agony of takeoff bearable.

But that was over — at least for now. Now he had a couple of days to recover and steel himself for the next flight.

He put a finger to her lips. "You can stop now. Thank you."

****

Kari stole a moment to savor the jolt of awareness that shot through her at his touch. However, she didn't have time to get turned on, not until she was sure Damien wasn't going to freak out on her. "Are you sure you'll be okay?"

Damien nodded. "Now that we're back on solid ground, I'll be fine."

Her heart plummeted. He didn't know they still had a connecting flight to catch. Judging by the way he'd been acting, she was afraid of that. "Didn't you look at the itinerary I gave you?"

This time, he shook his head. "I was too nervous about the flight to pay attention to the details."

"Then you don't know."

Damien frowned. "Know what?"

"This is Anchorage. We catch a connection here to Fairbanks."

All the blood drained from her husband's face. When his

face was whiter than a cotton T-shirt fresh out of the package, he spoke. "I have to get on another plane? Today?"

Kari nodded, wishing he'd bothered to pay at least a little attention to those pesky details.

"Can't we just rent a car?"

Now Kari was the one shaking her head. "Sorry. It's a six-hour drive, but only a one-hour flight."

A little of the color returned to his face. "No problem. I'll do the driving."

She eyed Damien skeptically. "After that long on a plane, you're up to driving another six-plus hours to get to our hotel?"

"I am."

Kari was still reluctant. "Won't we get put on some kind of terrorist watch list if we don't take our connecting flight?"

Damien wrinkled his forehead. "When does it leave?"

She checked her watch. "In forty-five minutes."

"Then let's go ask someone at the ticket counter."

After asking several airline employees and getting no satisfactory answer — all they would say was "you *might* get put on the TSA's no-fly list" — Damien turned to Kari. The scowl on his face spoke volumes.

"I guess we'd better get to the gate, then." He took off.

Kari bit her lip and raced to catch up with him. "I'm sorry, Damien."

He stopped and looked at her. His eyes were troubled. "It's not your fault I didn't read the itinerary, you know."

"I know that," she replied, confused. He thought she blamed herself for that? No. That was all on him. "But it *is* my fault that you had to fly to Alaska in the first place."

"I have to get over this ridiculous fear of flying sometime. Now's as good a time as any." Damien started walking again.

Kari hurried after him, glad her legs were long enough to keep up. As they made their way down the corridor, she studied his profile, wondering what had made him so afraid of airplanes.

Suddenly, he stopped again, looking thunderstruck. "Did you just say Cody told you I was afraid of flying?"

"About eight hours ago."

The corners of Damien's lips curled up almost imperceptibly. "I've been a little distracted."

"You told me to distract you!"

"And I appreciate your effort, sweetheart. I probably

wouldn't have made it through the first leg of our trip as easily as I did had you not been telling me about your early years." After a pause, he continued. "Cody did this at the apartment? In front of Sam?"

"Yes."

Damien groaned. "Great. Now everyone knows I'm a big chicken."

"There's nothing wrong with being afraid. Everyone's afraid of something." *Like me being terrified of getting close to you.*

"True enough." With that, he started down the hall yet again. "But most of us don't have to let the whole world in on our deepest fears."

He was right. Kari watched Damien for a few moments, admiring the way his butt looked in his jeans. Then she took off after him, vowing to herself that she'd make it up to him somehow.

Chapter Twenty-Six

"Finally!" Damien fell onto the queen-sized bed in their room at the Regency Fairbanks Hotel, relieved to be on firm ground at last. After lying there for several minutes, trying to gather his scattered wits, he sat up and looked around. Kari was still by the door, stowing her suitcase.

The room was a suite. The living area featured a cozy loveseat for two and the small kitchenette had a fridge, microwave, even a stovetop. He briefly wondered how much in-room cooking Kari was planning to do, but a glance inside the bathroom distracted him. There was a Jacuzzi tub in there, and it was big enough for two.

Immediately, his mind conjured a picture of himself and Kari putting that tub to good use. He shoved the image aside. Even though she was his wife, he had no right to expect her to act like they were married. He might be getting used to the union, but that didn't mean she was.

The picture popped back into his thoughts. He shook his head to clear it, and this time, it stayed cleared.

He had to hand it to Kari. If this swanky room was any indication, that wife of his really knew how to plan a trip.

"This is a great room."

She gifted him with one of her widest, brightest smiles as she approached. "I found this hotel online, and knew I had to stay here."

Damien found himself grinning back at her. He couldn't help himself. That sunny smile of hers was contagious. "I'm glad."

"Well, I didn't pick this room for myself. I was going to stay in one of the smaller rooms, but when I found out you'd be joining me, I upgraded us to the suite."

Her eyes went straight to the room's one bed and she froze, looking from it to him and back again. "I thought we were getting two regular beds."

He eyed Kari warily. Now she was back to wanting separate beds? When had that happened? His observation probably came out sharper than he intended. "I thought we'd already gotten past that."

When she sank onto the bed, looking like she was ready to burst into tears, Damien wondered if having Kari talk so much about her childhood had been such a good idea. She'd always been shy, sure. Now she seemed to be regressing into a mousy little thing right before his eyes.

He sat down beside her and put his arm around her shoulders, careful not to make her think he was trying to put any moves on her. "Sweetheart, if you really feel the need to have separate beds, we can switch to another room."

When Kari turned her head to look at him, her eyes brimmed with tears. "No, that's not what I want."

Damien felt himself relax slightly. She still trusted him — at least a little bit. "What do you want, then?"

He watched her take a few deep breaths, and when she looked at him again, she appeared much more calm and centered. "I think I'm just overtired after our long trip. Let's get some sleep."

"Now? In broad daylight?"

Kari giggled. "The rooms are equipped with room-darkening shades."

Damien supposed he did sound a little ridiculous. It wasn't as if he never napped in the daytime, after all, and that was *without* the help of room-darkening shades. "Okay, then. Let's get to bed."

He took heart when his innocent proposal, which admittedly sounded a lot more suggestive than he'd intended it to, didn't put a look of terror in his wife's doe eyes.

Instead, she smiled shyly and slipped her hand into his. "Thanks for understanding."

Damien made himself more comfortable on the bed, pulling Kari along with him. As she snuggled against him, he started to think that perhaps he did understand his puzzle of a wife just a little bit better this morning. With sisters who'd teased her mercilessly, it was no wonder she had a bit of an inferiority complex.

Soon, Kari's breathing deepened and evened out. Sure that she was asleep, Damien relaxed too. He fell asleep still trying to figure out exactly what made Kari tick.

****

The ringing cell phone awakened Kari several hours later. She groped for it, but it wasn't on the bedside table where it was supposed to be.

That was when Kari remembered she wasn't at home. She was in Alaska. With Damien lying beside her, snoring softly as her phone continued jingling.

Since it wasn't the "Funeral March," she knew it wasn't one of her sisters. It wasn't Bethany's ringtone, either.

She eased herself out of Damien's embrace and got out of bed. Then she crossed the room to her purse, which was sitting on the table in the dining area, and pulled the phone out of its pocket.

She glanced back at Damien, who was still dead to the world. She was willing to bet that he hadn't even heard the phone. Facing down his fear of flying — which, after seeing him on a plane, she no longer doubted was genuine — had really taken a lot out of him. The poor, dear man.

"Hello?" she asked, her voice groggy.

"Kari, it's Stacy."

She made a face. The cameraman's wife sounded way too chipper. "What time is it?"

"It's 3 p.m. Time to get some footage of the happy honeymooners enjoying the sights of the Land of the Midnight Sun. Sam and I are in the lobby."

Kari made another face at the phone. "Damien's still sleeping."

"Daylight's a-wasting."

She snorted, unmoved by that particular argument. "Since it is, as you just pointed out, the Land of the Midnight Sun, there's plenty of daylight to be had. It won't hurt to let my exhausted husband sleep a little longer."

"You can have two more uninterrupted hours," Stacy said. Her tone implied that she didn't believe for a minute that Kari and Damien had been sleeping. "But if you're not in the lobby at five, Sam and I are coming up to get you."

After disconnecting the call, Kari stuck her tongue out at the phone.

"Why does everyone seem to think Damien and I are having sex twenty-four-seven?" she wondered aloud.

"Maybe because we're newlyweds, and that's what newlyweds are supposed to do."

Kari looked over at Damien, who was propped on his side, his chin resting in his hand. She felt her cheeks grow hot. He wasn't supposed to hear that! And he certainly wasn't supposed to answer the rhetorical question. "Sorry I woke you."

"Don't be. I don't want to sleep away all our sightseeing time."

She wrinkled her nose at him as she strolled back toward the bed. "You don't have to lie to spare my feelings, Damien. I know you didn't really want to come to Alaska."

"Maybe not at first, but now that I'm here, I don't want to waste my time or yours."

Kari sat back down beside him, searching his face for signs of deception. She found none. Damien really was the kindest, most considerate man she'd ever met — nothing like he who would remain unnamed.

She trailed her index finger up his arm. "You know, I told Stacy we wouldn't be down until five."

Instantly, fire flickered in Damien's eyes. "I can think of a way to put two hours to good use."

Kari swallowed the frisson of fear that leapt to her throat. Ridiculous to be afraid of something she wanted, of something she'd started, even. Nope. She wasn't going to waste any more time letting fear ruin what could be the start of something beautiful.

With a boldness she'd never before summoned, she smiled — encouragingly, she hoped — and rose to strip off her shirt. With only a slight hesitation, she reached behind her back to unhook her bra. Her hands shook a little, but she managed to wrangle it open. She let it fall away, baring everything to her husband's gaze.

Kari stood there, biting her lip and feeling her cheeks grow warmer and warmer, as Damien devoured her with his eyes. She tried to see herself through his eyes, but all she could think about was how she'd been eating too much and exercising too little.

Finally, she couldn't stand the silence, or the not knowing what he was thinking, anymore. "You like?"

Damien reached out and settled his hands on her waist, pulling her back onto the bed. "I do. Very much so."

Relief washed over Kari in waves, cleansing away the memories of Rob telling her she was packing on a few too many pounds or, her least favorite phrase, "chunking up."

Arlene Hittle

She resolutely forced those thoughts back out of her head. They had no place in bed with her and Damien, not today and not ever again.

"I'm glad," she said, offering him another smile as she tentatively reached out to lay her hand on his chest.

His voice was both tender and firm when he replied. "I've told you before, you have a body that's meant to be worshipped."

Kari tried not to giggle, but she couldn't help it. She appreciated the sentiment behind his words, but he sounded ridiculous. "Thanks, I think."

Damien's eyes were serious. "Let me worship you."

Never breaking eye contact, Damien gathered her in his arms and touched his lips to hers. Instantly, she felt a spark of desire. No, it was more than a spark. An inferno raged through her as he kissed and cajoled, stroked and caressed his way from her lips downward.

He got to the still-fastened button on her jeans and paused, glancing up at her for permission to continue.

"Please."

Her single-word reply sounded breathless. It also sounded a little like begging, something she swore she'd never do again, but not enough to spoil the mood.

Damien unfastened her pants, and she raised her hips so he could pull them off. When she lay on the bed completely naked, she looked at him. Something was wrong with this picture. He was still fully clothed.

She put her hand on his wrist. "You should be naked, too."

"That can be arranged." He grinned and began to strip.

Kari watched as he took off first his shirt, then his pants. Knowing what she was about to see next, she waited, holding her breath.

There it was: Damien, in all his glory. She sighed happily. "You are magnificent."

His cheeks flushed and he nodded, but said nothing. Instead, he returned to the bed, covering her body with his. "Now we're even."

"Yes, we are," Kari agreed, relishing the feel of his weight on her. It felt so natural, so *right* to have these emotions, *this man* all over her.

It didn't take much for her to get swept back up in the

moment. As soon as Damien started kissing her again, the heat flared back to life. Fire burned low in her belly as she kissed him back, demanding as much as he did.

His magnificence nudged at her. Again being bolder than she'd ever been, Kari spread her thighs wider, encouraging him to take the plunge. She wanted so much to feel Damien buried to the hilt inside her. Finally ready to be honest with herself, she admitted she'd wanted it from the moment they'd met.

She arched her hips up to meet him, sighing with pleasure when he pushed into her. Their eyes were still locked together as he started moving inside her, slowly at first and then faster, building to a frenetic pace.

For a moment, Kari watched the shadows flickering through his eyes, wishing she knew what he was thinking. Then she lost all capability for coherent thought, concentrating instead on the delicious feelings spiraling through every inch of her body.

Everything tingled as Damien thrust into her. Harder. Faster. Then slow and sensual, then hard and fast again. She tore her gaze away from his eyes to watch the place where they joined together, fascinated by the sight of him plunging ever deeper into her.

He was tender yet forceful, demanding that she give him everything. And she did. Willingly. At the same time he shuddered to completion, she felt herself splinter apart.

Several minutes later, when her thoughts and all her limbs resettled into some semblance of normalcy, she found herself safe in Damien's arms. He had her spooned against him and his arms were loosely around her, his right hand splayed against her stomach.

She knew, without a doubt, that her life would never be the same. She was changed, completely and irrevocably, because this man loved her.

Oh, he might not have said the words yet, but Kari knew without a doubt that he loved her. He had to feel that way. He wouldn't be able to make love like that if he didn't.

Kari snuggled deeper into his embrace and drifted off, feeling safe and secure.

****

Bang! Bang! Bang!

Damien cracked open one eye at the sound. "What the—?"

He trailed off as he caught sight of his watch. It was 5:05, which undoubtedly meant that Sam and Stacy were the ones clamoring to come in.

"Just a minute," he called out crossly. Then he gave Kari a gentle shake. "Sweetheart, wake up. The wolves are at the door."

She stirred and stretched languidly, obviously still satisfied by their recent activities. She offered him a shy smile. "Hi, there."

That reserved little smile — so at odds with the uninhibited way she'd responded mere hours ago — made Mr. Happy stir to life. He longed to show Kari she had nothing to be shy about.

Damien bit back a groan. He wanted nothing more than to keep his lovely wife in bed so they could finally enjoy the honeymoon they hadn't gotten to have, but he knew Sam and Stacy would soon talk their way into the room if he didn't willingly open the door to them.

"You'd better get dressed," he told her as he climbed out of bed. He hated to do it, but it was necessary.

Her smile faltered as she looked from the spot where Damien had been until moments ago to where he now stood. She sounded forlorn. "You don't—"

Shit! He lunged back onto the bed and guided her hand to his swelling cock. The last thing he wanted was for what she perceived to be rejection to set them back another several weeks. Now that he'd gotten a taste of the heaven he could find between Kari's thighs, he'd hate to be denied again.

He shuddered as her fingers tentatively curled around him, fluttering over the sensitive skin. Gathering his wits, he forced his attention back to the dilemma at hand. "I very much do," he assured her softly. "Unfortunately for both of us, Sam and Stacy don't—" Another round of banging on the door kept him from finishing his sentence. "See? There they are now." He raised his voice. "Just a minute!"

Stacy's sharp reply rang through the door: "Your minutes are up, buddy. You're not on the unlimited plan."

Kari checked her watch and groaned. "It *is* after five."

"I think we both fell asleep."

As soon as he said it, he wanted to kick himself for stating the obvious. He sounded completely witless! However, Kari didn't seem to notice. Maybe she was still a bit witless herself, after sharing such a profound sexual experience. Damien couldn't remember lovemaking ever being so intense.

Instead of replying, Kari merely climbed out of bed and

started to put her clothes back on. Jeans in hand, she looked into his eyes and grinned. "Don't look so glum, Damien. Sam and Stacy can't follow us around twenty-four-seven. We'll lose 'em later and come back to christen the hot tub."

Something primal inside Damien responded to that mischief in her eyes. His voice dropped half an octave as his cock stiffened even more. "I'm going to hold you to that promise."

****

They tried — hard — to shake the camera crew. Ultimately, though, they were unsuccessful. Having lost more than twelve hours to travel time on separate planes, Sam and Stacy pushed hard to get enough footage for the next episode of "Just Married."

That meant he and Kari had to spend the next several hours — from 5:30 that night to 1:30 the next morning — playing up to the cameras. They browsed some of the shops in Fairbanks, shared a late dinner at one of the city's six fine dining establishments and took a midnight stroll in broad daylight.

"They might call it reality TV, but I don't see how any of this is real," he grumbled to Kari at one point, after Sam had finished posing them in front of a statue of a moose.

"You mean you wouldn't normally want your photo taken with—" She paused to turn and read the statue's plaque. " — Mortimer the Moose?"

The grin on his face belied the small, sad shake of his head. "I'd look much manlier in front of a statue of a bear, don't you think?"

Kari giggled. "Definitely."

After they finished filming next to Mortimer the Moose, they headed back to the hotel. They parted ways with Sam and Stacy in the lobby, promising to meet again the next day.

On the elevator, finally alone again, Kari slipped her hand into his.

Still holding hands, he and Kari made their way down the suddenly too-long corridor to their room. He wrestled the hotel key card out of his pocket with his free hand and shoved it in the door, glad when it worked the first time.

Kari pulled the door shut behind her and sagged against it for the briefest of moments. Then she straightened up and beamed at him. "Alone at last."

"That we are."

He waited, unsure what Kari was going to do next. He never quite knew what to expect from his lovely wife. When she stepped away from the door and stripped off her shirt, revealing her lacy, pink bra, Damien sent a quick thank-you heavenward for the gift he was about to receive — again. He couldn't wait to unwrap it. "I'll go fire up the hot tub."

It took him a few minutes to find the on switch and get the hot tub going. When he returned to Kari, eager to finish what they'd barely started, she was snoring on the bed. She hadn't even managed to finish undressing — one pant leg was off, one was on.

Sighing, Damien fell into bed beside her. He let himself wallow in disappointment for a moment before his eyelids, too, grew heavy.

As he sailed off to dreamland, Kari turned toward him, seeking the warmth he was only too happy to provide. He gathered her close, tucking her head under his chin. She made a contented sound and snuggled even closer.

Damien chose to take it as another good sign.

Chapter Twenty-Seven

Damien stood in the shadow of majestic Mount McKinley. It was truly a magnificent sight, with craggy snow-covered peaks jutting into the clouds.

However, he wasn't thinking much about the scenery. No, Damien was too distracted by his wife. His mind kept replaying their encounter that morning — any man's fantasy. Kari awakened as hungry for him as he'd been for her. Moments later, she straddled his waist and welcomed him to his personal heaven.

He closed his eyes, relishing the memory of plunging into her tight, wet sheath. He recalled how it felt to slide into her.

"Shit!"

"Something wrong?" Kari eyed him with what looked like alarm. Small wonder. The exclamation did seem out of place in the face of such majesty.

He slanted a sideways glance at Sam and muttered one word: "Bathroom." Being the only place the camera couldn't access, it had become their code for "We'll talk about it later, alone."

Her eyes searched his for a moment. Then she slipped her hand into his, smiling at him trustingly.

Her expression made him feel like even more of a heel. She apparently had faith in him, and he'd already violated that trust by forgetting all about safe sex.

How could he have been so stupid?

Sure, they were married, and married couples didn't usually worry about using condoms. But as much as he'd like to pretend it was forever, Kari had given him no indication that she wanted to stay married after the three-month cohabitation period ended.

Unless she was telling him that with every shy smile, every glance in his direction, every increasingly bold action. Kari truly was blooming these days, becoming less timid and surer of herself. Maybe it was because she'd realized she loved him and wanted to be with him forever.

Damien snorted. Surely *that* was wishful thinking. His life couldn't go that smoothly. He'd always had to work harder than that for what he wanted, from relationships to veterinary school.

It was better that he wait for her to tell him explicitly, in real words, that she wanted this to last.

Suddenly, Kari nudged him out of his thoughts with a whisper. "Bear."

Did she just say bear? "Excuse me?"

She pointed and his eyes followed her finger. Not one but two bears were frolicking a few hundred feet off the trail. Cubs, by the look of them. He enjoyed the sight of them while Kari snapped a few photos with her digital camera.

But as the bears gamboled ever nearer to Sam, whose camera was trained on him and Kari, Damien thought it best to warn him.

He turned to the cameraman. "I know you said to pretend you're invisible, but you might want to know there are bear cubs coming your way."

Sam turned away from Kari and Damien, training the camera on the cubs. Just then, another, much larger, bear came crashing through the underbrush.

"Oh my God," Kari squealed. "I think that's mamma bear."

Glad he'd taken time on the park tour bus to read the pamphlet on bear encounters, Damien took charge. "Do not run. None of us can outrun a bear; they run faster than even Olympic sprinters. We need to wait and see what she's going to do."

The three of them watched the bear for a few moments. She seemed to be keeping an eye on the curious cubs. After swiping at something on the ground, they bounded off toward the forest. Mamma bear wandered after them.

Kari exhaled loudly. "That was close."

"It was," he agreed. "I'm just glad she didn't seem to notice us."

"Why's that?"

Damien grinned. "We would have looked pretty silly backing away slowly while we waved our arms over our heads. And Sam would have had to drop the camera to join us."

"Who says that'd be such a bad thing?" Kari asked, giggling.

Damien had to admit she had a point. "But the network would probably deduct that from our pay."

She waved her hand. "A small price to pay for a little extra alone time, don't you think?"

BLIND DATE BRIDE

Damien's heart leapt. Yes, he definitely did think. Now, if only he was sure Kari felt the same way — for good, not just for the moment — they could be on their way to building a lasting relationship.

****

Kari didn't dwell on Damien's strange exclamation or the near-encounter with bears that followed it. She was too busy enjoying her Alaskan vacation. She was actually relishing the sweeping vistas and closeness to nature more than she'd thought she would.

Maybe that was because she was visiting in summertime. She wouldn't be enjoying it nearly as much if she were experiencing endless darkness and a daytime temperature in the single digits.

Her unexpected delight in her trip was more likely due to the company. She slanted a glance at Damien. The husband she hadn't even known she wanted might turn out to be the best thing ever to happen to her.

It certainly was the best escapade Bethany had ever gotten her into — far superior to the time Beth talked her into running a half-marathon for a charity that turned out not to exist (they'd both been duped), or the time she'd bullied Kari into the worst double date of her life. They saw her date, who'd seemed much more interested in Bethany's boobs than in anything Kari had to say, in the campus police blotter a week later, after he'd been caught peeping in the windows of one of the sorority houses.

She quickly shoved that thought aside. That guy wasn't worth remembering. Neither, for that matter, was Rob. She snapped the rubber band on her wrist when his name came up. That reaction was automatic now.

However, it was coming up less and less often now that she and Damien were intimate. Making love to her husband truly had changed her; for the better, she liked to think.

She certainly felt different. Bolder. Stronger, somehow. Ready to stand up to pushy people, even her siblings. And she had being with Damien to thank.

She smiled to herself. Her family might not thank him, but she would every day for the rest of her life, if he'd let her.

Starting now, right here on the tour bus. She slipped her hand into Damien's, which rested in his lap, and leaned over to give him a peck on the cheek. "Thank you."

Arlene Hittle

He looked surprised. "For what?"

Not ready to articulate all the warm, fuzzy feelings she was having, Kari shrugged. "For being you."

Watching him scan the bus for Sam and his camera, she was again thankful that she'd decided to visit Alaska in summer, its peak tourist season. With the bus filled to capacity, the cameraman had been unable to sit near them, so they had relative privacy, as much as could be had on a bus full of tourists.

Damien must have decided they could have that bathroom chat now, because his countenance suddenly turned grim. "I'm not all that, you know."

"Sure you are." What had gotten into him? Usually, he took compliments better than that. She was the one who struggled to accept the nice things he said to her.

"You wouldn't say that if you realized—" He lowered his voice ever further to whisper. "—we haven't been following the rules of safe sex."

Kari gasped. He was right. Condoms had been the furthest thing from her mind yesterday and this morning, when she woke up craving Damien's touch. She wanted nothing more than to feel him buried deep inside of her.

"By the sound of it, I can tell you hadn't thought of that yet." His voice was dry.

Kari nodded. "But it's okay."

"How can it be okay? We're just beginning to get to know each other; we can't bring a child into the world yet."

There was real anguish in Damien's voice, she marveled. This was something new. In her admittedly limited experience, men didn't worry about unintended consequences of their bedroom antics. She squeezed his hand. "Really, Damien. It's okay. I'm on the pill."

"You are?"

She nodded again. She'd started taking it back in college, for the creep she refused to name. Even though she hadn't dated anyone seriously since then, she continued taking it — at first out of habit and later because she was eternally optimistic, hoping that one of her geeky accountant coworkers would turn out to be Mr. Right.

Since marrying Damien, she hadn't skipped a single day. Knowing how attracted she was to him, she wasn't about to slip up. Now she was extra glad for her vigilance. She didn't want a baby right now any more than he did.

Not that she was going to tell him any of that. As her husband, it was probably something he ought to know, but she still wasn't ready to share the sordid details of her past. She settled for a simple declaration. "I'm not ready to be pregnant, either."

Damien grinned. "Then we're agreed. We need to spend time getting to know each other before baby makes three."

"Definitely."

****

Once Kari knew she didn't need Alaska to deliver her the man of her dreams, the trip continued to be more than she'd hoped for — their virtual honeymoon.

In the charming seaside town of Sitka, she gladly gave up the flightseeing tour that she knew Damien would hate. Instead, they took a two-and-a-half-hour kayak tour of the harbor and islands. She had to deem it an unqualified success. Their kayak didn't overturn once, and even though her arms felt like Jell-O afterward, the spectacular views justified all the hard labor.

When they got to Anchorage, the last stop on their Alaskan tour, Kari was more than tired. She was completely and utterly exhausted. Long hours of sightseeing, capped with hours of bedroom acrobatics, left little time for actual sleep.

Not that she'd have traded that time with Damien for anything, but as she collapsed on the bed at the Hilton in downtown Anchorage, she acknowledged that she needed a few hours of uninterrupted shuteye.

So when Damien lay down beside her and nuzzled her neck, Kari pushed him away.

"Something wrong?"

She shook her head, and then nodded. "I can't. I just need to sleep."

He checked his watch. "It's two in the afternoon."

"But it feels like two in the morning," Kari countered. The midnight sun wasn't as great as it sounded in the brochures, because it was wreaking havoc on her circadian rhythms.

Apparently reading her mind, Damien said, "You're going to have to get back on a regular sleep schedule sometime in the next three days."

She sighed. "I know, but not today. Right now, I just need sleep. Please."

Arlene Hittle

Damien's eyes searched her face, and she hoped he could read the message she was trying to send. She wasn't rejecting him, not at all; she was just tired. Bone tired. The kind of tired she hadn't felt since pulling three back-to-back all-nighters during finals week her junior year of college.

Finally, he nodded. "Okay. I'm going to head downstairs to the hotel bar."

She wanted to tell Damien she'd rather he stay with her, but she knew that wasn't fair to him. If he weren't sleepy, he'd be bored as hell sitting in the room staring at the walls, not wanting to turn on the TV for fear of disturbing her while she slept.

Better that he go explore. Besides, Sam and Stacy would be ecstatic because they'd have something to shoot. The thought made Kari grin as she waved to Damien. "Have fun."

She relaxed into the pillows and was asleep almost before the door thumped shut on his backside.

When she awakened, she felt a hundred percent better: refreshed, alert and ready to find something to do. She checked her watch, which read 7 p.m.

She chuckled. "That's what a five-hour nap will do for a girl."

Looking around the room, she realized that Damien was still gone. She hoped he hadn't spent five hours in the hotel bar getting drunk. Though she'd only seen him drunk once, when Cody brought him home, and he hadn't done anything too out of line, she didn't like him that way. She preferred it when he was in complete control of his faculties.

She swung her legs off the bed. "Best to find out now, before he has time to do any more damage."

Kari rummaged in her suitcase until she found the pick for her hair. As she unsnarled the tangles that had formed while she slept, she wondered if perhaps it was time for a haircut. Sometimes — like now, when she wanted to be on her way — all this hair of hers was more trouble than it was worth.

Her hair finally put in some semblance of order, she made her way to the elevator and pushed "L" for lobby. When the elevator dinged and the doors whooshed open, Kari stepped out, glad to be on solid ground again. Elevators weren't her favorite place in the world, especially when she was in them alone.

The hotel bar, Bruins, was easy to find. Once inside, however, Damien was not. By rights he should have been. Just look for Sam and his camera. However, Sam was nowhere to be found. Maybe he'd decided five hours was too long to spend shooting in a bar.

She scanned the room once and then twice before spotting someone who resembled her husband in a dark corner. But it couldn't be Damien. This guy was with a short, curvaceous brunette.

As she watched, the brunette with the sleek pixie haircut put her hand on his shoulder and giggled. It was Damien, she realized as he laughed along with her. She'd know that laugh anywhere.

Bile rushed to Kari's throat, leaving a sour taste in her mouth, and something deep inside her — her womb, maybe — contracted painfully. This was what happened when she told Damien "no" just once? He rushed out and found someone else to give him what she was too tired to give?

This was her worst nightmare. She'd let herself trust Damien and now he was betraying her. How could she have been so wrong about him?

She backed toward the exit, strangely fascinated by the scene in front of her and unable to tear her gaze away. The tears that had sprung to her eyes made Damien and his companion blur into one big blob.

I have to get out of here before he sees me. She picked up her pace.

Oh, God. It was too late. The blur that was Damien rose and walked in her direction.

"Kari, sweetheart! I'm glad you're finally awake."

She gaped at him. Was he kidding?

"I want you to meet someone."

He had to be joking. Why would she want to meet her replacement? Still, she let him hook his arm around her waist and propel her toward the corner where the brunette waited. She was too shell-shocked to protest.

The other woman stood when they approached, extending her hand in greeting.

"Hi! I'm Stella."

Reluctantly, Kari shook Stella's hand. Where had Sam gotten off to? Surely this would be the kind of scene that would make great TV. Viewers would love to see her most humiliating moment onscreen.

Arlene Hittle

Damien's voice was low in her ear. "Sweetheart, are you okay?"

She looked at him, surprised to see real concern in his eyes. Why did he care? "Fine."

The look he leveled at her said he didn't believe her for a minute. "Stella went to college with Cody and me. She was our third Musketeer, so to speak. I completely forgot she moved to Alaska."

Stella's laugh tinkled through the air. "And you could have knocked me over with a feather when I came in here for a drink after work and saw Damien sitting at the bar, watching a Cubs game. I thought I was seeing a ghost!"

Relief washed over Kari in giant, soothing waves. She glanced over at Damien and knew she probably wasn't imagining the mild reproach in his eyes. She deserved it, jumping to the worst conclusion possible. What had he done to deserve such an appalling lack of faith? Nothing, that was what.

She giggled nervously as she slid into the booth beside Damien. "You don't want to know what I thought I was seeing."

Damien raised an eyebrow. "Oh, I think I have a pretty good idea."

"Me, too," Stella chimed in. "It'd be the first thing on my mind if I saw a gorgeous blonde like you with my Hank."

"Hank?" She was too curious to know who Hank was to object to how the striking brunette had just called *her* gorgeous.

"My husband. He should be here any minute."

Damien squeezed Kari's thigh, a move she found reassuring. She certainly didn't deserve such quick forgiveness after thinking the worst of him, but she was glad he gave it. She flashed him a smile.

"Stella and Hank offered to take us out to dinner at their favorite local seafood place, Glacier Brewhouse," he said. "I was going to let you sleep until eight, then come wake you so we could head over for a 9 p.m. reservation. It's just a few blocks from here."

They chatted for a few more minutes until Stella waved at a lanky Alaskan Native who'd just walked into the bar. His eyes lit up as he ambled their way. Kari briefly wondered if Damien would ever look at her with that kind of delight.

Not if you don't stop jumping to conclusions. Kari gave the tramp a mental shove and vowed to stop dwelling on her mistake. If Damien had already forgiven her for the lapse of faith, the least she could do was forgive herself.

Stella made the introductions. "Hank, this is my friend, Damien Walker, and his new bride, Kari. Guys, meet Hank."

Hank smiled, revealing perfectly straight, white teeth. "Stella's told me about some of your college exploits."

"All greatly exaggerated, I'm sure," Damien said, chuckling. "Stella told me you're a dentist."

That explained his perfect teeth. Kari grinned to herself and listened as Hank talked a little about his job. When she checked her watch, it read 8:20. "Um … if we have a reservation for nine, I'd better run back upstairs to freshen up."

When she stood, Damien jumped up, too. "I'll go with her. We'll be right back."

Once they were in the elevator, Kari leaned against the wall. "You didn't have to follow me. I trust you."

Damien grinned lazily as he looped his arms around her neck and tugged her closer. "Now that Hank's here, maybe."

"Well—"

He silenced her with a kiss. When he pulled away, he said, "I saw the look on your face when you first saw me, Kari."

"Sorry."

"You don't have to apologize." He paused to rest his forehead against hers, his lips just inches away from hers. "I kind of like knowing you care enough to get jealous."

Do I ever, she thought. She wasn't about to admit exactly how jealous she'd gotten, but she had a feeling Damien already knew.

She lunged forward, closing the almost infinitesimal distance between his lips and her own. By the time the elevator doors opened, she was so lost in Damien's kiss that she didn't notice.

His hand shot out as the doors were about to close again. He pulled away, giving her an apologetic look. "This is our floor."

Kari grinned sheepishly and followed Damien down the hall toward their room. "I'm glad one of us is paying attention. How embarrassing would it be to end up back in the lobby, locked in an embrace?"

"Totally." He nodded.

"Speaking of getting caught, where's Sam this evening?" It wasn't that she really wanted the cameraman tagging along, but she didn't want the hassle they'd get from the network if they didn't let him in on their plans.

Damien waved as he pushed open the door to their room. "After about an hour of filming me nursing a beer while watching the Cubs game, he declared me 'insufferably boring' and went to his room to catch a few Zs of his own." He paused to grin. "Had he waited another few minutes, he'd have caught Stella's arrival."

Kari giggled. "Sam's poor timing is good luck for us."

"Unfortunately, we won't be camera-free much longer. After Stella issued the invitation, I called up to the room and left a message with Stacy about our dinner plans. She and Sam will meet us there."

She quashed annoyance that Stacy knew about their dinner plans before she did. Damien was only trying to give her what she'd asked for — a chance to catch up on her sleep.

Kari made a beeline for the bathroom sink, where she misted her curls with water. She stared at the mass of wild ringlets before trying to twist it into some semblance of order.

"I really should do something with this hair," she grumbled when, after five minutes of fussing, it still looked as if it had been styled with an eggbeater.

Damien came up behind her and snaked his arms around her waist. He nuzzled her neck. "I love those untamed curls."

She felt a rush of warmth for how Damien always seemed to know the right thing to say. "Thanks."

"You're welcome. Ready to go?"

Kari waffled. "Maybe I should change."

"You look beautiful, but change if it'll make you feel better." He released her and she retrieved a fresh pink T-shirt and pair of shorts from her suitcase. A few minutes later, she was ready, at least as ready as possible with a rat's nest of curls.

She wondered why the hair she'd loved for years was suddenly more curse than blessing. But she didn't have time to dwell on that right now, when she was about to have dinner with one of Damien's oldest friends.

Friend? Really? A part of her, the part that increasingly wouldn't be silenced, seriously doubted that.

Moreover, if Damien and Stella had once had a fling, she had a right to know. But how could she find out without sounding like a jealous monster?

As Kari followed him back to the elevator, she kept her tone casual. "Stella's gorgeous."

"Hmm?" His eyes on her chest, Damien seemed distracted. "I suppose so."

That was all he was going to give her? Kari frowned. The subtle approach obviously wasn't working here.

She put her thumb under his chin, directing his blue gaze upward, to her eyes. "Since you're not taking the hint, I'm going to just come out and ask: Did you and Stella ever date?"

Chapter Twenty-Eight

Damien's laugh filled the elevator chamber. He knew her question had been a serious one, but damn, her gutsiness had taken him completely by surprise.

His meek little mouse of a wife was turning into quite the tigress, and he liked it a lot. She was becoming the woman he'd thought she was from the start: beautiful, poised and assertive. *This* Kari he could definitely see rocking that strip-aerobics workout video he'd found in their entertainment center.

She narrowed her eyes at him. "Well?"

With difficulty, Damien wiped the smile off his face. Jealous or not, she deserved a straight answer. "No, Stella and I were never attracted to one another like that. She had a bit of a thing for Cody, but even though she seemed to be just his type — a curvy brunette — they never clicked romantically." He lowered his voice to a whisper. "I'm pretty sure Cody thought she was gay."

"Stella?" Kari snorted. "How could he be that dumb?"

Damien shrugged. He personally couldn't see how anyone could mistake the bubbly brunette for a lesbian, either, but Cody had remained convinced for two years. "People usually see what they want to see. I think Cody needed her to be gay at that time in his life."

"Really? Why?"

Damien shrugged again. That story wasn't his to tell. It belonged to Cody. "I've said too much on that subject already. You'll have to ask Cody."

Kari suddenly stretched up on tiptoe to peck him on the cheek. "Thank you."

Curiosity and wariness warred inside him. He wasn't used to hearing those words from her, yet she'd been uttering them frequently these last few days. "What for?"

"For defending Cody's secrets when he's not around to do it for himself," she said. "You're a good friend."

"I try, but he doesn't always make it easy."

Kari laid her hand on his upper arm. "They never do."

Damien's skin heated where her fingers touched it. He stifled a groan. He and Kari were about to have dinner with friends, not jump into bed, so it was ridiculous for Mr. Happy to be stirring.

The elevator doors opened. Damien jumped at the chance to put a little distance between himself and the sweet little temptress that was his wife. He didn't want to walk back into the bar with an erection.

He took several swift steps alone and then realized how odd it would look if he and Kari arrived separately. He paused to let her catch up, all the while telling himself to think about something less sexy, something like the Cubs' loss that afternoon. That, coupled with a quick adjustment, dampened his ardor quickly enough, and soon the four of them were seated at a table at Glacier Brewhouse.

Kari perused the menu for a few minutes before she laid it on the table and looked around. "Everything looks delicious. You're the regulars here. What do you recommend?"

"That's easy: fish. The halibut and salmon are both fantastic." Stella paused. "And you have to try the blue cheese salad. It's one of the house specialties."

Fish and salad weren't going to do it for Damien. He was scanning the menu for something a little more appealing when Hank made a recommendation of his own. "I always get the prime rib and king crab."

Now *that* was something Damien could sink his teeth into. His mouth started to water at the thought of a nice, tender steak and fresh crab legs.

Kari decided on the herb-crusted halibut, and they ordered calamari to share. Dessert was what the restaurant billed as its world-famous bread pudding or, as Kari described it, heaven in a bowl.

"Everything was delicious," Kari said as they walked back to the hotel. "Thanks for inviting us."

"Thank you for agreeing to come," Stella replied. "I've enjoyed catching up with Damien and getting to know you."

Damien found himself nodding. It really had been great to see Stella again. How could he have let himself lose touch with her when she'd once played such a big part in his life? "Let's not wait so long to catch up next time."

In the hotel lobby, he and Kari exchanged email addresses

with Stella and Hank. As they rode up in the elevator, he watched Kari's face, trying to get a handle on how she really felt about the evening.

Once she'd realized he and Stella had no romantic interest in one another, she'd seemed to relax and enjoy the evening. Still, he wondered if she was holding back, waiting for a chance to hurl this back at him later.

That was what his ex would have done. He could apologize for a wrong and go about his business, blithely thinking all was forgiven until days, weeks or even months later, when Teena threw whatever it was back at him, usually in the heat of an argument.

God, he was glad Kari didn't hold a grudge like that. With her, what he saw was what he got. She couldn't hide her feelings from him if she tried. Her thoughts, perhaps, but not her feelings.

He watched his wife closely until her cheeks flushed pink and she turned her head away, letting the hair that had come loose from its twist curtain her features.

However, Kari didn't stay in hiding for long. A split second later, she turned back to him, stretching up on tiptoe to plant a kiss on his lips. When she pulled away, her voice was throaty. "I'm ready to be worshipped."

Even though the giggle that bubbled from her throat immediately afterward somewhat spoiled the words' effect, Damien was all too happy to comply.

Sweeping Kari off her feet, he carried her to their room and deposited her on the king-sized bed. Then he stripped off her clothes and made love to her slowly, telling her with every stroke and caress how important she was to him. He wanted her to feel cherished and loved.

****

When Kari opened her eyes the next morning, Damien was caressing her breast. A shiver of anticipation ran through her as his thumb brushed over her nipple, bringing it to a peak.

"Mmm. That feels nice."

"She lives!" Damien's tone was light. "I was starting to wonder if you were ever going to wake up."

She turned to face him and grinned, ready to free her inner tramp. The less control she tried to exert over the slut inside her, the easier she was finding it to relax and enjoy their sexual play.

And with Damien, it was definitely play. Sure, it had its

serious moments, but there was always an undercurrent of fun. She liked that she felt safe enough to enjoy herself.

She let loose a giggle. "Maybe you just needed to try a little harder."

"Like this?" He guided her hand to his erection.

Her fingers curled around its length, sliding over velvet steel. "That's a good start."

She relished the way he grew even larger as she stroked him, filling her hand. The place between her thighs dampened, and she unhesitatingly straddled Damien's waist, ready to accept him.

Kari gasped as he plunged into her. Right away, he tensed up and his eyes filled with concern. "Too much?"

She shook her head, offering what she hoped was an encouraging smile. "I can never get enough of you."

Damien relaxed again and Kari moved her hips in a slow circle.

He groaned. "Keep that up and I won't last long."

Kari smiled again, relishing the position she was in. On top, she held all the power. She got to set the pace; she was in control. That made exposing the flab he didn't seem to mind anyway well worth the risk.

Control firmly in hand, she rode him until they were both fulfilled. Then, with Damien still inside her, she collapsed on top of him. Her ear to his chest, she listened as his heartbeat slowed.

She lay there as he stroked her hair with his free hand. His other arm was draped over her waist, anchoring her to him. She wouldn't be able to move even if she had the energy to go anywhere.

Kari took a moment to marvel at that. It was as if he couldn't get enough of her, either. Good.

Feeling safe, comfortable and completely cherished, she'd nearly drifted back to sleep when Damien mumbled something that sounded like "love you."

Immediately alert again, Kari froze. Did he just say what she thought he said?

She cracked one eye open to see the look on his face, but that was no help. He seemed to be sleeping as soundly as she'd been about to be before he'd awakened her with his declaration.

Still stunned by what she thought she heard, Kari rolled off Damien, who mumbled a sleepy protest. He loved her? Even with all her hang-ups?

Impossible.

Not impossible, she corrected herself as she watched Damien slumber — the untroubled sleep of someone who knew his place in the world. Highly improbable, maybe. But definitely not impossible.

She took a deep breath. Then, sure he was sleeping and wouldn't hear what she wasn't quite ready to tell him, tested the words on her tongue. "I love you, too."

"There. That wasn't so hard," she told herself.

No, it wasn't difficult at all to say those words to Damien and mean them wholeheartedly. And that in itself frightened her more than she could say.

****

Later that morning, Kari was enjoying some alone time at the mall in downtown Anchorage.

Okay, she wasn't really alone. Stacy trailed her, a small camera in hand. Stacy and Sam had encouraged her and Damien to spend a little time doing their own thing because, as Sam explained, "all that mushy gunk makes for boring TV."

Kari giggled to herself. Damien watching a ballgame was boring; so was their happy togetherness. There was no pleasing Sam unless they were embarrassing themselves.

She was willing to bet people watching at the mall wasn't going to rate any higher on Sam's scale than Damien's Cubs game. Tough, because that was what she wanted to do. At least Damien was doing something interesting. Hank was taking him fishing.

She wandered the corridors, window-shopping, until she came to a trendy salon. Her hand flew to her hair. Yep. It was still a curly mess, the same way it had been for about a decade. Some products worked better than others, but none of them truly tamed her unruly mop.

"Why have I put up with this all these years?"

As she watched two women leave the salon, each with adorable short hair, her mind flashed back to Stella's cute pixie style. Suddenly, she couldn't think of a single reason to hold onto her long blond curls.

She turned to Stacy. "I'm going in."

"I'll be right behind you."

When Kari pushed open the door, her ears were

immediately assaulted by cutting-edge hip-hop music.

What did you expect from a salon named Cutz?

Kari brushed away her doubts and approached the counter. "Is someone available to cut my hair?" she asked the young brunette whose hair was cut in an asymmetric wedge.

"Sure. Wait here."

The brunette disappeared behind a black screen. She came back seconds later. "Franc will be right with you."

Less than a minute ticked by before a man appeared at her side. His name tag said "Frank," but the receptionist had pronounced it like the former French currency.

When he smiled at her, she was struck by his resemblance to Kevin Bacon. "What are you wanting done with your beautiful blond locks?"

Kari gulped. Was she really about to put her head in the hands of someone with questionable style sense? Frank was wearing black leather pants and a loose white button-down shirt unbuttoned practically to his waist.

At least he has nice hair, her conscience pointed out. True enough. His well-kept sandy brown hair was just long enough to give him a slightly dangerous look — an image her inner tramp embraced.

"Surprise me." The tramp's words were out of her mouth, hanging in the air, before she could stop them.

Behind her, Stacy gasped, but Frank didn't look surprised. He stroked his chin thoughtfully. "You'd like it fairly short, no?"

"No," she echoed. Then she shook her head. "I mean yes. Cut as much as you think you should — just so long as I don't end up looking like a fuzzy blond Q-tip."

Kari's cheeks grew hot as Frank's eyes swept up and down her body. "My dear, you will look fabulous no matter what I do to you."

She straightened her spine. She wanted to be clear. "That may be, but I still don't want to be forced to rock a Q-tip look."

"Don't worry. When I'm done, you'll look marvelous."

Kari managed to stay calm as the stylist shampooed her hair, treating her to the most relaxing scalp massage she'd ever had. She kept her eyes closed as Frank started to snip away, knowing she'd be better off not watching the transformation.

But when he was still cutting after what seemed like forever, she made the mistake of peeking at the floor. A small mountain of hair was piled around the chair.

She shifted in her seat. "Umm — maybe you should stop now."

Frank shook his head. "I am not yet finished."

Suddenly panicked at the result, Kari bolted.

"We have a runner!" Frank shouted. His scissors clattered to the floor as he took off after her.

Before she could make it to the door, a stout Alaskan Native woman stepped into her path. The woman spoke in soothing tones, as if Kari were a frightened wild animal. "Now, miss, Frank is good at what he does. You must let him finish what he has started. Frank will not let you down."

As she listened to the woman's calming voice, Kari felt sanity begin to return. She breathed in and out. Of course she couldn't leave with half a haircut. Well, she could if she truly did want to look ridiculous.

No, she had to suck it up and let Frank finish demolishing the blond hair it had taken her almost ten years to grow.

She let the woman guide her back to Frank's chair, where she offered him a sheepish smile. "Sorry about that."

Frank waved away her apology. "Do not worry. I understand it's traumatic to lose so much hair at once. It happens often. This is why we employ Juanita — precisely for these types of situations." He paused, beginning to snip again. "How long have you had your long, beautiful locks?"

"Almost a decade."

Kari's response was automatic, but something clicked when she said it. "Oh my God."

Frank's scissors stopped. "What is wrong?"

Kari shook her head. "Nothing." Or perhaps everything. She'd been growing out her hair ever since she left Rob. Was it significant that she was cutting it now, when she was finally shaking off his death grip on her heart and mind?

Making a mental note to ask Dr. Spaulding about that when she got back to Chicago, Kari closed her eyes again and tried to relax as she put her hair in Frank's capable hands.

What seemed like hours later, but was more like forty-five minutes when she checked her watch, Frank put down his scissors and clapped his hands.

"You can look now. It is done!"

Kari opened her eyes to a pleasant surprise. Now chin-length, her hair was full without being bushy. It fell from a center part in nice, orderly waves.

"How did you get it to behave like that?"

"It's all about the product, darling."

She groaned. "I've heard that before."

"But it is true, my dear. Good product makes any good cut better."

Kari shook her head adamantly. "I have lots of good product, Frank, but you saw my hair when I walked in."

The stylist shook his finger at her. "I said a 'good' cut. You need to fire your regular stylist."

Kari blushed. Despite their rocky start, she liked Frank, so she might as well fess up. "Umm, would you believe I haven't been to a salon in about three years?"

Frank raised both eyebrows. "People amaze me. No one would dream of working on their own car without knowing what they are doing, but they'll pick up a pair of scissors to trim their own hair without a qualm."

She shrugged. "I guess we all think we have enough expertise to undertake a little trim."

"But you rarely do." Frank shook his finger at her again. "Promise me you will not try to cut your own hair again."

Seeing what a skilled stylist could do with her hair, she wasn't all that tempted to muck it up on her own. Still, she couldn't commit to Frank. "But, Frank, I'm from Chicago. That's a long way to come for a trim."

The stylist waved. "I have friends in the Windy City. I will give you a recommendation."

Kari left the salon with the name and number of one of Frank's friends securely tucked in her purse and a bag of Frank's "most excellent" product in her hand.

Stacy flashed her a thumbs-up. "Lookin' good, Kari."

"Thanks."

As she continued exploring the mall, Kari found herself reaching up to play with what was left of her hair. She loved running her fingers through the short, tousled waves. Her head felt at least ten pounds lighter, but that was nothing compared to how much lighter her psyche was.

Shedding her hair was like discarding her past once and for all. She couldn't wait to get back to the hotel to show Damien the new Kari Walker. With that thought in mind, she waltzed into

Frederick's of Hollywood and bought a racy red negligee. It was something the old Kari never would have dared to wear, but now, powered by her recently freed inner vixen, she had just enough daring to pull it off.

At least she hoped so. If she succeeded, she and Damien would definitely enjoy their last night in Alaska. She envisioned an evening filled with strawberries, whipped cream and sex with her hunk of a husband.

****

"Alone at last!" Damien grumbled after bidding Sam goodbye in the hotel lobby. He sagged against the back of the elevator, glad that ordeal was over.

He never should have agreed to go fishing — not with Hank or with anyone else. It turned out he didn't like boating much more than flying.

Why he'd had no trouble kayaking in Sitka, he didn't know. All he knew was that getting on another boat was nearly as low on his list of things he enjoyed doing as getting back on an airplane tomorrow morning.

Somehow, between bouts of hurling over the side of the boat, he'd managed to catch a good-sized salmon. They'd had it cleaned, packed and shipped back to Chicago. It might actually beat him and Kari back to the apartment. He'd have to call Cody to go check at the appointed delivery hour.

When Damien got to the room, he swiped the key card and pushed open the door.

As tired as he was, a certain part of his anatomy stirred when he caught a glimpse of long, tanned, bare legs on the bed. He hurried over to the bed, his eyes skimming upward as he walked. The legs led to a pair of hips he'd know anywhere, flaring out from her trim waist.

He froze. Wait just a darn minute! That couldn't be his wife dressed — if you could call it that — in a barely there red lace teddy.

"Am I in the right room?"

The girlish giggle confirmed that it was, indeed, Kari lying practically naked on the bed. That was when his eyes focused on her face and he realized she had a lot less hair.

Gut-punched by her sheer beauty, Damien sucked in a breath. Sure, he'd always found her gorgeous, but now, with her hair framing her face instead of hiding it, everyone else would see it as clearly as he did.

Jealousy stabbed at him. What if he didn't want to share his wife with the world?

It occurred to him then that her transformation was complete. In the six weeks he'd known Kari, she'd gone from blushing almost-virgin bride to voluptuous vixen.

It was that vamp who boldly beckoned to him, crooking her finger. Her other hand held out a ripe, red strawberry. "Hungry?"

The slight quaver in her voice was the only hint that Kari might be less at ease than she looked. He marveled at how good she was getting at masking her fear.

Not that he wanted her to fear him, he amended. No, that was the last thing he wanted. Been there, done that, and he was elated she finally felt comfortable with him.

Damien nodded, wasting no time in stripping off his clothes and covering her body with his own. He nudged aside the small strip of cloth that didn't leave anything to the imagination, idly wondering where she'd gotten such a garment. Surely the mall didn't have a shop called Porn Stars R Us.

Yet there she was, looking like every man's fantasy. Damien threw a quick prayer heavenward, thanking his lucky stars that fate had thrown them together, and pushed into her. She arched her hips to meet him, and soon he was lost in the frenzied rhythm of love.

Later, as he cradled his sleeping sex kitten in his arms, Damien knew without a doubt that he never wanted to let her go. Not now … not six weeks from now. He wanted her at his side, forever.

Now, if only she felt the same way, they'd be set.

Chapter Twenty-Nine

"Kari! Your hair!"

Kari's hand flew up to the now-tame locks Bethany was seeing for the first time. "What? You don't like it?"

"No, it's not that," Bethany rushed to reassure her. "You look great. I was surprised, that's all. You should warn your best friend before you chop off a decade's worth of hair."

Kari shrugged. Back in Chicago for less than forty-eight hours, she was having a much-needed catch-up lunch with Beth before she headed back to work in the morning. "It was a snap decision. I was strolling through the mall in Anchorage and walked right in."

"You who deliberates for half an hour before deciding to buy generic over name brand at the grocery store?" Bethany snorted. "Not likely."

"I'm not the same person you said goodbye to a week and a half ago, Beth."

When she endured Bethany's intense scrutiny without looking away — and with barely a blush — her friend looked thoughtful. "No, I don't think you are." Her eyes took on a mischievous gleam. "Does this mean you and Damien finally did the deed?"

Kari's cheeks grew hot. Still, she held her friend's gaze as she nodded.

"More than once, I hope." At Kari's second nod, Bethany chuckled. "About time, Kar."

She grinned. "I think so, too." After glancing around the café and seeing no one was paying a bit of attention to them or their conversation, Kari added, "I have to say, I don't know why I waited so long."

"He's that good, huh?"

Kari stopped mid-nod. She didn't want to overshare, especially with Sam hovering somewhere nearby. In her primmest voice, she said, "A lady doesn't kiss and tell."

Bethany nudged her. "Good thing, then, that you're no lady."

"Maybe I've turned over a new leaf."

Her friend snorted. "I certainly hope not." Then she grinned. "Wait. Maybe that's not such a bad thing. They say men want a lady in the drawing room and a whore in the bedroom."

Kari rolled her eyes. "Careful, Beth. Your 1950s-era sensibilities are showing again."

Still, she had to admit, at least to herself, that Damien was most docile and agreeable right after they finished making love, and it had been much easier to distract him on the flight home. Vomiting details of her childhood hadn't been necessary. All she'd had to do was whisper a few naughty suggestions in his ear. He'd nodded off with a cheesy grin on his face. A good thing, too, because she doubted she had any childhood stories left to tell.

She didn't, however, have to admit it to Bethany. Some things were better left unsaid, and letting Beth know how right her 1950s throwback ideas were was one of them. She wouldn't be the one to set women's lib back a half-century.

****

"Hey, Cody," Damien greeted his friend when he picked up the phone. "While Kari's having lunch with What's Her Name, how would you like to ride with me to the suburbs?"

"Didn't you just visit your parents a few weeks ago?"

Damien sighed, making no effort to hide his impatience. He wanted to get out and back as quickly as possible so he and Kari could spend a cozy evening together before reality smacked them in the face in the morning. "Not to see them. I'm going to Kari's sister's neighborhood."

"Don't tell me you have a thing for her sister, man. I didn't like the look of her."

"Not that sister — the other one, Shannon. There's a house for sale nearby that I want to take a look at."

Cody whistled. "A house? I'm definitely coming with you to keep you from doing something you'll regret."

About an hour later, Damien was pulling up to the house in Shannon's neighborhood. It was as inviting as he remembered, with its white picket fence and oversized porch swing.

Cody seemed less than impressed. "Are you channeling Ward Cleaver here, bud?"

"You know I've always wanted a house in the 'burbs."

"But — "

"Hold off on any judgments until we've seen the inside, will you?" Damien asked as a Lincoln Town Car pulled into the driveway.

"Okay, okay," Cody grumbled.

A stout woman with short, graying hair got out of the vehicle and hurried toward them. "I'm sorry I'm late, Mr. Walker. I got stuck in traffic."

Damien shrugged. Having spent more than his fair share of time in traffic jams, he knew what that was like. "We just got here a minute ago ourselves."

A vehicle screeched to a stop at the curb and Sam jumped out, camera in hand. "Wait for me."

The Realtor glanced at Damien, eyes wide with alarm.

Damn. He'd been hoping to take the tour without an audience. Apparently Sam had gotten his message in time. He gave her what he hoped was a reassuring smile. "He's with us." Then, unsure how to explain, he tried to change the subject. "I can't wait to see the house."

The woman's gaze darted from him to Cody to the cameraman before she shook her head and led them inside.

"The house was built in the mid-80s, and extensively remodeled in 2002. Now that their family is out of the house, the Stapleys want to sell and move into a smaller place."

Damien liked what he saw. The interior was perfect, from the foyer to the spacious kitchen, and the backyard was big enough for Sunny to run in.

"If you'll follow me upstairs, I'll show you the bedrooms. The master bedroom is beautiful."

Cody held up his hands. "I don't need to see that."

She stopped and turned around, surprise evident in her face. "You don't?"

Cody shook his head and pointed at Damien. "Nope. But he does."

"You mean, you two aren't—?"

Suddenly, her hesitation made more sense. "No. I'm considering buying this house to surprise my wife."

She blinked and then turned back to the stairs. "Oh. Well then—" She broke off and whirled back around, her blue eyes twinkling with excitement. "Wait a minute. You're that guy on TV — the one on that newlyweds show."

Damien nodded, somewhat embarrassed to be recognized.

"Guilty."

"That explains him." She pointed to Sam and then rubbed her hands together. "I can't wait to tell my coworkers who I showed the Stapley house to!"

As she turned away and headed up the stairs, Cody chuckled softly. "You're famous, dude."

Damien, too, kept his voice low. "Thanks to you."

He followed the Realtor upstairs to continue the tour. She was right: The master bedroom was as perfect as the rest of the house, from the window seat to the oversized Jacuzzi tub in the master bath.

"I love it. I'll take it!" he said to the Realtor, who flushed with pleasure.

Cody raised his eyebrows and put a hand on Damien's arm. "Don't you think you should let Kari have a say in such a major purchase?"

"I thought it'd be fun to surprise her."

Cody shook his head. "I may not be an expert on the subject, but I'm pretty sure girls don't like surprises of this magnitude. Besides, didn't you say her sister lives near here?" When Damien nodded, Cody prompted, "And didn't you also say she doesn't like her sister much?"

"I'm pretty sure Shannon, the one who lives around the corner, is the sister she can stand. Claire's the bitchy one."

Cody merely looked at him. "Is 'pretty sure' good enough?"

Under his buddy's steady gaze, Damien's thoughts crystallized. "Pretty good" would never be good enough for Kari. She deserved the best of everything.

"Okay, Cody, you win. I'll bring Kari here for a tour before I sign anything."

"Wise decision, dude."

****

"Surprise!"

Momentary panic crashed over Kari as a pair of arms locked around her waist. She was used to Damien sneaking up on her since he'd done it many, many times in the last few days. However, this time was different — probably because of the blindfold he'd slipped over her eyes before sliding his arms around her waist.

Even so, the certainty that it was Damien and not some unknown assailant made her brave enough to fight off the rising fear. She whirled in his embrace and turned up her lips for a kiss. Damien readily delivered one. When he pulled away, she asked, "Why the blindfold?"

"Trust me."

His voice was a husky whisper in her ear. She nodded, melting into his embrace. That was when he swept her up in his arms and carried her. Toward what, she didn't know. The bed, she hoped. With Damien in charge, she was willing to take a stab at a little light bondage.

No such luck.

She quashed a bubble of disappointment as she heard the door click shut and the elevator doors slide open. Moments later, she was sitting in what had to be the Element. Damien fastened the seat belt, securely buckling her in.

Now more curious than anything, she asked, "Where are you taking me?

"That's the surprise, sweetheart."

"Not even a hint?"

His "no" was firm. "And if I catch you trying to peek, I'm going to bind your hands with this ugly paisley tie I've never liked."

Having seen the tie in question hanging in the closet several times, Kari giggled. "That is quite possibly the ugliest tie on earth."

"Earth?" Damien snorted. "Try the entire universe. I don't know what possessed my mom to buy it for me."

"She probably thought you'd look handsome in it."

"Does any man look good in turquoise, pink and purple print?"

Kari giggled again, having fun despite her initial alarm. "Maybe in 1985."

She paused, considering the power she was about to give Damien over her. Certain that he wouldn't abuse it, she held out her hands, wrists together. "Tie me up, please."

"Really?"

There was definite surprise in his voice. She nodded. "Really. I don't trust myself not to peek."

"Okay." He wrapped the tie around her wrists — tight but not too tight — and then put the car in gear.

They were off. To where, she didn't know, but she was sure it would be a wonderful surprise.

About forty-five minutes later, the Element rolled to a stop.

"Don't move," Damien instructed. "I'll come around to get you."

"Where am I going to go like this?" She held out her still-bound hands.

He chuckled. "Good point."

Kari waited impatiently for him to help her out of the vehicle, curious about what was coming next. Damien set her on her feet and pulled off the blindfold. "Here we are."

It took a moment for her eyes to focus after being covered for so long. When they did, she noticed the yard, the porch swing and the big grin on her husband's face.

"Where is here?"

His grin got even wider. "Our new house."

Kari's heart stuttered. "Did you say house?" Surely not. She had to be hearing things.

Damien nodded. "Well, it's ours if we want it. Cody insisted I let you take the grand tour before I made the deal."

Overwhelmed, she tried to wrap her mind around the idea of a house. She couldn't do it, so she focused on something much less immense instead. "Where are Sam and Stacy?"

He flashed a guilty grin. "I gave Cody a hundred bucks to distract them for me. I wanted to give you the grand tour without the camera hanging around."

"Sam'll be ticked about the bait-and-switch."

"Probably." He shrugged. "But I bet whatever Cody does is a thousand times more entertaining than us walking through an empty house. Besides, I get tired of the camera watching us all the time."

"Me too, but it's what we signed up for."

"Not my brightest moment," he grumbled under his breath. Then he took her hand and tugged her toward the door. "Wait until you see the fireplace."

Kari followed Damien through the two-story, three-bedroom home. It was a beautiful house, with mosaic tile floors, high ceilings and lots of windows to let in natural light. A gigantic fireplace dominated the living room.

"What do you think?"

What did she think? "It's gorgeous, but—"

"There's a but?"

"Yes, and it's a big but. Don't you think we're rushing

things?"

"Rushing?"

He acted as if he'd never heard the word before. "Yes, rushing."

"We're already married. Buying a house is the next logical step, and I've been wanting to move to the suburbs for a while now."

Kari looked at her husband's matter-of-fact countenance. When he put it that way, it made complete sense. Forget the fact that he'd given her no indication that he wanted to stay married after the contest ended.

She froze. Maybe buying a house was his way of telling her that. A guy didn't buy a house with someone he'd only be with for another month.

Kari didn't want to deny Damien this — or anything else, for that matter. She wanted him to be as happy as she was. She flashed him a smile. "Then let's do it."

Damien grinned back. "We're about to make the Realtor's year."

****

"Catching up at work after two weeks off is a bear," Kari grumbled on the El ride home later that week. Then she thought of the real bear she and Damien had seen on the trail at Denali and giggled.

The extra hours she was putting in to clear the work that had piled up in her absence sobered her up quickly enough. When she wasn't working, Kari was busy packing for their move. In the down economy, the house had stood empty for so long that the previous owners jumped at Damien's offer, so they could move in almost immediately.

It didn't take much to gather up the few belongings she had at Damien's apartment, but he had years' worth of stuff to go through, and it was no more fun that playing catch-up at the office.

Between all the working and packing, she also sandwiched in another session with Dr. Spaulding. The doctor seemed pleased with the progress she'd made.

"You look great, and it's clear from what you're telling me that you feel fantastic, too." She laid down her pencil and took off her glasses. "But I want you to be careful, Kari."

Kari narrowed her eyes, trying to comprehend the warning.

She didn't know what she should be afraid of, and she didn't want to, either. She was tired of being wary. She'd been that way for nine long years, and it had gotten her exactly nowhere. "Careful of what?"

"You think you've turned over a new leaf, and you're done being who you once were, right?" When Kari nodded slowly, Dr. Spaulding continued, her eyes serious. "I hope that's true. But we human beings have a way of slipping back into old, comfortable behaviors."

"Then I'll be fine. My old behaviors weren't comfortable at all. They were holding me back." From everything. Living life. Finding love. Thank God she finally found the wherewithal to realize it.

The doctor shook her head. "Perhaps I misspoke. I should have said 'familiar' behaviors. Just be wary, my dear." With that, she picked up her pencil again and smiled. "When do you want to meet again?"

Kari picked a date two weeks away. As she entered the appointment into the calendar on her cell phone, it occurred to her that was the last month of the contest.

In five short weeks, she and Damien would be free of Sam, Stacy and all the Romance TV madness. She could hardly wait for their real life together to begin, even if it did have to start right around the corner from her sister, Shannon. Yes, that fact hadn't escaped her attention, but the house was so gorgeous that she didn't mind. Besides Shannon was the one sibling she could stand in more than short doses.

That night, night three of their packing marathon, Kari glanced across the living room at Damien. He was on his knees clearing off the bookshelves while she packed up all but the most basic of the kitchen supplies. All that remained out were two mugs, two plates, two sets of silverware and, of course, the coffeemaker.

She shoved a stray curl behind her ear and blew out an exasperated breath. Three straight nights of packing was too much, especially when she thought about the need to do the same thing at her apartment. She'd be stuck in packing purgatory for the duration of their contract with the network.

"Sam will report us to Romance TV HQ soon if we don't do something more interesting than throw things in boxes."

Damien turned to face her. "Good point." He grinned.

"Whaddya say we drive out to the new house with a carload and *un*pack a few boxes instead?"

Kari shook her head. "Let's forget all about boxes for the evening and go out for dinner or something."

"That's an even better idea." He waggled his eyebrows suggestively. "I'll race you to the shower."

She giggled. "On your mark, get set—"

"Go!"

With the head start he got by jumping the gun, Damien beat her to the bathroom. They showered together — to be environmentally conscious, of course — and then headed out for dinner at Stavros'.

Stavros welcomed them to his restaurant, throwing open the door for the camera crew as well.

"You two are good for business, no?" he greeted them, throwing his ample arms around Kari and pecking her on each cheek.

Kari laughed as she looked around at the restaurant's updated decor. It looked quite different than it had their first few visits. "I guess we are."

Damien playfully nudged the restaurateur out of the way. "Keep your hands to yourself."

Secretly thrilled that Damien was guarding her, she let him put his arm around her waist and guide her to a table — the same one they'd had on their first visit to Stavros'.

She ordered the exact same meal, too — right down to the baklava for dessert.

Later, as she lay in Damien's arms, Kari smiled to herself. Life couldn't get much better than this.

Chapter Thirty

Damien whistled a happy tune on his way home from the office the next afternoon. He was going to pick up a load of boxes before he and Kari drove out to the house.

Life can't get much better than this. Now that she was no longer afraid of him, Kari was the perfect partner: one part helpmate, two parts playmate.

Why, she'd even ditched the rubber band on her wrist. That had to be an excellent sign that she was as comfortable with their relationship as he was.

With a load of boxes in the back of the Element and Sunny in the backseat, they headed to the suburbs. Only one short traffic jam impeded their progress. Damien was conscious of Sam and Stacy following behind them. He couldn't wait for the day he and Kari would no longer have the camera crew stuck to them like a third arm.

They unloaded the vehicle in silence, distributing boxes in the appropriate rooms. When he delivered the last box to the kitchen, Kari stopped him by putting her hand on his arm.

"I'm getting hungry."

He took a good, hard look at his wife, trying to determine what she meant. Was she truly hungry for food, or was she talking about something else altogether? It wouldn't be the first time she'd surprised him with her sexual appetite. As he studied her, her stomach growled.

"That answers that question," he muttered under his breath. Food it was. He raised his voice. "I saw a shopping center down the street. Want to see what they have in the way of restaurants?"

Kari nodded. "But let's walk over there. I've been skipping way too many workouts lately."

"Sure." He agreed easily. A walk wouldn't hurt him any, either.

They held hands as they strolled the three blocks to the shopping center, settling on a place called China Moon. Not surprisingly, it was a Chinese restaurant. He loved Chinese food nearly as much as Mexican.

He and Kari split orders of spicy sesame chicken and egg rolls, and then walked farther down the strip mall to an ice cream parlor. Kari ordered chocolate ice cream mixed with peanut butter cups and hot fudge; he was in the mood for a strawberry shortcake blend — strawberry ice cream, sponge cake, whipped cream and real strawberries.

Damien smiled to himself as he watched Kari enjoy her dessert. It still amazed him to see her attack foods most women would shun with such gusto.

When she polished off the last bite of her ice cream, she grinned. "It's getting late. We'd better get back so we can head back to the city."

"You're right," he agreed. "Sunny has probably explored every corner of the backyard by now."

Kari slipped her hand into his as they left the ice cream shop and started walking back toward the house. His steps slowed as they passed a grocery store. A boy who looked to be about nine stood next to a box with a sign that said, "Puppies free to a good home."

"There are better ways to find homes for puppies," he whispered to Kari, who nodded.

He was about to go tell the kid that when someone else walked up. Damien frowned. Was that — Nah. Couldn't be. That would be too much coincidence.

He took a second look. It was definitely Stan Thompson, a man Damien had hoped never to see again. After helping get Stan locked up two years ago for animal abuse, he'd never expected to see the man again. He must be out on parole, living somewhere near here.

Damien tensed as the other man reached into the box and picked up a puppy. The little rascal, some kind of terrier, nuzzled him trustingly.

"Don't even think about it," he growled at Stan, scowling.

For a second, the other man looked surprised to see him. The shock, however, was quickly replaced by a sneer. "What are you going to do about it?"

Damien recognized that sneer. It was the same one he'd worn throughout the trial.

He knew without question that he could not let that asshole have that dog — or any other. Instinctively, he lunged at Stan, knocking him to the ground. The puppy scampered out of danger and Damien proceeded to punch the other man once ... twice ... three times.

It felt good to do what he'd wanted to do the day Stan Thompson had brought a bloodied, battered pit bull in to his office. He'd known right away the poor animal had been in a dogfight. It hadn't taken him long to figure out Stan was involved in a dogfighting ring.

"I told you I never wanted to see you with a dog again." He punctuated each word with a jab, punch or poke.

As his rage receded, Damien became aware of two sounds: a wailing child and a distant siren coming this way. He glanced in the direction of the crying, guilt washing over him as he saw the boy's tear-streaked face. He hadn't given any thought to how his actions might traumatize the kid.

What kind of parent are you going to make if you don't stop and think about things like that?

The thought brought him up short. Parent? Who said anything about being a parent? He wasn't ready for that. Then again, wasn't having living space for a child or two part of the reason he'd wanted the house in the suburbs? If he was honest with himself, the answer to that question was "yes."

The sirens grew closer. Undoubtedly, they were coming for him. He was, after all, the one who started whaling on someone seemingly for no reason. The crowd that had started to gather to watch the melee had no idea this guy was a dog killer.

I really didn't think this thing through.

Getting arrested was really going to put a damper on Kari's desire to get back to the city anytime soon.

Speaking of Kari. Damien scanned the crowd, looking for his wife. Sam and the camera were there, apparently having figured out Cody's deception. Fantastic. Now his humiliating arrest would be captured for the whole world to see.

Kari, however, wasn't present. He was torn between delight that she wouldn't have to see him in handcuffs and worry about where she was.

Sure, she was still shy enough to hate making a scene, but where could she have gone? As a cop handcuffed his wrists behind his back, delight won out. He didn't want her to see him like this. Still, he vowed to find her as soon as he explained himself to the police.

Arlene Hittle

Explain himself to the police? Now *that* was a phrase he'd never thought he'd to have to utter!

****

When Kari's husband went from affable to homicidal in a split second, her flight instinct kicked in. Without thinking, she started to run — away from the shopping center, away from her big, suddenly very scary husband.

She'd never seen him so angry before and for no apparent reason. Sure, there were better ways to find homes for unwanted puppies. Still, her mind raced. If Damien could start beating a man for picking up a free dog, what on earth would he do to her the first time she somehow displeased him?

She ran without thinking about where she was headed, covering the distance to the new house in a few short minutes. When she let herself into the yard, Sunny trotted up and nosed at her hand, whining softly.

"I know, girl," she murmured, stroking the dog's soft head.

What was she going to do? She had to get out of there — fast — before he came after her. He'd probably be all kinds of pissed that she ran off and left him. No way would she let herself be his next punching bag.

She went to the kitchen to get Sunny a bowl of water. She filled it to nearly overflowing and set it on the back steps before glancing around the yard. The fence was solid, without any gaps. Certain Sunny would be safe while waiting for Damien's return, Kari latched the gate behind her and headed around the corner to her sister's place.

Spending the night with Shannon wasn't ideal, but it was better than stealing Damien's car or — God forbid — waiting for him to come find her.

She'd put up with one violent man in her life. No way was she going to go through that again.

When she knocked on Shannon's door a few minutes later, Tim opened it.

"Kari! What are you doing here? And what did you do to your hair?"

She sighed. "It's a long story. Mind if I crash here tonight?"

He shook his head. "Shannon's in the laundry room, I think."

"Thanks."

She found her sister folding underwear. Shannon took one

look at her and dropped the boxer shorts.

"Kar-Bear! I love the new 'do."

Kari grimaced. When would her hair cease to be such a hot topic? "Thanks."

Shannon's eyes searched her face. "Something's wrong. What is it?"

She shrugged. "Damien and I are going to move into the house around the corner, but—"

"You two are having a tiff, right?"

Kari nodded. That was the understatement of the decade, but it'd do. Better to let Shannon think it was a simple argument than to try to explain ten years' worth of history to someone she didn't want to know all the dirty details of her past.

Her sister grinned. "Our guest room is yours for the night. You know where it is."

Kari headed for the guest room and closed the door behind her in an attempt to shut out Shannon's well-meaning questions. She sank onto the bed, burying her face in her hands and then rubbing her eyes. It was no use. Nothing could block out the image seared into her brain of Damien beating that poor man.

She pulled her cell phone out of her pocket and dialed Bethany's number. It went straight to voicemail.

Great. Her friend was probably off somewhere with Cody, having a fine time.

"At least one of us is happy," she grumbled.

Kari closed her eyes and tried to relax. When it didn't work, she got up off the bed and started her favorite calming yoga routine.

When her phone rang fifteen minutes later, she was so deep into a corpse pose that she almost didn't hear it.

It was Bethany's ring. Good. She answered the call. Bethany spoke before she could say a word. "Kari, where the hell are you? Damien's in jail!"

"That's what happens when you beat up a guy in front of the Shop and Save."

"What?"

Bethany's shriek made Kari pull the phone away from her ear. "We were walking back to the new house after dinner, and he just started hitting some random guy who was about to take a free puppy from a kid standing in front of the store."

Bethany shrieked again. Kari heard her yell, "Cody, what

kind of maniac is Damien, anyway?"

Suddenly, a male voice was speaking to her on Beth's phone. "Those two have history together. You don't know the whole story."

"I know what I saw, Cody."

Cody's voice was patient. "But you don't know Damien helped put that guy in jail for dogfighting."

"Really?" Perhaps she'd overreacted — just a little — by running away.

Her inner tramp scoffed. *Perhaps? It's practically a certainty.*

"Yes, really," Cody continued, his voice steely. "I suggest you get Damien's car and meet us at the Glenlawn Police Department. It's time for you to stop running."

Before she had time to protest that she wasn't running, which would have been a lie since that was exactly what she'd done, or demand more details of the past Damien shared with the man from the store, Bethany came back on the line. "Sorry, Kar."

"You told him about me." It wasn't a question. Cody's attitude, somehow patient and snippy at the same time, made it obvious.

"He made some crack one night while we were watching your show, and I had to defend you by explaining what made you *you.*"

Kari almost heard the shrug in Bethany's voice. Well, there was nothing she could do about it now. "No worries, Beth. You can't unring the bell."

"So we'll see you at the station?"

The idea of facing Damien scared her, even if they'd be surrounded by police officers sworn to protect and serve. Still, it wasn't fair to him to run off without giving him a chance to explain. "Yes, I'll get there as soon as I can."

Kari dashed down the stairs, pausing in the living room long enough to announce, "I might or might not be back later. I'll call and let you know."

Then she headed back to the new house, where Stacy leaned against the SUV. The camerawoman sprang to attention. "Where have you been?"

"Around." Kari waved vaguely. Maybe Stacy wouldn't remember that her sister lived around the corner.

Without further comment, she grabbed the Element's keys

off the kitchen counter and hefted Sunny into the backseat. Man, she hoped the dog's cast came off soon. A few minutes later, after realizing that she had no idea where the police station was, she pulled into a gas station for directions.

Thank goodness she — unlike a man — wasn't afraid to ask for directions. It turned out she was a few blocks away. By the time she and Stacy pulled into the cop shop parking lot, Cody and Bethany were exiting a flashy red Camaro. It had to be Cody's, because Beth drove a Prius.

Cody's eyes were considerably warmer than his voice had been on the phone. "Let's get in there and rescue our boy."

Kari nodded and followed Cody and Beth up the police station steps. With no idea what to do, she was more than content to let someone else take charge.

Cody strode up to the officer at the reception desk. "We're here for Damien Walker."

"The guy with the TV camera on his tail?" The officer glanced up from his paperwork and shook his head. "He's still in booking. He won't be ready for visitors for at least another thirty minutes."

Kari surprised herself by saying, "We're not here to visit. We want to get him out."

Eyes wide, she clapped her hand over her mouth. She wasn't in the habit of mouthing off to policemen, or anyone else for that matter.

But the officer didn't take offense. He merely chuckled. "That'll have to wait until morning, after he's seen the judge."

Uncertain what to do next, Kari looked at Cody, who shrugged. "We'd better wait here to tell him he'll be stuck here tonight."

"Suit yourself." The officer gestured to some chairs. "Sit there. I'll let you know when Walker's ready for visitors."

Kari sat beside Bethany, plucking at the edges of a hole in the chair's upholstery and trying to ignore Stacy's presence. What was she doing in a police station, waiting to talk to a man she no longer was sure she wanted anything to do with?

Give him a chance to explain, you dope.

Kari scowled. Some things were unexplainable and unforgivable.

This isn't one of them. It's not like he hit you, after all.

But he could have. If he could hit a man, he was capable of

hitting a woman.

Kari shook her head to clear it. What had Dr. Spaulding said about old, familiar behaviors? Running was one of those behaviors. She owed it to both Damien and herself to give him a chance to explain.

"Mrs. Walker?"

Lost in her thoughts, Kari didn't answer.

Bethany poked her. "He's talking to you, Kar."

She jumped. "Sorry." Then she smiled at the policeman. "I'm not really used to the name."

"Walker can have visitors now."

Her resolve to listen to Damien's explanation still firm, Kari stood. Stacy did too. *Blast!* If any moment begged for privacy, it was visiting your husband in jail.

The officer held up his hand. "Family only. Chief's orders."

Resisting a childish urge to stick out her tongue at the camerawoman, Kari followed the officer down the hall to the holding cell. She'd hear Damien out, and probably end up begging him to forgive her for running away when he needed her.

Then he stood to greet her, and fear came rushing back.

The officer unlocked the door and pushed it open. "You can go in."

Kari stared at Damien. Instead of seeing the man who loved her — even though he still hadn't said those words while fully conscious — she saw his face contorted with rage, the way it had been as he punched that guy repeatedly.

Dread rooted her to the spot. He was so large, looming over her like that. It was exactly the way Rob used to hover every time he'd wanted something she didn't want to give, either badgering her until she gave in or simply overpowering her to take what he wanted.

Bile surged to her throat. She turned and bolted back down the hallway, managing to choke out an apology of sorts as she ran. "I'm sorry. I can't."

****

Damien watched Kari turn tail and run, wondering what in hell had gotten into her.

Here he'd been glad to see his lovely wife coming down the hall, but as soon as she saw him, she froze, staring at him with that deer-in-headlights look in her eyes.

BLIND DATE BRIDE

It dawned on him: There still was a scared mouse hiding in Kari, and he'd managed to coax her back out of hiding with his ill-thought-out attack on Stan Thompson.

Great. Now he was going to have a police record and a wife whose trust he needed to earn all over again. He didn't have time for that. There were just five short weeks to the end of the contest-mandated cohabitation period, and if Kari didn't trust him, they might as well file for divorce.

He spat out an expletive. Now he could hate Stan Thompson for killing dogs *and* slaying his marriage.

He heard footsteps approaching. Maybe she'd changed her mind. Yeah right.

Sure enough, when he looked up, it wasn't Kari but Cody coming toward him, his steps never faltering. The officer opened the door and ushered his buddy into the cell.

Damien didn't feel much like grinning, but he did. He had to hang onto his sense of humor or he'd go crazy. "At least you're not running scared."

Cody took a seat on the cot beside him and cleared his throat. "About that—"

"What do you know about it?"

"I saw Kari streak out of here like the hounds of hell were hot on her heels. Beth went after her and I came back to see you."

"Beth?"

His buddy looked at him as if he'd lost his marbles. Maybe he had. Beating up Stan Thompson in front of the Shop and Save certainly hadn't been his sanest idea.

Finally, Cody nodded. "You know, Kari's best friend. The one I've been dating for almost eight weeks."

"You've been dating Kari's friend?" Damien was surprised on more than one level. First, he couldn't believe Cody had managed to sustain a relationship for nearly two months. Cody still subscribed to the Don Juan school of women: love 'em and leave 'em.

Perhaps more importantly, he finally knew What's Her Name's name. Beth. It suited the redhead.

Cody nodded again. "And Beth told me something you probably ought to know about your hot little wife."

After several moments passed in silence, Damien raised his eyebrows. "Well?"

"Sorry, man. I got sidetracked there for a second. When

you're stuck in jail, you have nothing but time to think."

"You've been in 'the big house' for all of five minutes, Cody," Damien snapped, impatient to hear what his friend knew about Kari. He was up for anything that would help him make sense of his wife's behavior.

"Kari had a bad relationship in college."

He looked at Cody expectantly. There had to be more to the story than that. "I figured that much out on my own."

"Apparently, it wasn't pretty. Beth said he bullied Kari into doing whatever he wanted — in bed and out."

Someone had done that to his Kari? It explained so much: her lack of self-esteem, her initial mistrust of him, her reaction to their chat about what his mother did for a living, the way she ran every time he got close.

The same red veil of rage he'd experienced earlier, in front of the store, fell over Damien as he thought of some guy forcing himself on Kari. He pictured her struggling, futilely trying to fend him off. "Who is he? I'll kill him."

Cody touched Damien's shoulder. "Don't you think maybe that's what Kari's afraid of?"

Damien felt sanity start to return. Cody was right again. If she had a problem with displays of strength, she wouldn't thank him for a show of force — even if the guy deserved it.

It also explained why she bolted earlier, when she'd witnessed him punching out the dog killer. "Now all I have to do is figure out how to convince Kari that I'm nothing like that jerk — what was his name?"

"Rob."

"Rob." Damien tasted the name on his tongue. He wondered if that was the same guy Kari's brothers had mentioned. Rob, Bob … could very well be. "I knew there was more to that than her brothers let on!"

"I doubt they knew. Beth said Kari didn't tell anyone the whole story. Not even her — she filled in the blanks on her own, and Kari never denied it."

Damien smiled grimly. Kari's skeleton was out of the closet now. "I'm not going to give up until I flesh out the truth."

"If she's been not talking about it for nine years, dude, that's gonna be a lot easier said than done."

"I'm pretty sure I'm up to the task."

****

When Damien got back to their apartment the next morning after his arraignment, he wasn't surprised that Kari was nowhere to be found. He also was far from flabbergasted that she'd taken her stuff with her. Even the cats were gone.

After what she'd seen, she probably thought she'd stepped back into her worst nightmare. Of course she was going to run. Prize money be damned. They'd already made more than enough off "Just Married" to offset the lost prize money.

Damien walked through the empty apartment, looking for anything she might have left behind, anything that would give him an excuse to go over to her apartment.

He pushed open the door to the bedroom, half hoping to see her waiting there. Of course, she wasn't. But there, on the nightstand, her wedding ring twinkled up at him. It hit him like a punch to the gut. Leaving that behind meant she was really gone.

Sighing, Damien pocketed the ring. It was flashier than he would have picked, but he'd gotten used to seeing it on Kari's finger. What's more, he liked seeing it there.

He vowed to see that ring on her finger again, and soon.

Chapter Thirty-One

Kari sat in her office a few days later, staring at a pile of papers in front of her without really seeing it. She tried to force herself to focus. If she didn't start working instead of thinking about her husband, she wouldn't have a job for much longer.

Even knowing that, she welcomed the interruption when her office phone started to ring.

"McClatchy, Berkley and Beck Accounting. How may I help you?"

"Hello, dear. It's Ella."

Ella? Why on earth was Damien's mother calling her? Surely he'd told his mom about the demise of their marriage.

Well, maybe not. Kari certainly wouldn't be eager to tell her parents she'd spent the night in jail, and since that was part and parcel of their problem, perhaps Ella didn't know. She'd best not let on that anything was wrong.

"Hi, Ella." Politeness compelled her to add, "It's good to hear from you."

If Damien's mother doubted the statement, she didn't let on. "I know I'm probably overstepping here, but I have a favor to ask of you."

"A favor?" Kari was intrigued. What could a woman like Ella want from her?

"Yes, dear. There's a bug going around among my volunteers, and I can't find anyone to work this afternoon. I'd love for you to come down to Hope House and help me out."

"Hope House." Crap. Maybe her voice didn't sound faint to Ella as it did to her.

"Yes, dear. We have a couple of new arrivals scheduled for today. All you have to do is help the women settle in and offer to listen to them if they want to talk."

Ella wanted her to hear other women's tales of abuse? She wasn't strong enough for that.

Wait just a minute, her inner tramp — or maybe her inner goddess — piped up. *That's the old Kari talking.*

The vixen was right. Old Kari would avoid meeting new

people and shy away from listening to problems that would only remind her of her own. However, she wasn't that girl anymore. She was a changed person, and, as Cody had pointed out, it was time to stop running.

Even if seeing Damien was too much right now, she could help his mother. After all, Ella was still her mother-in-law until she and Damien were officially divorced.

If they were officially divorced, that is.

Her desertion most likely gave him grounds to sever all ties. He'd be well within his rights to file. So would she, for that matter. Getting married because a TV network told you to had to provide ample grounds for divorce.

Kari shook off the unwelcome thought. She might be running scared for now, but she couldn't quite give up on a future with Damien. Not yet.

She squared her shoulders. "What time should I be there?"

****

Damien perched on the arm of his couch, drumming his fingers on his thigh as he waited for the phone to ring. Finally, it did.

"Well? What did she say?"

He heard his mother sigh. "She agreed, reluctantly."

"How did she sound?"

His mother clucked her tongue. "Really, Damien. You should just pick up the phone and talk to her. Kari's still your wife."

"And I scared the hell out of her, Mom." He snorted. "I even scared myself. I think it was the first time I acted first and thought about the consequences later."

"Yes, and now you have a criminal record to remember your folly."

Damien thought he heard laughter in her voice, though he had no clue why his mother was so amused. She certainly wouldn't have thought an arrest was funny during his teen years. "You never answered my question, Mom. How did Kari sound?"

"Sad, confused, scared, determined."

He seized on the last word. "Determined is good."

"I think so."

"So what time do you want me there?"

"Hold your horses, Mr. Jailbird."

Damien scowled. His mother would be needling him about his arrest for months — years, even. If he hadn't needed her help getting through to Kari, he'd have been tempted to keep his run-in with the law from her. However, his mom knew abuse victims, and since that was what his wayward wife was, he'd shared the whole sorry tale, adding what he knew about Kari's past, courtesy of Cody. "You yourself said I need to see her."

"I said you should call her," Ella corrected. Her voice was crisp. "You know the rules: no men allowed at Hope House."

He felt his scowl deepen. "You make the rules. Surely you can break them for your only son."

A merry laugh tinkled over the phone line. "Hope House is a safe place for women, Damien. I hate to break this to you, dear, but you aren't exactly the poster boy for making women feel safe."

"What are you talking about, Mom? I've never hit a woman in my life, and I'm not about to start at my age."

Her voice took on a professorial tone. "You and I know that, but at your size, you're most of these girls' worst nightmare. And don't think I'm unaware of what you got up to in college. You may never have struck a woman, but I'm fairly certain you left plenty of broken hearts behind."

Damien swallowed hard. He wasn't exactly proud of his behavior back then, and thought he'd successfully kept the Don Juan years from his mother. "I doubt that. We all got exactly what we wanted."

"That's neither her nor there, Damien." He imagined her giving an airy wave to push the conversation back in the desired direction. She was always gesturing with her hands. "You are going to stay right where you are while Kari and I meet Hope House's newest tenants. If all goes well, Kari will realize she's lucky to have you."

He forced himself to smile. "You know best."

As he hung up the phone, Damien hoped that was true. He felt like a rat, enlisting his mother's help in winning Kari back, but she *was* the expert. And since he was clueless, he needed all the help he could get.

He supposed he could go to Kari's family, but he doubted she would thank him for getting them involved. Her friend, Beth, would side with Kari over him, no matter what Cody said. He'd expect nothing less. Their decade-long friendship had to be stronger than new bonds with men — even fine men like him and Cody.

Damien groaned. Right now, he didn't feel like much of a man. He felt like an ass, an ass who missed his wife. He missed everything about her: her laugh, the sound of her voice, her quiet strength in facing down her fears. He especially missed her playful spirit, both in and out of the bedroom.

When Mr. Happy stirred, Damien cursed. Whether he was cursing the direction of his thoughts or his stupidity for beating Stan Thompson senseless, he wasn't sure. Still puzzling over that question, he went to take a cold shower.

He sure hoped his mother was right, because he wanted Kari back where she belonged — in his life and his bed. The sooner she came home, the sooner they could begin their life together.

****

Kari took the El to Hope House's neighborhood after work and used the time on the train to give herself a pep talk.

You are stronger than you think you are. You can't run from everything that scares you. You can help these women just by listening.

As she repeated those statements like a mantra, Kari began to believe them, especially that last one. How often had she felt better after venting to Bethany? Granted, she'd kept a lot to herself, but even sharing the things she had always lifted her mood.

Offering others that same kind of comfort was the least she could do.

Still, Kari dragged her feet as she approached the brownstone housing Hope House, resisting her inner tramp's prodding to hurry. "I don't think I'm ready."

Oh yes you are. You can do this. Besides, maybe Damien's inside.

Instead of hurrying her along, as the vixen no doubt intended, that thought stopped Kari in her tracks. She grabbed the compact from her purse and checked her appearance. Yep, sunken eyes, pale cheeks, hair that, while not quite the rat's nest of a few weeks ago, definitely wasn't living up to the promise of Frank's gorgeous cut. She couldn't run into Damien now, when she looked like she'd been through hell.

The door to Hope House swung open as Kari debated turning tail, and Ella stepped onto the stoop. Kari made herself wave and walk toward her mother-in-law, even as part of her wanted to bolt in the other direction as fast as her legs would carry her in high-heeled pumps.

Dr. Spaulding was right about old, familiar behaviors coming back to bite her on the butt. She was a runner and had been for years. Only sheer will would allow her to break herself of that habit.

Kari greeted Ella with a smile that didn't feel too forced and followed her mother-in-law inside for the grand tour. The living room was warm, painted a burnt orange and decorated in rich brown tones. The kitchen, too, was inviting, with its cheery yellow walls and white cabinets. However, the bedrooms were most comforting of all, decorated in calming blues and greens and filled with lots of soft bedding and throw pillows.

"Like a cocoon," she said under her breath.

Ella reached out to squeeze her hand. "Exactly like that. I knew you'd understand."

Kari glanced sharply at Damien's mother, wondering what, exactly, the older woman knew. She couldn't know everything about Rob because no one did — not even Beth. Even so, Mrs. Walker seemed to understand more than Kari wanted her to. "Forget I said that."

Ella shook her head. "I can't do that, dear. But if you're not ready to unburden yourself, I won't say another word about it." Her eyes crinkled with her smile. "Now let's head back downstairs. Our first arrival is due any minute."

Kari followed her mother-in-law back to the living room. The doorbell rang as they reached the bottom of the stairs, as if she'd timed it. Mrs. Walker answered it, ushering a young woman with a ratty duffel bag inside. Kari had to bite her lip to stifle a gasp when she saw the poor girl's face. She looked like she'd gone several rounds in a boxing match and lost. Both her eyes were purpled by old bruises and her lip was split. Even more frightening, she looked to be about nineteen.

The look Ella gave her told her the non-reaction was the right one. "Kari, please escort Carla to the first room on the left."

Kari led the way to the designated room, wondering what, if anything, she should say. She opted for the obvious. "Here's where you'll be staying."

Carla's facial expression didn't change much, but her posture was one of disbelief as she turned on Kari. "You're going to let me stay here?"

Kari nodded. "This is your safe haven."

"Safe? Nowhere's safe."

At one time, Kari might have agreed, but she knew without question that Hope House would protect anyone within its walls. "This place is," she said, her voice firm.

"Won't be when Joey finds me." Her reply was bleak. "He always finds me."

"Not this time." Kari paused, searching for the right words. "Do you mind if I ask what happened?"

Carla shook her head. "Crazy bastard said I was flirting with my little brother's best friend. He's only fifteen — a kid, for cripe's sake. What would I want with a fifteen-year-old?"

"How old are you?"

"Eighteen."

Younger than she'd thought. Kari had to fight hard to keep her expression neutral. "And how old's Joey?"

"Twenty-three." Her chin jutted up. "And don't tell me he's too old for me. I'm figuring that out for myself. That's why I'm here. I want him out of my life for good this time."

"This time?"

Carla nodded. "I tried to leave him last year, and he threw me down a flight of stairs. Broke my arm and my ankle. Then he pretended to be sorry and, fool that I was, I believed him when he said he'd never hurt me again." Her laugh was harsh as she gestured to her battered face. "This is what I got for my trust."

Kari felt her stomach lurch as memories of Rob's abuse — most of it merely verbal — rained down on her. She had to get out of there before she lost what little lunch she'd managed to choke down. "I'm sorry to hear that, but I know you'll be safe here. Please excuse me."

She rushed into the hall and barreled straight into Ella, who caught her by the elbows to keep her from falling.

"Are you okay, dear?"

Keeping a tight lid on rising bile, Kari shook her head. She squeezed out one word. "Bathroom."

Ella pointed. "Down the hall on the right."

Kari managed to get there just in time. She vomited the meager contents of her stomach — half a ham sandwich on wheat and some coffee — into the toilet and then stayed on her knees, staring unseeingly at the wall as she considered what she'd just heard.

Arlene Hittle

She should consider herself lucky. For the most part, Rob's abuse had been mental, telling her she was getting fat, that she'd never find another guy who loved her the way he did, that she had to put out because she was a prick tease. Oh, there had been times when he'd menaced her into having sex with him, but in the end, she'd always given in. Grudgingly, perhaps, but she'd always let him have his way with her. It had seemed the least she could do after leading him on.

New Kari snorted. *Ri-ii-ght. Rob was just a boor. Look at how many times you led Damien on, and he never once tried to push you farther than you wanted to go.*

Damien. She wasn't ready to face him yet. When she finally did summon the strength, she hoped he'd be the man she thought he was. He'd have to be something special to forgive her for her chicken-hearted desertion.

What kind of woman left the man she loves sitting in jail?

Kari knew the answer to that: a scared, scarred one who needed to stop living in the past. Now she just needed the courage to do what had to be done.

****

Despite her resolve at Hope House, Kari still struggled to find her backbone the next week.

She trudged from the El stop to Dr. Spaulding's office at lunchtime Thursday, six days after what she'd taken to calling the "Hope House Epiphany." Her heart wasn't in this session. She knew the doctor was going to encourage her to let Damien explain, to reconcile her irrational fear with reality.

That's precisely why you need to go.

She gave her inner tramp a mental swat. No doubt the slut wanted the spectacular sex she and Damien shared.

Kari missed that, sure. However, she also missed their companionship and friendship. She missed the way he seemed to know what she was thinking, even when she didn't want to admit it to herself. She missed having someone besides the cats to come home to. She missed simply cuddling and waking up in Damien's arms.

"Why'd he have to go and ruin it all by acting like Rob?"

When she asked Dr. Spaulding that question, the doctor raised an eyebrow. "Did your husband really act like your ex-boyfriend?"

Kari sighed. A week and two days had gone by, a week and

two days of missing Damien and being miserable. It was time to stop lying to herself. Damien truly was nothing like Rob, and the sooner she faced it once and for all, the better. Wasn't that what she was paying Dr. Spaulding the big bucks for? "Not really."

"Then what, exactly, are you afraid of?"

That was an easy one. She answered quickly. "The potential."

"So you're letting the possibility that Damien might hurt you keep you from the certain happiness you've already found?"

When she put it like that ... "It sounds pretty silly, doesn't it?"

As always, the doctor's response was neutral. "You feel what you feel, Kari."

"But..." She turned the thought over in her mind a few times. "We can't let a possibility that something might go wrong keep us from living. If everyone did that, no one would fly or get married or go to work."

This time, Dr. Spaulding smiled. "You, my dear, are infinitely sensible. Who told you that you need therapy?"

Kari giggled. "Bethany said it more than once, but I arrived at the conclusion on my own."

"As you did with today's breakthrough. Fear can't keep us from living. Now get out there and experience life."

When Kari left the therapist's office, her step was considerably lighter. Dr. Spaulding was right. People were meant to enjoy life, not hide away from what might, but probably wouldn't, happen.

She was going to tell Damien that, as soon as she could. Even though her early exit had caused them to forfeit Romance TV's prize money, she had a feeling he'd be happy to see her.

Strange how that prize money, which once had been so important to her, hadn't even entered her mind when she ran off and left Damien at the police station, thus negating their contract with the network. Luckily, she'd gotten enough pay from the completed episodes of "Just Married" to help her parents out of their financial jam.

Turned out, Kari's chance to talk to Damien came sooner than she thought. He was waiting at her apartment door when she returned home after yoga class that evening.

He held out a scrunchie she'd never seen before. "I think you left that at my place."

"Thanks." Even though she'd never wear a mint green scrunchie, she took it and stuffed it in her pocket. The brush of his fingertips against hers sparked heat so intense she was surprised not to see flames.

In a bid for time to get a grip on her reaction, she ducked her head. When masses of hair didn't fall forward to hide her face, she wished she hadn't gotten so brave in Alaska.

No, that wasn't true. She didn't regret a minute of their time in the Land of the Midnight Sun. Well, maybe the minute or two she spent doubting Damien's fidelity was regret-worthy, but that was it. She wouldn't change anything else about that trip.

Lifting her chin, she leveled her gaze on Damien. "Damien, I—"

"Kari, I—"

They both spoke at the same time, and then laughed.

"I guess great minds still think alike," he teased.

"Guess so." She took a deep breath. This was no time for jokes. Their future might well depend on this encounter, so she had to make sure it went in their favor. "Damien, I'm sorry for running out on you like that."

He shrugged, but didn't break eye contact. "I understand why you did it. Cody told me about Rob."

Kari sucked in a breath, even though she'd figured as much when his mother stepped in. Once Beth told Cody, she couldn't expect it to remain a secret. "He did?"

Damien nodded. "I know everything."

"I doubt that."

He reached for her hand, lacing his fingers through hers. "Why don't we walk to that coffee shop around the corner and you can fill in the blanks?"

That familiar tingle jolted through Kari where their hands touched, and this time she was ready for it. She nodded and let Damien lead her downstairs.

An hour later, she'd told him everything, from the subtle little emotional digs to the big one. Just thinking about it made her shudder. Even now, she was loath to call it what it was.

Damien, however, had no such qualms. "That's rape."

"Shhh!" Despite the 90-degree temperature outside, she shivered. "That's such an ugly word."

Damien frowned. "What that jerk did to you *is* ugly, sweetheart, and you have my word I will never, ever force myself on you."

"I know that," she told him. She did, too. Despite a penchant for punching out potential puppy abusers, Damien and Rob couldn't be more different. More than likely, Rob would have joined the guy in torturing dogs.

"Then you're ready to come home with me? I move into the house tomorrow."

He looked so hopeful that Kari hated to say no, but she did, shaking her head slowly. "We really rushed into this marriage of ours."

Damien nodded. "Yeah, we did."

"So don't you think we'd be better off spending a little more time getting to know each other before we move in together?"

After a long pause, he nodded again. "I suppose it couldn't hurt." Then he grinned. "Will we still get to spend some time getting to know each other in the sack?"

Kari giggled and lowered her eyelids. "You bring the bacon."

Damien chuckled. "You bet."

****

Damien spent the next two months courting Kari — the way he should have done before they even thought about getting married. This time, it was just the two of them — no TV cameras, no fans.

Actually, they still encountered a few fans. Even though they'd been off the air for weeks, people still seemed to recognize them more often than not.

He watched as Kari started to handle these situations with increasing aplomb. The day she merely smiled and gave a gushing waitress her autograph, Damien knew her transformation really was complete.

That night, they sat in the house he hoped to be sharing with Kari soon. It was a cool September evening, so a fire crackled in the fireplace. They were cuddled together on the couch, enjoying the ambience.

It was time. He pulled away from Kari to fish something out of his pocket.

Determined to do things right this time, he dropped to one knee in front of her. Her eyes widened.

"Oh my God, Damien! Is this what I think it is?"

He nodded and held out a small, velvet jeweler's box. As he

popped it open, he delivered his speech — the one he'd practiced in the mirror about a hundred times over the last few months, ever since she'd agreed to get to know one another.

"Kari Parker-Walker, I love you. Will you marry me for real this time?"

She looked at him, her eyes shining with excitement. "Of course." Only then did she look at the ring. "This isn't the ring from the network!"

"You're right. It's not. Does that matter?"

Personally, he thought this one, a tasteful marquis-cut diamond in white gold, was much prettier. Even better, it was theirs and theirs alone.

Kari shook her head. "Not a bit. I love this ring even better because you picked it for me."

He wrapped his arms around Kari and started planting kisses all over her face. "That was just the right thing to say."

"I'm glad." After a pause, she asked, "What did happen to the other ring?"

"I had to give it back to Romance TV. Did you know that thing cost $3,000?"

"So it was real after all. I wondered about that."

Damien nodded. He, too, had been surprised that the ring wasn't cubic zirconia. But Hayworth had divulged its cost when he asked for the ring's return. "As real as my feelings for you, sweetheart."

He rose to his feet, tugging Kari upright with him. "Now, what do you say we go christen another room?"

Kari's giggle bubbled up, warming his heart. He still loved that sound. "Haven't we already hit them all?"

"Not the laundry room." He grinned, sweeping her into his arms. She weighed practically nothing. "If you're very, very good, there might be a spin cycle in your future."

She giggled again as she threw her arms around his neck. "Bring it on, Damien. Bring it on."

Chapter Thirty-Two

"You couldn't have picked a better day for a wedding."

Kari nodded, agreeing with Bethany, who walked on her left. Her sisters were on her other side. The crisp October morning didn't deter them from walking the few blocks from her and Damien's house, where they'd spent the night, to the church.

Two weeks had flown past in a whirlwind of activity, and today was the capstone: the wedding. In a few short hours, she and Damien would speak their vows — and mean them. This time, the ceremony would be no made-for-TV farce.

It had been planned too hurriedly to be the exact wedding Kari had always dreamed about, but at least this time it wasn't the wedding of her nightmares. Then, she'd had absolutely no input. This time, she'd had a modicum of control over her gown, the bridesmaid's dresses and even the music.

Sure, choices were limited by the quick turnaround time. Now that she and Damien were getting married for real, she didn't want to wait any longer than she had to. It was past time for them to begin the rest of their lives together.

As they approached the squat little church that resembled a grocery store, but not the Shop and Save Damien had been arrested in front of, thank goodness, Claire's perfect nose lifted in the air. "It's a little plain, don't you think?"

Kari gritted her teeth. Leave it to Claire to try to spoil her special day. She refused to regret asking both her sisters to be in the wedding party, though. She wanted to establish normal, adult relationships with them — both of them — no matter how tough it might be.

She turned her gritted teeth into a smile, albeit a weak one, and explained. "It's nondenominational, and the only one that had an opening. Did you know most churches are booked for weddings a year in advance?"

"We booked mine eighteen months out."

Shannon spoke up. "Tim and I ran off to Vegas. They have so many wedding chapels you can't turn around without seeing one."

Kari flashed Shannon a grateful smile. Who'd have thought that Shannon, once Claire's sidekick in the let's-torment-Kari game, would rush to her rescue?

Her bridesmaids wore dresses the colors of rich fall leaves — a burnished gold for redhead Bethany, burnt orange for blond Shannon and a red for dark-haired Claire.

There hadn't been time for Kari to order a real wedding dress, but the cream-colored gown hit all the right notes. Floor-length satin, spaghetti straps, curve-skimming. She liked, make that loved, the way she looked.

"You ladies look lovely."

The voice in the doorway could only belong to one man, and it wasn't her husband. Kari whirled around. "Frank! You came."

Her Anchorage miracle worker beamed at her and swished into the room. She wasn't surprised to see he still wore tight leather pants and a billowy white shirt. On him, the look somehow worked.

"Of course I came. It's not every day I get a postcard from one of my runners."

Kari felt her cheeks flush as her hand flew to her hair, still expertly cut, thanks to the friend Frank had recommended. "I hope I apologized for that."

"You did, but like I said then, we have so many runners that there's a policy in place to keep them in-store." He paused. "Whose hair shall I arrange first?"

"Frank, I didn't expect you to come and do our hair. I didn't think you'd come at all. I just wanted to let you know your haircut helped me change my life."

Frank waved away the praise. "You'd already changed inside, where it counts. I just altered the wrappings."

Kari relaxed back into the well-padded bride's chair, letting Frank work another miracle on her hair. He deftly arranged her curls into a beautiful cascade, somehow making it look like she had the amount of hair she'd had before he took scissors to her head.

As Frank worked, Bethany hovered near Kari's right elbow with a bottle of water and a straw. She glanced at Beth. "I can't get over how much more relaxed I feel this time around."

"That's because this time you want to get married, you dope."

Kari looked at her friend, surprised. So *that's* where her

BLIND DATE BRIDE

inner tramp got that particular phrase. "Did I ever thank you for getting me into this mess?"

"Not in so many words."

"Well, thanks. If you hadn't entered me in that crazy contest, I never would have met Damien." She took a sip of water.

Bethany grinned. "And I wouldn't have gotten to know Cody, so maybe I should thank myself, too."

Kari laughed. Leave it to Bethany to be thinking of herself on a day that was supposed to be all about the bride. "Maybe you should."

Not soon enough, the opening notes of "The Wedding March" sounded. Kari eagerly stepped down the aisle, toward her future. She didn't once worry about tripping over her own feet.

She glided to where Damien waited. As she walked, she took note of the familiar faces on all sides. Her parents sat in one of the pews with her brother, Chris, and his family; Damien's mom and dad were in another. Her other brothers, Steve and Sean, joined Cody at the front of the church as Damien's groomsmen.

What a sharp contrast with their last wedding, where all the guests had been members of the media and she hadn't known a single one.

Kari shook off that unpleasant memory and took her place beside Damien. Moments later, she spoke her vows as surely as he did, and the minister pronounced them man and wife.

"You may kiss the bride."

Some inner devil prompted her to purse her lips for a quick, chaste peck, just like she had the first time.

Damien grinned and shook his head. "No way, sweetheart. It didn't work then, so what on earth makes you think you'll get away with that now?"

He settled his hands on her hips, tugging her close as his tongue teased her mouth open. She willingly let his tongue sweep inside, relishing the sweet heat that started to build between them.

She heard Cody whisper just loud enough for Damien — and her — to hear. "Dude, this time the family's watching."

Damien reluctantly pulled away, giving her a one-word promise. "Later."

Her entire body tingled. She looked forward to later — later

Arlene Hittle

tonight and the rest of their lives. She and Damien would be together.

"Forever," she whispered back.

"You bet it's forever, sweetheart. Forever and a day."

If you enjoyed BLIND DATE BRIDE, watch for Bethany and Cody's story, TROUBLE IN PARADISE. Coming in Spring 2015.

"You want to what?"

Cody stared at his girlfriend of a little more than six months, unable to comprehend what he was hearing. He glanced from her pretty heart-shaped face to the pancakes, sausage and bacon on his breakfast plate. He knew by the double meat that she was trying to butter him up for something — but he never would have imagined this.

"You heard me the first time. I want to apply for Romance TV's new reality series."

"After what Damien went through? No way, Beth." Cody shook his head as he put the half-full plate on the coffee table.

"You don't even know what the show's about."

He shook his head again. "Doesn't matter. I'm not subjecting either one of us to that kind of torture."

Bethany's emerald eyes narrowed and she pointed the remote at the TV. "Just watch."

"Don't tell me you TiVo'ed a commercial."

Ignoring his objection, she pressed "play." A picture of a white sand beach lined with palm trees replaced Bugs Bunny and Cody paused. He was man enough to admit the white sands and turquoise sea looked inviting. It beat winter in Chicago, for sure.

Then the words "Trouble in Paradise?" replaced the tropical scene. He darted a glance at Bethany. Did she think they were in trouble? He was about to ask her when the announcer started rambling about "sizzle," "fizzle" and "insignificant others."

Oh, hell. That clinched it. For some crazy reason, Beth did think they were in trouble. "Just because — "

She shushed him, so he made it a point to listen to the rest of the ad before he tried to defend himself. He held out hope that it might get better. It didn't.

"'Invitation to Sin'?" he repeated. When she nodded, his stress level shot up two notches. The woman he loved with all his heart apparently thought the relationship was on the rocks. Why? Because he wasn't the Energizer Bunny in bed? "So what if we don't have wild, crazy sex every night? I'm almost thirty-three years old, for God's sake. Even in my twenties, I needed a break once in a while."

"Once in a while is fine. But lately we've been lucky to have sex once a week. It's like we're an old married couple."

Cody rubbed his temples. What had started as a good morning, complete with his favorite breakfast, was quickly heading south. "What's wrong with that?"

She fluttered her naked left hand in front of his face. "We're not married. We shouldn't be acting like we are."

Not quite sure what to say next, he scrubbed a hand over his face. The moment he'd met Bethany, he knew she'd be a handful — in bed and out. Most days he welcomed the challenge. She intrigued him, excited him and made him feel alive. She even made him glad he'd developed an addiction to Romance TV, despite all the ribbing friends gave him about it. If he hadn't been watching the network while convalescing from his broken leg, he'd have never entered his buddy in the contest that brought Beth into his life.

"You want a proposal? Is that it?"

When she looked at him like he'd just suggested they castrate Michaelangelo's David, he wondered if the Christmas morning surprise he had planned would go over as well as he hoped. "I just want to make love more often than I take out the trash!"

Well, crap. The woman he loved was telling him he didn't satisfy her — and if that was true, maybe their relationship really was on the rocks. It wouldn't be the first time. She'd always held herself a little aloof, been more reticent than he was about their being together. He'd assumed she was just less flamboyant than she seemed. He spoke in his quietest voice. "I didn't realize I was such a disappointment."

Her eyes widened. "I'm not disappointed."

"You just compared me to the garbageman, Beth. Forgive me if I took it the wrong way."

She laid her hand on his chest, her green eyes beseeching him to understand. "I've always been a sensual being."

"Tell me something I don't know." He raked his eyes over her from head to toe, paying special attention to the curve of her ample breasts and the flare of her hips. His body responded instantly and he wondered why Bethany was suddenly so sure they had a problem. Just because he'd been working until he dropped didn't mean he wanted her any less than he had the day they met. He guided her hand to his crotch and smiled in satisfaction as her eyes widened again. "When I'm not dead on my feet, everything's in working order."

He watched her expression brighten and knew he'd managed to say something right. She smiled her winningest smile. "All the more reason for us to apply for the show. You've been working too hard. You need a vacation."

Cody groaned. How could he have walked straight into that one? "Spending a month in front of TV cameras isn't my idea of a vacation."

"But we'd be on a tropical island ... having fun in the sun, sand and surf."

He was tempted, sure. What sane man wouldn't be when it would mean escaping the sub-zero wind chills of a Chicago winter? However, Damien's experience with meddling TV execs and an intrusive camera crew was more than enough to convince him he wanted no part of another Romance TV production. Just because it worked out for his buddy and his new bride didn't mean he and Bethany would be so lucky. "I don't think so, Beth."

Her smile dimmed. Damn, he hated to disappoint her, especially when she seemed convinced they were in trouble. He didn't want trouble. He didn't even want a minor hassle. He was quite pleased with the direction of his life with Bethany. He liked being comfortable — and he was glad he didn't need to pretend to be something he wasn't.

On the other hand, if she thought they were *too* comfortable, maybe he did need to put in a little more effort. Maybe he should agree to apply. Filling out an application was no guarantee they'd be chosen for the show. In fact, when he thought about how many poor saps were probably clamoring to be on a show like this, being one of the eight couples selected for "Invitation to Sin" was highly unlikely.

And when he factored in the fact that he'd already "won" once by submitting Damien's story for the "Get a Love Life" contest, it became even less likely. No way would Romance TV lightning strike their circle twice.

He gave Bethany's hand a squeeze. "Okay, sweetheart. Let's apply."

Bethany squealed and sat on his lap. Her silken hair teased his shoulders as she planted kisses all over his face. "Thank you, thank you, thank you." When she was done kissing him, she smiled. "Let's work on the application today."

"Right now?" When she nodded, he directed her attention to the part of him brought to life by her enthusiastic response. "I can think of something I'd rather be doing right now."

She didn't wait for a second invitation to yank down the sweatpants he'd slept in and straddle his waist. He watched as she tugged her T-shirt over her head and tossed it aside. Then she flattened herself against him, pressing the points of her nipples into his chest, and a wave of pure pleasure washed over him. He groaned.

No, their relationship wasn't in a bit of trouble — and if he had to apply for a stupid TV show they didn't have a chance in hell of getting on to convince Beth of that, so be it.